THE HOLLOW:

The Keeper's Legacy

Ladean Warner

Linda,
They are back to
haunt your dreams!
Ladean Warner

Open Door Publishers, Inc.
Malta, NY

See, I have placed
before you an open door
that no one can shut.
Rev 3:8

Open Door Publishers, Inc
P.O. Box 2871
Malta, NY 12020 (518) 899-2097
http://www.opendoorpublishers.com

Printed in the United States of America

First Edition

First Printing 2012

ISBN: 978-1-937138-09-7

This third book in the Keeper series is dedicated to my three children, Jami, Katie, and Joshua. I am blessed that you are mine and love you all so much! And as always, I wouldn't even be an author without the ongoing support of Joe, my best friend and husband. I love you!!

Special thanks to my close friends, Barb Griffin and Karie Garrow, who always encourage, support and pray. You are the best kind of friends!!

CHAPTER 1

A t the top of the mountain, Jake Peterson paused and breathed in the woodsy mountain air. The long hike to the Hollow, deep in the Blue Ridge Mountains, had been invigorating. Jake slipped the backpack off and let it fall to the ground. He could see the Blue Mountains for miles, and just stood looking at the panoramic view.

"Hey, Pastor Jake, we're not that far from the Hollow here. Why you stopping now?" his companion said as he caught up to where Jake stood looking across the mountains.

"Just wanted to see the view. Isn't it great, Tom?" Jake asked not taking his eyes off the distant mountains. Jake's blue eyes almost matched the deep blue in the sky that met the top of the highest peak.

"Seen one hill, you've seen them all," Tom Meyer just grunted as he sat down on a fallen log. He dug into his pack looking for a water bottle. A smile played across Jake's handsome face knowing Tom had been ready for a break for a while. The sun sparkled on a lake that Jake could barely see in the distance. He stepped further out of the woods to get a better look.

Living in upstate New York in the Adirondack Mountains, Jake did his fair share of hiking. But here in the mountains of Virginia, Jake found something really special. Although he loved these mountains with their deep blue hue, the clouds that settle on the mountain peaks, and the unbroken miles of trees, it was really the people that kept Jake coming back for the past several years. The people living in deep poverty in the Hollow were those that Jake wanted to help.

Jake heard Tom struggling to his feet and turned back to the barely discernable path. Tom was ready to get moving. The long trip to the Hollow wore him out, but the missionaries from Granelle, New York, only stayed a week. They paid Tom good money to be their guide to the mountain people that were related to him.

Tom took over the lead and soon came to the first of the rundown shacks in the Hollow. "Clancy, you home?" Tom yelled as they approached the shack. There was no response, but Jake hadn't expected one. A man just seemed to appear from the woods near the shack. He just stood watching Tom and Jake as they walked up to him.

"You remember Pastor Jake?" Tom asked as they approached. The older man, dressed in ragged clothes, spit tobacco juice near a tree. His dirty grey beard was stained from years of chewing tobacco. Jake waited for Clancy Boon to acknowledge him.

There was a long silence as Clancy just stared at Jake. He then turned his attention to Tom. "Ya brung them things?"

"Yep, yep," Tom said dropping his pack. He rummaged around in the bag and finally pulled out a tin of tobacco and an object wrapped in a dirty cloth. Clancy took the stuff from Tom and looked it over. He stuffed the tin in his dirty overalls and looked over at Jake.

Clancy regarded Jake again. Jake still waited for Clancy, knowing the only way to reach the Hollow was through him. Finally, Clancy nodded. "Preacher," he said as he turned and disappeared into the woods near his shack. Jake followed knowing that he was once again accepted into the Hollow.

"Yep, you're in," Tom said with a big goofy smile. He slapped Jake on the back as they followed him.

Clancy walked ahead until they came to another shack. An old woman sat in a rocking chair on what passed as a porch. Clancy went to the woman and leaned down and kissed her weathered cheek. Her long silver hair was up in a bun and she wore a dingy grey dress.

"Mama," he began. "Preacher from the city come back to see ya."

The old lady looked up through rummy eyes. A big smile lit up her face. "Pastor Jake," she said. She took Jake's big hand in both of hers. Jake knelt down next to the chair.

"Ma, it's good to see you again," Jake said with sincerity.

"Y'all brung that wife o' yours?"

"I couldn't bring her this time. She's expecting a baby in the fall."

"Another child. I's got me fifteen youngns now. Sissy had one few months back."

"Was it a boy or girl this time?"

"Boy?" She looked up at Clancy who just nodded. "Boy."

"That's great!" Jake said smiling. "It would be wonderful if we had a girl since we already have our little boy."

"Havin' a girl ain't a good thing. Hard life for a girl here. Well, come in and get ya some cider."

THE HOLLOW

The men followed the old woman into the shack. Like most of the shacks on the mountain, it was one big room, with an old wood stove in one corner of a haphazard kitchen. The other side of the room was a small bed with a worn quilt draped over it. A curtained area provided the only privacy in the room, held clothes and some personal items. Jake noticed the newer stains on the wall where rain had been seeping in.

"Looks like you need some tarring done," Jake said acknowledging the water stains.

"Git to it by winter," Clancy said a bit defensively.

"I was just thinking that I could give you a hand while I'm here. Big job for one person."

"Don't need no…," Clancy began.

"Let im help ya." Ma poured some cool cider into mugs. "Lots of other stuff ya need doin' fer winter."

"I can manage." Clancy took one the mugs and gave her a warning look which she ignored.

"I know ya do, son. But that's why theys here, to help. Ya needin' to keep up two places, Jonesy leavin', it's too much for ya." She finished handing out the cider and sat in a wooden rocker. "So, Pastor, ya fixin' on doin' some preachin' whils ya here?"

"If the people want me to," Jake said looking at Clancy. He was looking hard at his mother, but shrugged at Jake's half asked question.

"Course they's do. We need it now too. Been bad goings on here in the Hollow. Devil comin' here now."

"Now, Mama. Ya know that ain't true," Clancy rebuked her.

"I's see it. Pray to God. But now…," she stopped shaking her head.

"What are you talking about?" Jake asked with a bit of concern.

"She just an ole woman talkin' ole tales," Clancy said in a hard voice.

"I seen it myself. Say what ya want. But I know it were the devil," she replied.

"What's going on?" Jake asked Clancy. He looked away and crossed his arms. "Clancy, I care about your people. After all these years, you can tell me. I might be able to help."

Clancy shook his head. "Nothin' to tell ya." Jake looked to Tom for support. But Tom looked at his feet and didn't say anything.

"Clancy thinks I old and gettin' on. But I know'd what I seen. He was big and dark, happen that night Erica…."

"That's 'nough talk like that, woman," Clancy's tone stopped Ma. She looked hurt and her chin trembled. "Ain't no good talkin' 'bout it. If y'all want to help the preacher, no more talkin' bout this devil."

Clancy had a hard look that Jake had never seen, so he decided not to push it. "Okay, if that's the way you want it. Can I still go up the knoll and let people know my teens will be coming tomorrow?"

Clancy nodded and left the shack. Jake knelt down and hugged Ma. She hugged him back, whispering, "Pray fer us." Jake just nodded and nudged Tom.

As they left the shack, Clancy was standing on the porch. "Don't pay her no mind, Preacher."

Jake not knowing how to respond, reached out and shook Clancy's hand. "I appreciate being able to come and help your people. You won't have trouble from me."

Jake and Tom went together up to the knoll where a cluster of shacks stood. Jake was back. He glanced back and saw Clancy watching him. Jake felt the warning that the look implied. As Tom yelled to a group of kids that Pastor Jake was back, a dark cloud covered the sun casting dark shadows around them. Jake looked around and felt something sinister coming from the woods. He shook it off as a few kids came running up to him.

A few hours later, Jake and Tom were heading back down the mountain to the little town. The visit had been overshadowed by the warning from Clancy. They reached the end of the woods and entered the little town of Creek River. The small Baptist church that hosted the missionary trip was a ways down the dirt road.

"Tom, I won't ask you to betray Clancy, but if there is something going on in the Hollow, I need to know before I bring my youth group up that mountain tomorrow."

"Pastor Jake, you know how superstitious these mountain folk are."

"Yes, but a lot of superstitions are based on some fact."

"I thought preachers didn't believe in that kind of stuff."

"I'm not just any kind of preacher. I used to be a cop. I learned the hard way that some of what people think are just superstitions are actually real."

"Well, there is one real thing I can tell you," Tom said with a shrug. "You'll know soon enough anyway. Clancy's youngest run away few weeks back. He's real bitter about it."

"Who is his youngest?"

"Erica. She was goin' on sixteen. Jus' left one night."

"I think I remember her. Didn't she get baptized a couple of years ago?"

"Yep, Clancy thinks it was the religion that got her turned against him. But Ma, she's sure it were the devil that got her."

"Why would she think that?"

"That night, Ma was sure that she saw the devil go by her house," Tom laughed. "It's really kind of funny. Like the boogey man got her. Probably just her boyfriend Ma saw."

As they got to the church, Tom waved and kept walking down the road. Jake stopped at the door and prayed for Erica. He remembered her and how she had changed after her conversion and baptism in the river. The girl he remembered wouldn't have run off with a boy. But now he understood Clancy's hardness. The sounds of singing drifted from the church as a meeting started, and Jake went into join the teens.

CHAPTER 2

Jake could hear the women before he saw them. It had been a long day at the Hollow and he was beat. The tar on Ma's roof had turned into a major project with new timber beams needed to replace the rotten wood. Jake was hoping for a long hot shower before the teens, who were wound up, dragged him into a night of activity.

"...he was in the backyard one minute, and then he was just gone," Jake heard the voice. As he entered the kitchen he saw Margaret Zimmer, the pastor's wife, stirring a large pot on the stove and Norma Golden making sandwiches. "Pastor Jake, how did it go today?" Margaret asked.

"Everything was fine. There's a bunch of people down by the post office. What's going on in town?"

"Oh, it's a shame really. Little Timmy Novak is missing. He was playing in the backyard and now he's just gone. Pastor Zimmer and a few of the men are helping look for the boy. Pastor Jake, are you okay?"

Jake just felt a sense of déjà vu wash over him. He just stared at Margaret who stopped stirring the soup and came over to Jake. He looked down and saw such concern on her face. It brought him out of his reprieve. "I'm sorry to startle you. It's just that it is so reminiscent of something that happened in my town a long time ago. I'd like to help out."

"If you're sure your okay...." Jake nodded. "Well, the search is taking place from the sheriff's office. It's right near where you saw the crowd. You can't miss it."

Jake went into the fellowship hall and found Keith Richards, the youth pastor from Granelle Gospel Church. Pulling him aside, he said, "There's a young boy missing in town. Since we're here to help out the whole town, not just the people who live in the Hollow, I think we should see what we can do."

"Are you sure?" Keith looked concerned and then dropped his voice lower. "Not that many of these kids would remember, but is it wise considering what happened in our town?"

"I had a moment of déjà vu myself. But it's probably some little boy who wandered off. If we help out, maybe the people in town will give us a chance to hear our message."

Keith let out a sigh. "You're right. Let's see if the kids want to go with us."

"Alright, but if they come, let me talk to the sheriff alone first."

Keith called the team together and explained what was going on. They all agreed to help in the search and followed Jake to the Sheriff's Office. Keith stopped with the teens at the Post Office to give Jake time to talk to the sheriff. As Jake opened the door to the office, the men inside stopped talking. The sheriff glanced out his window to the group of teens standing with Keith.

"Can I help you?" the sheriff asked.

"I'm Pastor Jake Peterson. I'm in town with the youth group from my church working with the Baptist Church up in the Hollow. Mrs. Zimmer told us there's a missing boy, and we came to see if we can help you in the search."

The men looked at each other, a few of them snickered. "No offense preacher, but I don't think we really have a place for your group. These woods are pretty thick, and the boy probably just wandered off. We don't want to lose any of you and have to send out another search party," the sheriff replied.

"No offense taken sheriff. But just so you know, we live in a mountainous region too. I've lead search parties myself…."

"When was that?" one man asked laughing. "When one of your parishioners lost her bingo chip?" A few joined in the laughter.

Jake smiled. "Actually, it was when I was a detective with the Granelle Police Department, in Upstate New York." The laughter died, but only for a moment. As the man tried to say more, the sheriff interrupted.

"You'll have to excuse Paul, Preacher. I'm Jesse Mueller," he said reaching out to shake Jake's hand.

"We'd be glad to help in any way we can."

"I'm really not trying to dismiss your help, but you're here with a bunch of kids. It might be better for you to stick to your activities and let us handle our own."

"From my experiences, I can understand you not wanting a bunch of teens coming into your search. But when I was on the force, we had several women and a small boy abducted. I was lead investigator on the case. I'd like to offer you my experience should you feel you need it."

"To be honest, we think Timmy just wandered off. He's been getting in trouble at school. I'll keep your offer to help in mind though."

"If you need me, the Zimmers will know where I am." Jake nodded to the men and left. As the door closed behind him, he heard Paul making another joke at his expense.

"So, what's going on?" Keith asked. A bunch of the teens were playing ball with a small group of younger children.

"They respectfully denied our help. Let's go back and eat our dinner. When we have our prayer meeting at the church, we can pray for Timmy. The sheriff knows we're willing to help if he needs us."

Keith called to the teens who complained about not being able to help in the search. Back at the church, the women put out the soup and sandwiches. Jake sat with the Zimmers and Goldens listening to them discuss Timmy.

"Lori Novak has certainly had her hands full with Timmy since Roy ran off with the hussy over in Beaumont," Mrs. Golden said shaking her head.

"Norma, you don't know the whole story…," her husband began.

"You siding with the man! What kind of a man walks out on his pregnant wife with a little boy at home to boot!" Norma exclaimed.

"What do you think, Jake?" Cal Zimmer asked him knowing his police background.

"There's always a price to be paid for the break up of a family. Usually, it's the children that suffer," Jake said being careful to word it so that Norma didn't go off into gossip again.

"Well, of course. I understand that," the pastor said with a smile. "But I was wondering if it could be true that the boy just ran away?"

"I don't know the family. But troubled kids have been known to run away. I find it hard to believe that he got lost since he was raised here and spent a lot of time in these woods."

The others murmur agreement. "It's a shame that the sheriff won't let you help search," Margaret said as she began to gather the dirty plates.

"I understand his concerns. Maybe the best place for the teens is right here helping watch some of the children while their parents search for Timmy."

"Maybe," Margaret said with a scowl. "But I still think that he should have respected you as a former police officer."

"I agree," Norma chimed in as she glared at her husband.

"It's fine, ladies," Jake said. "If he needs me, he knows where I am. They'll probably find him soon anyway."

"Well, I certainly hope so," Norma said standing to help clear the table. The two women took the dishes to the kitchen, and the teens started clearing their own tables.

"I'm not sure how many people will come to the prayer meeting," Cal said. "Do you still want to hold it if only a few people come?"

"I think we should," Jake responded. "We've already got a good size group with us, Keith and the teens. A few of the girls can play games with the children in the gym."

"Well, Roger and I were going to continue with the search," he replied. "So, it's really you and your team. Norma and Margaret were going to go over to stay with Lori Novak after dinner."

"Even if it's just us, we'll still pray. If any of your members come, they can join us."

The two older men exchanged glances. "Thing is, I don't think our members will come out without me here. They think you're here for the people up at the Hollow."

"Cal, that's fine. I'm here to help, however you need me. We haven't got anything else to do tonight since we can't help in the search. So, we can either do the meeting in the sanctuary, or right in the fellowship hall."

"I guess that'll work."

"In fact, why don't you and your wives go on ahead and get back to the search. We can clean up the kitchen and be ready for the meeting."

The older men exchanged glances again. Roger shrugged and shook his head. The women complained about leaving the cleaning to a bunch of teens, but their husbands gently led them out of the door. The team had a great time cleaning and getting ready for the meeting. But when the time rolled around and no one joined them, the group got serious.

"It seems so unfair, Pastor Jake," one boy complained and a few other teens agreed. "We came all the way down here and no one wants us to do anything. We can't help look for the missing kid. We can't have our meeting. We can't do anything, but go up in the mountain."

"Why did we come?" Jake asked.

"We came to be missionaries to Creek River," Beth said. Jake knew she was heading to Bible college in the fall with big dreams of being a missionary.

"And what does that mean to you?"

"It means we teach Bible studies, pray with people, and minister to their needs," Beth said with a flourish and a few agreed.

"And we've been doing that."

"No," the boy said again. "We're stuck here in the church...."

"Stuck?" Jake asked. "Scott, we spent all day up in the mountains. We held a Bible class for some elementary school kids, gave the clothes and supplies we brought to some of the families, and even played some games with the older kids. Keith and I even got to help repair a roof. Isn't that why we came?"

"But they don't want us here in town," Scott complained again.

"The town is hosting our stay here. They have provided us with a place to sleep, food, and we've been a part of their meetings...."

"A part of *their* meetings. We're the missionaries, how come we have to sit back in a stuffy, boring church service and just watch. John and I practiced all these songs for months and Pastor Zimmer won't even let us play in the sanctuary. Then they don't want to hear the message we prepared. It's not fair!"

Jake looked around at the group and saw many disappointed kids. He raised his eyebrows to Keith, who was sitting behind the group. Keith just shook his head in disappointment. "Okay, I see where you're coming from," Jake finally said.

"So, what can you do about it?" John asked piping in.

"To be honest, I think we should pack up and go home tomorrow."

"Yeah, because we'll never get to be real missionaries here," Scott said looking around for support. Jake noticed a few kids weren't agreeing with Scott and were waiting for Jake to respond.

"Is that what you think, Katie?" Jake asked one of the girls.

"No," she replied shyly.

"You don't think we should just go home in the morning? Give up on Creek River?"

Katie glanced around at the other kids. Pink stained her cheeks at the attention she was getting from everyone. She looked down at her hands. "I didn't come here to sing in front of people or to tell people stories. I came because I thought if even one person heard about Jesus, it was worth coming."

"So, do you think coming down here was a waste of your time?"

"No."

"Why?"

"Today, Emma told me that the people in the Hollow have been waiting for months for us to come back. She told me that they need us because without the stuff we bring, her family wouldn't have made it through last winter. I thought that's what a missionary did."

"And it is, Katie," Jake replied. "That's even what Jesus did. He met the physical needs of the people first. It might seem insignificant to you that we bring used clothes, canned goods, and other stuff to these people. But without those things, they wouldn't be open to hearing the Word. The people here in town don't have those same needs. We help where we can."

Emboldened by Jake's support, Katie went on. "And if you want to sing so bad, Scott Murphy, lug your guitar up the mountain and sing with them. They love music and won't care about there being no organ."

Everyone turned and looked with surprise at Katie. Her cheeks were glowing red, but she held Scott's stare until he finally turned away. Jake opened his Bible and read about Jesus feeding the multitudes and then led them in prayer. It was long after the teens turned in for the night that the Zimmers stopped by to tell Jake that Timmy was still lost.

CHAPTER 3

Sam Craig watched the two girls as they mingled with the crowd at 'The Venue.' He watched as they worked their way across through the gyrating bodies of the dancers moving to the loud pulsating music. Sam leaned on the railing on the upper balcony which overlooked the dance floor and the circular bar. Even with the strobe light splashing dark spots, he still watched the girls as they stopped at the edge of the dancers.

In his early 20s and dressed simply, Sam fit easily into the crowd that filled the club. Sam stood out as the stranger in the room. The Venue was the only nightclub in the county, and it drew all those old enough to drink. Within the tiny towns, everyone knew each other, so Sam stood out, even though he tried to fade into the community.

"Hi," a brunette said that was near to Sam. He glanced over at her.

"Hi yourself," he said turning back to watch the two girls.

"I've noticed you before. Are you here alone?" she went on. Sam almost sighed at the distraction, but straightened up and finally looked at her. She was tall, thin, and gorgeous. She was wearing tight black jeans and a bright blue silk shirt. It complemented her dark hair and eyes.

"Not now," Sam said with a smile. "I'm Sam."

"Sam, nice name. I'm Bobbi. Anyone ever tell you that you look like Michael J. Fox?"

"No, that's a new one."

"Same sandy brown hair, brown eyes, and he's a bit short too! Why, he could be your brother!"

"Except, he's a bit older than me." Her enthusiasm was dampening his interest.

"You live around here?"

"You know, I'm not big on twenty questions. Why don't we just dance a little, get a drink, you know, just see how it goes. Is that okay?"

"Sure," Bobbi said taking his hand. She led him to the dance floor as a slow song started. She was a little taller than Sam in her heals, so she draped her arms over his shoulders and leaned in close. Sam found his eyes searching the floor for the two girls again. He watched them walk up the stairs to the second floor balcony he just left.

"You must be from up North. You don't sound like you're from here," Bobbi said as she pulled back to look into Sam's face.

Sam just smiled. "Does it matter?"

"I just want to get to know you, that's all."

"Why don't we dance and see where it leads. Okay?"

"Sure," Bobbi said with a little pout. "I've been known to dance a bit."

They danced in silence while Sam kept watching the two other girls. High above the dance floor, the DJ was encased in a glass room. He watched the two girls climb the spiral staircase to the room. When they were let in, Sam lost interest and focused on Bobbi. As the song ended, she took Sam's hand and led him to a table.

Very animated, she introduced Sam to everyone, "Hey, everyone, this is Sam. These are my friends."

Sam just smiled and said hi to the group. Bobbi sat, patted the seat next to her, and motioned for a waitress. Sam looked around and caught the eye of a guy who was introduced as Ryan. Ryan took his girlfriend's hand and pulled her to her feet. As he passed Sam, he leaned in and whispered, "Good luck with her, man."

"Well, come on over, silly," Bobbi said with a wary look at Sam.

"Will you excuse me for a minute?" Sam asked starting to turn away.

"Wait!" Bobbi exclaimed as she jumped up. "Where are you going?"

When she got near him, he noticed tears brimming in her eyes, desperation. Not good, Sam thought. "Men's room," Sam whispered and headed to the back of the nightclub.

"Bet you won't see him again," Sam heard someone say as he walked away.

Sam passed the two girls who had had his interest earlier, but now he just wanted to get away. He went into the Men's Room and stood in front of a sink. Trying to kill time, Sam washed his hands and checked his watch. When someone else finally came in, Sam walked out. He noticed Bobbi right away watching the Men's Room door. As she stood and started toward Sam, he saw another girl standing near him with a drink watching the dancers.

"Excuse me," Sam said getting her attention. "Would you like to dance?"

"Sure," she said with a big smile. She set her drink down on a small table and let Sam take her hand. He didn't pay attention to Bobbi, but hoped she would get the idea. Sam danced several songs with the new girl, found out that she worked in a small law office, and left with her number. The few glances at Bobbi told him that she was miserable. It was after midnight, and Sam had enough. All Sam had wanted was a brief distraction and nothing serious. With the new girl's phone number in his pocket, Sam went to the door. As he reached for the handle, Bobbi stepped in front of him.

"What she got that I don't got?"

"Look, I'm just not interested," Sam said trying to get around her.

"Do you think she's prettier than me?" Bobbi asked as a tear slid down her cheek.

"I don't want to hurt your feelings, honey. But have a little self respect. I'm not interested," Sam said in a very low voice.

"But why?" Bobbi wailed.

"Everything okay?" a bouncer asked coming over.

"Everything is fine. I'm leaving," Sam said finally pushing past her. Once outside, Sam breathed in the night air. He heard a shuffle behind him, and saw Bobbi following him. Groaning to himself, Sam pulled his keys out of his pocket and hurried to his car.

"Wait, Sam!" Bobbi called out unable to catch up to him in her heels.

Sam ignored her and got to his car. Once inside, he locked the doors and started the car. Bobbi came up to the driver's side and pleaded with him to open the window. Sam put the car into reverse and she stumbled back away from the car. As he drove away, he looked in the rearview mirror and saw Bobbi standing, watching him drive away, crying.

Sam turned on the radio, relieved that he got away from her. It wasn't the first time Sam saw the desperation that Bobbi showed in this area. The hard economic times hit Steuben County hard. In this little town, businesses continued to close and more and more people were unemployed. Though Sam lived modestly, he realized that he was drawing attention to himself with his lifestyle. It was time to move on and away from Beaumont.

As Sam drove back to his rented house, he began his plan to move again. Living this transit lifestyle afforded freedom, but he was lonely. His frequent trips to night clubs helped ease some of his loneliness, but these girls were looking for more than Sam could offer. Pulling into the driveway,

Sam turned off the headlights. He shut off the car and got out. The isolated house, surrounded by the mountains, reminded him of his childhood home in Granelle, New York.

Sam longed to return to Granelle, but his secrets couldn't be hidden there. Too many knew his past and would try to make him face the hidden things he didn't want to face. So he chose, instead, to live in small mountain towns until it became necessary to move. He wished he had realized that Bobbi had been keeping tabs on him. His work in Beaumont wasn't done yet, but he knew he needed to leave. He was sure that Bobbi would track him down if he stayed.

Sam unlocked the door and went inside. The sparsely furnished monthly rental would make it easy for him to pack up and leave. Even though it was late, Sam went to the small downstairs room that he had made into an office. He went to the computer intent on writing a letter to his landlord. He had to make plans and figure out where to go from here.

As Sam waited for the computer, he found himself drawn to the old leather journals. Those old journals were part of the reason he had come to Beaumont. The old hand written journals that Sam had found in an old house in Granelle. He had a connection to the journals and the man who had written them. He spent hours trying to understand the broken English and older Irish language that were blended in the journals. He picked up the oldest one and turned again to the worn pages.

Sam remembered the day he found the journals at the old house in Granelle. When Sam was eleven years old, he had been abducted by a man after he had killed Sam's mother. He was held in the basement of an old abandoned house with four women. The man, Trevor Grant, thought himself to be a keeper of some dark creatures and needed Sam and the women for some ritual. After he was found, Sam's father moved away. It was years later when Sam went back to visit his childhood friend. He found the journals, in that same old house.

As Sam sat holding the old journal, he thought about those dark creatures and the hold they still had on him. He traced an old scar on one of his fingers, the scar left by the creature when it bit him. He remembered feeling the power, having control over that creature, even as an eleven-year old boy. But it was during his return trip to Granelle that he realized the creatures had bound him to them and an old legend with that bite. The legend that these old journals spoke of, Trevor Grant believed in, and that belief turned him into a killer.

Sam never knew Shamus O'Leary, the man that had abducted Trevor as a boy and forced him to live a life of darkness. Sam didn't even know the legend, but these journals gave him a glimpse of something he longed to know more about. After searching for years, he finally found someone he thought could read the old Gaelic language and tell him the secrets of the creature…if he could trust him.

One day, he would know the whole story, but for tonight, he went back to his letter for his landlord. After writing a brief letter, he turned to his computer to find a new rental. He needed to stay close to the college where the man worked, but outside of Steuben County and away from Bobbi.

CHAPTER 4

It had been a great week. It was the last night and they would be leaving in the morning. The worship team was playing and the church members were singing. A few of the girls were getting the kids ready to do the skits they had been practicing. Jake leaned against the back wall and said a silent prayer for the last sermon he would preach to the group gathered in the hall.

Working with the people from the Hollow was rewarding. They lived in such poverty that the clothes, personal items, and food that they brought from upstate New York were appreciated. They listened as the teams shared their faith in Christ. Jake was delighted to hear the children saying their memory verse and sing songs about Jesus. But the greater community of River Creek didn't feel they needed the missionaries to come to them. Oh, they appreciated the work with the people from the Hollow, but they felt they were above the need for more religion.

As the song was finishing, Jake looked up and was surprised to see Jesse standing next to him. "Sorry to interrupt your meeting, but can I speak with you outside for a moment?" the sheriff whispered.

Jake nodded and got Keith's attention. Outside, Jake could see flashlights in the woods and a small crowd by the sheriff's office. All week searchers had been looking for Timmy and the search was winding down. Jake leaned against the church building.

"Detective Peterson, I would have waited to talk to you after the meeting, but things have changed," Jesse began.

"Sheriff, it's been a long time since anyone's called me that."

"I decided to check you out. You have a pretty impressive history in law enforcement."

"It was a long time ago."

"Maybe, maybe not," the sheriff shrugged. "Timmy Novak still hasn't been found. Last night, a girl from town went missing from a club in Beaumont."

"I told you earlier in the week, I'd be glad to help you search for the boy. It's been several days now, so I'm not sure how easy it will be to find him now."

"That's the thing. If Timmy was in the woods, our folks would have found him. He didn't just wander off. You mentioned you had been involved in a case where several women and a boy went missing. Seemed strange to me that two girls are missing here and Timmy."

"Sheriff, ours was a local crime. The men responsible for it are deceased now."

"The stuff on the Internet confirmed that women were missing with a boy. They were found at some old house…that you found them at the house. But it got kind of weird. There was some creature involved and a ritual about passing on power of the keeper. Facts got mixed up with the fiction, so I thought I'd come ask you. Get it right from the horse's mouth."

"Like I said, it was a long time ago. If you'd like me to help in the search, I'd be glad to do that. In either case, I'll be praying."

"Thing is, I'm asking you for more than that. I want to know about your missing people."

"Are you trying to find out if I'm qualified to help you find a missing boy?" Jake asked perplexed.

"Well, I checked with the Granelle Police Department. Captain Bennett, who was your boss, is retired. Megan Riley, your former partner, doesn't work there anymore. It was so long ago that your jacket isn't even on file anymore. The person I spoke with knows you as Pastor Jake, the nice preacher from the Pentecostal church. Speaking of that, does Rev. Zimmer know you're one of those Pentecostals? We're Baptist in this town."

"That's a lot of checking out to do to help find a boy that wandered off. But I've got nothing to hide. First of all, Reggie Bennett is a personal friend of mine and if you want to talk to him, I can give you his unlisted number. Yes, Rev. Zimmer knows my church is Pentecostal, and we have the same mission, to see the people of the Hollow and Creek River come to Christ."

The sheriff looked past Jake to the woods. He stood with a faraway look for a few moments. "I got to reading those news articles and something clicked. I think what happened up there in your mountain is happening here."

Jake shook his head. "Can't be. I already mentioned that those responsible are dead."

"Then, maybe a copycat. Can you just humor me and tell me what happened, what's real and what wasn't?"

"It wouldn't be a copycat. It had to do with an old Irish myth and these creatures. No one could replicate the crimes because they were all tied to the creatures. And they were real, I saw them for myself. I saw the control they had over that man."

"After you left, I started digging around for stuff about you. Then I saw how similar things were. Can you come down to my office? Let me show you what I have?"

"Sheriff, I'd like to help you. But there is no way what happened in Granelle all those years ago is happening here in Creek River."

"If I tell you that people have seen that creature of yours, would you believe me?"

"There's no way...."

"Big animal, like a wolf, sharp razor-like teeth, eyes that glow red in the night like something being reflected in them."

"Who saw it?"

"I did, few weeks back. It was right after Clancy Boon came down from the mountain to find the kid his daughter was shacking up with."

"Erica. Where is she?"

"Don't know. Contrary to what the Hollow folks will tell you, Erica was seeing a boy in town. But he's still here and upset that she ran off."

"I remember Erica. I didn't think she'd be the type of girl to just run off."

"The other girl that is missing is from Creek River. She goes over to Beaumont to this dance club. Her best friend, Mindy, was there with her last night. Roberta had been keeping tabs on this young fellow that isn't from around here and looks like he has money. The bartender said he kind of dumped her at the bar, but she followed him out when he left. She didn't come back in. She even left Mindy and her car behind."

"Did you check out this guy?"

"Can't get a handle on him. The police in Beaumont have had Mindy there most of the day. They think they got a sketch of him."

"It sounds like you've got it all covered. I could take a look at the sketch to see if he looks familiar. But...."

"Listen, Detective. This is the second missing girl from our little town. While it's not uncommon for our kids to leave this god-forsaken mountain, these girls just vanished. Put it all together...the girls, Timmy, and that creature. Can you tell me now, Detective Peterson, that there is no way what happened in Granelle isn't happening here?"

"I was very close to all the cases, and there is no way...."

"All? This happened more than once?"

"Yes, the first time, we had the wrong guy. The second time, we got both Grant and O'Leary. But after O'Leary died, Grant escaped from jail trying to reclaim his place as the keeper."

"That's the part I don't understand."

"I understand your concern, Sheriff, but that's the part that makes it impossible for this to be happening here in Creek River. Grant was obsessed with the creatures and being their keeper. When he got the letter that O'Leary had died, he broke out of jail to reclaim his place with the creatures."

"Do you know more about this keeper thing?"

"Yes, but it will be a dead end to you. I'm positive. Grant was killed after he escaped."

"There's something else too. When Timmy disappeared, we searched everywhere. In back of his house, there's this creek that runs through it. Back in the day, his grandfather used to keep livestock by the creek. Still are sections of the old barb-wire fence along the riverbed. When I started checking you out, I went back and searched that area again. I found hair stuck in the wire. It came back from the lab today. It's some kind of animal hair from an unknown origin. Thing is, it matches the hairs found in the cases you worked on. It has human DNA."

"Human...?" Jake looked past the sheriff to the dense woods.

"Mean something to you?"

"Can't be human. It would be impossible."

"Yeah, I thought so too. Called the lab to complain about the mix up. It's not a mistake. I found a mention about animal hair in your case records."

"But animal hair is common in mountain regions like ours," Jake said feeling uneasy. He remembered saying something like that to Meg years ago when she was investigating one of the cases.

"Animal hair with human DNA? What did your reports say?"

"I don't recall anything about that. But there is someone who would know."

"Who?"

"My old partner, Meg Riley. She was lead investigator when Grant was captured, and she was really focused on the animal aspect of the case. If anyone would know, she would."

"Well, the police department in Granelle didn't think I should involve her. Wouldn't even give me an idea of how to reach her."

"Let me tell my team where I'm going. I want to see your evidence. If I think Meg needs to be involved, I know how to reach her."

Once they were at the Sheriff's office, Jesse showed Jake the evidence he gathered. The sense of unease grew as Jake read through pages of notes Jesse had written.

"Jesse," Jake finally said, "I'd like to do more than just offer my advice on this case. There's things that I know about this case. They're just intuitive, but in order for me to be involved, I need to have my badge."

"That would be great Jake. But the problem is, you've been off the force for so long, your jacket is no longer in the police files."

"It shouldn't be a problem on a temporary basis. If you call Reggie Bennett, he'll give me the go-ahead. I worked with him for many years, and we have a good relationship. I know that he'll approve of this."

"Are you sure? Bennett is retired and not on the force either. People I talked to in Granelle kind of felt you shouldn't be involved…fact is, I just got the run around from them."

"The last time I got involved in this, my wife had been abducted. Do you know who you spoke with in Granelle?"

"Let me see, I wrote it down," Jesse went to his desk and found a piece of paper. "Guy named, Greg Matthews."

"Oh, him. He's just an officer, not anyone with authority in the force. The new Captain is Steve Crandall, I worked with him when I was on the force and with Reggie's reference, I should be able to be reinstated, at least on a temporary basis."

"That Matthews guy didn't think so. He didn't have a high opinion of you."

"Look, since I'm here, you have missing people, and I know things that might be able to help this case. Let's call Reggie. He's the one, not Matthews, that can give you the truth about my background in law enforcement. Don't get me wrong though, I will help you even if I can't have the badge. But I know from past experience that it's better if I'm working this case as a cop, and not a civilian."

Jesse didn't need any more convincing and called the number Jake gave him. He listened as Jesse explained the situation in Creek River. A couple of times, he could hear Reggie's voice getting loud, but just waited.

Finally, Jesse handed the phone to Jake. "Says he needs to talk to you before he'll consider giving me any support."

Jake took the phone. "Hey Reggie. Before you say anything...."

"Before I say anything?" Reggie exploded. "Has it been that long that you've forgotten who you're talking to? Just what do you think you're doing, Peterson?"

"Look, I understand that you're concerned Captain. But from what I've seen of the evidence, it appears that what happened in Granelle is happening again...only it's happening here. I know it seems impossible, but I'm beginning to think that maybe someone has followed me here and is trying to hurt these people because of me."

"Think about what you're saying, Jake. If that's true, why get involved? It would be better for you to just come back to New York and get away from that place and draw whoever it is away."

"But the problem with that, Reggie, is that there's missing people already. We have to find those people first. If I leave before we find them, those people are as good as dead. Do you remember what Trevor said to me back at the police station all those years ago? He said he took Trudy because he wanted to play with me. Do you remember?"

"Of course I remember. I was the captain and Trudy worked for me. But that was Grant, not some nameless person. You're the one who said then, that it was personal. Grant was playing with you. And that's why he kidnapped Riley too, because he was trying to get to you. But now, this is nothing to do with you. Grant is dead."

"How can you say this has nothing to do with me? I have been coming to Creek River now for three summers and the people in Granelle know that. Is it possible that someone wanting to resurrect the Keeper myth is following me, wanting to play with me? If this was just some random act, then why here, why now, when I'm here?"

"You haven't been a cop in a long time. I get what you're saying. But you have a pregnant wife waiting for you at home, a great church, and a lot of people who love you. Why get involved?"

"Because I care about the people here too. And while I don't have the evidence yet, I think this does have something to do with me. I can't just walk away from it."

"And what about your wife?"

"Sarah's been to Creek River. She loves the people here too. I already told her about the missing boy earlier in the week. Knowing Sarah, when I tell her what's going on, she's going to agree with me."

"I don't like this at all. It was bad enough having you back on the force back when I was in control. You have been off the force for a long time now," Reggie sighed. "Is anything I'm saying getting through to you? Are you determined to do this foolish thing?"

"I need to help these people. I found out the hard way that if I'm going to play cop, I should just be one. And since I'm qualified to do it, it's just easier for me to have my badge. As you know, I've kept up my certification and my gun permit after the whole Grant escapade. All it takes is for you to give the okay, as my old captain."

"Put that Sheriff back on the phone," Reggie said gruffly.

"One more thing." Reggie grunted at that, so Jake continued, "The sheriff over in Beaumont got a sketch of a guy that was hanging around the club where the second girl disappeared. He's got to be in his early twenties. I want to fax it up to you. The friend said he called himself Sam."

"Sam? You think it might be Sam Craig? After all these years?"

"I don't know. I never saw him when Sarah was missing. But I know you did."

"That kid was bad news, even though he had nothing to do with Sarah. Big trouble maker in school."

"Can you see if he's still in New York?"

"Yeah, I'll get Crandall to check with Poughkeepsie. See what happened to the kid."

"Thanks, Reggie."

"Don't thank me yet. I still think it's a bad idea for you to be on the force."

"Just this information alone is helpful. If we're looking for Sam Craig, we have the history with the kid."

"You don't need to keep convincing me Jake. Just put Mueller on the phone."

Jake sat listening to Jesse's side of the conversation. He knew that even though Reggie didn't agree with what he was doing, he was giving his consent. He knew the next call he needed to make was to Sarah.

CHAPTER 5

Sam put the last carton in the trunk of his car. He had left the keys to the rental house on the counter before he locked it. He really liked this house and the little town. But he had learned a long time ago to not get attached. Sam stuffed a duffel bag full of clothes around the boxes and closed the trunk. The car was packed, but the majority of his possessions were in a storage unit in New Jersey. Someday, he hoped he could settle somewhere, once he knew what was required of him.

Sam didn't know where he was headed, but first he needed to talk to Roscoe Harman. The young history professor might finally have some answers for him. The small community college just outside of Creek River had been a private boys' school that was established close to 100 years ago. But when the economy in the area changed in the 1970's the private school went under and the property was bought by the state for the college.

Sam had looked for over a year for someone with Roscoe's qualifications. A few others who claimed to have knowledge of the older Irish language had disappointed him, but he felt that he finally found the person who could really translate the old journals for him. Sam's whole reason for coming to Beaumont was to befriend and hire Roscoe to look at the journals.

Sam had called Roscoe earlier to tell him he was stopping by. Now, as he walked toward the history department wing, he felt anticipation and excitement. Roscoe was waiting for him in the front hall of the old stone building.

"I'm so glad you came," Roscoe said to Sam as he reached out to shake his hand. "I've been anxiously waiting to hear from you." Roscoe led the way to his office down the narrow hallway. "I am so excited to read the excerpt you sent to me."

They went into Roscoe's office. Sam sat in the offered chair and waited for Roscoe to sit behind his desk. "So, you were able to figure it all out?" Sam asked.

"For the most part. Of course, the handwriting is atrocious and the use of the language is awful, but from the period it was written, I wouldn't have expected much more from someone who wasn't very well educated."

"Can you tell me what it says?"

"I did transcribe it for you like you asked. It was really fascinating. Since I know Irish history, I can tell that this family is living in the early years of the potato famine. The boy writes of his father's anger at the black potatoes and hunger."

"Is that all?"

"It's a start! You mentioned this was just a portion of a diary you have? Is there more?"

"Yeah, but I'm…," Sam began hesitantly.

"If it's my cost of transcribing it, I can negotiate that."

"It's not the money. I'd be glad to pay you for your time. It's just that my plans have changed, and I'm going to be leaving the area soon."

"Does that matter? I can always email the transcriptions to you. If you can leave the diary…."

"No, that's impossible. I can't part with them."

"I understand. Family heirloom," he said a bit saddened. "But you could copy them like you did this excerpt."

"There are parts that are extremely personal, and I'm just not sure."

"Please, Mr. Craig," Roscoe began as he fumbled on his desk for a folder. "I understand the confidential nature of the work you gave me. It's just that it was exciting for me. As a historian, I know this diary has such historical significance."

Sam took the folder and looked inside at the typed pages. He read a few lines quickly, and felt disappointment wash over him. "It seems so simple."

"Well, this was only a small entry. The boy is probably 11 or 12 years old."

"Boy? I thought it was a girl. The name is Paddy."

"Yes, short for Patrick…Paddy. How much more do you have?"

"A few journals."

Roscoe gave a low whistle. "From a historical view, that could be a gold mine! If it's complete, it would be a wonderful document to show what these people endured." His enthusiasm made Sam uneasy. He couldn't allow this man to know the truth about those journals.

"Well, I'm not interested in making money from these. It's personal to me."

"What a find!" he went on as if not hearing Sam. "I imagine even a museum would love it!"

"How much do I owe you for the work you've done?" Sam asked standing.

Realizing his blunder, Roscoe tried to cover, "Oh, you can wait and pay me once I finish...."

"I'm sorry, but it is finished."

"I would be honored if you would let me finish transcribing the diary. Just for me, I'll sign a confidentially agreement, if that's what it takes."

Sam thought for a moment. He knew that those journals held the answers that he needed to understand the creatures. "I'm not sure. But I will discuss this with my attorney and see what he thinks. I cannot stress to you the need for your complete cooperation in keeping what you've already seen to yourself."

"Oh, certainly! And thank you for the work. I look forward to hearing what you decide."

Sam nodded and turned away. As he walked out of the building, the heat hit him. It was a lot hotter down south than it was in upstate New York. He quickly walked across the parking lot to his car. He sank into the bucket seat and turned on the car. Glancing up at the building, he could see Roscoe standing in the window of his office watching him. The bag on the seat next to him held one of the journals.

As Sam pulled out of the lot, he glanced at the bag. He longed for the answers the journals held, but wasn't sure it was worth the risk of exposing the creatures to anyone. He drove toward the small town of Creek River, but just before reaching the first of the small shacks, he turned down a mountain road. The narrow road led to a few shacks before disappearing into the mountains. Sam drove to the end of the road, then kept going until the woods became too dense for the car to pass through.

Sam took the journal and locked it in the glove box before getting out of the car. It was much cooler in the woods with the tree cover blocking the sun. Sam walked deep into the woods and up to a mountain face. Following a barely discernable trail, Sam gave a few sharp whistles. As he continued to walk through the woods, dark shadows appeared near him keeping pace as he walked toward a fresh mountain stream. He sat down on the bank and waited. Soon, he felt the presence near him.

"We may have to leave soon," he said without turning. "I'm trying to find a place close, so we can stay in these mountains, but I'm attracting attention again. I wish I knew how to do this without all the moving. It's great here in these woods, but...."

Sam sighed and turned to the two large dark creatures sitting near him. He could see another still in the woods. It was these two that held his affection and dedication, the alpha male and his young son. They sat as if comprehending what Sam was saying to them. There was knowing in their eyes.

"I want to read what's in those diaries. I know they will tell me about where you came from and how I can take better care of you. I found this guy that can read them, but I'm afraid he will tell people about you. I can't let anything happen to you after what happened to your father."

Sam dropped his head. He couldn't help remembering how the old creature had saved his life, more than once. Anguish washed over him as he remembered burying him deep in the woods after he died from a gunshot wound. He felt a nudge behind him and buried his face into the dirty rough fur. He felt strengthened in his resolve to protect these creatures, whatever the cost. They were all he had now.

Sam pulled back to look into the creatures face. It was a large wolf like creature, with a massive jaw holding sharp needle-like teeth. The creature's eyes were brown with a red glow that shown brighter in the darkness. His son was just as massive and dangerous as his father. Four others stood apart from Sam, including the mate of the alpha male. While she accepted Sam and seemed to sense his intention, she was elusive. The three smaller creatures were just pups and always held back unless prompted by the alpha, as they sensed their mother's apprehension of the human. Sam watched her knowing that he needed to do something to gain her acceptance. Something he knew was hidden in those journals.

"Sometimes, I wish you could talk to me." Sam stood and followed the stream up deeper into the woods and the mountain. The creature walked by his side, the pack following behind. Near a rock wall, the three pups raced ahead and entered a den. The female followed ducking to enter the small opening. Sam sat down again and watched the stream. It was peaceful here in the woods, with the sounds of the pups playing, the stream rushing past, and the security of the only love Sam now knew. A long time passed as Sam just sat lost in thought trying to figure out his next move. Finally, physical need began to weigh on him, and he knew he needed to leave. It was getting late in the day, and Sam knew he needed to find a place for the night. As he got to his feet, the male was alerted and came over to Sam.

"I wish I could just stay here forever…," Sam felt an excitement grow in him. "Why can't I? I'll just get some camping equipment and stay here with you! Then Roscoe can keep working too. Why didn't I ever think of that before?"

The creature sensed his change of mood and even the female came out of the den and looked at Sam. "This will be great! I better get to a store, so I can try to get something set up before dark."

Sam headed back down the mountain to where his car was. The two males kept pace with him, watching the woods for any predator that could harm Sam. But none would approach the evil that emanated from the darkness that surrounded the human.

CHAPTER 6

"Where do we go from here?" Jesse asked Jake. Jake had been going over all the details of the case, but felt like something was missing. The search for Timmy ended a few days before, and the police in Beaumont had no leads on Bobbi. The evidence in the Novak case provided nothing for them to pursue. Reggie couldn't be sure that the sketch was Sam Craig since the faxed picture was so grainy. According to information obtained from Sam's father through the police in Poughkeepsie, Sam had left home two years ago and he hadn't been heard from since.

"If it were up to me, I'd get some backup from Granelle," Jake finally replied.

"As far as I'm concerned, it is up to you." Jesse got up and went to the coffee pot. "It's one thing to look for a lost kid in the woods, a marital dispute, you know, routine things. But if this is somehow connected to New York, to this Craig fellow, I don't have the resources or men to handle this."

"The Granelle Police force is about the size of Beaumont's. I don't think they will send anyone down to work with us. But there's a PI firm in Saratoga that I know of that can help us. It's run by my former partner."

"Meg Riley," Jesse quickly added.

"Yeah."

"Reggie Bennett told me not to let her anywhere near the case."

"Reggie is biased. Meg's a good detective."

"From what you've told me about these cases, you're the expert here. Do you really think she knows anymore than you do about this?"

"She figured out the stuff about the myths long before anyone else. She knew about the creature first, saw it first, and was even kidnapped by Grant because of what she figured out."

"How's this going to work? Bennett ain't going to go along with this."

"Reggie doesn't have to. Meg works for herself as a private investigator. We hire her to work with us. When we were partners, we were a good team. Besides, if she finds out what's going on here, I don't think I'll be able to keep her away."

"Well, go ahead and call her. Bennett ain't running the show here in Creek River. I'm just hoping we find these kids alive."

Jake pulled out his cell phone and went outside. He didn't know if this was a mistake or not, but he knew she was the only one person he felt could help. Dialing from memory, Jake sat down on the steps. He listened to the phone ringing.

"Hello?"

"Hi, Meg. I'm probably the last person you expected a call from," Jake said feeling a bit unnerved. When there was no response to what he said, Jake continued. "It's kind of a long story, but I've gotten involved in a police investigation. This.... It's just.... Man, this is harder than I thought it would be."

"Okay Jake, what's going on?"

"Two teenage girls are missing and a young boy. Meg, you are the only one I know who would understand the relevance of that." Jake waited for the response from his former partner. The long silence stretched out, and Jake began to feel like calling Meg was a big mistake. Finally he added, "A few of the mountain folks think they saw the devil. What they described to me is that creature."

Meg let out a long sigh. "Did you forget that you're a minister?"

"I haven't forgotten. But there are too many things that match what happened in Granelle. So many clues that tie to the past that I couldn't just walk away without trying to help law enforcement find these missing kids."

"Where are you if you're not in Granelle?

"Virginia."

"This is happening in Virginia? Then how is it the same creature? And missing kids? This isn't the same case Jake. Forget it and just go home."

"I'm not walking away from these people. This place has become like a second home to me. I care about the people of the Hollow the way I care about the folks in Granelle. Two teen-age girls are missing, one from the mountains and one from town. It's all the pieces that point to similarities to what happened in Granelle years ago. As incredible as that sounds knowing Trevor is dead, it's happening here."

Again, there was a long silence when Jake stopped talking. Finally, Meg said, "Okay, you've sufficiently spooked me. But this is all over, Jake. Trevor is dead. Shamus is dead. There's no one else...."

"Yes, there is. The only one I can figure who is starting this again is Sam."

"No, there's no way that Sam is doing this. I was with him in that basement when we were both abducted by Trevor. He was only ten-years old. He knows what it feels like, and I can't believe he would take another child and put him through what he went through."

"There are two teenage girls missing too."

"Last time, we thought it was Sam and it wasn't him then either."

"Well, I can't find him anywhere. It's like he fell off the planet," Jake said pacing. "We have a police sketch from a witness who was with the second girl just before she disappeared. I can't tell, but it could be Sam grown up."

"Okay, back up. Start at the beginning, so I know everything."

Jake went back to that day on the mountain with Ma. He told Meg everything up to where the sheriff came asking for his help.

"But I'm doing this by the book, Meg," Jake said as he finished. "I took my badge back."

"What? Jake...how...," Meg stammered.

"After what happened last time, I want to make sure that if I'm supposed to be working on this case, that I'm really working on it. Jesse Mueller, the local sheriff, asked me to help after he checked me out. I said the only way would be if I was officially on the case."

"So, how...Jake, you haven't officially been in law enforcement since we were partners! That was like, what ten, twelve years ago. How in the world...?"

"Believe it or not, Reggie Bennett."

"Bennett? He agreed with you being on the case?"

"Well, after he got done yelling at me he did. He said all the same things you did. But when Jesse and I told him what evidence we had, he gave me the reference and dug up my jacket."

"What do you want from me?"

"My old partner back."

Meg laughed. "Well, Bennett's not going to give me the same treatment. Oh, he'll yell at me, but he won't give me the reference."

"It's not up to Reggie. It's up to me."

"You? What about this sheriff...Jesse, you said?"

"This is a bit out of Jesse's comfort zone. He's used to dealing with jay walkers and family feuds. He's officially given me the case. I can hire whoever I need. You're a private investigator that I'm asking to help me out with some investigative work."

"Jake, I'm in the middle of a bunch of cases...."

"Do you think you can stay away from this? This is the same, Meg. I feel it in my gut. Those creatures are here in Creek River and up in the Hollow. A little boy and two girls are missing, just like you were. Someone is behind this.... Sam or someone who thinks this needs to keep going...I don't know. But I need back up and you are the only one I trust."

Meg sighed. "Okay, where do you want me to start?"

"I thought I'd email you the sketch. Sam was in Granelle three years ago. If that sketch is him, someone will know."

"Did you send it to Bennett? He saw Sam three years ago."

"He said he wasn't sure. The fax was pretty grainy. I wanted to scan it and email it, but the technology down here is a bit out dated."

"Then what?"

"Are you ready to travel?"

"Where?"

"A few places, Poughkeepsie, Virginia..., maybe Ireland."

"You serious?"

"Can you go by my place when you go to Granelle? I need my passport and a few other things. I'll have Sarah get it all ready for you."

"You're serious," Meg stated. She got up and went to her closet. As she talked, she pulled out a suitcase and began to pack. "How soon do we leave for Ireland?"

"Depends on how soon you can find out what we need to know about Sam. If we find him, we might not need to go. But even using Reggie's connections, we cannot find him. Either he's dead, which is highly unlikely, or he's living under a pseudonym."

"What are you working on in Virginia?"

"I'm trying to follow our victims from this end. Erica Boon was our first victim. Her trail is a bit cold. She's been missing almost a month now. Sheriff believed she ran away, so he didn't pursue any leads. The boy that went missing was a troubled kid, sort of like Sam was. So that leaves me with Roberta Jackson. She went missing day before yesterday."

"Anything else I should know?"

"Well, there's something a bit strange. It's probably a mix up at the lab, but…do you remember the theory you had about those animal hairs?"

"How can I forget? It's what alienated me from Bennett and led to my leaving the force."

"The sheriff found some animal hairs stuck in barb-wire at the scene where the boy disappeared. It's just…never mind this is too farfetched."

"Oh, let me guess. There is human DNA in the sample."

Jake was silent for a moment. "Then it's true. These are the same creatures. Why didn't you ever tell me about that?"

Meg stopped packing and sat on the edge of her bed. "I figured that no one would believe me. The only one I ever told was my dad when he was helping us track down Grant."

"Brian knew and never told me?"

"Would it have made a difference then? I figured if you knew it, it would drive you further away from the case. Then afterwards, it didn't seem to matter."

"What do you make of it? How is that possible?"

"The only explanation I could come up with is that all the old myths are true."

"Well, obviously Grant and O'Leary believed them to be true or they wouldn't have done what they did to complete those rituals."

"I'm not talking about the rituals, or about certain people believing they are true. The heart of what the keepers have done is that they believe that those creatures are part human and that they require a blood sacrifice."

"Meg, how in the world can they be part human?"

"Because they are part werewolf."

"That's impossible…."

Meg cut Jake off. "Let me finish. When I was working the case, I found this guy, Chevers, a PhD that was working at Albany State College. He said that the original creatures were from a mixture of a werewolf being bred to a wolf. It created this hybrid animal that we've seen."

"That's nonsense!"

"Then you explain the human DNA in the sample."

"I can't. There's no logical explanation."

"Believe what you want, Jake. Personally, after all I've seen over the past twelve years, I believe it wholeheartedly."

"Well, I guess for now that doesn't matter. I'm going to go over to Beaumont tomorrow and see if there's a place I can scan the sketch. Are you ready for this?"

"I don't have a choice. This needs to finally end. This time, Jake, we take out those creatures too. Without them, it really is over."

"Okay, call me tomorrow after you get done in Granelle. I want to know what Reggie thinks of the sketch. I'll let him know that you're coming by. But Meg, be nice to him."

"I'll try. But I'm not promising you anything." After Meg hung up, Jake called Sarah and Reggie to update them on Meg.

CHAPTER 7

Meg sat on the edge of her bed after she hung up the phone. She looked at her reflection in her closet door mirror and realized she was pale. Her green eyes looked huge with her shoulder length blond hair pulled back into a ponytail. Meg couldn't believe it was possible that history could be repeating itself again. With the death of Shamus O'Leary and Trevor Grant, how could anyone know to continue the rituals of the keeper? And why? From what Meg remembered, the blood ritual was to make a new keeper, and the only one who could perform the ritual would be Sam. She pulled her attention away from her reflection and made a call.

"Hey, Dad," Meg said when the phone was answered. Brian Riley, Meg's father, was a cop in Albany when Trevor Grant broke out of prison three years before. To protect his daughter, he got mixed up in the investigation that Meg and Jake were pursing to find Grant. Mauled by the creature, it took Brian almost six months to recover, only to find himself without a job. His involvement in the investigation and giving out confidential police information led to his forced resignation from the department. Feeling responsible, Meg asked him to be her partner in her PI firm. There were days when Meg really enjoyed working with her father, but other times….

"How's my favorite daughter?" Brian asked.

"Well, I've got a new case that I need some help on," Meg said hedging a bit.

"A him or a her?"

"It's not a matrimonial case. Thing is, Dad, I'm not sure if I should involve you."

"Why? What's the problem? Think I'm getting too old?"

"The cycle is starting again. I just got off the phone with Jake."

Brian was quiet for a few long moments, and Meg just waited for his response. "Jake? Not his wife again?"

"No, no. As far as I know, Sarah's fine. It isn't even happening here. Jake's in Virginia."

"Okay, Meggie. You better start at the beginning."

Meg recounted what Jake told her. Brian listened only interrupting for clarification. Finally, he said, "Jake's right. How can we stay out of this? We know more than anybody about these creatures and the crimes. He's doing it the right way this time too. But, I think his wife and anyone else who was involved in the past need to go to safe places. Until we know who's behind it, anyone of them could be in danger to protect those creatures."

"You mean any of us. We could be in danger, Dad. That's why I'm not sure you should be involved."

"If you really thought I shouldn't be involved, you wouldn't have called me."

"The last time you were hurt, and I almost lost you."

"I don't plan on going into the woods this time though. Besides, you said this was happening in Virginia."

"Who's to say that something isn't happening here too? Last we knew that animal was living in the mountains behind Granelle."

"Sounds like they've relocated according to what Jake is saying."

"And like I said in the past, that means a person is involved, someone who moved them. Look, I'm going over to Granelle tomorrow and talk to some people, including Sarah. I'll see if I can convince her to visit her family out of state. If not, I'll ask Bennett if he can keep an eye on her to protect her."

"You're going to talk to Bennett?" Brian asked knowing the history between them.

"I don't have a choice. I've got to see if that sketch looks like Sam."

"Okay. What do you want me to do?"

"Jake wanted me to go to Poughkeepsie and track down Stanley Craig, Sam's father. I think maybe it would be better if you did that. My history with the family isn't very good. I didn't handle Sam's disappearance very well when he was a kid and I'm not sure if Mr. Craig will open up to me. If you head down there in the morning while I'm in Granelle, we can meet at the office when you get back and see if we can figure out where Sam actually is living."

"I can do that. Do you have an address or should I find it?"

"I had an old address from three years ago. I'll give you that to start. Hopefully, he's still living in Poughkeepsie."

"Do you really think the person is this kid?"

"I don't really know. It seems like it would be impossible. Especially since the last time we thought that, we were wrong. I think we need to find out more about these creatures and the hold they have on people."

"Then what?"

"We've got to end this. Like I told Jake, this doesn't end until we finally get rid of those creatures. Without them, this can't keep on happening."

They talked for a while longer going over everything they remembered about the past. Meg found the addresses of Sam's family members who lived in Poughkeepsie and gave them to Brian. After she hung up, she went through her old files and began to painstakingly go through all the details of the past. The theories, the animal hairs, and the people. As she traced back the line from Shamus O'Leary's abduction of the ten year old boy, who was Trevor Grant, she stopped and thought about Sam. Grant had become so deranged in the end of his life with those creatures and his obsession with continuing a legacy of evil, he murdered and kidnapped people.

Meg sat thinking about that time locked in the basement of the old house in Granelle with Sam. She thought about how scared the little boy was, but he was found and reunited with his father. Sam hadn't been involved three years ago when Grant broke out of jail and tried to resurrect his power of the keeper. Sam had no connection to be making this happen again. Or did he?

Meg remembered being locked in the cage with the child who commanded the creature to turn on Grant. And watched as ten-year old Sam commanded the creature to leave Jake alone and declaring himself the new keeper with authority that surprised her. Could that be all it took? So many questions about the power of the keeper plagued Meg's mind. It was time to end this once and for all. If it was Sam, she would stop him or die trying.

* * *

Meg barely slept as she was so keyed up about the case. After leaving a message about the change in plans for her assistant at her Saratoga PI office, Meg headed to Granelle. She realized it was early, but she hoped to see Bennett first and then go to Jake's for his stuff. Neither visit appealed to her, but she would handle it. She had long accepted the fact that her ex-partner and fiancé had moved on, both professionally and personally. Begrudgingly, Meg found that Sarah was a really nice person. But she often wondered how different her life would be if Jake hadn't turned religious and they had had the future they had planned together. Meg's life had become her business, and she was fine with it. Her reputation had grown and she even had a few cases in California.

As the dense woods thinned, the small town of Granelle spread out before her. It had changed little from the town she remembered. She drove to the far side of town, where the Bennetts lived. Reggie's two sons were grown and had moved away, but Reggie and his wife still lived in the small town. Jake lived in the small white house near the church. As she passed the house, Meg couldn't tell if Sarah was up yet.

The middle of town was small, and Meg was soon on a dirt road leading to a few of the isolated houses. It had been great living in the small town where everyone knew each other. But Meg had left Granelle a long time ago, and now preferred the anonymity of living in the city of Saratoga Springs. Well, as anonymous as she could be with her reputation as an investigator.

Meg pulled into the driveway in front of the Bennett house. Reggie must have been waiting for her because the front door opened while she was walking up the stone walkway.

"I hoped I wasn't coming too early," Meg said stopping in front of the porch.

"Nope, I've been waiting for you," Reggie replied and then opened the storm door. Meg walked up to him. Now that he was retired, Reggie spent even more time at the gym. Meg was impressed with how well-built he still was. Years ago, Reggie had moved his family up from New York City where he had worked on the police force on the harsh city streets. He was well over six feet tall, with a deep booming voice. Meg could quickly tell that body building wasn't the only thing that had stayed the same.

Reggie led the way to a sunny kitchen where his wife, Clarissa, was having a cup of coffee. There were two other cups already waiting at the table for her and Reggie. Clarissa poured coffee into both cups and excused herself. As Meg settled at the table, she couldn't help wondering what Reggie was thinking about her involvement.

"So, did you get the email from Jake yet?" Meg began fussing with her coffee cup. She realized that Reggie was scrutinizing her.

"Just before you came. I think that sketch is Craig."

Meg looked up at him surprised. "I just can't believe that Sam would do this. Not after what he's gone through."

"I didn't say that he did it. I just think the sketch looks like him. Might not even be him. That sketch could be any number of people." Meg didn't respond, just took a sip of the coffee. There was a long silence between them. "Anything else?" Reggie finally asked.

"There are a lot of things I'd like to ask," Meg murmured.

"Well, then ask."

Meg looked up at him again. "It's not that easy. Not after what happened between us."

"Riley, are you forgetting that I was the one that helped you keep your PI license after you interfered in my investigation three years ago?"

"No, I haven't forgotten. And I haven't forgotten what happened when I was on the force either."

"I was your superior and you wouldn't respect that position or take orders."

"But I was right about Grant."

"Yeah, you were. But that didn't give you authority on the force that you tried to take when the case was solved. I was still your boss. Not the other way around," Reggie said in a matter-of-fact tone of voice.

Meg felt herself getting defensive anyway. "But you didn't respect what I did...and neither did anyone else."

"Actually, we all did. But you made it hard for all of us to work with you. Look, Meg, I'm not your boss anymore." Surprised at the use of her first name, Meg was taken aback. "Against my better judgment, Jake wants your help. It's not that I don't think you are a good investigator, the problem is that you always think you're right and won't listen to anyone else."

"But I was right!"

"Yes, you were right about Grant and that creature...a long time ago. But you were wrong about Sam. I'm willing to help you so that it will help Jake. But you need to realize going into this, that Jake is the one in charge. I understand he wants to use you and you are a PI. I strongly discouraged him, but you do know things that no one else knows. Like the stuff about those creatures."

"I can't believe you! After all these years...."

"...you're still hot headed. I am too. But this isn't about either one of us. This is about Jake, some missing people in another small town, and some nut case has followed him to Virginia. Jake is my friend, and I don't want anything to happen to him."

"He's my friend too."

"Then let's agree to disagree about the past and focus on what Jake needs right now to find this person. Now what do you need to ask me that is relevant to this case? What resources did you...and, I assume, your father... discuss that you might need?"

"Okay, for the sake of those missing people in Virginia, I'll put the past in the past too. There are a few things that Dad and I talked about last night. Do you still have any case notes or records from three years ago?"

"Some, but mostly it's just stuff I remember. So, let's go over what we both remember and see if we can develop a theory." Meg agreed and for the next few hours they went over the details of the past. When Meg went to leave, Reggie walked her to her car.

"I've been thinking about another rabbit trail you might want to follow before you leave Granelle," Reggie said as Meg settled in the car.

"You don't think I've got enough here?" Meg gestured at the pages of notes she had compiled.

"The old house on Dunning. When we arrested Grant, a bunch of stuff got left there. We figured the Hanson family would clean it out before they tried selling it. But they never did. There might be something there that could help."

"That house…," Meg said staring up at Reggie. "I haven't gone back inside that house since…."

"I know… since you were found in that basement with those other women and Sam. But it's another place you might find clues."

"Maybe Dad could check it out."

"Yeah, maybe."

"You don't agree?"

"I think that it should be you. You were down there with Grant. Maybe you saw something or he did something that you'll remember that can direct you now. Or maybe you'll just find a bunch of old rotting junk."

"Or, I'll find myself reliving the nightmare. Sorry," she quickly added. "I'll talk it over with Jake. Anyway, thanks, Captain, for helping. I'll keep in mind the other stuff you said too."

Meg closed the door and backed out of the driveway. She drove off toward town to go see Sarah, but with a feeling of fear about Reggie's suggestion that she go back to that old house. She shuddered as she remembered being locked in that cage with the little boy, seeing that creature waiting for them, and watching Grant plan their deaths. That place caused her deepest darkest nightmares and she did not want to go back there…ever.

CHAPTER 8

The trip to Poughkeepsie was long for Brian. Waking up a bit later than he intended, he got stuck in the morning rush hour traffic around Albany. The GPS led Brian directly to a big, white, colonial house in the outskirts of Poughkeepsie just before eleven in the morning. Brian pulled into the driveway and could see there were no cars in the garage. Deciding to try anyway, he stepped out into the heat and went to the door. No one answered the door, and Brian looked around for some indication that this was the Craig's house.

Brian turned and looked around the neighborhood. The neat row of big houses with large yards spread out down the street. This was the type of neighborhood where there was no one home during the day. Brian still walked to the several houses only to find no one was home. Walking back to the white colonial, he went back to his car and got in. The blast of the air conditioner felt great when he turned the car on, and he took a long drink from a bottle of water. After sitting for a few moments, he backed out of the driveway. He drove around the neighborhood and finally found an older lady working in a flower bed.

"Excuse me," Brian called stepping from the car, but staying near it. The lady looked up and squinted in the sun. "I'm friends with the Craigs, live at 511. Do you know them?"

"The Craigs?" she replied getting to her feet.

"Yes, Stanley and Anne."

"Oh, yes, the accountants. I don't think they are home during the day."

"I must have gotten the times wrong or something. Do you know where they work?"

"I'm not comfortable telling you stuff about them. If you know them, you would know how to get in touch with them."

"I'm sorry for bothering you. I'll call Stanley later."

She stood watching as Brian got back in his car and drove way. After he was out of sight, he pulled out his cell phone and asked directory assistance for a listing for Stanley Craig, CPA. He called the office and got the address. Fifteen minutes later, he was in front of an office complex with lawyers and accountants. Apparently, Stanley was one of the partners in the accounting practice. Brian found the office and went in. He told the receptionist he had an appointment with Stanley and made a big scene when she told him he wasn't in the appointment book.

Stanley came out of a back office looking concerned. He was wearing a polo shirt and kayak pants. His sandy brown hair was thinning and turning grey. "I'm sorry, Mr. Craig. He's not on the schedule."

"It's alright, Becky. What did you say your name was?"

"Can we talk in private?" Brian looked at Becky with a frown. "I prefer not to discuss personal matters in front of others."

"Oh, of course," Stanley replied leading the way to a conference room. Reluctantly, he closed the door. "Now, what is your name?"

Brian sat down at the table and waited for Stanley to sit. He knew he would be a while before he left once he told Stanley why he was really here. "My name is Brian Riley."

"How did you get my name? I don't believe we ever talked."

"You're right, we haven't spoken yet."

"Then why…," Stanley said looking toward the door.

"I'm a private investigator from Saratoga Springs. I'm trying to get some information about your son, Sam."

"Sam?" Now, Stanley looked confused. "You aren't here for…."

"No. I thought if I said I was here looking for Sam, you might not want to talk to me." Stanley just looked even more confused. "I'm working with Jake Peterson on a case."

"Jake Peterson? Isn't he…I mean, he's my old minister. Working on a case?"

"Can I start at the beginning?"

"Maybe that would be best."

Brian told Stanley about Jake's trip to the Hollow, the missing women, and the mystery man who met up with Bobbi. "We aren't sure if this person is Sam. But Reggie Bennett thought that sketch could be him. Meg sent me the picture just before I got here." Brian pulled out his cell and found the picture. He showed it to Stanley.

"Well, this does look a little like Sam. But you should know that I had a falling out with my son. It was so hard for us after his mother was killed. It wasn't his fault. I know that now. But I had a rough marriage to Clara.

After we moved to Poughkeepsie, I took it as a chance to start over again. I got this job and worked hard to become a partner. Then, I met Anne when she came to work here. For my part, rebuilding my life, starting over again, I failed Sam. I didn't realize how troubled he was and just ignored him most of the time."

"In your opinion, could he be doing this? Trying to resurrect the old myths?"

"I would have said no until he spent that summer in Granelle. Were you around that summer that Grant broke out of jail?"

"Yes, I was in the woods when my daughter killed Grant."

"Your daughter...Riley. Oh, I see now. Do you work on the police force?"

"I did until that summer. I guess our lives, all our lives, were changed in ways we never thought that summer. Sounds like Sam's changed too."

Someone knocked on the door and an older man stuck his head in. "Is everything alright in here, Stanley? I heard there was a commotion."

"Yes, Kevin. This is Brian Riley, from Saratoga. We have mutual friends upstate."

Kevin regarded Brian with skepticism. "Are you sure?"

"Yes, I believe we are almost done." The man nodded and stepped out, closing the door.

"I'm sorry about that. Everything going to be okay?" Brian asked concerned.

"Yeah, he's the managing partner. I'll explain things once you leave."

"So, what happened after that summer that changed Sam?"

"I got some calls that fall from a lawyer in Ireland. I can't remember his name right now. But he said that somehow, Sam was mentioned in a will, but it wasn't a good thing. He wouldn't give me details. Sam for his part, began to spend a lot of time in the woods. Sometimes he would spend days out there. He stopped going to school and wouldn't get a job. I tell you, we were relieved when he left home after he turned 18. Apparently, the inheritance he got was enough for him to get his own place."

"Who did he get the money from?"

"I don't know. The lawyer said it was all confidential. After Sam left, I never heard from him again. It was all strange."

"Do you have any pictures of Sam that I could get copied?"

"I don't have anything really recent. He stopped having school pictures taken in high school. There might be something in a snapshot. I wish I could be more help. I wanted so much better for my son."

"Even if he doesn't end up being the person we are looking for, would you mind if I looked for him for you? Just to see how he is?"

"Oh, I can't really afford...."

"I'm not doing this for money. I guess maybe I'm trying to make up a bit for that summer. Fact is, we thought that Sam was the one that kidnapped Jake's wife. We were looking for him in those woods. It ended up being Sam that found Sarah and his friend, Johnny."

"Well, if you were wrong about that, is it possible that this person isn't Sam?"

"It probably isn't Sam. But he has a tie to a crime that matches the one we are investigating and a picture that resembles your son. Plus, you said yourself that he changed. Is there a possibility that the inheritance is somehow connected?"

"I don't know how."

"If I track Sam down...?"

"If you find my son, tell him I'm sorry. Tell him that he can come home anytime. We always have a place for him."

Stanley took a lunch break and took Brian back to the house. He found some pictures of Sam and showed Brian Sam's old bedroom. Stanley left Brian to look around the room. Anne had cleaned the room and it looked like a spare room in any house. There were very little personal effects left. Brian looked out the window into the dense woods behind the house. He wondered why Sam would spend so much time in the woods, alone. Brian pulled out his cell phone and called Meg.

"I got a question," he began before she could even say hello. "What ever happened to those animals that were in Granelle?"

"You mean that creature that attacked you?"

"Yeah, ever hear anything about them after Grant was killed?"

"No. Jake and I went into the woods trying to hunt it down after we knew you were going to recover. I wanted to make sure that no one else was attacked."

"Is it possible that it left Granelle?"

"Dad, those woods are endless."

"Is it possible?"

"Yeah, they were originally from Ireland. O'Leary and Grant brought them to the states. But they traveled with Grant and O'Leary."

"Ireland? That lawyer is from Ireland."

"What lawyer?"

"The one that contacted Stanley about Sam."

"Fill me in."

"Look, Stanley's going to have to get back to work and I need to check out a couple of things with him. Meet me at the office around three." Brian hung up and went to look for Stanley. He found him sorting some mail.

"I didn't think there was anything left in his old room that could help you," Stanley said as he put the mail down on a small table.

"Actually, I was looking at the woods and remembering you saying he spent a lot of time there. Do you have any idea why?"

"No, I figured it was just to get out of the house. Sam didn't have friends here. He spent a lot of time alone."

"Is it possible that he was in the woods with those creatures from Granelle?"

"Absolutely not. Sam was terrified of that animal. It bit him when he was kidnapped by Grant. He had nightmares when we moved here."

"Hmmm.... Did you by any chance write down that name of that lawyer from Ireland?"

"No, I know I didn't. Is that significant?"

"I think it might be. This all started in Ireland. That's where O'Leary was from and those animals."

"I really don't remember. I'll check with my wife to see if she remembers."

"Here's my card. If she remembers anything, please call me. I'm sure that Sam isn't the one we are looking for. I appreciate that you took the time to talk to me."

"Just remember if you do find Sam, let him know that I'm here if he needs me."

CHAPTER 9

Meg was pacing in the office when her father finally arrived from Poughkeepsie. She had been on the phone with Jake who was anxious to hear about Stanley too. When he finally walked in an hour late, Meg had a hard time holding back. "Why didn't you call me? I was getting worried."

"Oh, sorry. I took a walk through the woods behind the Craig house. It was...."

"Hold on, Dad. Jake wants an update too. We thought it would be easier to do a conference call." They went into the conference room, and Meg set up the call. "Okay, go ahead Dad."

"Hey, Jake," Brian began. "Been a while."

"I just wish it was under different circumstances. Sorry for the lousy connection. It's these mountains."

"You sound fine to me. I thought Stanley would be a bit evasive after what Meg told me, but he was quite willing to talk about Sam and his failings as a father. He's a pretty nice guy and remembers you as his pastor."

"We got pretty close when his wife died all those years ago."

"Maybe the connection to you is what made it easy for him to open up and discuss Sam. Anyway, he saw the sketch. It was the same as Bennett's reaction. Could be Sam, but maybe not. He gave me some pictures." Brian pulled them out of his pocket and put them on the table for Meg to see. She quickly took the photos and compared them to the printout she had of the sketch from Beaumont.

"I see what you mean," Meg said. "It could be Sam. In the pictures, his hair is long and shaggy. He looks like a hoodlum. But in the sketch is a guy that could be a preppy college student."

"Well, there is a kicker in all this. Apparently, Sam came into an inheritance when he turned eighteen. With some money, he could have changed his appearance or could really be a preppy college student."

"Who was the inheritance from? His mother?" Jake asked.

"Nope. Some benefactor, get this...from Ireland!"

"You're kidding? Would Grant have left him money?"

"That's what I was thinking. Some lawyer from Ireland tried to get Stanley to intervene before Sam turned eighteen. The problem was he wouldn't tell Stanley anything about the money. But the connection has to be there somehow. I made the connection when Meggie told me those animals originally came from Ireland."

"Who is this lawyer?" Jake asked. "If we can follow the money, we can find Sam."

"Stanley didn't remember. He was going to ask his wife."

"It wouldn't be Grant," Meg said matter of fact. "I remember how Grant hated Sam before he was arrested. He called him a failure and a disappointment. If it came from that source, it would have to be O'Leary."

"But why? Why would O'Leary, or even Grant leave money to Sam?" Jake asked.

"It's those creatures and that old myth. Somehow it all goes back to that. I think I need to see if that historian guy still works down at Albany State."

"Was he the one that gave you the original information about those creatures?"

"Yeah, Harry Chevers, PhD in medieval folklore. Who gets a degree in medieval folklore?" Meg shook her head. "Guess I can understand how Bennett felt with that piece of information when I tried to tell him all those years ago."

"Would Dr. Chevers know anything about the money, though?"

"He knew about the blood ritual that passed the power of the keeper to the next generation. If he doesn't know, maybe he knows someone who would know."

"Or maybe this is why we need to go to Ireland," Jake's voice began to break up.

"What did you say, Jake?" Meg sat up and leaned toward the phone.

"I said, maybe we need to go to Ireland. Find out from O'Leary's family if he had money. It might not be from him."

"You really believe that?" Meg asked.

"No, but we have to be objective and realize that it might be someone else. Maybe there was an inheritance from his mother that Stanley didn't know about. I know that Clara didn't always get along with her husband."

"There's one other thing from Poughkeepsie," Brian interrupted. "Then, I want to hear about your visit with Reggie. After that summer Sam spent up here, he changed. Something happened to him. When he went back to Poughkeepsie, he became a loner, spent hours and sometimes days in the woods. After Stanley left, I went into the woods. There was a barely discernable path."

"Dad!" Meg exclaimed. "You promised me you wouldn't go into the woods."

"Well, nothing happened, but I did find a den deep in the woods. There were some camping supplies and a lot of hairs in the cave. Since hairs seemed to be such a key to linking these cases, I took a sample. Hope Bennett will allow us access to a lab."

"If he can't, I can," Jake said. "So, it is possible that Sam had those creatures in Poughkeepsie. That would explain why we never found them."

"Sure does," Meg agreed. "And if these hairs are a match to what Jake has, we can rightly assume that Sam is involved with these disappearances. It has to be part of that myth. Maybe the money is contingent on Sam committing the blood ritual like Chevers talked about."

"I'd say it's time you tracked down your old friend Meg," Brian said. "I've got a contact who might be able to help me get the records from probate court about the inheritance."

"If you guys can scan those pictures from Stanley, Jesse and I can go back to the witnesses and see if they recognize Sam. Just like before, we are in a race against time in getting our victims back alive. I'm really worried about Erica and Timmy. We've even stopped looking for them," Jake said.

"I'll get them right over to you, Jake," Meg said getting up.

"Hey, aren't you forgetting your update?" Brian asked. "What happened with Bennett?"

"We played nice, Dad." She walked to the door. "Turns out, Bennett isn't as big a jerk as I remembered him to be."

"Well, I already have an update from Reggie so I'll check in with you later today." Jake hung up and Brian followed Meg into the reception area. Meg went to a scanner and began to scan the pictures to email to Jake.

"Well, spill it. How bad was he?"

"We agreed to disagree about the past and help Jake. Then, we went over what we both remembered and that was it."

"You expect me to believe that? With your history with Bennett?"

Meg looked up innocently at her father. "Of course. We are both professionals. You need to call him about your sample hairs, ask him yourself."

Meg smiled as he went to the conference room to call Reggie. While she wasn't really happy with what Reggie said about her conduct, in retrospect, she had to admit that she did have a chip on her shoulder back then. Well, maybe still did. As the scanner brought the pictures up on the computer, Meg could hear Brian's voice as he talked to Reggie. It seemed all her problems with working on the force began with the O'Leary/Grant cases. Her talk with Reggie that morning continued to absorb her thoughts. Maybe Reggie was right and it was time to let the past be the past. Once this case was closed, she intended to finally move on with her life and let go of the demons that haunted her. She heard Brian laugh and smiled.

CHAPTER 10

The heat in the canvas tent was unbearable, so Sam sat next to the stream with his feet dangling into the cool mountain waters. He was intent on working on his plan to move into the mountains and barely noticed the sunburn he was getting. The creatures were out in the woods hunting. He finished his list and tore it out of the notebook, knowing he needed to get moving because of the long hike back to the car. An off-road vehicle was the first thing on his list.

As Sam went to put the notebook back into his knapsack, he saw the folder with Roscoe's notes of the journal. He took the folder out and read again the first pages of the journal. He felt a kinship with Paddy and wanted to know more about him. Well, going back to the college was definitely on his list. But for now, he needed to get some supplies. Sticking the knapsack inside the tent, Sam then took off down the hill. As he started down the hill, he noticed a dark shadow following next to him in the woods. He smiled feeling safe with one of the creatures protecting him.

Sam was lost in his planning as he took the long trip down the hill. Suddenly, he heard growling and looked toward the creature. "Move boy, unless you want to get shot!" a voice called out.

Sam turned the other way to see a man aiming a shotgun in his direction. "No!" Sam shouted. "It's alright. He's mine."

The man lowered the gun, but only slightly. The mountain man was dressed in dirty clothes and his long grey beard was just as dirty. He was taller than Sam and squinted down at him. "What you doin' up here boy?"

"Getting away from everything. That dog is mine, and he won't hurt you unless he thinks you're going to hurt me."

"There's more than one and they ain't dogs. Mountain belongs to me. You aren't welcome."

"Mister, I don't mean any harm to you. I need a place where I can just be alone with them." Sam pointed toward the creature that stood still, waiting. As Sam watched the man, he saw another creature creeping up behind him.

"You aren't welcome. This mountain is mine!"

"Okay, I get it, but I want to stay here. These animals won't hurt you if they know that you are my friend. If you force me to leave, I can't stop them."

"I can with this," he indicated the gun.

"You might get one, but not the pack." Sam saw to his right edging down the hill, the third adult. She blended into the shadows, barely discernable. Sam knew they could easily tear the man apart.

"Then I'll take you out too." The man grinned. The creature behind Sam began to growl again and the man cocked the gun.

"Wait. We can help each other."

Lifting the gun to shoulder height, the man said, "And what can a kid like you do for me?"

"First, I'll call off the pack. You're surrounded, and they will kill you. Second, I've got money and I can help make your life a bit easier if you help me. But if you don't stop aiming that gun at me, I won't be able to stop them." The one behind the man was crouching to jump. Sam knew it was the alpha. The female was almost upon them too. The man saw her and slowly lowered the weapon. He turned and looked behind him seeing the third.

"What's your name boy?"

"Depends, you going to let us stay on your mountain?"

"Seems I don't have much of a choice."

Sam walked over to the man. He could almost feel the tension between the man and the creatures that surrounded them. "This mountain is the perfect place for us. I don't want to live near people. I want to be with them. If you're my friend, you will be safe."

"What's that suppose to mean?"

"Just what I said. Don't you want to be my friend?"

The man narrowed his eyes. "I don't want to be anybody's friend. I live here alone, taking care of myself."

"That's all I want too. Just to be alone. Don't you think this mountain is big enough?"

"Depends, what's that you said about money?"

"I've got some."

The man looked hard at Sam and then looked around at the creatures. They had stayed back, in the shadows. "And them? What are they? Wolves?"

"Not really. Something else."

"Something wild. You train them?"

"No. They can't be trained. Like you said, they're wild. It's more like I belong to them."

"Don't like the sounds of that. Why do you belong to them?"

"Let's just say it's my destiny. And in return, I don't have to worry about anyone trying to hurt me. They protect me, and I them."

"Don't make sense. Why'd you pick my mountain?"

"Maybe I'll tell you, someday. For now, we need to come to terms with each other. I'm not here to cause you problems. But on the other hand, I could use some help."

"You hiding out because the law's after you?"

"No. It's just as I said."

"What kind of help you needing?"

"I need a shelter. I have a tent, but that's not going to be much good in the bad weather. I figure I can get supplies, but I don't have much experience with building things. If you'd help me, I'll help you."

"The money?"

"Or whatever else you might want in exchange."

The man looked around at the creatures again who still hadn't moved. He looked up the mountain the way Sam had come. "How far up you planning on going?"

"Right now, I'm camped where the stream breaks through the mountain rocks. I thought that'd be a good place."

"How intent are you in staying away from people?"

"Very. I have to protect them."

"If you stay where you're camped, you'll have hikers by the end of the week. How much money you willing to give me?"

"How much money do you think its worth?"

"After you get set, you plan on being neighborly and such?"

"No. After I'm set, I'm hoping that we never see each other again."

"Fair enough." The man squinted. "You can promise these animals will leave me alone?"

"In my experience with them, they've protected those that have been my friends."

"I'll help you build a one room place. Nothing more."

"Actually, I wanted something a bit bigger than that."

"I've lived up here for close to 10 years. One big room, with a place to sleep, cook, and wash. You heat with wood in a cast iron stove that you cook on too. Any bigger, you won't stay warm in the winter. Nothing fancy. You want fancy, get off my mountain. You see those shacks on the way up?" he nodded down the hill.

"Yeah, I saw them."

"Those folks are kin to me. I don't bother with them, haven't seen some of them in years, but they are still kin."

"I won't bother them and neither will they. One more thing, can you teach me to shoot?" Sam nodded toward the shotgun.

"That'll cost you more."

"Fair enough." Sam stuck out his hand. "So, do we have a deal?"

The man shook his hand. "Now, what you are called boy?"

Sam thought for a moment, almost telling him he was Paddy, but quickly changed his mind. "You can call me Sam. And you?"

"Boon. I'll show you where you'll live."

Sam hesitated as the man began to turn to go up the mountain. "I was going to go into town and get some supplies first."

Boon turned back and looked at him. "You know what you need to get?"

"I made a list." Sam pulled the paper out of his pocket. Boon read it and then headed up the mountain. "Hey, that's my list."

"Dumb list. Let's see what you really need."

Sam looked at the back of the man walking away. He sighed and began to follow. Boon walked up toward the female. She slipped deeper into the woods away from the human. The two males took up the rear following Sam and Boon up the mountain. As they reached the stream where Sam had his tent, the female went into the den.

Boon stopped near the tent. "Another problem here is how the woods open up." Around the stream, the trees thinned and the sun shone down on them through the break. "When the weather is bad, you have no protection." Boon walked into the stream and splashed to the other side. Sam followed, knowing the two males were right behind them. They walked to the top of the ridge. Boon pointed down the mountain to his left.

"Down that way is the Hollow. That's more kin." He turned and looked toward the dark shadows. "That means they stay away from them too. I know they've been there, that's why I was hunting them. You might have an agreement with me, but not my cousin, Clancy. He's been hunting too."

"How can we stop your cousin from hunting for them? They will kill him if they are threatened."

"Only way is to bury you so far in the mountain that Clancy can't find you." Boon turned and walked deeper into the woods. They walked for hours, the woods were getting so dense at times, it was hard to break through. Boon pointed to a small shack and indicated that was his place. Then he continued to walk deeper and deeper into the woods. Finally, Boon stopped and looked around. A rock mountain was to the left and just deep woods surrounded them. "This will do."

"What! You've got me so far out in the woods, I have no idea how to even get here. And it has to be a good place for them. They need a cave or something for shelter too."

Boon made a disgusted sound. "You said you wanted to live totally away from people. Well, this is it."

"Away from people, but not away from food, water, and basic necessities. How can I survive out here?"

Boon looked hard at Sam. "You can survive because I survive."

"Well, that might be fine for you, but you were raised like this. I wasn't." The silence between them showed Sam he had made a big mistake. But this wasn't what he had in mind. He wanted to be away from everyone, not lost in the woods. Boon went to turn away. "You can't just leave me here."

"Follow your animals. They will take you back to their den."

"We have an agreement."

"That didn't include you insulting me or my life."

"I just figured, you live in the mountains…." Boon turned and glared at him.

"And people wondered why I disappeared into the mountains. I'm not an illiterate cracker. I was once married, with a family, working at a university. I chose to leave life behind."

"I'm sorry. I didn't know."

"But you chose to believe what you wanted just because of the way I look. I brought you out this far, so that no one would ever be able to find you."

"Okay, okay. But I don't know if I can do this."

"How important is it for you to protect them?" he said pointing at the creatures that were barely discernable in the woods.

"I will protect them with my very life."

"Why?" The rage from Boon caused the alpha to come closer to Sam. Boon clearly saw the creature for the first time as it came to stand near Sam. "My God, what is that?"

Sam laid his hand on the enormous head. The eyes glowed deep red in the darkness of the woods, every hair on the back of its neck stood on end, and a low growl started deep inside its chest. "I don't really know what kind of creature he is. His father chose me to be his keeper. I have made a pledge with my life to protect them."

"I think you made a pact with the devil, boy."

"I made a promise to his father who gave his life to protect me. Are you going to keep your promise to help me?"

Boon looked toward the other who was standing now closer to Sam. It was identical to its father, except his fur was black, and was creeping closer to Boon. Fear ripped through Boon as the realization of what he was seeing began to press down on him. These creatures emanated an evil that Boon could actually feel. Now, they were on his mountain and he had promised to help them. He had no choice. Swallowing his fear, Boon nodded. "Yeah, I'll help. But you better be rich because this is going to cost you."

CHAPTER 11

"All set, Dad," Meg yelled as she finished packing her bag and tried dragging it into the living room. Brian came down the hall and took the bag from her.

"What did you do? Pack everything you own?"

"I don't really know how long I'm going to be gone. I doubt I'll have time to wash clothes."

"You could always buy a few things if you need them." Brian struggled with the suitcase and finally stopped at the front door. Meg's carry-on was jammed and bulging with stuff too. "Seriously, Meggie, I think you've got way too much stuff. I doubt the airline is going to let you take this heavy bag."

"Okay, drag it over to the sofa. I'll pull a few things out."

After he put the suitcase near the sofa, Brian sat in the recliner. He watched as Meg opened the suitcase and started rearranging things. "Do you really think you're going to find Sam in Virginia?" he asked.

"I'm not sure what to think yet. He's the best suspect we have so far. But yet, I can't imagine Sam being the one behind these disappearances."

"That's not really what I was asking. Even if he was the guy, do you think he's in Virginia?"

"That's where the crimes are happening. Someone's in Virginia doing something, even if it's not Sam. Why are you asking? Do you think I shouldn't go?"

"Are you sure you've followed up on everything here?"

Meg sighed. "Dad, you're no good at beating around the bush. What are you asking me?"

"Are you going to be okay with Jake?"

"I'm fine, Dad. That was a long time ago. We've both moved on. I'm even on friendly terms with his wife."

"Well the last time we worked with Jake, you weren't really over him. Now you're going to be alone with him in another state. Are you ready for that?"

"Like I said, it was over a long time ago. My interest is in ending this thing once and for all. Even if we don't find the person, we have to get that creature. According to Jake, it's in Virginia."

"Well, we've got to get moving if you're going to get on the plane. You sure you're ready for this?"

"Dad, I'd rather be doing this kind of investigative work. I really hate these scumbags that cheat on their wives with younger girls. I'd like to slap them with charges of child molestation, but they are always so careful to get them once they are of legal age. To tell you the truth, Dad, my not being married doesn't have anything to do with Jake. It's because I'm not wasting my time on a guy who's going to screw me over in the end."

"Not all guys are like that."

"Well, sorry. But that's the way I see it."

"Then maybe you should get out of this kind of work. Do some consulting like you are now."

"Yeah, I could do that. But there's good money catching those cheats. I really have been enjoying the trips I've been taking lately and being able to choose which cases I want. I've got a pretty good life now."

"Okay, I'm done being the worried dad. But if you feel any kind of conflict, you call me. I am your partner now and you can't have any conflict of interest working on a case. Let's get to the airport before you miss your flight. You done packing?"

"I think it's lighter now."

Brian got up and took the bag. "You're kidding right? Did you really take anything out of this bag?" he laughed as she pointed to the pile of stuff on the couch.

It was a quiet ride to Albany, each lost in their own thoughts about the case. Meg was anxious to get to Creek River and see the evidence for herself. She was surprised when Reggie gave her the Granelle police files from the old cases. She felt that finally, she was being respected by Reggie. At the airport, Brian pulled the car up to the drop off area.

"Sorry, I can't wait with you, but I got an appointment with that probate guy."

"I'll call you when I get down there," Meg said as she stepped out of the car. Brain got her suitcase from the trunk and set it up onto the platform. Meg reached out and hugged her father, surprising him. "Please be careful, Dad. I'm still mad at you for going into the woods in Poughkeepsie."

"Well, you were the one who said that the creature is in Virginia now."

"Still, you need to be careful. You're the only dad I've got and I want you around for a long time.

"You be careful too. We know for sure you're headed right into this thing." Meg nodded and turned away, choked up with emotion. As Brian watched her walk away, he couldn't help but remember that just a few short years ago, Meg wouldn't even talk to him. She had blamed him for the breakup of his marriage to her mother. Her resentment of his new wife had pushed her further away from him. But when Grant broke out of jail, they joined together to find him and stop him. The bond they shared made them closer than ever. Brian regretted the lost years, but ultimately, he loved his daughter and was proud of who she was.

Brian left the airport and drove to some corporate offices on Washington Avenue Ext. He found the building he was looking for and parked in front. The receptionist had him wait in a conference room. Finally, an older well-dressed man came into the office with a folder.

"Brian, good to see you again," he said shaking Brian's hand. The two men sat facing each other.

"Were you able to find out anything on Craig?"

"Nothing. Are you sure of the year?"

"Positive."

"There was nothing filed in any probate court in New York for the name Sam or Samuel Craig that year. I even checked out Trevor Grant and Shamus O'Leary. Nothing. Are you sure you had the right information?"

"Thought so. But maybe there was a catch to it somehow. Is there any way to check it out in Ireland? That's where O'Leary was when he died."

"The laws are different there, and I have no access to records. But if you find out who their families are and see if there was any money, you might be able to access the court system over there."

"Meg might be going to Ireland. We think that this money is the key to finding this kid. Do you have any suggestions?"

"Have there been any hits on his social security number?"

"Nothing. It looks like he never worked, no taxes filed, nothing."

Brian thought for a moment remembering something that Jake had said. "It is possible that he could have changed his name?"

"There would be a record that he did that."

"If the money goes back to Ireland, the name change could have happened there."

"But again, it's going to be hard to trace without any point of contact."

"Isn't there a way to trace a trust fund?"

"Do you know the name of the trust?"

Brian shook his head. "This is like a big circle. There's no way in."

"You need to go back to the beginning, get the relevant names, find out where the will was recorded. Once you have that, we can dig into where the money is now."

"I just hope it's not too late to save those three kids who are missing," Brian said with finality, standing. The lawyer stood and walked Brian out.

"I'll help in any way that I can. If Meg is going to Ireland and does find out that O'Leary had money, have her find out where that came from. Since we can't find anything in Craig's name, I bet that he kept the same lawyer and funding sources."

"Thanks for all your help, Pete."

"I didn't do much. But call me if you think I can help with something."

Brian walked back to the car. Storm clouds were gathering and he knew that the rain would only add to the humidity. He sat in his car considering his options. Going back over what he knew, he wondered about the junk that Meg mentioned was in the Hanson house in Granelle. Maybe there was something there that would help find the elusive money.

CHAPTER 12

Back at Boon's cabin, Sam ate some kind of stew that Boon had heated on a propane stove. Sam was impressed with the one room cabin, the handcrafted furniture, and the realization that Boon had built it. They hadn't spoken much since their argument in the woods. Sam could sense that the creatures were close by, and so could Boon. They carried with them a presence that could be felt.

Boon finished his meal and began to clean up the few dishes they had used. Sam didn't know what to do, so he just sat at the table looking around at the furnishings. He realized how inadequate his list had been and almost felt embarrassed by it. Boon came back to the table and pulled out a pad of paper.

"Probably should just stay till morning," Boon said as he began to write things on the paper.

"I can't. I have to go back to the tent."

"Why? They'll be fine without you."

Sam shook his head. "It's not them. There's other stuff in the tent that I can't just leave there. You said before, they could lead me back to the den."

"What's so important that you can't stay here overnight?"

"Just some of my stuff. It's personal."

Boon looked up at Sam with a look of disapproval. "That's ridiculous. You're already here, and we can get an early start in the morning. What's so important about this stuff that it can't wait?"

"What difference does it make to you anyway?"

"If you want to get working on this before the hikers come up for the weekend, you've got to get an early start in the morning. We've got ground to break…."

"I want to get my stuff before any hikers come across it. Besides, I'm going to have to go to town tomorrow anyway. If I'm further down the hill, it will be faster for me to leave in the morning. I'm going to have to get my things anyway."

"What's the big hurry about getting to town that it can't wait?"

Sam sat thinking for a minute wondering how much to let Boon into his private life. "There's someone I have to see in town."

Boon sat back in his chair regarding Sam. "Some girl?"

"What! No, nothing like that. I have to go to the college."

"College?"

"Look, it's a personal matter. I can't talk about it."

"Just like you can't talk about what's in the tent that you can't leave overnight." Boon got up and got a jug, taking a long drink. He wiped his hand across his mouth as he turned back to Sam. "Your biggest secret is already out, boy. Those animals you're hiding are worse then anything else you can tell me."

"No, there's more. Right now, I'm not ready to tell you about it." Sam got up and walked toward the door. "I'm not sure I can find my way back up here though. So, can you come back to the tent...?"

Boon laughed. "You think you got this all figured out. I'm just going to be at your beck and call. Forget that! I'm letting *you* stay here, not the other way around."

"Are you forgetting them?" Sam said darkly.

"No, but you're forgetting that without me, you can't survive here. Without me, you'll be living in a tent where anyone can find you. And if your animals forget that I'm helping you and kill me, you're back to running from whatever it is you're running from, without me."

Sam just glared at him. After living these past years on his own, he resented that he needed this man. He knew Boon was right, but he wanted to call the shots. Sam could hear them just outside the door. He saw Boon look toward an opened window. "Okay," Sam said unclenching his fist. "I get that I need you. But there are certain things about who I am to the creatures that I'm not ready to talk about. That includes what's in my tent and my need to go into town. But I'm paying you for that help too."

"What you don't understand is how long it is going to take to get you set up and how quickly winter comes to this mountain. There's a lot of work that I need to do to my own cabin before winter, wood that needs to be gathered, and food to see us through until spring."

"With my money, it's going to make that process easier."

"Maybe, but I don't want to draw attention to us either. We can't just go into Beaumont throwing a lot of money around. I don't want anyone to know where I live."

Sam could hear the creature at the door knowing it could feel the tension between the two men. "Guess I'm not the only one with a past to hide. Seems like you've been the only one with questions. What are you hiding? Why do you live up here all alone?"

Boon narrowed his eyes at Sam. "My life is none of your business."

"Then we agree. My life isn't any of yours. Now, I have to go back to the tent."

"Okay, get your things from the tent. But it's pointless for you to go into town and lose a day when you don't know everything you need to get. I don't want to waste that kind of time, so wait for another day to go to Beaumont."

"That's not for you to decide."

"That's my compromise." Boon took another drink from the jug and waited.

"My cell phone doesn't work up here. I have no way of contacting the college unless I go there."

"Another day or two won't matter."

Sam took a couple of steps toward Boon. "You don't get it. I have to make sure he doesn't say anything."

"About them?" Boon said cocking his head toward the door. The one creature kept pacing in front of the cabin, waiting.

"No. He doesn't know about them. It's just…Roscoe was so intent about this being of historical importance. I have to make sure…." Sam realized he was about to say more than he intended.

"Look boy. I get that you're in some kind of trouble. But you're not making any sense. Roscoe? The only Roscoe that I know that lives in Beaumont is a twit at the community college. Have you gotten yourself mixed up with him?"

"How do you know him?"

Boon went back and sat in the chair, taking the jug with him. He set it on the table and pointed for Sam to sit too. Sam sighed as he came back to the table. "You talking about Roscoe Harman?"

"Yeah, he's doing some work for me."

"Big mistake. I used to be his boss until he stole some of my work and passed it off as his own."

"You were his boss? But how, when…?" Sam broke off remembering how mad Boon got when he questioned his life before.

Boon went on, almost eager to talk about Roscoe. "Started off simple enough. I was looking for a research assistant, someone to help me organize notes on the local history and help with an archeological dig that I was heading up in the back woods. Some artifacts from the Civil War were found on Boon land. Harman was right out of college, smart, but lazy. I had a bit of hard luck. He stole the work, and had it published under his name."

"I don't understand. If he worked for you, how could he take your work?"

Boon looked away, his mood turning dark. "I came here looking for kin after my folks died. I found Clancy and his Ma. I was fascinated with their lives and spent a lot of time here. Eventually, I moved my wife and family down to Creek River and got a job at the college. Life was good." Boon looked back at Sam as if realizing he was still there. "Whatever it is that you have Harman doing for you will end in ruin. He has no ethics. If you're already afraid he will talk, be assured he will."

"He said he would sign a confidentiality agreement...."

Boon laughed and took another long drink. "What good is an agreement when he has no ethics? He's a liar and a thief. Whatever he knows, he will tell others. It's getting late, if you want to get your stuff, let's go so we can get back."

"But, all of his credentials say he's the expert in his field. I've read his book, *The Creek River Battles*. He cannot tell anyone about me or the journals," Sam began to get upset. Boon looked toward the door where the creature was once again scratching, and took a long slow drink.

"Boy, that book was mine, based on my research," Boon said quietly. He stood and went to the door. "He built his reputation on my back. Let me ask you this—how important is it for you to protect these animals?" He looked back at Sam with his hand on the doorknob.

"I said it before, I'll protect them with my life."

"If you continue to work with Harman, that's what it will cost you. I don't know what you're hiding except these animals. But if it's tied to something he feels is financially valuable to him, he will expose them and you. Is it these journals you want to share with Harman that you need to get from your tent?"

Sam nodded, feeling foolish for exposing so much to this man with so few words. Boon opened the door and the alpha male pushed his way into the room. He walked up to Sam, and the other stood in the door, waiting.

"It will be dark before we get back, so get the lantern that's under that window. I have some kerosene in the woodshed."

"You're going with me?" Sam asked innocently. Boon watched as Sam absentmindedly pet the head of the creature. There was something childlike about Sam that made Boon feel the need to protect him. The creature was staring right into Boon's eyes as if he understood what Boon was feeling.

"I don't understand what you're involved in and still feel like this is very wrong. But I'll help you." Sam grabbed the lantern. Boon turned to leave the room, but the creature in the doorway didn't move. He felt the other one behind him and just stood still.

"It's okay, he's a friend," Sam said pushing past Boon. The younger creature turned and ran toward the woods. The alpha stayed close to Sam watching Boon.

"What do you call him?" Boon asked nodding toward the creature.

"I don't have a name for him. He's not my pet," Sam said surprised by the idea.

"Should call him something so we can tell them apart?" Boon walked around the small cabin to a shed that was beneath tall pines. Sam wouldn't have known it was there if Boon hadn't walked to it.

"That seems almost…stupid." Sam looked down at the creature and then shrugged. "What kind of names were you thinking?"

Boon opened the shed and pulled out a gas can. He poured kerosene into the lantern base and put it back. As he turned back to Sam, he looked down at the creature that was standing next to him. "I don't really know, like Wolf, Boss, King…."

Sam frowned. "That's dumb."

"You have a name. Why not him? He seems smart enough too, even though he is a wild animal. Almost seems like, even now, he knows what I'm talking about." The two men began to walk to the tent, with the creature walking with them, instead of in the woods like the younger male. "It's like that one," Boon pointed toward the dark shadow deeper in the woods keeping pace with them. "He's younger, and his fur is blacker. You could call him like Blackie or Prince."

"Why is it so important to you that they have names? What does it matter?"

"Guess it doesn't. But if he doesn't care," Boon looked around Sam to make eye contact with the creature, "I'm going to call him Boss. Seems like that's fitting. Is that alright with you?" Boon asked more to the creature than Sam, who just shrugged. The creature walked along for a while with them and finally took off into the woods, joining the younger one. Boon watched as the two became part of the shadows of the woods and disappeared.

As they walked to the tent, darkness began to descend on the woods. The usual night sounds of the wood's animals were silent, making Boon realize that he too joined Sam's pact with the devil. He had long ago given up on God, but this revelation made something in his heart became harder and darker, and he wondered if he could ever go back again.

CHAPTER 13

Sam woke up and for a moment and wondered where he was. The grey light filtering into the dirty windows made Sam realize that it was very early in the morning. He groaned as he stretched. The hard wood floor of Boon's cabin wasn't comfortable, and even the blankets offered little comfort. He smelled coffee and wondered if that's what woke him, but quickly realized it was the sound of pounding coming from outside. He looked over at the bed, and saw that Boon was already up and gone.

Getting up, Sam found a mug and poured himself some coffee. Taking it with him, he went outside to find Boon. He followed the sounds of the chopping which led down an embankment. Boon was chopping up an old tree and looked up when Sam came over.

"Finally out of bed I see. After your coffee, we need to gather some stuff and head over to your site."

"I still want to get to town soon."

"I figured," Boon said, starting to chop at the tree again.

"Why are you doing that anyway?" Sam sat down on an old stump.

"Need to stay warm this winter. Wood doesn't just come in neat little pieces that fit in a woodstove."

"You don't need to talk to me like I'm an idiot."

"Yeah, well, seems appropriate sometimes."

"Why? Cause you got a college degree and I don't."

"Look boy, we need to get along at least for a few months. Let's stop before we get mad again."

Sam grunted and took another drink of coffee. He looked around for the creatures and didn't see them. He sat watching Boon for a while, noticing just how muscular the man was and how much work it was to chop the wood. Finally, he went back to the cabin. On the table was a list that Boon had been working on. He was surprised by the size of the list. Taking a piece of paper from the notepad, Sam started his own list. There were things that he felt were important that he figured Boon wouldn't. He figured he would just buy what he wanted when he eventually got to town. He was working on his list when Boon came in.

"Do you know how to cook, boy?" Boon asked pouring himself some coffee.

"Some, but not much." Sam folded his list and put it in his pocket.

"Eat out a lot, huh?"

"Some, I eat a lot of sandwiches." Sam got up and picked up his bedding. He figured he'd do his part to not irritate Boon.

"Sandwiches will only get you so far in the dead of winter when you can't get out. Guess, I'll show you a few things. Do you have stuff for living? Dishes? Pots?"

"What I have is in my car, which isn't too much. I've got some furniture in storage in New Jersey."

"New Jersey? Why there?"

"It was where I was living at the time. Didn't make much sense to rent a U-Haul. I needed to get away."

Boon grunted at that. "Before we finish that list, we should see what you have. What are your plans for the car?"

Sam looked surprised. "I was planning on trading it in."

"Trading it in? For what? Where?"

"There's a car dealership in Beaumont. I wanted to get a truck that I could drive up here."

"Up here? Boy, you can't drive a truck up this mountain. You walk up a mountain."

"Some people drive trucks off road. There's a lot of stuff on your list, how did you figure we'd get that stuff up here?"

"Carry it in, like I did."

"You're kidding, right?

"Nope. Besides where'd you think you would keep it?"

"Wherever it is that I end up living. If I need to get off the mountain in a hurry, I need a vehicle."

"You'll never get a truck through these woods."

"Well, I'll drive the truck in as far as I can get it, then a four-wheeler. I can't walk, you've got me too far into the woods."

"And when someone finds it and reports it to the sheriff, he'll know you're in these woods someplace."

"I'll find a place to hide it."

"It will still be found, just like the tent."

"Why are you asking me anyway? I'm sure you've already figured everything out." Sam said, starting to get aggravated. "Even when you're asking me questions, you have this know-it-all attitude. Why not just tell me what you think I should do?"

71

"Don't have it all figured out, like you think. I like your idea of having the ATV. But not having a truck or any vehicle that needs to be registered. It's a good idea to have something to bring the stuff up from town. But we need to consider going to Langford or Stroudsburg, bigger towns, further away." Sam stood quiet, not expecting that kind of a response. Boon went back to his list and began to add a few things.

After a few minutes of just watching Boon, Sam finally asked, "When do you think we can go to Beaumont?"

"Did anything I said about Harman make a difference?"

"Some. I'm worried that he's going to say something."

"If you just go away, he has nothing. Does he have any part of your journal?"

"He has copies of a few pages. I wouldn't give him the originals."

"Then, you disappear. Without the original, he cannot authenticate the pages he has. Where'd you get them from?"

"I...I inherited them," Sam said hesitantly.

"Don't seem too sure," Boon narrowed his eyes at Sam. "It's one thing to tell me straight up that you don't want to tell me. But don't lie to me."

"I'm not. I got them from the same person I got the money."

Boon looked doubtful. "Let's get to that car of yours and see what you've got."

"It's going to take us most of the day to get there and back. Why don't we take my tent and stay down there tonight?"

"If I stay down the mountain, I stay in the Hollow, especially with Boss and his pack out there."

"See, that sounds stupid, Boss."

"Never mind that, you know how to make sandwiches. Go make us some for the day. See that door in the floor? It leads to a cold cellar. There's a large cooler with some meats."

"Is that the same meat that was in the stew?"

"There's some salt ham down there too." Boon wasn't paying much attention. "This list is going to cost a lot of money. I don't have any idea how much one of them ATV costs. You sure you want to do this boy?"

"Yes," Sam said with conviction. "Why do you like your meat so salty?"

Boon looked up and chuckled. "Salt curing the meat keeps it from spoiling in the summer. The cellar only keeps things cool, not cold enough for it not to go rancid. Don't worry, winter months we can leave the meat in the shed where it freezes."

As Boon went back to his planning, Sam went to the cellar and got the meats. He made a bunch of sandwiches, and found some wrap to put them in. As he finished, Boon got up, picked up a gym bag, and his shotgun. He walked out the door without saying anymore to Sam. Sam caught up with him outside as he headed back toward the mountain road.

"Boon, were you serious about staying with your family tonight?"

"Depends. I'd rather not."

"If it comes to that, I'll just stay with the creatures or in my car."

"Got a problem with my kin?"

"You told me to keep them away from your family. If I stay there, they will be there protecting me. You said your cousin was hunting them. That makes it dangerous for him and them."

Boon walked in silence contemplating what Sam said. It wasn't long before he saw the dark shadows following them in the woods. He knew that Sam was right about them following Sam into the Hollow. "Let's make it fast so we can get back to my place."

"Why don't we go to town and get some of the stuff on your list? Depending on how much money this is going to cost, I might have to get some money from some of my other accounts too."

Boon grunted. "I don't stay in town."

"That's fine for you. But I…."

"Boy, if you trust me with knowing about Boss and that somehow you need to hide out, then trust me about Harman. Stay away from him."

"I actually wasn't thinking about him. I had a look at your list and have some things of my own to add. I know you don't want me to start getting stuff yet, but your list is getting long. If you don't want to draw attention to us, isn't it better for me to get things a little at a time?"

Boon didn't respond, but thought Sam had a point. As they walked near the den, Boon saw the other creature join them as they headed toward the mountain road. The car was so well hidden that Boon was surprised. He had been underestimating Sam. They quickly went through everything, and as Boon thought, there was little to help Sam get through a long winter.

"Okay," Boon said standing up. He pulled the list out of his back pocket and opened it up onto the trunk of the car. All of Sam's stuff was piled near a tree. Boon had the list split up and he marked on area. "This stuff is pretty easy for you to find. When you get the building materials, as much as I hate it, I should go with you. Don't lose this list cause I don't want to start over again."

"So…you're agreeing that I should go to town?" Sam asked feeling sure of himself.

"I'm agreeing that you can get some of these things and like you said, bring them in a bit at a time. But I got a really bad feeling about Beaumont. I don't know if it's cause of Harman, or them." He gestured to the shadows that were barely discernable in the woods. Boon had seen the pups for the first time with the female, and the idea of a growing population of these animals frightened him. He turned the paper over and made a crude map. "If you go past the college, there's a road that veers off to the left. It's a shortcut over to the interstate that takes you around Beaumont. At the end of that road, take a right. The interstate is there. Go north about ½ hour or so, you'll see the exit for Langford. Right at the exit is one of those big Wal-Mart's."

"There's a big Wal-Mart in Beaumont. I'll be back this afternoon. If I go all the way to Langford, it will be getting dark. We won't be able to go back to the cabin today." Boon narrowed his eyes and stared at Sam until he felt uncomfortable. "Okay, okay. I'll go to Langford."

Boon nodded and handed the paper to Sam. "I'm going to do some hunting. Then go down to the Hollow, see if I can get Clancy to back off. Let's cover this stuff and get moving."

Finally, Sam was in his car and headed toward the mountain road. Boon stood watching for a few minutes and then turned toward the Hollow. He looked around and realized Boss was following him. "You need to stay away," he warned the creature. Boon stopped and the creature got closer to him, but far enough that he was still shrouded in the shadows. "Somehow, I know you understand me. Clancy is my kin, and I don't want any harm to come to him. I'm helping the boy protect you so, stay away from the Hollow."

Boon headed toward the ridge that would lead him to the tiny community in the mountain. He looked around and didn't see the creature, but he couldn't be sure that the creature wasn't still following.

CHAPTER 14

The flight to Virginia was uneventful. After getting a rental car that was just a mid-size standard vehicle to drive around, Meg was on her way to Creek River. Jake was going to have someone pick her up, but Meg preferred to have her own vehicle, so she wouldn't have to depend on anyone. It took over an hour to get to the little town. Meg kept looking at the desolation and mountains on the ride out, realizing they were looking for a needle in a hay stack. The three kids could be hidden anywhere.

On the flight, Meg had started compiling a list of the differences between the New York cases and this one. The most significant was that Erica was already missing for a month. In the previous cases, the keeper had collected his victim to perform the ritual by the new moon. But he gathered them quickly, so he didn't have to hold them captive for too long.

Of course, Meg realized that Shamus O'Leary had been the keeper for a long time and hadn't been able to pass along this knowledge to the new keeper, who Meg believed was Sam Craig. As the expert on the keeper's rituals, Meg knew that the ritual would have to be performed on the night of a full moon. But this month, the full moon had already happened just before Bobbi disappeared. It would be another 24 days until the next full moon. Plus, he needed two more girls to complete the ritual. Meg knew that she would have to see all the evidence to make sure this is really connected to the keeper.

The small town of Creek River appeared around the next bend. Meg had seen some small shacks on the hills surrounding the winding road. Some of them didn't even have driveways, but dirt paths. She realized life down here was different than anything she had seen. As she came into the town, there were few cars and those she saw were older models. Her rental looked like a luxury vehicle.

Jake had told her to go to the parsonage and that the pastor would tell her where he was. Instead, Meg stopped at the Post Office and got out. She saw the small Sheriff's Office across the street and decided to see if Jake was there first. As she stepped out the car, the heat of the day hit her. Wanting to look professional, she pulled a blazer out of the backseat and slipped it on, putting her credentials in the large pocket.

There was no traffic and everything was still in the heat of the mid-day. After meeting the local law enforcement, she was definitely going to get into shorts and a tee shirt. Meg was surprised to find the Sheriff's Office empty. The one room office with a few holding cells was only the size of a storefront. She looked in a small backroom that looked more like a supply closet, but no one was there either.

Resigned, she went back to her car to go to the parsonage. She took off the blazer and tossed it into the backseat. Turning the air conditioner on high, she hoped that at least there was air conditioning at the parsonage. Pulling into the driveway, an older white haired woman looked out of a window at her. Meg saw the curtain moving and then she was at the side door.

"You must be Meg," the woman said as Meg got out of the car.

"Yes, that's me." She walked up to the lady and put her hand out, but was quickly hugged.

"I'm Margaret Zimmer, the pastor's wife. I hope you didn't stop for lunch on the way out. I have the fixin's for sandwiches and thought we could get to know each other over lunch."

She smiled at Meg as she led her into the house, right into the kitchen. "No, I didn't stop for lunch. Is Jake here? I thought he would be here, so we could start working."

"Oh, the men are talking to some folks."

"Do you know where they are? Perhaps I should join them."

Margaret set a tray of cold cuts on the table. She turned and looked astonished at Meg. "Why would you want to do that? That's men's work."

"Mrs. Zimmer, didn't Jake tell you that I'm a private investigator? This is what I do for a living." Meg was able to keep her voice calm even though she felt herself getting defensive.

"Oh dear! Yes, he did say something like that, but I wasn't expecting someone so pretty. Please forgive me and have lunch too. I have all this food."

Meg gave her a tense smile. She didn't come all the way to Virginia to just spend time with the church ladies. "I do need to eat. But then I need to find Jake and get to work. After all, there are some missing kids."

Margaret patted Meg's hand as she continued setting the table. "I really didn't mean to offend you. It's just that we have a different way of life than in the big city."

"Actually, we aren't from New York City, but upstate New York. Certain parts of New York are just as rural as the mountains I came through to get here."

Margaret chuckled, "Seems like I'm getting everything all backwards with you. Instead of my presuming things, why don't you tell me a bit about yourself?" She sat down at the table and Meg sat down across from her. As Meg reached for bread, Margaret bowed her head and said a prayer. Meg was embarrassed and put her hands on her lap. What had Jake gotten her into? "Well, go ahead, don't wait for me," Margaret said when she looked up from her prayer.

Meg sighed as she finally started to make a sandwich. Margaret asked her all kinds of questions while they ate, most of which Meg didn't directly answer. Finally as they finished and Meg helped put the food away, she sent a text message to Jake asking where he was and when he would be back.

Margaret took Meg to a guest room with a small private bathroom. "No, I can't possibly stay here. Is there a hotel in town?"

"No dear. The closest motel would be in Beaumont. Pastor Jake is staying here and thought it would be best for you to be here too. This room was my daughter's when she lived home. Isn't this alright for you?"

"It's a great room. I just don't want to put you out."

"You aren't putting me out. I love having company and we have more than enough room, since our children have all grown up. While you're waiting for the men to come back, you could bring your suitcase in and get settled. We have a Bible Study tonight at the church if you would like to come."

"I'm sure that I'll be working. I just need to find Jake, so we can figure out where to start."

"Make yourself at home. I'll be in the kitchen if you need anything. There are clean towels and toiletries in the bathroom for your use."

"Thank you." As Margaret left the room, Meg closed the door and called Jake's cell. He didn't answer and she left him a terse message saying she was in town. She went to her car and got her bags. After she hung a few things in the closet, Meg sat down with her notes and wrote down all the things she had thought about on the drive to town.

Finally, an hour or so later, Meg heard men's voices and felt relieved. She went back toward the kitchen and found Jake with several other men. Meg was introduced to Jesse Mueller, his deputy, Earl Graves, and Cal Zimmer.

"So," Meg looking at Jake, "did you find out anything new during your interviews?"

"Nothing new. It's like we really are hitting a brick wall."

"Well Jake," the sheriff interrupted, "Earl and I are going to head back to our office. You know how to reach me if you come up with anything."

"And we're going to head over to the church to make sure everything is ready for the study tonight. Are you going to come tonight, Jake?" Margaret asked, glancing at Meg as she asked.

"Depends on how far we get. I'll let you know at dinner."

Margaret smiled, "If you come, then Meg can come too." Before Meg could reply, they left the kitchen.

As soon as she heard the door close, Meg unleashed on Jake. "I'm not going to any church meeting. I didn't come to Virginia to get religion crammed down my throat. I came to help work this case."

"Whoa, slow down! I didn't ask you down here to go to church. I truly need your help here. Mrs. Zimmer is a wonderful woman who just wants to bring people to Christ."

"I'm not falling for it Jake Peterson. So don't include me in your little Bible Study. I won't go!"

"Okay, okay. Are you ready to lay out our notes and see what we have?"

"I've been ready to do that for over two hours."

"Well, come on." Jake went into the dining room where papers were spread all over the table. He had a laptop set up at one end too.

"You're kidding me. We aren't going to the station?"

"There's no station in Creek River. I can take you over to the Sheriff's Office later. But it's little more than a big room with a few desks. There's no place to spread out and work like here. The Zimmers have been really great about giving me this space."

Meg sighed. "Are you sure there are no other options?"

"The only other option would be to work in the conference room at the church. There are no other big rooms in this town that we would be able to have access to. If it gets to be too overbearing for you, just let me know. I'll talk to Mrs. Zimmer."

"No, I don't want you to hurt her feelings. I just wasn't expecting this."

"That's my fault. I didn't even think about how it would appear to you. I'm just so used to being around church folks."

"Forget it, let's just get to work."

They went over all the notes and forensics that Jake had already discussed with her over the phone. Meg explained her time frame issues regarding Erica and the moon cycles. "So, I'm actually thinking that whoever is behind this isn't going to try to do the ritual, but set Sam up. Otherwise, he will have Erica locked up someplace for two months. It's just too long."

"Unless he doesn't have all details of performing the ritual."

"I found out from an expert in Albany. If this person has any of the information, it would be easy enough to know that the ritual always happens during a full moon."

Meg's cell phone rang. "It's Dad. Let me take this. He was going to talk to some buddy of his who does probate work." Meg took the call as Jake looked over her notes. She sighed as she hung up the phone. "Well, that was another dead end. It's like trying to find a single pine tree in the whole mountain."

"I've got an idea that might help us getting a starting point. I think we need to go to Ireland and trace the money. I know we talked about it before you came down. But it seems the only logical place to go. We can't keep searching these woods, asking the parents the same questions. It's all leading us no place. Maybe if we can find the money, we can figure out who is doing this."

"Dad's lawyer friend pretty much said the same thing. Find the money trail, so we can find Sam."

"Let's check out flights to Dublin and then see if we can track down O'Leary's daughter. Do you remember her name?"

"I don't know if I ever knew it. Would it be in the old police files?"

"Let me check with Reggie. If it's there, he would have it. I remember that she was the one that turned him into the police when he arrived in Dublin."

"You call Reggie and' I'll check overseas flights. Oh, Dad said he found a lead that Sam lived for a while on Long Island. He's going to go down and check it out. Maybe if he traces Sam the old fashion way, he'll find him before we do."

Jake agreed and took his cell outside onto a deck. Meg went to the laptop and looked up the local airports to find the next flight to Ireland.

CHAPTER 15

S am took the long drive to Langford with mixed feelings. He didn't like being told what to do, and he definitely would be stopping on the way back to see Roscoe. But on the other hand, he *had* left Beaumont because he was attracting attention to himself. If he went there, traded in his car, bought a bunch of stuff, it would raise a lot of questions. Bad enough Boon knew as much as he did, Sam didn't want other people to find out about the creatures and his bond with them. But Boon was willing to help him, even if it did cost him money, that's what that lawyer had told him the money was for anyway.

Sam pulled into a gas station and filled his car with gas. He got a soda from a machine and drank it down. One thing on his list was a few cases of soda. He didn't know what Boon was drinking in that jug, and he didn't want to know. It was an hour later, when Sam pulled into the Wal-Mart parking lot. It was crowded and Sam drove around until he found a place to park. Grabbing a cart, Sam started with his list, sodas and junk food quickly filled the cart. He put back some of the junk food to make room for clothes. Figuring he wouldn't have much access to wash clothes, he filled the cart with jeans, shirts, and socks. He found new sneakers and work boots. He liked the old broken in boots that Boon wore and wanted to get a pair for himself.

After going through the checkout, Sam took stuff to the car and went back in to get some of the stuff on Boon's list. Most of the items were in the sporting goods section. Sam found himself looking at the shotguns and wondering if he should get one. He moved on when he saw a salesperson watching him. He picked up a case of small propane canisters figuring they were for Boon's small grill. Sam found the tarps and air mattress with a small pump before moving to the find some pans and towels.

After checking out, Sam was stopped at the door. His second trip leaving the store with a loaded cart caused suspicion. The greeter checked his receipt against what was in the cart. As Sam stood waiting, his attention was drawn to a bulletin board with flyers. One flyer in particular stood out from the rest, and he stood staring at a sketch of himself, wanted for questioning in the disappearance of Bobbi. Bobbi! That girl from the bar!

THE HOLLOW

Sam looked away and watched the greeter checking off his receipt. Finally, she handed him the receipt and Sam left. His hands were shaking as he loaded the car with his purchases. Sam got in the car and was trembling so much, he could hardly start the car. Missing! How could she be missing?

Sam took off toward the interstate, but ended up driving down a side road instead. His thoughts were in turmoil thinking about the events of that night at the bar. Clearly, Bobbi was looking to be picked up and was desperate. Sam thought about going to the police and telling them he never saw her after he drove off. But he remembered Reggie Bennett's reaction and belief that he was somehow responsible for that disappearance three summers ago. He remembered his last troubled years in high school, the run-in with the police in Poughkeepsie over fights in school, and then rejected the idea of going to the police. Besides, his lifestyle over the past three years, no ties to any community, and the creatures he swore to protect, made him realize he was the prime suspect in Bobbi's disappearance.

Sam wanted to get back to the mountain as quickly as possible. Any more trips to town, Boon would have to go. The drive back toward Creek River took a lot longer taking back roads, but Sam didn't want to risk the interstate. Finally, he was on the road leading to the mountain. As he approached the college, he thought again about Roscoe Harman. He pulled into the parking lot and looked up at the window that was Harman's office.

Sam got out and walked to the door of the old building. Plastered on the door were flyers about Bobbi missing. Sam pulled one off and looked around. With the summer session closed, there was no one around. He read the flyer, which told of Sam being a person of interest. Folding the flyer, he stuck it into his pocket and went into the building. His thoughts were confused, but he knew he had to speak to Roscoe, tell him he was leaving the area, and the work was finished. As he started going up the stairs, he stopped as he realized anyone working in the building would have seen the flyer and would recognize him.

The late afternoon sun shone through a window in the stairwell. Sam could almost hear Boon telling him not to trust Roscoe. He turned and practically fled from the building. Getting to his car, he looked up at the window and didn't see anyone looking out. The drive back to the mountain was quick. After he hid the car, he headed toward the stream and the den. He kept looking around for them, but didn't see them anyplace.

Collapsing at the riverbed, Sam allowed himself to begin to calm down. He pulled the flyer out and read it again. The reality of what he was reading began to sink in. He was being blamed for Bobbi's disappearance. The decision to move to the mountain made more sense than ever and Sam needed to find Boon. They had to get working right away. No more arguing with Boon, whatever he said, whatever he wanted, no amount of money would be unreasonable. He wanted to be free from running and that was only possible on this mountain.

Sam went to the den and ducked to look inside. It was empty, so he gave a sharp whistle, waiting. After a few minutes, he headed toward the Hollow hoping Boon was still around. He felt panicked. He wanted the familiarity of the creatures' protection or Boon. Finding the Hollow was harder than Sam thought, but finally he was in back of a small shack. It was in pretty dire condition compared to Boon's. He stood not knowing what to do.

"What'cha doin' boy?" Sam turned expectantly, but it wasn't Boon. There was a strong resemblance to the rough mountain man, but it wasn't him, and this man was pointing a shotgun at him.

Sam stammered, "I'm looking for Boon. I thought he might have come over here."

The man lowered the gun and narrowed his eyes, just like Boon. "What'cha want with him?"

"I… I need to talk to him. Do you know where he is?"

"Boon don't talk to people." Sam didn't know how to respond. "You ain't wanted here. Go back to where y'all come from."

Out of the corner of his eye, Sam saw movement. The dark shadow was slowly making its way toward them. "Listen, I have to find Boon. Are you his kin?"

The man brought the gun back up and looked mad. "What y'all know 'bout us?"

"Boon pointed out the Hollow to me and said that his kin lived here. I thought he might have come over here."

"Y'all knowin' too much boy. I ain't likin' that."

"I'll leave if you just tell me where I can find him." Sam glanced toward the shadow and saw that it had stopped a ways off. Sam was relieved to see one of the creatures, but was afraid that it would attack this man if he continued to threaten him. "If you can't help me, tell me where I can find Clancy. Boon told me that Clancy was his cousin and he would know how to find him."

The man lowered his gun. "I's Clancy."

"Has Boon been here today?"

Clancy nodded and started walking toward the cluster of shacks on the ridge. Sam followed Clancy, but kept looking around to see if any of the others were around. He only saw the one, from a distance. It didn't follow them toward the shacks, much to Sam's relief. They passed the first several shacks and finally stopped at one that looked in better condition than the others. Clancy knocked once and then entered. As Sam stepped into the shack, he saw Boon with an old woman. Boon stood when he saw Sam.

"What'cha doin' here boy? I run you off this mornin'!" Boon practically yelled.

Clancy looked between the two. "Told him a lot for someone ya run off."

"What?" Boon said looking at his cousin. "What did he tell you?"

"Enough. Ya's kin to us, so we trust ya. But this boy knows that we kin and 'bout the Hollow."

Boon was furious. His anger turned dark and menacing. Sam quickly started to talk to cover his blunder. "I went back to the college. I couldn't believe that Harman stole your work like you said. He had me convinced that the book was his. I know now that you were right and I wanted to apologize to you for not believing you."

Clancy squinted at Boon. "After all this time, ya's still havin' troubles with that fella?"

"I wouldn't be having any trouble if this kid hadn't shown up!" Boon stormed out the door. Clancy followed him, and Sam stood not knowing what to do.

The old woman chuckled. "Ya better go with em, else Boon will be gone."

Sam went outside and didn't know which way to go. He went back the direction he came and saw the dark shadow had come closer to the Hollow. "Which way?' Sam asked. The shadow turned and took off, and Sam followed. He caught up with Boon and Clancy away from the Hollow. They looked up surprised as Sam approached, but Boon quickly looked around until he saw the darkness.

"Why are you following me, boy?" Boon demanded.

Sam looked at Clancy and hesitated. "Thinks ya need to just leave," Clancy said pointing off into the woods.

"Boon, I'm sorry I came to the Hollow. But I...," Sam stammered afraid to say anything in front of Clancy. He desperately wanted to talk to Boon about the flyer, needed to talk to him about it. But he also knew that he couldn't let Clancy know he was staying with Boon.

"What boy?" Boon was furious with Sam.

"I'm sorry. I found out something at the college. I needed to find you, to talk to you. I couldn't find you...."

"What y'all talkin' to that boy for anyhow, Boon?" Clancy asked. Behind the two men, Sam could see another creature approaching.

"Okay, I know I shouldn't have come back, Boon. But I'm lost and don't know how to get back to my car."

"Goes back the ways ya come," Clancy said matter of fact and pointed again into the woods. Boon stared off into the woods. Sam could see him looking around, knowing he was furious with Sam, but knowing that the creatures were surrounding them. Sam just waited. Finally, Boon turned and started walking. Sam waited only a moment and then followed. Clancy stood watching and then shook his head.

Boon walked, saying nothing, until they were on the other side of the ridge. In a low dangerous voice, Boon said, "What were you thinking boy?"

"I wasn't. I was just desperate to talk to you. I couldn't wait until sometime tomorrow when you figured I would be back. I couldn't spend the night alone, and I couldn't find the creatures."

"What did that bastard say that made you risk the lives of my kin?" Boon stopped and glared down at Sam. He heard the creature approaching, nearing them, but didn't even care.

"Nothing. I never talked to Harman. It was this," Sam reached in his pocket and pulled out the flyer handing it to Boon. "It was at the Wal-Mart too. I took this one off the door of the building Harman works in."

Boon quickly read the flyer. "This what you're hiding from boy?"

"No, I didn't have anything to do with this. I left her at the bar. I really did come here to be with them, away from people."

"So why'd you lead them right to Clancy? Especially after I told you that he was hunting them?"

"I couldn't find them. Besides if anyone led them to the Hollow, it was you. That's where I finally found them."

Boon looked around him, and then back at the flyer, rereading it. "If you didn't do this, then go to the law and tell them."

"It's not that easy."

"Why not? If you didn't do this thing?"

"I can't explain it all. It has to do with the creatures and my need to protect them."

"You better start explaining now that you got the law involved. This flyer was at the college?" Sam nodded. "How much you want to bet that your good friend, Roscoe Harman, has already told the police about you and the work you had him doing?"

"Let's get going then! We need to get back to your cabin." Sam started to go down the side of the ridge.

"Before we go anywhere, you better explain yourself, boy."

"What if someone goes to the police and says that they saw me today? I bought camping equipment. Don't you think that police will start looking…."

Boon interrupted approaching Sam and grabbing his arm. "You went to Beaumont after I told you not to!"

"No! I went to Langford, like you said. But this flyer was hanging up there too."

A deep growl near them made Boon drop Sam's arm. The alpha stood near them, staring right at Boon. "Maybe you should find another mountain boy. Take your animals and go."

"I can't! I can't do this by myself and you promised to help me."

"What if I changed my mind?"

"Then you aren't my friend any longer and the agreement we have doesn't exist."

"You threatenin' me?"

"No, but they will. I didn't do anything to this girl. But I can't have the cops find me or them. Right now, I don't care how much money you want. I'll do whatever you say. But don't make me leave."

"What about Erica? Did you do anything to her?"

"Erica? What are you talking about?"

"Do you know why Clancy has been hunting them?"

"I don't know. Because he saw them and thinks they are dangerous."

"The night that those animals were seen in the Hollow, Clancy's youngest daughter went missing. My aunt thinks she saw the devil."

"What are you saying?"

"You know anything about Erica being missing?"

Sam looked surprised, then shook his head. "If you think I had anything to do with that, you wouldn't be helping me."

"I didn't know everything, like about this Roberta, from Creek River, the town at the bottom of the Hollow."

"I didn't do anything to anyone. I wouldn't do anything like this after what I went through."

"Start talking boy."

"Can't we talk at your cabin? My car is packed with stuff. I can't just leave it down there now. If they find my car, the cops will tear this mountain apart until they find me."

Boon thought about that for a moment. He looked down at the creature near them and then to the dark shadow standing in the woods. "Okay, boy. But I want to know everything. No more secrets and no lies."

"And I expect the same from you."

CHAPTER 16

The next morning, Meg was driving her rental back to the airport with Jake. The flight had a long layover in Atlanta before the thirteen hour flight to Dublin. Reggie and Brian were tracking down O'Leary's family. They hoped to have the information for them when they reached Dublin.

The layover in Atlanta was boring and Meg found that she was restless. Jake was content sitting reading a Bible which Meg was finding annoying. Finally, she decided to stretch her legs. "I'm going to see if there's a store or something. See if I can find a magazine."

"Sure," Jake replied without really looking up.

Meg went down the escalator to a big lobby where lines of people were waiting to get cleared to board flights. She stepped outside into the hot, Atlanta air. She couldn't believe it was actually hotter here than it was in Creek River.

Pulling out her cell, she looked through her contacts and finally found a number. She looked back inside to be sure Jake hadn't followed her before calling. "Hey, Mick, this is Meg. I'm working on a private case and need some help."

"Sure, you know my rates."

"Yeah, I always pay you."

"That's why I like your jobs. What's going on?"

"Well, I got pulled into a police case with Jake Peterson, my old partner from Granelle." Meg explained the case and how they were on their way to Ireland. "So, I got thinking, if anyone can track down someone in Ireland, why not my good friend, Mick Finley."

Mick laughed. "Why, cause I got an Irish name?"

"Nope, because you're the only person I know with family still living on the Emerald Isle. You know people that will talk to you when they won't to cops and those who won't want to be found."

"Sure you don't need a tour guide? Been there plenty myself, know my way around."

"I can barely afford your non-traveling rates, Mick. I'm looking for Shamus O'Leary's daughter. She's the one that would know the most. And don't let my father know that I've hired you. He thinks because he's a partner, he needs to know every penny I spend."

"You know you can trust me. When are you supposed to land?"

"We won't be getting into Dublin until around seven in the morning. Our time."

"Alright, I'll see what I can find out and call you tomorrow."

After she hung up, Meg found a small store and bought herself a paperback. She wandered back to the waiting area and found Jake still engrossed in the Book. She sat near him and slouched down in the seat. It was going to be a long flight, but she had a good feeling about Mick. She couldn't wait to meet O'Leary's family and see for herself the place where those hateful creatures had come from. Maybe they'd finally learn the truth about the keeper and how all this darkness began.

* * *

Boon hated sharing the cramped tent with Sam. But it was better than being out in the opened with those dark creatures and the mosquitoes. Those bugs seemed merciless tonight and the tent offered some protection. Boon rolled over again and sighed. He looked over at Sam who was fast asleep, oblivious to his restlessness. Finally he sat up, intending to leave the tent, when he heard sniffing near his side of the tent.

Even in the darkness of the night, Boon was suddenly very aware of the creatures and Sam's protection from them. He flopped back down on the hot thick sleeping bag. As he stretched his feet out, he kicked Sam's duffel bag. Boon sat back up again and looked at the bag. He glanced over at Sam again, making sure he was sound asleep.

Gingerly, he opened the bag, making sure the zipper was quiet. He pulled one of the journals out. Feeling around near him, he found a flashlight. Turning so his body would block the light from Sam, Boon opened the journal. As he focused on the old Gaelic words, Boon began to read about Paddy. He stopped reading and glanced over his shoulder and then to the dark shadows outside the tent.

Boon put the first one back and took one from the middle of the pile. The binding was different and the writing was different. But Boon immediately realized it was the same kid, only now with maturity in the handwriting and in the words written. Seems Paddy had grown up. It had been so long since Boon had read any of the old Irish words, so it took him a while to translate the text. But the more he read, the easier it came and with it the horrifying details of Paddy spying on his father as he held a girl captive in a cave.

Boon found himself so wrapped up in the story, he was unaware of changes in the darkness as early morning began to break through. But it was movement outside the tent that caught his attention. He looked around and realized that it was almost morning. With regret, he put the journal back in the bag and closed it.

Lying back on the sleeping bag, Boon thought about the story and how young Paddy had been taught by his father. He was captivated as the young boy wrote of his introduction to the hounds and forced into a life of darkness and damnation as his inherited right as the keeper. Exhaustion began to wash over him as he thought about the boy sleeping in the tent with him. As he finally began to fall asleep, Boon wondered how much Sam really knew about the O'Shea's and their secrets. But, he figured it couldn't be much or he would never have let Roscoe Harman read that first journal. Boon intended to read those journals for himself, not because he wanted the fame like Harman, but he knew that his life and Sam depended on knowing all he could about the past and who those creatures really were.

CHAPTER 17

Mick came through for Meg and got her the name of Kristen Nolan, Shamus O'Leary's granddaughter. But when Meg called the number Mick had given her, Kristen hung up refusing to talk to her. Jake had booked a hotel and they checked in. Meg told Jake she needed about an hour to get showered and get cleaned up.

Meg closed the door to her room, and called Mick. "Okay, she won't talk on the phone," she said without hesitating. "Do you have an address?"

"Got it from the Internet. I've got some feelers out for Mum too. My uncle knows the Nolan's in Dublin and I have a lead."

"That would be great 'cause it sounds like Kristen doesn't want to talk. If I have her mother as leverage, it might help her spill the family beans."

"You still looking for the money trail?"

"Yeah, if we can find the money, we can track Sam. I've got to meet up with Jake in about an hour. I'm going to go to Kristen's and see where that takes us. If you can find out where the mother is before that, let me know. We can go right to her place if we get nowhere with the daughter."

Meg took down the address and then got ready. She was just going to call Mick again, when he called her, with the Kelly Flannigan's address, a nursing home on the other side of Dublin. Writing down all the information, Meg felt satisfaction that she had enough leverage to get information from Kristen.

When she went to the room across the hall, Jake didn't even wait for her to knock. He seemed excited. "Okay, what gives?" Meg asked.

"I found out where O'Leary is buried."

"Okay," Meg shrugged.

"It's worth more than just a shrug Meg. I set up a time for us to meet with the groundskeeper to see the graves and see what information they have about O'Leary."

"Okay, what time are we doing that?"

"Later this afternoon. I thought we could get the lay of the land and see if we can find out more about O'Leary."

"Then we have time to go see his granddaughter. I found her on the Internet. She lives right her in Dublin."

"Did you call her?"

"I figure it's best if we just go to the address. I imagine with O'Leary being a criminal, it isn't something she will want to talk about on the phone."

"Yeah, well…."

"We've got the time, that's why we're in Ireland. I have the address, let's just go. Worst she can do is not be home. Then we'll do your cemetery trip."

"I have a feeling you've got more on your mind than you're saying."

"We have to find out all we can about the past. We need to know about those creatures, so we can destroy them. We need to know where the money came from. Once and for all, I want to know whether that stupid legend is true. The only way we can find out all that is to ask questions of the people who are right in the middle of this, O'Leary's family. Grant was a kid when O'Leary kidnapped him, so his family knows nothing. But not the O'Leary family…or the Flannigan's. Seems O'Leary's daughter got married and changed her name."

"Okay, let's go talk to them. But they aren't the criminals, so go easy on them."

Meg looked at him with an innocent look and then smiled. He shook his head and followed her out the door. Within an hour, the rented car stopped in front of a modest cottage on the outskirts of the city.

"Well, there's a car in the driveway. Let's see if anyone is home." Meg opened the car door and stepped out.

Jake hesitated and then followed her. As they walked to the door, it opened and a young woman stepped out onto the porch. "My husband's not home," she said and crossed her arms.

"I'm not sure who you think we are, but we are actually looking for Kristen Nolan," Jake said as he stepped onto the porch.

"I'm Kristen," she said uncertain as she looked between them. Her eyes rested on Meg. "You…you the one that called?"

"I'm Meg Riley and my partner, Jake Peterson. We are private investigators from the United States. There are some missing kids there, and we believe that it is tied to some things that Shamus O'Leary was involved in."

"I know nothing," Kristen turned to go back inside and Meg reached out and put her arm across the door, stopping her.

"Look, we came a long way to get some answers about your grandfather. I don't know about my partner, but I'm not leaving until I find out some things. And if that means, I wait for your husband to get home…."

"No, I don't… I can't dig up the past. I can't do this…."

Meg removed her arm. "Well, then we wait for Mr. Nolan. Or we go talk to your mother."

Kristen's eyes got big and she shook her head. "Please, don't bother my mum."

"Then answer some questions about Shamus O'Leary. We need to know about this legend that he was involved in and about the creatures."

Kristen looked around and saw curtains move across the road. "Okay, but come in. I don't want my neighbors hearing anything."

Kristen led Jake and Meg to her small living room. She sat and was visibly nervous about her visitors. "I don't know a lot about my grandfather. My mother tried to protect us from knowing anything."

"What did your grandfather do for work? He traveled so much, he had to make a living doing something."

Kristen looked annoyed at that question. "Make a living! He was rich and never gave my grandmother a dime to help support her and my mother."

"Rich? Where did the money come from?"

"We never knew. An unknown benefactor. There was this lawyer who handled financial affairs. A few times, my grandmother got a little money from him when she threatened to expose my grandfather."

"Do you know who this lawyer was?"

"No, I never asked. I don't care," she said standing. "I don't have anything more to tell you. These myths destroyed my mother's childhood and part of my own. This Shamus O'Leary was nothing to me. My grandmother died a very lonely, unhappy woman. So, please leave us alone."

"I'm sorry that we bothered you, Kristen," Jake said as he stood. "We wouldn't have come if we didn't need answers. But maybe we can find them someplace else." Jake looked to Meg who was still sitting watching Kristen. "Meg, we should get going."

"Actually, I have a few more questions," Meg said not moving.

"Well, I'm finished," Kristen walked toward the front door.

"Fine," Meg said standing. "I can save my questions for your mother."

"No!" Kristen exclaimed. "My mother has been through enough. I won't have you bothering her."

"Then what's a few more questions."

The two women faced each other, each standing their ground. Kristen broke first, "I have tried to answered your questions and understand your need to ask them. Please understand mine. My mother is old and very ill. She cannot be disturbed."

Jake started saying something, and Meg lifted her hand to stop him. "I don't have questions about Shamus O'Leary. Quite frankly, he is of little use to me. My questions are about those creatures."

"The creatures?" Kristen asked incredulous. "They are a myth."

"No, they aren't. I've seen them. In fact, I was a prisoner of Trevor Grant's and saw those creatures face to face. They are real."

"Well, then you know more about them than I!"

"Actually, I know what they look like. I know what control they have over the person that is known as the keeper. I know a little of the history. But what I really want to know is where did they come from? Whose lineage do they belong too? This money you talk about, it had to come from that person. Who was the werewolf?"

Kristen sighed. "You are asking too much of me."

"Then who do I ask? Certainly, your mother knows."

"Do you not realize that the Irish are full of tales? We love stories and folklore. This is just another."

"No, it's not. I think you're protesting so much because you know where this started. It was your family. The original clan didn't really die out. It came from the O'Leary's, didn't it?"

"Do you not realize how this has destroyed my family? Why did you come back now and try to bring this back to life? It's over. My grandfather was the last. It ended with him. I want my family to live in peace."

"That's the problem. It didn't end. That boy declared in the basement that *he* was the new keeper. I was there, I heard it and so did Jake. Now, he is a man, and people are missing again. If we don't know how to stop it, it will just continue on and on. We need to stop this and you are the key to helping us understand how to stop it."

"I don't know how. No one does. Don't you think people tried to stop this in the past? Just go back to America and to your lives," Kristen said, starting to cry.

"Meg, let's just go," Jake said quietly trying to end it.

"No Jake," Meg said, walking over to Kristen. "Maybe you're family is out of it. But my father was mauled by one of those creatures. I need to know how it continues to survive."

"I don't know. Please, just leave us alone," Kristen said sobbing. She turned and ran from the room leaving Meg and Jake standing alone in the living room.

"Well, that didn't end well," Jake said walking over to Meg. "You certainly took the bad cop role to heart."

"Don't give me that Jake. She knows the answers."

"Does it really matter?"

"Why are we here then? Did we come all the way to Ireland to go home with more questions than we had originally?"

"We aren't going to get any more answers here," Jake said walking to the door. "Come on. Let's check out that old cemetery."

Meg followed Jake outside to the car. She was quiet on the ride back toward the town. When Jake was ready to take the road toward Dublin, Meg stopped him. "Why don't you go without me? I'm getting a headache and just want to go back to the hotel."

"Are you alright? We can go later to the cemetery," Jake said in concern.

"You go on ahead and get the names from the tombstone and ask the caretaker the questions. I don't want you to lose time sitting around waiting for my headache to go away."

"Are you sure?"

"Yeah," Meg said leaning her head against the window. Jake looked over in concern as he drove to the hotel. He dropped her off in front and waited while she went inside. As he drove off toward the cemetery, he didn't see her come back out and flag down a taxi.

CHAPTER 18

The drive was quiet, and Jake used the time to gather his thoughts. He didn't understand why Meg was so concerned about the legend. As far as Jake was concerned, he needed to find out if it was possible for someone from Ireland to be starting this up again in the states. While Brian was tracking down leads in New York, this side trip was becoming about the past and offering little in terms of who could be behind the crimes.

Finally, Jake found the old cemetery and drove into the drive. There was a stone building on his left, where Jake had been assured he would find a caretaker. He parked near the building and got out of the car. Looking around at the expansive acres of headstones and mausoleums, Jake knew he would never find O'Leary's grave without assistance.

Jake walked to the small building and knocked. A young man answered with a smile. He was a bit shorter than Jake, dressed in work clothes and boots.

"You must be the preacher from the states," he said sticking his hand out. "I'm Tom O'Brien. You spoke with my father."

"Jake Peterson," Jake replied shaking his hand.

"Pop's a bit superstitious. So, I offered to show you the graves."

"Graves? I was hoping to just find Shamus O'Leary's."

"Showing you that grave wouldn't be complete without showing you all the keepers, would it?" Tom gestured toward the graves, and they started walking through the cemetery.

"All the keepers? Your father didn't give me much information on the phone."

"Pop ain't one for telling people much. Personally, I think it's odd that these men are all buried here together. You'd think in death, they'd want to be with their clan."

"I don't understand. All the keepers are buried in this cemetery? Are you sure?"

"Not just in the cemetery, but in a special place. Far north corner... away from everyone else."

"How is that possible? How would they know they could be buried together?"

"All set up by O'Shea. He's the first. The story has another man as the first, but that wasn't true. The cemetery has the original documents. Man named, Rue O'Shea, was a potato farmer. Dirt poor too. Many believed he entered into a pack with the devil. Died wealthy tending to wild dogs in the mountains. Here we are, the Keeper's Gate."

Jake stopped outside a fenced area with a plaque engraved with 'The Keeper's Gate' on it. Tom opened the gate and stepped inside. "Well, come on now. Rue O'Shea was buried right smack in the middle."

Jake followed not knowing what to say as he looked around at the ten or so graves that were scattered around the area, with room for many more. The monument that was O'Shea's headstone declared him to be 'The Keeper of the Hound of Darkness' with the dates of his life.

Jake pulled out a small pad and wrote down all the information from the stone. The next grave was marked, Patrick O'Shea, Rue's son. Jake walked slowly around the gated area until he found himself before Shamus O'Leary's grave. Simply stated, the headstone just gave his name and dates.

"Tom, can you explain to me how all these men ended up here?

"In order to be buried here in this place, each man's name was given to the one who was before him. I checked the documents. After O'Leary, there was to be one called Trevor Grant, but that name was removed. The next grave will be one of Samuel Craig."

"Sam? But how is that possible?"

"I know what you mean. He's not Irish, but I guess the decision is from the one before."

"I don't mean his nationality. How was the name given to cemetery?" Jake asked.

"Oh, that, very formal, legal documents from the estate. It's all very clear."

"Can I see those documents?"

"My father was wondering, and so am I now that you're here. What does a preacher want with all this nonsense?"

"I explained all this to your father."

"Tell me Reverend. Like I said, Pop ain't too big on words."

"I'm not only a minister, but a police detective. Right now, there are two girls and a boy missing from a small town. This is the fourth time this has happened in the states, and it all traces back to Shamus O'Leary and his belief that he was the keeper of those creatures. What do you know about the legend?"

"I don't know anything about a legend. I just help keep these graves looking nice."

"Listen, I've been able to stop this from happening before, mostly by accident. But this needs to stop for good. People have died because of what O'Leary did, and I'm sure many others because of the actions of the other men buried here."

"Reverend, the answers you seek ain't here in the graves."

"You know more than you're saying. I saw the news articles going back centuries about the Hounds of Darkness. How are these men connected?"

"From what I know, each was chosen by the one before. That's all I know."

Tom walked to the gate, and Jake just stood looking around the area. He pulled out his cell phone and took some pictures of the graves. When he was done, he walked over to Tom.

"I'd still like to see the documents that show the trail of these graves," Jake said falling into stride beside Tom.

"You won't be able to see them and if they knew I looked, well, my father would be out of a job."

"I need to know who is behind all this. You mentioned an estate. That means there must be lawyers involved. Even O'Leary's granddaughter mentioned a lawyer."

"The cemetery is paid a lot of money each year to keep up those graves and for burying them that die. Dead people in Ireland ain't gonna find your lost people. There's nothing more that I can say without getting me and my family shut out."

"What do you know about the creatures?"

"Just that they existed. Never seen them. No one I know has either, unless some of the old folks did. But they won't talk to you."

"Can I talk to your father?'

As they came up to Jake's rental car, Tom stopped. "Like I said, my father's superstitious. He won't speak of the hounds to you out of fear. There's nothing more I can tell you."

"Where do I go from here? I still need answers."

"It makes sense that if Samuel Craig is to be next one buried here, he has to know something. Find him."

"I'm trying. Thanks for your help. I won't bother your father," Jake said turning to his car.

"I hope you find what you're searching for Reverend."

Tom went around the building and took off in a small car. Jake kept standing there thinking. He went up to the caretaker's building and turned the handle. Tom had forgotten to lock it. Looking around, Jake slipped inside the one room building. To one side of the room, there were tools, tractors, and other gardening equipment. But on the other side was a desk and filing cabinet. Dim, filtered light poured through a dirty window. Jake went to the desk and began to look at the papers scattered there.

Jake searched the papers on the desk and only found a scrap with Sam's name on it. He figured it was from Tom. He turned to the filing cabinet and looked through invoices and receipts. Wherever Tom had found Sam's name, it wasn't in this room. Finally, Jake decided to see if Meg was up to finding this law firm. Someone was financing this whole operation, and the law firm was mixed up in it.

CHAPTER 19

Sitting in the taxi, Meg felt a little guilty about lying to Jake. But she didn't agree to not bother Kristen's mother, and she wanted those answers. Until those creatures were stopped, everyone was in danger. Going to an old cemetery to look at O'Leary's grave wasn't going to help them at this point. But confronting O'Leary's daughter about what her father had done might provide answers that Meg so desperately needed

The ride to the nursing home didn't take very long, and Meg was sure she'd be back before Jake. The taxi dropped Meg off and she stood in front of the large complex. She went to the door of the complex and found it locked. She pressed a buzzer and waited. Finally, an orderly answered the door.

"I'm here to see my aunt," Meg said with a smile.

"No one told us they were expecting a visitor," she said with suspicion.

"I'm here from the states. My father wasn't aware that his sister was no longer living in her home. I came to surprise her."

"I cannot give you permission to see any of our residents. You'll have to talk to the administrator. I'll have to take you to her office. Follow me," she opened the door to allow Meg to come in.

"Thank you," Meg said as she walked into the building. Its bright reception area had a few residents sitting watching her. She followed the woman down a narrow hall of offices and was directed to sit in a chair in the hall. After a while, a door opened and an impeccably dressed woman came out.

"Ms. Riley, I presume," she stated.

Meg felt a little chagrined at being caught. "Kristen called."

"Yes, and she was very concerned that you or a Jake Peterson would be coming to talk to her mother."

"Look, I'm not here to cause Mrs. Flannigan any trouble. I just need to ask her some questions about her father."

"I know why you're here Ms. Riley. But I don't take to deceptions when it comes to our residents. It is my job to protect them from predators of all kinds."

"My intentions are not to harm her. In fact, I'm trying to figure out who is behind some disappearances of three people in the states. Her father was involved in these crimes in the past and I just need a few answers."

"That is not my concern. Since you allowed your taxi to leave, you will wait in my office until another can be hailed for you."

Realizing it was pointless to argue, Meg nodded and followed the woman into her office. She listened while she called for a taxi to come pick her up. The administrator turned to a computer and began to do some work, while Meg sat feeling dejected. Some commotion in the hall sent the woman to see what was going on. Using the opportunity, Meg tried to see if there was a list of residents on the desk. When the door opened again, Meg sat back in the chair.

"Well, it appears that Mrs. Flannigan is taking it upon herself to talk to you anyway. Against my better judgment, I will allow you a few minutes while your taxi comes. But I will stay present and will stop you if you get her upset like you did her daughter."

Meg was shocked when an older version of Kristen came in. Meg began, "Mrs. Flannigan, I truly am sorry to disturb you. I didn't mean to upset your daughter either."

Mrs. Flannigan settled in the chair next to Meg. "It was a difficult life for me, and my daughter is trying to spare me any more pain. What is it you need to know?"

"Let me start by saying that I am an investigator. I was involved in several cases involving missing women that your father was responsible for and I was also kidnapped by Trevor Grant. I was fortunate to have been rescued, but the cycles are repeating again. Three people are missing in the same way, one is another small boy. I'm trying to find out the origin of this legend to discover who is behind all this."

"I see. Well for my sake, I can only tell you that my father left us when I was small. Had I been born a boy, I'm afraid I would have been in Mr. Grant's place. My mother could have no other children after me. My father had money and it left with him. We were left penniless and had to rely on the kindness of relatives so support us."

"I'm sorry your life was so hard. Your daughter told me the same thing."

"The problem was the stigma that was attached to us, not the loss of the money. Everyone knew that my father had become the keeper when Liam passed. He had been chosen, inherited the money, and was to carry on the legacy. My mother did not know all this when they married."

"How was your father chosen?"

"That I don't know. My mother refused to speak of it as did my other relatives. Better that Shamus had left, driven out of the country with those hounds, so they could pretend it didn't exist."

"Driven out? Your family drove Shamus out of Ireland?"

"Yes, they were bound to murder him for he became obsessed with needing a male heir. He kidnapped a small boy and tried to make my mother care for him. But he cried so for his own mother that one day, my mother took him back. Shamus raged against her. She took me and ran to her uncles. They drove him out. He went to France first. It was there that he found little Trevor. Mother knew Shamus had taken Trevor, but he quickly disappeared with the boy. I never heard from him again until about ten years ago when he came back. He claimed to want to see me to appease his lost soul. I handed him over to the police."

"Where did this all start? Where did the money come from?"

"The money belonged to the werewolf, if you believe the myths. He gave the money to the man who kept him so he would keep him alive and protect his offspring. The money just keeps getting handed down along with the power."

"That's the part that is so hard to believe. What is this power? How does the keeper control the creatures?"

"No one really knows. I suppose the keeper must know. Mother told me that Shamus had these old leather journals that contained great secrets. Perhaps they held the secrets that you seek. All I know is that Shamus destroyed my mother. Had it not been for Peter Flannigan, I would have been destroyed too. He saved me and made a way for me to find some happiness."

"That's not the way your daughter describes your life."

"My daughter wants to protect me, Miss Riley. When Shamus came back ten years ago, what little peace we knew was crushed. The destruction of his life fell on our heads and reminded everyone of a powerful evil that prevailed. His death finally brought closure to our clan. Now you come here talking about the hounds and asking questions. It's disconcerting."

A phone rang disrupting the conversation. The administrator answered, then quickly hung up. "Your taxi is here. So, please leave us and don't come back."

"I have just one last question. Do you know who the lawyer is that Kristen mentioned?"

"I suppose that would be Robert Donovan. He defended my father in his trial. Poor excuse of a lawyer though."

"Does he have any answers?"

Mrs. Flannigan stood, and Meg stood with her. "I don't really know. And if he did, he would be sworn to secrecy. Miss Riley, let me give you a warning. If you expose these hounds or the keeper, you won't be expected to live. My family was terrified of the consequences of turning on Shamus. Several of my family members disappeared, some were found dead. I believe the only reasons I am alive is that I have my faith in God."

"I've already survived the worst."

"The worst? No, you haven't even seen the worst. From what my father told me, your survival back in that day was due to the prayers of some young minister. That is the only Power that will win against this evil. You cannot fight this without God."

"I don't believe in God."

"Then you have no hope of bringing down this new keeper."

"Why? This is just a man, like any other," Meg began to feel herself getting defensive. She saw the administrator coming around her desk. Mrs. Flannigan put her hand up to stop her.

"I don't know why you fight so much against God. There are some evils that only God can stand against. You are fighting against an evil that goes back over 150 years. You think you, a young woman, alone, can win a battle that so many fought before you? Find that young minister whose prayers stopped Shamus in his tracks. That man has the answers that you need."

Mrs. Flannigan patted Meg's arm and turned to leave. Meg stood speechless knowing that the young minster she spoke of was probably waiting at the hotel, wondering where she was. She followed the administrator to the front door and climbed into the taxi. On the drive to the hotel, Mrs. Flannigan's words echoed in her mind, "That man has the answers that you need."

CHAPTER 20

B rian stood in front of the old house in Long Island Sound. The realtor told him that she had rented this house to Sam Hanson two years ago as a month-to-month rental. He saw curtains move and knew that someone was watching him. He climbed the steps to the front door and knocked.

"Can I help you?" a nervous woman asked with the safety chain on.

"Yes, I'm looking for an Elizabeth Boyd. I'm a private investigator from upstate."

"I'm Liz. What do you want?"

"A few years ago, you rented this house to a Sam Hanson. I'm trying to find him. His family is looking for him."

"Sam?"

"Yes, I have a picture of him if it helps you recall him." Brian pulled out the picture Stanley had given him of Sam. Liz glanced at the picture then back up at Brian.

"I remember him. He left abruptly. I had to move back in here because I couldn't get a new tenant."

"What do you remember about him? Did he ever leave you a forwarding address?"

Liz relaxed a bit. "He was kind of quiet, kept to himself. He just left though."

"Did he work someplace?"

"Oh, he didn't need to work. He said he had a trust fund or something. He always paid his rent with no problem. He even paid me a month extra when he left."

"Trust fund?" Brian jotted that down. "Did he have any friends?"

"There was this one kid who visited him. Johnny something. I think he had a dog in here too. When he left, it smelled like dogs."

"Hmmm. Did he leave anything behind?"

"Just some junk that I got rid of."

"There's nothing left?"

"No, I cleaned the whole place out. Took a bunch of junk to the dump."

"Well, can I give you my card? If you think of something, can you call me?"

"Okay," Liz stuck her hand through the opening to take the card. She looked at the name. "Riley? I remember Sam saying something about a Riley. But it was a girl's name."

"Meg Riley? Was that the name?"

"I think so."

"Meg Riley is my daughter. Do you remember what he said about her?"

"It had something to do with the Barker's divorce. I can't really remember it all, but he saw the article in the paper…wait a minute, it was shortly after that he left. Why would your daughter have anything to do with a divorce?"

"She's a PI like me. She probably found out one of them was having an affair."

"Do you think Sam was involved?" her eyes got big.

"No, it was probably a coincidence. If you think of anything else, will you please call me?"

"Sure, but you think Sam was having an affair with Mrs. Baker?"

"I doubt it. But I'll look into it. If I found out he was, you'll be the first one I call."

"Really? WOW! That would be something."

Brian turned away before rolling his eyes. Some people just like scandal. Brian drove back to town to find a library. He knew that the old newspapers would give him the Baker's story, but he already figured that Sam got spooked by Meg who was investigating one of the divorces. At the library, Brian quickly found the article on the Baker divorce and Meg's court appearance for the wife. He scanned through several issues and one caught his attention.

Local Farmer Loses Prize Chickens. With all the news focused on the scandalous divorce, it was easy to miss the article on the disappearance of several chickens and other small animals in the area. Perhaps Sam had those creatures in Long Island Sound at that time. Meg was close to those creatures again, because Sam had them here. That was why the house smelled like dogs. He left to protect the creatures, not to hide himself. Meg wouldn't have recognized Sam, but she would know those animals.

Brian sat in the cubicle reading the article on Meg again, and thought about the case in Virginia. Sam had to be traveling with those creatures. So, if people really did see them in Virginia, Sam had to be down there.

Quickly closing the volume, Brian put it back on the shelf and left. Once outside, he called Meg's cell phone only to get her voice mail.

"Meggie, I figured out something. I'm heading to Creek River right now. Call me back when you get this message."

Brian hung up and then called the office and asked Allison to book him a flight to Virginia from LaGuardia Airport in New York City. He called his wife and told her of his plans. While he was waiting on standby, he called Mick Finley to get some help on the case.

"Mick, Brian Riley, here. Look, you can't tell Meggie, but I need some help on a case. I'm on my way to Virginia to track down a lead on Craig. I need you to go check out some stuff in the Albany area that I got stuck with."

"Sure, you know my rates."

"Yeah, yeah, but send your bills to my residence, not the office."

Mick laughed good naturedly. "What's up?"

Brian told Mick about the case and Mick compared what Brian told him to what Meg was working on. After being assured that Mick wouldn't tell Meg, Brian called Creek River to talk to the sheriff about coming down. The deputy had him call Jesse at the Zimmer's house.

"Oh, Mr. Riley, it is so nice to talk to you," Mrs. Zimmer said. "Well, the sheriff is over at the church with my husband."

"I wanted to notify him that I'm on my way down to your town to help with the case. I have a new lead."

"When does your flight come in?"

"Looks like I'll be leaving on this next flight. I should be coming in this evening around 7 PM."

"That's wonderful!! You can stay here with us. Would you mind waiting for an 8 o'clock flight to land and bring a passenger with you to Creek River too?"

"Uh, I guess that would be alright. I just wanted to get to town before dark."

"Well, the sheriff was going to take the trip the airport to pick her up, but if you can do it, it would help him out."

"Okay, who will I be looking for? And how will you let her know?"

"It's Sarah Peterson and her little son, Richie. They are flying down to surprise Pastor Jake. Oh, you probably know them anyway, seeing how your daughter is working with Pastor Jake." There was a long pause while

Brian thought about picking up Jake's wife. "Hello? Mr. Riley, are you still there?"

"Yeah, sorry. I was just surprised."

"We all are! What a wonderful surprise for Pastor Jake when he gets back from Ireland. I can't wait to see his face when he sees Sarah. They haven't seen each other since before he came down for the mission trip."

As Mrs. Zimmer went on about how wonderful the Petersons were, Brian wondered how this was going to affect his daughter, Jake's ex-fiancé, when she got off the plane from Ireland to see the Peterson family reunion.

CHAPTER 21

Meg got to the hotel before Jake and pulled out her laptop. She was carefully documenting everything she could remember. She wrote about all the information she got from both Kristen and her mother. But her talk with the women left her with more questions that needed to be answered. As she sat thinking, her cell phone rang.

"Hey, it's Mick. Any luck with the O'Leary women?"

"A little bit from the daughter, the granddaughter was totally closed."

"My uncle found a few other relatives. They might not open up though. He told me the family believes they are cursed and any mention of the 'hounds,' as they call them, leads to death."

"The daughter said something like that too. But you might as well give me the names so I can follow up while we are here. Oh, I did get the name of the lawyer. It's Robert Donovan. I absolutely hate to ask you this, but Dad had a contact that said if we got the name, he might be able to trace it in the probate courts to find Sam. I can't seem to get in touch with Dad."

"Apparently, your pop is on his way to Virginia to follow up on something he found out on Long Island Sound."

"Yeah, he left me a convoluted message. But I can't reach him."

"Probably in flight as we speak. He ran into some brick walls of his own, so he called me. He didn't want me to tell you that he hired me, too."

Meg laughed. "Guess Dad and I are a lot alike."

"Yeah, you're both sneaky. But it works out for me. He gave me some more work, and it's the other side of your case. So, I get to help on both sides."

"Okay, so why are you telling me about Dad? Did you tell him about me?"

"Well, he called me before he got on the flight. Apparently, there's been a little hitch in his plan. He has to wait in Langford airport to pick up a passenger for the Zimmers. He wanted to give you the heads up."

"Why?"

"Your pop is picking up Sarah Peterson tonight at the Langford airport."

"Sarah? In Virginia?"

"Yep, she decided that she misses her husband and is going to surprise him when he gets back from Ireland by being there. Just thought I'd give you a bit of a warning, so you aren't surprised to see her at the airport when you and Jake come back from your trip."

"I'm okay with Sarah now. She seems like a nice person."

"For some reason, your pop thinks you'd be upset by her. Anyway, let me give you those addresses for the relatives. Good luck with them. If they're anything like my uncles...."

"I get it. Just give me the info. I'll figure it out."

While she was waiting, Meg called a few of the relatives and got nowhere. No one wanted to claim to be relatives of Shamus O'Leary. Finally, she heard Jake coming back and went to her door. As she opened the door, Jake turned from his own and asked, "Are you feeling better?"

"Come on in, we need to talk," Meg opened the door wide and stepped aside.

"Are you sure you're up to it?"

"Yeah, I'm okay...."

Jake sat in a stuffed chair that was near the window. "Meg, it's too bad you didn't get to come with me. There's this section in the cemetery that's just for the keepers. There's actually a place for Sam Craig there."

"What! That's unbelievable! How?"

"Apparently, O'Leary made all the arrangements before he died. Some lawyer set the whole thing up."

"Robert Donovan."

"Who?"

"O'Leary's lawyer is Robert Donovan."

"How did you find that out? The caretaker's son refused to give me that information."

"Kelly Flannigan, O'Leary's daughter."

Jake shook his head, "How?"

"I went to the nursing home where she's living."

"We told Kristen we wouldn't bother her mother."

"Correction, you told Kristen. I never agreed to cut off a lead."

"Meg, come on. I want to do this ethically."

"It didn't matter anyway. She willingly talked to me. Kristen called and told them not to let me near her mother, but she wanted to talk."

"Still, you went behind my back."

"You're right, I did. But I got some really good information from her, including the lawyer's name. What else did you find out at the cemetery?"

"It's really pretty sad. These men gave up everything, families, lives, and even in death are bound to those creatures."

"I got that same message from Mrs. Flannigan. There's such an air of mystery around the whole story."

"Well, maybe we can get some answers from Donovan."

"She didn't think so. He'd be sworn to secrecy. She even told me that if we expose this story or the keeper, our lives would be in danger."

"I doubt we'll be able to expose the real story. The only people who know the truth are older people who won't talk."

"There might be a way. She talked about some old journals that held the story. But where those could be…who knows?" Meg shrugged.

"Sam?"

"How? O'Leary went to prison when Sam was ten. There would have been no way he could have them."

"That lawyer. If it was his responsibility to take care of the will and make sure Sam had a place in the cemetery, he could have easily given him the journals when O'Leary died."

"Mrs. Flannigan talked about O'Leary being rich and that the money was handed down between the keepers. Sam must have inherited a lot of money with the cemetery plot. How else can he be hiding?"

"Yeah, but how much money are we talking about?"

"Guess we better find that lawyer. He's got a lot of explaining to do."

"Okay, let's see if we can find him." Meg hesitated for a moment. Then shook it off, but Jake knowingly asked, "What else?"

"It's nothing."

"I know you too well, Meg. What else did Mrs. Flannigan say to you?"

"Alright. This is where you and I always part ways…so I wasn't going to mention it."

"We've been pretty much in sync through this whole investigation so far."

"Yeah, it's been like the old days when we were partners. It's been great having my old partner, and I don't want to mess it up. I guess I should have told you that I still was planning on going to see Mrs. Flannigan."

"Yeah, you should have. But that's not what's bugging you though. What is it? Is it something I need to know?"

Meg shrugged. "I don't really think so, but...."

"Then just tell me."

"Part of it is her story about Shamus. She told me that her family drove O'Leary out of Ireland when she was a child. Shortly after, a lot of her relatives died, or just went missing. They believed it was retaliation for turning on him."

"But if he wasn't in Ireland anymore, he couldn't have been responsible."

"I don't think that mattered. I got the impression that it was the creatures that made them pay. Then she told me we haven't seen the worst yet. That things are going to get really bad for us if we go after the creatures."

"So is this where it gets back into the stuff that we don't agree on?" Jake asked. "We don't have to be afraid of these things. These are just myths and they can't hurt us."

"Well, according to Kelly Flannigan, you don't have anything to worry about. But I do."

"Well, that doesn't make any sense."

"She told me that when O'Leary went to jail, he said his plans failed because a young minister was praying. The only young minister I knew back then was you. She said that I should find you. That you have the answers that I need to fight the evil that those creatures have."

Jake sat just staring at Meg and then dropped his head. "Meg," he said softly. "I don't think she's right. This thing has been going on for over a 100 years. How is it that I am the only one with the answers?"

"She said that your power was in your prayers, and they stopped O'Leary." Meg got up and went to the window. "I don't believe in any of this. We've fought so much over the years over your religion. But she believes that it was her faith that stopped O'Leary from sending someone or something after her when she turned him over to the police. She said that you have that same faith, that same power."

"Maybe O'Leary finally got a conscience and couldn't hurt his daughter. Or the creatures were in the states," Jake offered.

Meg shook her head. "I can't believe I'm even going to say this. But when she said that you had the answers, it was like something inside of me made a connection. It's like the creatures are so evil and you're so good. How did you manage to find me and Sam in that basement all those years ago? What compelled you to go with me and Dad into the woods that day when you said you were finished with helping us? And then, you just happened to be there to save Dad's life. Are those really all coincidences, Jake? Or did God really have you in the right places at the right time?"

Jake didn't answer. So many times, he would have jumped in with Bible verses or quick answers to her questions. But he just stayed still, hardly breathing, listening as she talked it out for herself.

"Could God really have brought you to this place to end this evil? I've never known anyone like you whose faith is so real. I used to think it was because you became a minister. But now that I've seen how you live, the way you are with your family, and even on this trip…."

Meg sighed and turned from the window. She saw Jake sitting there quietly, waiting. "Well, we better see where this lawyer is, so we can get back to the states," she said going back to the desk. She shut down her laptop and grabbed her purse. She looked at her cell phone and saw the missed call from her father. "Oh, I should mention I got a message from my Dad. He is on his way to Creek River."

"Maybe you should call him back."

"Dad's probably in flight right now. I'll just wait and see if we find out anything from Donovan and then call him back."

"It's too late today. The office would be closed. Anything else we can do that you came up with?"

"I got the names of other O'Leary relatives. If Kristen is any indication of the response, it's probably a dead end."

"Yeah, but like you said, we came to Ireland to get answers. Let's see what we can dig up. Then first thing tomorrow morning, we are at the law firm of Donovan & Donovan."

"Okay, let's go."

CHAPTER 22

Boon couldn't stay away from the journals. He watched where Sam had hidden them and every chance he got, he would read more. The things he read scared him about the man whose legacy Sam claimed to be his. Paddy didn't seem too bad...yet. But his father was another story, one that Boon read with increasing anxiety.

After they had hauled all the stuff Sam had bought in Langford up the mountain, Boon went to the site of Sam's future cabin. He showed Sam how to clear the land and get it ready for digging the cellar. Although Boon hated the idea, he knew he would have to be the one to go back to Langford for the building supplies. He didn't want the law to find out Sam was hiding on his mountain. But for now, there was enough work to do without the need to get more supplies.

While Sam began to chop down trees and clear the area, Boon wandered back to the cabin and the journals. The day started getting away from Boon, but he was so engrossed in the journal, he didn't realize it was getting late. The tone in the journal was changing. Paddy was becoming like his father. Boon could feel the change as he read more about the child who had become a man. One that was about the same age as Sam was right now.

"What are you doing?" Sam asked snatching the journal away from Boon.

Boon was so lost in the story that he stared at Sam for a few long moments trying to comprehend who Sam was. At the doorway, one of the alpha stood watching, waiting. "Sam," Boon finally replied saying the name almost like a sigh.

"What are you doing? These are mine!"

Sam went over to his corner of the room and looked at the place where he had carefully hidden the journals. They were pulled out from underneath the other stuff Sam had stacked on top of them. "Let me explain." Boon got up and went to the kitchen area.

"Explain? How can you explain going into my personal belongings. You had no right!"

Boon picked up his jug and took a long deliberate drink while trying to calm his nerves. Finally, he set the jug down and watched as Sam put the journals back into place. He looked over at the creature who had stepped further into the cabin, standing between the two men. "Look Sam. When I started reading them, I just wanted to see if I remembered the old Irish, but then I got caught up in reading. I have a right to know what I've gotten myself into."

"No, you don't. I've told you all you need to know."

"But you don't feel that way yourself. You want to know what those old diaries say as much as I do. Problem is, you can't read them."

"And you can?"

"Yeah, I can. As much as I hate to admit that to you, I can."

"They belong to me!"

"So, you don't care that I can read them? You don't really want to know how this all started?"

Sam got up and walked up to Boon. "That's no excuse. You shouldn't have touched them without my permission."

"Look boy, those journals hold the answer that you can't even comprehend. Are you listening to me, boy? That O'Shea Pa was not a nice guy. He started all this. And now, you've inherited it."

Sam was seething, but a bit of what Boon was explaining was getting through. "I've wanted to know what those books have said since I got them. You know I was hiring Roscoe to tell me what they said, but that doesn't mean you could take them for yourself. They are mine."

"Okay, I get it. But I told you that I could read Gaelic, so why didn't you already ask me to read them?"

"Well, maybe it had to do with the way you've been treating me, like I'm some stupid kid. Or maybe it has to do with the fact that I don't know if I can trust you. Which by the way, taking them sure shows me how much I can trust you!"

Boon looked at Sam and then down at the alpha who continued to just stand watching them. He took another long drink from the jug and wiped his mouth on the back of his hand. He took the jug with him and went back to the table where he had been sitting reading the journal. There was another journal on the floor near his chair. As he sat down, he pushed it under a stack of old newspapers that was stacked in the corner.

"Sorry, kid. I didn't mean to upset you. But I have to know, just like you, what's behind all this. I understand now what you mean about how they kind of own you. Paddy talked about that too. He got bitten by one and it kind of changed him. His Pa called himself the Keeper, said with that bite, he was passing it on. But he also said there was some ritual. I didn't finish reading that part though. That's when you came back."

Sam looked down at his finger at the long white scar. "I got bit too."

"When? Recently?"

"No, back when I was ten."

"Ten? Ten years old?"

"Yeah, I think that his father," he pointed to the alpha, "knew that Trevor wasn't going to be able to keep them safe anymore. He was kind of mentally screwed up. So, he chose me to take care of him."

"But you were just a kid?"

"Yeah, I didn't even know it." Sam came over and sat at the table too. He looked down at the scar and rubbed it. Boon saw it and then looked at Sam's face. He looked so young and innocent to be facing such a task even at this age. He couldn't fathom how a ten year old would have been able to take care of those creatures.

"Ten. How did you take care of them?"

Sam shrugged. "I didn't really do anything. He followed me when my father moved us away. We lived in a wooded area. They lived in the woods behind my house, making sure I was okay and waiting for me to grow up."

"Where's his father?"

"A couple of years ago, he got killed." Sam eye's filled with tears, and he struggled to continue. "I didn't know that I was supposed to be taking care of him. I was confused because Trevor had come back somehow, and I saw them together. But then, I realized he was trying to protect me from Trevor and the cops."

Sam stopped and wiped his eyes. The creature came over and laid his huge head on Sam's lap. He absentmindedly reached down and pet him. Boon watched knowing that the bond between them was stronger than he first realized. After a few minutes, Sam continued, "I found him and the female in the woods by themselves. I took them back upstate, showing them where their father used to hide. But I couldn't just stay there because I didn't have a job or anything. I had gotten this letter from an attorney telling me that I would have this inheritance that belonged to the keeper, but couldn't get it until I was eighteen. So, I had to go back to my father's house. When the weather started to change, I went back to them. I found they had a litter, but they had all died. I felt horrible, so I brought them back to Poughkeepsie. I left as soon as I got the money."

"Where did you go?"

"At first I thought it would be cool to live where rich people lived, but it was really bad for them. So, I moved to all kinds of places where there were mountains and I could stay close. I ended up here because I got information about Roscoe thinking he could help me with the journals."

"So how old is Blackie?"

"He's about a year old, born last summer. It's hard to keep them alive. I don't know why."

"But there's the new ones...."

"Yeah, like last summer. The other was the only one that lived. That's one of the reasons I wanted to read the journals. Did you read anything about babies?"

"So, now you want to know about them?" Sam started to say something and the creature looked up at Boon. "Calm down, I'm joking with you. I didn't read anything about offspring. But I didn't get through all the books either. You're willing to let me read them?"

"I want you to read them to me and teach me how to read it, so I can read it for myself."

"Look, it's not easy to translate a foreign language. It takes students years to be proficient enough to read a book. You've got to remember that Paddy isn't writing grammatically correct either."

"Let's just call this a part of what I'm paying you for. I've got the money and you said you used to teach, so teach me."

Boon desperately wanted to finish reading the journals, but knew this wasn't going to be an easy task. Driven more by his need to know, Boon sat back in the chair. "You remember how to use that propane stove that's outside?"

"Kind of."

"You get me the first journal, we'll start there. While I read, you heat up some of that stew I made yesterday. Maybe we can get through that first one this evening."

"Yeah, but Roscoe already started that one. All it talks about is how poor they are and hungry."

"It started in the beginning, so that's where we are going to start. One journal at a time."

"You'll show me how to read it?"

"I'll show you some things as we go along. But in order to teach you Gaelic, I'll have to get some materials from the library."

"I only want to know how to read those journals, so teach me from them."

"I'm the teacher, remember? I do remember *how* to teach. You have to start with the basics in order to understand the harder stuff."

Sam finally conceded and pulled out the first journal. After looking at it, Boon went to the pile and pulled out another one. Sam sighed as he went to start the stove. The creature watched Boon for a while, then he took off for the woods. Boon watched him go and remembered that he was an offspring of whatever the hound was that Paddy was terrified of. Driven by the need to know, both men quickly got the meal out of the way and turned to the old journal that held long lost secrets of a past haunted by famine, starvation, and desperation.

CHAPTER 23

Meg was right. None of O'Leary's relatives would talk to them.
In fact, by the time they went to the first couple of addresses on
her list, all the other homes were darkened and closed. So, they gave up and
went to an Irish pub for dinner.

Earlier the next morning, they went unannounced to the Donovan law
firm. There they were surprised to be lead to the office of Robert Donovan,
Jr. Robert, as he preferred to be called, sat behind his desk in disbelief as
Jake finished explaining the purpose of their visit. Finally, he interrupted.
"I'm sorry to disappoint you, but my father is not the man you seek."

"So, you are telling us that Kelly Flannigan was wrong? That your
father didn't defend Shamus O'Leary?" Jake asked before Meg could jump
in. He could sense her tension and didn't want to ruin this small chance
they had to get information from Shamus's lawyer.

"My father defended him, but Shamus O'Leary was not this legendary
'keeper' you talk about. That whole story is preposterous!"

"Even if you removed the story of these creatures, O'Leary was
found guilty of crimes that went back years. How long was your father his
attorney?"

"I don't know and that would be privileged information. Are we
through? I have real business to attend to."

"Mr. Donavan," Meg said in a cool voice. "I understand that you
have other pressing business. But Shamus O'Leary committed horrendous
crimes in the United States that someone is now trying to copy. Your father
was his attorney. Now, you can either help us, or I will go to the local
authorities and have them get the information from your father."

"My father and my entire family are well respected in this community.
If you think you can intimidate me, try it...."

"Hold on," Jake interjected, glaring at Meg. "She does not speak for
both of us. I'm not here to threaten your father. We have reason to believe
that O'Leary left an inheritance to a boy named Sam Craig. This was the
boy that Trevor Grant kidnapped. Is it possible to find out about any will
that O'Leary might have left?"

Robert's face turned red. "Inheritance? To some boy?"

117

"Yes, Mrs. Flannigan said her father was wealthy and left nothing to her family. The caretaker at the graveyard where O'Leary is buried said that a plot has been already set aside for Sam Craig. All we are trying to do is follow the money to see if it leads to a person who is responsible for the disappearance of some people in the States. We believe your father would know."

"My father would know nothing about that. He never did estate work, or for that matter, criminal law. He was a contract lawyer for a publishing company."

Jake looked puzzled. "Then why did your father defend O'Leary for those crimes?"

"I don't know. My family has been doing corporate law for generations. My father was no exception."

"I'm sorry to keep asking you questions, but something doesn't make sense. If you don't know why he defended O'Leary criminally, then how would you know if he helped him with a will?"

Robert was clearly upset, and was blustering. "I know he would not have!"

"How? How would you know?"

"Enough!" Robert put his face in his hands. Jake stopped and shrugged at Meg. She motioned to Jake to let her ask a question, he nodded.

"Why are you so adamant about saying your father wouldn't have done a will for O'Leary?" Meg asked in a gentle non-threatening voice. "Certainly your father did work for O'Leary before his death. It would make sense that he would help settle his estate. We know that O'Leary's family got nothing from the estate."

"My father worked for a publishing house! He was not involved in this keeper affair."

"But he was," Meg went on. "You can't sit here and say he wasn't. He defended him in the criminal case. Why can't you believe that your father was involved in this? He clearly was."

Robert got up and looked out a giant window, his back to Meg and Jake. Jake started to stand, and Meg stopped him. Finally Robert sighed, "When I was a child, we used to hear stories about these demon hounds that roamed the countryside. We would scare each other with stories of them around campfires. But they were just another part of our Irish lure. As an adult, I even forgot the stories. I decided to become a lawyer, like my father and grandfather before him. I joined my grandfather's firm to take over for him, since my father had left as a young attorney to venture out on his own."

He finally turned and faced them. "Several years ago, I got a call from my father that his old childhood friend was back in Ireland, that he had been arrested and was asking Father to defend him. My father did a lousy job, and he finally accepted a plea deal. The papers linked not only my father, but this firm to allegations of past crimes. Kidnappings and murders at the hands of the one known as the keeper of the hounds. It took a long time for it to die down, and it came back after O'Leary died several years ago. Our lives have returned to normal. Then you come here asking questions, going to the cemetery, upsetting many of the older residents in our city."

"I'm sorry that we are dragging the past up again," Jake said. "But there is a small boy that has been missing now for weeks. Erica Boon is the daughter of one of my friends. She's been missing for over a month. These are real people missing under the same circumstances as the crimes that O'Leary was convicted of committing. I don't want to do as Meg suggested, get the local authorities involved. All I want to do is ask your father if he knows if Sam Craig has money and how we can trace it. I believe if we can find him, I'll find my missing people. I just hope that it's not too late to find them alive."

Robert shook his head. "My father wouldn't know."

"But what if he does. What if he has information that can help save Erica or Tommy's lives?"

Robert looked between them and shook his head. "He knows nothing. If you try to cause problems for us, I will contact the authorities myself. Now, please leave." He turned his back again and looked down at the city below him. Meg started to say something, but Jake shook his head, got up and walked to the door.

She stood and followed Jake, but stopped to turn back, "I'll give you fair warning, Mr. Donavan. When we solve this case and find out your father's involvement, I will make sure that every national newspaper knows that we came to you and you refused to help us, especially if it's too late to save the lives of these kids." She waited a moment and he never moved. They walked to the car in silence, aware that they were being watched.

Jake got behind the wheel and started driving. "Where now?" Meg asked.

"Thought that would be obvious to you. The Donavan residence."

"Really?" Meg asked in surprise. "Do you know where he lives?"

"I wasn't sure until we got here. I'm almost positive it's the smaller house on a side road in the city. I figure Junior owns the mansion on the outskirts, the family house, that was his grandfather's."

"Do you think Junior will tip off Dad?"

"Even if he does," Jake shrugged, "we can find the publishing house he worked for. If we can't trace O'Leary's money, then we trace Donavan's. Someone paid him for the legal services he performed for O'Leary."

"Hmmm, you think maybe we should split up?"

"What are you thinking?"

"I'm thinking Junior is making calls. Maybe to Dad, then to friends in high places. How many publishing houses do you think there are in Dublin?"

"Depends, is Dublin like New York City or like Saratoga Springs?"

"That's what I think I should find out. If you drop me off at our hotel, I can do an Internet search and find out. I'll start checking them out and see if I can find his employer. You can go talk to Donavan."

"I thought you'd want to visit Donavan." Meg sat quiet until Jake finally glanced over at her. "What's up?"

"I don't know. I just got a gut feeling that I should stay away from him. There was a big difference between the way Junior reacted to you than me. Maybe because I'm a woman."

"But you're the one that finally got him to talk. I was ready to just leave."

"Jake, just trust me on this. Drop me off and go see Donovan."

"You do realize that the old man is retired. It's not going to be easy finding his old employer."

"I can try. I also want to check in with Dad and see what's happening in the states."

Jake pulled up in front of the hotel. As Meg started opening the door, Jake said, "Please call me if you end up finding anything out. It might make him open up if he knows we're going to his employer."

"To be honest, I think you're going to hit a brick wall with Donovan after what Junior said. I've been thinking about it. If Donovan has been behind O'Leary all this time, hiding the money, protecting him from prosecution, there's no way, after all these years, that he is going to start talking and tell you anything."

"If that's what you think, then why should I bother going there?"

"Because maybe he will slip and give us something. Well, get going. This whole town is totally shutting down on us. I doubt even the local police would give us the time of day right now."

Jake watched Meg go into the hotel with mixed feelings. As he drove off, he looked back to make sure she wasn't going to leave like before. It was a quick drive to the small townhouse on the quiet side street. Jake pulled up in front and looked around. A car was parked in the short cobblestone driveway. He went to the front door and rang the bell.

Hearing sounds from within, Jake stood waiting, but no one came to the door. As he stood waiting, he looked around and saw a mailbox next to the door. The mail was sticking up. He rang the bell again and listened. Jake saw a curtain move to his left. He stepped to the edge of the stoop and looked at the window, but couldn't see in through the curtain. Jake looked around the street, and knocked on the door this time. When no one came, he took the mail out of the box and leafed through it. He took out a pad of paper and wrote down all the return addresses.

CHAPTER 24

Brian hated the waiting. But he was in no shape to hike up that mountain to the Hollow. There was little he could do but wait. After visiting the Novak's and Jackson's, he hit a dead end. He really wanted to talk to Clancy Boon, but he had to leave that up to the local sheriff. Jesse seemed competent enough, but there were things that Brian could pick up on that he wasn't sure the local sheriff would notice.

Sitting at the parsonage having lunch with the Zimmers and Jake's wife, Sarah, was helping kill time, but Brian didn't come to Virginia to have a nice meal with nice Christian people talking about the wonderful mission trip. Brian hated getting older, hated feeling that he couldn't keep up with Meg…and now Jake. Sarah seemed to sense Brian's mood.

As the meal ended, she offered, "Brian, I was thinking about going over to Beaumont. I was wondering if you could drive me."

Brian frowned. "I thought I'd just wait here for the sheriff to come back."

"Oh, Jesse won't be back until mid to late afternoon," Mrs. Zimmer said as she started to clear the table. "You've got plenty of time to run over to Beaumont. Besides, if he gets back before you, I can call Sarah."

"Why do you want to go over there?" Brian countered hoping for an excuse to stay put.

"Jake and Meg will be flying in tomorrow morning, and then I'll be heading back to New York. Things are so much cheaper down here and I wanted to pick up a few things for the baby."

"Well, you can go. Why do you need me?"

Sarah laughed and put her hand on her big belly. "I can't fit behind a steering wheel."

"I could always take her," Mrs. Zimmer said coming back in the dining room for more dishes. "My husband is going to be going over to the Rotary Club for his weekly Bible study with the men. You can go hear the Word."

Brian shook his head. "That's okay, Mrs. Zimmer. If Sarah wants me to take her to Beaumont, guess I can do her that favor."

Sarah smiled in amusement. She knew that Brian was conceding, so he didn't have to go to a Bible study. As Mrs. Zimmer left with a plate of leftovers, she winked at Sarah. After putting Richie down for a nap under the care of Mrs. Zimmer, Sarah took her purse and went outside to the waiting Brian.

After settling in the passenger side, Sarah turned to him. "I know that you didn't come to Virginia to be my chauffer. But I could see that you couldn't take much more preaching either."

Brian sighed as he pulled out of the driveway. "Are all you religious people like this?"

"Is Jake?"

"What do you mean?"

"Is Jake always preaching at you? Trying to get you to Bible studies or church meetings?"

"Okay, I get it. No, you're not all like the Zimmers."

They drove toward Beaumont falling into comfortable small talk. The drive didn't seem to take that long. Sarah went to a few stores and bought some things for the baby. She found a few small toys and clothes for Richie too. They stopped at an ice cream stand for some soft serve cones. As they took the mountain road back to Creek River, Brian found that he was grateful to Sarah for the diversion.

The winding road took them away from Beaumont with the mountains on either side of them. It was a beautiful drive with the deep blue hewed pines framing the road. Brian saw movement off to his right and took his eyes from the road. With surprise, he recognized one of the creatures standing just inside the woods.

"Do you see…," Brian started as Sarah screamed. He looked at the road and saw another creature standing right in front of them. He jerked the wheel to the right and hit the soft shoulder. Brian couldn't control the small car as it bounced down the incline gaining speed. When the car hit a tree head on, the airbag deployed smacking Brian hard in the face. He blacked out.

As Brian came to, he was aware of heaviness in his chest and found it difficult to get a deep breath. The car was head first into a tree that had stopped it from going all the way to the bottom of the ravine. Looking around, he saw Sarah pinned beneath the dashboard, unconscious.

"Sarah," Brian said weakly. He tried to reach her, but couldn't, so he unbuckled his seatbelt and slid into the steering wheel. Brian tried to push back against the seat, but the angle of the car made it difficult. For a few panicked moments, he struggled against gravity. He opened the door and leaned out taking in gulps of the fresh pine scented air. As he pushed against the steering wheel, Brian fell out of the car, hitting the moss-covered ground with a thud.

He laid on the ground as pain radiated from his hip down his left leg. The pain caused black dots in his field of vision. Struggling against the pain, Brian pulled himself up using the car door. Leaning heavily on the car, he looked back in at Sarah who still hadn't moved. He felt in his pocket for his cell phone, but it wasn't there. He saw it on the floor under the brake pedal. Groaning, he leaned into the car to get the phone.

The pain in Brian's chest caused each breath to be a new experience in pain. He tried to calm the ragged breathing as he dialed 911. He listened to nothing. Looking at the display, he saw 'No Service.' Brian had to get to Sarah and get her out of the car. He looked up the incline and realized no one would even know that they were down here. With the thought, Brian remembered why he went off the road...the creatures!!

Brian scanned the woods around him, but didn't see them and began to hobble to the other side of the car. With no airbag to keep her up on the seat and her seatbelt broken, Sarah was just crumpled under the dash with part of it collapsed on top of her from the impact of the crash. To Brian, hanging onto the car to stay upright, the walk to the passenger side seemed to take an eternity. When he finally made it to the door, he struggled to open it as it was damaged from the slid down the hill. Kneeling on the seat, Brian reached in and touched Sarah's face.

"Sarah?" Brian said softly. He reached her neck and felt a faint pulse. Relief flooded him, but only for a moment. "Sarah, honey, you need to wake up. Can you hear me?"

Brian sat in the seat and gently pushed her long black hair out of her face. There was blood on her face from the multiple cuts caused by the shattered windshield. From this angle, Brian could see that Sarah's legs were pinned under the dash and it would take the Jaws of Life to extricate her from the car. Brian picked up her hand and realized she was still holding a melted ice cream cone. How long had it been since the crash, Brian thought. Sweat was pouring down his face, from the heat and the excursion around the car.

THE HOLLOW

"Come on, Sarah. You need to open your eyes." He gently removed glass fragmented from her face and hair. Brian kept talking trying to get a response, as he felt her arms and legs to assess the damage. He could tell that one leg was definitely broken by the angle it was pinned. The blood on the floor of the car scared him, as did Sarah's ash colored face and lips.

"Sarah, you hearing me? Stay with me. Help is coming," he said trying to fight his own rising panic. He saw Sarah's purse on the floor and reached for it. The movement caused pain to shoot down his leg again, and the gasp against the pain caused his chest to flare up again. He managed to reach the purse and opened it. Somewhere, Sarah had a cell phone too. When he finally found it in the bottom of her purse, Brian almost cried when he saw that one bar.

Brian's hands were shaking when he dialed 911. The static was so bad, he couldn't tell if anyone answered. "I cannot hear you. This is Brian Riley. There's been an accident on the mountain road between Beaumont and Creek River. The car is down the embankment. My passenger needs an ambulance. Please hurry." He repeated his message several times with only static as a response.

Brian took the phones and decided to try to climb the incline to see if he could get better reception. As he stepped out of the car onto his left leg, the pain caused him to go down. It took Brian several long minutes for the pain to calm enough for him to climb back into the car. He sat on Sarah's seat gasping for breath, drenched in sweat. Even with the canopy of shade from the pine trees, the car was like a furnace.

"Okay, that was a big mistake. I guess I messed up my hip. I'm just going to stay right here with you, Sarah. Help is coming soon."

Brian was thirsty and there was no water in the car. For a few fleeting moments, he thought of the melted, and now drying ice cream cone on Sarah's lap. But knew it would only make him thirstier. He looked into the backseat and saw some bottles on the floor. Turning gently so not to enrage the injury to his hip, Brian reached for one of the bottles. His hand grazed one and it slipped away. He continued to reach, struggling for a bottle, until he got one. The tiny bit of water in the bottom was warm.

As Brian brought the bottle to his lips, he realized Sarah must be parched as well. He wet his lips as he poured a few precious drops of water into Sarah's mouth. He then lifted the bottle to his lips and saw him. Fear

125

jolted through Brian and he dropped the bottle. It bounced on the seat and fell on Sarah's lap. Forgetting about his pain and pushed by adrenaline, Brian pulled his feet in the car and slammed the door.

Slowly, the dark creature moved forward, its eyes glowing red in the shadowed woods. Brian's heart began to race with fear as he stared at the creature. As it neared the car, Brian saw the second creature coming from the back of the car. The second was a bit smaller than the first one, with black fur, and soon a third joined them.

Moving slowly, Brian reached in his pocket for the phone. He pushed the send button to redial 911. He heard the static again. The pain in his hip screamed again as the car shifted. For the first time in years, Brian felt helpless and terrified. "Oh God," he whispered. "If You really are real, please protect us."

The car moved as one of the creatures jumped on the trunk. With a metal groan, the car slid a bit from its hold on the tree. The creature jumped down, causing the car to move a little bit more. One creature jumped up on the door and snarled at Brian through the window. They began to circle the car, driven by the smell of the blood, looking for entrance into the car. One of the creatures jumped on the hood coming at Brian through the broken windshield. Brian reached down finding the water bottle. As the creature got close, Brian hollered and threw the bottle.

When it leaped off the hood, the car slid further sideways. A large low hanging pine branch pushed into the broken windshield. Long bluish pine needles hit Brian in the face. The branch wedged into the car holding it against the tree, keeping it from sliding further down the embankment. When the creature jumped back on the car, the branch prevented it from getting into the car and at Brian. Watching them through the closed window, Brian prayed for an end to this nightmare.

Throughout the never ending day, Brian talked softly to the unconscious Sarah, assuring her that help was coming, watching the creatures as they took turns trying to get into the car, and praying for help. He fought fatigue and pain as he lay across the seat. A few times, Brian heard a car or truck passing on the upper road. But he knew that until someone began looking for them, no one would find them. He managed to get another water bottle and drank the few tepid drops of water. It did little to appease his thirst.

Finally, the creatures took off. Brian tried to sit up to see where they went, but they just disappeared into the deep woods. It wasn't until deeper shadows filled the woods that Brian heard noise at the top of the embankment. He heard shouts, and soon, Jesse was near the car.

"Brian! We've been searching for you for hours. Paramedics are coming."

Jesse left the window, and soon activity was all around them. Brian was lifted out first, and carried up the embankment on a stretcher. From the angle, he could see emergency personnel using the Jaws of Life on the car, while Jesse sat in the passenger seat, holding Sarah still. Brian asked for water, but was told to wait until he was checked out at the hospital. He finally closed his eyes, feeling the drip of some pain medication from the I.V., as the ambulance took off toward Beaumont.

CHAPTER 25

Jake was on the phone with Phelps Publishing House when Meg knocked on his door. "I understand you have confidentiality rules, but this is a police investigation," he said into the phone as she opened the door. Meg came in with her laptop, and a few hand written notes. "Well, we will get that subpoena and have your financial records open. We believe that while in your employ, Robert Donovan was involved in illegal actions and ran money through your company....Depends....your cooperation, now, can make the difference in how the D.A. handles your company's involvement....Of course, there is always the possibility of individuals being held legally responsible....I understand, but you might want to consider consulting a different law firm than Donovan & Donovan. We aren't sure how deep this goes in the family's business."

Jake listened for a few minutes with a look of satisfaction. "Absolutely, I can be reached at 518-555-9871. I'll be waiting to hear from you....I'll be back in the States tomorrow...Thank you."

Jake hung up. "Well, I found it! He worked for Phelps Publishing House. And get this, it's actually in New York City!"

Meg stood dumbfounded for a minute, and then put down her stuff on the small table. "Well, guess I can quit guessing. I never thought he would just tell you."

"Oh, he didn't," Jake said smugly. "I did some old fashion detective work. You know it feels really great!"

Meg laughed. "So, you want to become 'real' partners again?"

"No, I still like being a pastor, but this is only a start. We still haven't found Sam or the missing kids."

"True. So, tell me. How did you find out who he worked for?"

"You mean works for. He's not retired, still gets a regular paycheck for being on retainer."

"They told you that?"

"Well, actually, I found that out at Donovan's."

"He talked to you?"

"No, the house was closed right up. I heard someone inside, but they wouldn't answer the door. But the mailman had come. He got a paycheck today, from Phelps."

"So…now, we go back to the States, get a subpoena for their records, and see who is on their payroll," Meg finished. "Very well done, partner."

"Then hopefully, we find out whose…," Jake and Meg's cell phones rang simultaneously. For a moment, everything just stood still, then Jake picked up his phone.

"Jake, this is Jesse. There's been an accident on Mountain Road. Sarah asked Brian to take her to Beaumont. They got into an accident on the way back."

"Sarah? What are you talking about?"

"Sarah came down to Creek River last night. She wanted to surprise you with a visit from her and Richie."

"This makes no sense. Sarah's in Creek River?"

"Jake,` I'm sorry."

"Are they…?" The question hung in the air.

"They are both in the hospital in Beaumont. Sarah's in surgery right now. You need to get back as soon as you can."

"Richie? What about my son?"

"He was with Mrs. Zimmer. He's fine."

Jake took a shaky breath, and felt Meg touch his arm. "Okay, we'll get the next flight back."

Jake hung up and looked down at Meg. Her eyes were filled with tears. "Who was yours from?"

"Jesse. You?"

"My stepmother. She's at Albany getting a flight to Virginia. What did they tell you about their conditions?"

"That Sarah's in surgery, and Richie was with the Zimmers. He didn't tell me how Brian is."

"She didn't give me many details either. Let's just get out of here."

"Wait. Did your stepmother say anything about Sarah?" Meg hesitated. "Meg, tell me, please. What is it that Jesse wouldn't tell me on the phone?"

"She doesn't know anything for sure. Why don't we just wait until we get to Beaumont?"

"Meg, don't…just tell me."

"I'm sorry, Jake. Dad told her that Sarah lost the baby. She's in surgery to stop internal bleeding."

Jake sank down in a chair. Meg stood there not knowing what to say or do. She knew that her father had also had surgery, and was still in critical condition, but that seemed so small in comparison to Jake's loss. Finally, she said, "I'll go pack and call the airport. See if there's a flight out sooner. I'm so sorry."

Meg went to her room and made the calls. There was a flight out that would get them to Virginia in the middle of the night. She made arrangements to rent a car at the airport and then packed her bags. When she got back to Jake's room, she found he was packed and waiting.

"Are you okay?" she asked hesitantly.

"I'm okay right now. I need to get to Sarah and make sure Richie is taken care of. I called Sarah's mother in Wyoming. She's going to fly in too."

"Well, there's a flight that takes off in less than two hours. Because of the circumstances, they are going to get us on that flight."

They took their bags and checked out of the hotel. Meg drove the car back to the airport, led a quiet Jake through security, and onto the flight. Meg kept a watchful eye on him and felt a deep sense of remorse for him. Most of the flight, Jake had his eyes closed, but Meg knew he was awake, praying. She wondered how this was going to affect his faith.

The long flight, the delay at the airport for the car, and the long drive to Beaumont left Meg wiped out. She couldn't even imagine how Jake was feeling. He had been so quiet, she was worried about him. Once at Beaumont General Hospital, Meg left Jake at the ICU in search of her dad.

Meg found Rachel sitting next her father in a semi-private room. He was sleeping with wires and tubes hooked up to him. Meg went in and laid her hand on her step-mother's shoulder. Rachel looked up and sighed, "Oh Meg, I'm so glad you finally made it here."

"How is he doing?"

"Resting now. He broke several ribs in the accident which made it hard for him to breath. Then he cracked his hip when he fell out of the car. But he will heal."

"Have you heard anything about Sarah?" Meg asked relieved that her father was going to be okay.

"It's not good. She lost a lot of blood. The doctors wouldn't tell me too much. They were waiting for Jake to get here feeling he deserved to know first."

"It's that bad? Is she going to make it?"

"I don't know. How's Jake holding up?"

"It's hard to say. He's been quiet. I think he's been praying, at least that's what it looked like to me."

"That's probably all they can do now. She's been operated on, and been given transfusions. Only time will tell."

"How long has Dad been asleep?"

"For a while now. But he's being sedated. They had to put a pin in his hip. I think his days of doing private investigating are over."

"How did this happen?"

"I think it's best you hear this from your father." Rachel looked back to Brian avoiding eye contact.

"Why?"

"You'll know when he tells you."

"Come on, Rachel, just tell me. I'll just ask the sheriff if you don't tell me."

"Look, it's too personal to your Dad. He wants to tell you himself."

Meg stood looking down at her father trying to figure out what it could be. "Too personal? That doesn't even make sense. It was an accident right? He wasn't drinking was he?"

"No, it's nothing like that."

"How long will he be sleeping?"

"I don't really know."

"Well, if Dad is going to be alright for now, I'm going to check on Jake."

"Well, if he wakes, I'll let him know you're back. Tell Jake, I've been praying for Sarah."

"Sure," Meg said absentmindedly thinking about the accident. What is this big secret? Meg went out into the hall and asked how to get back to the ICU, then followed the hallways until she found the wing. A few beds held patients and Meg found Jake near a bed with Sarah. Like Brian, she was hooked up to monitors, IV's and tubes, but she was also on a respirator. Jake saw Meg and stood. He walked out into the hallway where Meg waited.

"How is she?" Meg whispered aware of the quietness of the wing.

"It doesn't look good," Jake said in a choked whisper. "The doctor talked to her OB-GYN in Saratoga. I didn't know this was a high risk pregnancy. Sarah never told me."

"What's that mean?"

"Means she had been advised against getting pregnant again. She was having complications. She wasn't supposed to travel, and then the accident just…," Jake took an uneasy breath. "She didn't want Richie to be an only child like she was. Had I known, I would not have let her risk her life like this."

Meg didn't know what to say. She looked at Sarah on that sterile hospital bed, and felt horrible for them. She knew how much they loved each other.

"Is there anything I can do for you?" she asked.

"The only thing anyone can do now is pray. I don't know what else to do."

"My Dad is in Room 210. If you need anything, have a nurse call me. Okay?'

Jake nodded and then went back into the room. Meg watched for a few more minutes before turning away. She stepped outside into the hot day. It seemed like an eternity since they were in Ireland. She pulled out her cell phone and called directory assistance. She knew one person that Jake needed, that he turned to again and again. Somehow, talking to him might even help her. After getting the number, she made the call.

"Hello?" a woman answered.

"Hi, I'm looking for Pastor Ryerson. Is he available?"

"Yes, do you mind me asking who is calling?"

"My name is Meg Riley. I'm a friend of Jake's." There was a moment of silence and then she heard the phone being put down. A few moments later, Pastor Walt answered the phone. Pastor Walter Ryerson had been the senior pastor of Granelle Gospel Church when Jake took the associate pastor's job. As a mentor to Jake, a spiritual father, and a good friend, Jake turned to Walt for answers in the past. Meg knew that Jake depended on Walt and knew that Jake needed him now.

"Meg, this is Walt. How can I help you?"

"I'm not calling for you to help me. I'm actually calling to see if you can help Jake."

"Why isn't Jake calling me himself if he needs me?"

"I don't suppose you've heard yet. Sarah has been in a bad car accident. She's in ICU in the hospital in Beaumont, Virginia. She's not doing very well. I hate to even tell you this, but she lost their baby."

"Oh my! No, we hadn't heard anything yet. Is Jake alright? Was he in the accident too?"

"No, my father was actually driving the car. It happened yesterday, and Jake and I were in Ireland investigating some leads in the case we are working on down here. Jake seems so...almost lost."

"How is your father, Meg?"

Surprised by the question, Meg answered. "He's going to be okay. A few broken bones and a lot of pain. But I'm worried about Sarah...and Jake."

"What can I do?"

"Well, Jake said the only thing people can do is pray."

"I can certainly get the prayer chain from the church praying. But I sense there is something else."

"I just remember in that past, when Jake needed support, he turned to you. I hate to even ask this, but as his friend, I wanted to know if you can come here. He needs something that I can't give him. I'm really afraid that if Sarah doesn't make it, he's really going to need you."

"I'll get there as soon as I can. What about you? Do you need anything?"

"I guess I can use some of those prayers for my father too. His heart isn't very strong."

"I'll do that and put him on our prayer list as well. Let me make the travel arrangements. Is there a number I can reach you at?"

Meg gave her cell number to Walt and hoped that she had made the right decision. She then put in a call to Reggie to update him on what had happened. Reggie said he would make arrangements to join Walt on the trip to Virginia and contact Jake's parents in New Jersey about Sarah's accident. With the calls made, Meg went back to her Dad's room to wait for him to wake up.

CHAPTER 26

Meg met Pastor Walt and Reggie at the airport. She was surprised when the aging pastor walked right up to her and hugged her.

"Any news?" Pastor Walt asked searching her face.

"No, nothing has changed."

"And your father?"

"Dad is resting. I haven't been able to talk to him because he's under sedation. I still don't know what caused the accident. My stepmother knows, but won't tell me. I can't leave to them to track down Jesse. I feel so…." Realizing she was rambling, she took a deep shaky breath.

"Well, maybe that's where I can help," Reggie said picking up his carryon bag. At 6'5" Reggie towered over Pastor Walt and Meg. Usually, Meg felt intimidated by Reggie's size and his deep gruff voice. But today, she felt Reggie was a strength that she needed right now.

She looked up at him. "What are you thinking?"

"After we check in with Jake, we can talk about where you are with the investigation and look up the sheriff. See what's going on here, find out about the accident."

"Okay," she said gloomily leading the way to her rental.

"You, alright Riley?"

Meg looked up at him and half shrugged. "Yeah, sure."

"That doesn't convince me. I'm here offering to help you. What's up with you?"

Meg didn't know how to respond to that and just shrugged again. She felt so weary and fatigued. Pastor Walt glanced up at Reggie who gave him an 'I don't get it' look. They got to the car and put their bags in the trunk. As they got in the car, Meg said, "I'll take you to the hospital first. I made arrangements through the church for you to stay right in Creek River. I didn't tell anyone but the minister that you were coming. I wasn't sure how Jake would take it."

Walt and Reggie made small talk during the drive to the hospital. Meg kept thinking about Reggie's offer to help with mixed emotions. It was a long time ago she quit the police department because of conflicts with Reggie being her boss. She was worried about her father, Jake, and Sarah.

She couldn't understand how Jake was remaining so calm. Both men were aware of how quiet Meg was, but let her be in her silence. When they arrived at the hospital, Meg led the way to the I.C.U. and Jake.

Going on ahead, she went into the cubicle where the respirator continued to breathe for Sarah. Jake sat holding her head talking softly to her about Richie. Meg touched his arm, and when he looked up, she saw the tears in his eyes.

"Hey," she said. "Can you take a break for a few minutes? I brought someone here to see you."

Jake nodded and kissed Sarah's hand before laying it on the bed. He followed Meg into the waiting room. Surprise and then relief spread over his face as he saw the two men.

"What...? How did...?" Jake started getting choked up. He went to Walt and hugged him then reached out to shake Reggie's hand. But Reggie caught him in a big bear hug too.

"It was Meg," Reggie said nodding toward Meg who was hanging back. Jake looked at her and she shrugged. "She called us yesterday, and we came as soon as we could."

"I don't even know what to say," Jake replied.

"Well, why don't you start by catching us up on how Sarah is doing," Pastor Walt replied as he gestured toward the chairs.

After they all sat, Jake just shook his head, "It's not looking good. She was having a high risk pregnancy as it was. The accident...," he swallowed hard. "The baby didn't survive the impact. It was hours before they were found. She bled so much...." When Jake's voice broke, Meg's eyes filled up with tears.

"I think just about everyone in Granelle is praying for Sarah right now. The ladies' auxiliary has started a 24-hour prayer chain that is meeting in the church. Keith and Lori have the teens meeting for the weekend at the church hall for another prayer vigil. That entire town loves you and Sarah."

Jake nodded when Pastor Walt finished. "I can't even begin to tell you how much it means to me that you came. Both of you."

"I've asked my church in Saratoga to add you to their prayers too," Reggie added a bit more gruffly than usual.

"That's all we have left," Jake replied. "They are only allowing family in the room to see her. I think they will let you in as clergy, Walt, but I don't think I can pass you off as family Reg."

Reggie chuckled. "It's okay. I'll go see Brian and hang out with Riley for a bit. We've got some catching up to do."

They all got up to go in different directions, but Jake stopped. "Meg," he waited until she turned back. "Thank you for this."

"That's what friends are for," she said and turned away before Jake could see her tears. Reggie followed her down the corridors to an elevator frowning. She didn't talk to him at all as they went to the other side of the hospital. She found her father awake, but very groggy, trying to talk Rachel.

"Hey Dad, look who I found," Meg said in a cheery voice.

"Reggie Bennett?" Brian asked in a raspy voice. "Am I still out of it?"

"Nope, it's really me." Reggie wanted to joke around a bit, but was still feeling somber from his encounter with Jake and Meg's despondency.

Brian noticed the sober expressions. "It's bad or you wouldn't be here. Oh God, what did I do?"

"It was an accident," Rachel said quickly defending him. "It wasn't your fault."

"How is she...really? Rachel won't tell me a thing. Don't lie to me either, Meggie. I got to know."

Meg walked to the side of the bed and plucked at the blanket. "First of all, Dad, Rachel's right. It was an accident. And it's not your fault that it took a long time for them to find you. Sarah's had surgery and is on a respirator. It's just a waiting game now."

"I tried to help her. That's how I broke my hip. The airbag on her side didn't deploy. She just went under the dash...," his voice was turning into a harsh whisper.

"Excuse me, but Mr. Riley cannot be getting this distressed," a nurse said bustling up to the bed. "I think there are too many visitors."

Meg and Reggie backed up toward the door. The nurse fussed with some machines, shooting them dirty looks. Meg nodded toward the hallway, and Reggie followed her. The nurse came out and complained about them upsetting her patient.

Meg didn't argue, just apologized and left the floor. Reggie followed her, concerned by her lack of zeal. This wasn't the Meg Riley he knew. She left the hospital and leaned against the side of the building.

"Okay, Riley," Reggie began. "What's going on with you?"

"I feel so helpless. I can't help Dad. In fact, I seem to make things worse. I can't help Jake. I can't do anything," she said in a tired voice.

"Riley, you got Jake exactly the help he needs. Walt Ryerson is the one person to get him through this. As for your father, he feels guilty about the accident. He has some broken bones that will heal. But *your* feeling... what? That it's somehow your fault?"

Meg didn't respond. She shrugged and swiped at some tears on her face. "I don't know."

"What? What don't you know?"

Meg looked at Reggie in a helpless way. Frustrated at her, Reggie exploded, "I just figured out why I'm here. I'm here to kick your butt!"

Meg stared at Reggie with wide eyes. It had been a lot of years since she got yelled at by Reggie. "Hey, you can't yell at me. I don't work for you. I'm my own boss here."

"Well then act like it! Where is the hard-nosed detective that worked for the Granelle Police Department? Where's that Det. Riley who dared stand in my office and yell at me because I didn't want to believe your theory?"

"I'm right here," Meg said getting riled up.

"Are you? Cause what I see standing in front of me is a little girl, not a once decorated detective that worked for me!"

"In case you forgot," she yelled back, "I have a friend whose wife is in critical condition and a father who is not doing much better."

"Oh, really? I saw your father, and he's going to be fine. And what good is this pity party doing for your friend? You're down here feeling sorry for you, not Jake."

"Why are you doing this? What do you want from me?"

"I want you to wake up and remember why you're down here in Virginia. I want you to remember that you are looking for two missing girls and a little boy. I want you to remember that somewhere, someone has decided to revisit *your* past. And unless you get off your duff and get good and mad, this case won't get solved."

"But you're here now. You can take over."

"Yes, I am. But you've already been working this case. You've already built rapport with this police force, and you've just come back from Ireland. I've been retired for a couple of years. But you...oh, that's right, you chase cheating spouses. You've forgotten how to do *real* detective work. Guess I should find Jesse Mueller and tell him that you're feeling sorry for yourself, so forget about those kids."

Meg was mad. "Okay, okay! I get it! But that doesn't take back how I feel about Dad and Jake."

Reggie dropped his voice, "Yeah, and how do you feel?"

"Like a fool! I'm the one who's falling all apart about this accident, but it's Jake who should be. You know, O'Leary's daughter told me that Jake is the one with all the answers to this. Jake? Really? She told me that I couldn't stop the creatures, but he could. He's a minister!"

"Glad to see you're finally talking, but I don't know what you're talking about," Reggie grunted. "Look, I'm starved. Let's find a diner someplace, get something to eat, and talk. I need you to get me caught up, now that you're in the talking mood."

"Well, you might not want to hear all I have to say."

"That won't be the first time," Reggie laughed. "Then, we'll find that sheriff and find out what happened."

"Okay, but first," Meg said heading to the parking lot. "I want to make it clear that I'm the lead investigator, not you."

Reggie held his hands up in mock surrender. "As long as you don't play the little girl act again, I'll defer to you...maybe. But I'll kick your butt if I have to."

CHAPTER 27

Boon stormed to the site where Sam was busy digging a big hole. Sam had figured Boon would be doing this work for what he demanded in payment. But Sam was the one in the filth, digging a giant hole for a cellar. Boon had taken off earlier in the day.

"Get out of that hole!" Boon yelled. "You've got to get those animals and get off my mountain, now!"

"Hold on," Sam said not moving. "We have an agreement. I'm not leaving."

"Well, they're all going to be up here looking for you. Those animals of yours caused an accident. Clancy told them that you were with me on the mountain. So you got to leave."

"First of all, I'm not running anymore. I'm where I belong. You've taken money from me, too. I'm not leaving."

"Get out of that hole!" Sam picked up the shovel and scooped dirt, flinging it out of the hole. "They will come up here with guns and shoot those animals. Is that what you want?"

"After what you read in that journal, do you really think so?" Sam rested on the shovel staring up at Boon. There had been a shift when Sam realized the power that was at his command. He wasn't going to be bossed around. Boon stared back and then started to walk away. "Yeah, I didn't think so."

Boon stopped and spun around. "I'm done. You figure this out by yourself."

Sam put the shovel down and hopped out of the hole and followed. "We had an agreement. You promised you would help!"

"That was before you got mixed up in some accident. Preacher's wife might die because of those animals." Boon kept walking away.

Sam ran to catch him and grabbed his arm stopping him. "I don't know what you're talking about. I've been up here working, trying to get this cabin built, so I can get out of yours. You made a deal with me, for which I've paid you a bunch of money. You owe me - and them."

"They'll tear this mountain apart to get to them. Don't you get it?"

"I get it, but I also know from those journals that they were able to hide from people before. I've even seen that. You need to help me, and I need to make sure that they are safe. This mountain is huge, they will never find us."

"Yes, they will. Clancy will lead them right here." Boon glanced around and realized the creatures were near. "You think that they won't have guns? You think that they will really be safe if they come up onto this mountain?"

"Yes!"

"I don't. I have no faith in man. Not after what happened to me. They will come, and they will want blood for that accident."

"What accident are you talking about?"

"Two days ago, a preacher's wife and some cop were coming from Beaumont. Story says he looked away and one of them," he pointed to the dark shadow, "was in the road. He swerved to miss it and ran off the road. It was bad."

"How is that my fault? Or theirs?"

"Don't matter if it is or isn't. Town folk always want revenge."

"For an accident?"

"For an accident and for those kids that are gone. You showed me that poster, Clancy knows you're here. He's seen those animals. Now they are being blamed for the accident. I am trying to help you, don't you get that? If you leave, go somewhere else...."

Sam was looking off in the distance. Boon looked around and saw the alpha standing near as if listening. Sam looked back to Boon, "We are where be belong. They will take care of this 'problem.' I've got a hole to dig."

Sam walked back to the hole and jumped in. Boon followed him, "What's that suppose to mean?"

Sam started shoveling dirt. Boon heard a howl and spun around. The creature was gone, and he could hear a distant howl echo off the mountain. Boon looked back down at Sam and whispered, "What did you just do?"

"Go back to work. I think you're getting paid enough to help do some of this digging. If I have to do it all alone, this cabin won't get built before winter."

"Sam, what just happened? Where are they headed?" Sam looked up at Boon with a hard look. "You promised that nothing would happen to my kin. Where are they going?"

"You know where. Clancy is the problem. They will take care of it."

Boon cursed and took off. Sam called after him, "Choose your side carefully, Boon. You read those journals. You know that power that they have."

Boon stopped at the edge of the clearing, hesitating for a moment, then took off running. Sam continued to dig the hole knowing that the creatures would keep people away. He would be safe.

* * *

Boon ran back to his cabin. Branches raked his face as he ran totally oblivious to the surroundings. He was intent on getting his shotgun and heading to the Hollow. Out of breath, he threw the door to the cabin opened. Grabbing the gun, he took a handful of shells and put them in his pocket. As he bolted out the door, he stopped short. The young, black male stood still staring at Boon.

"Out of my way, Blackie," Boon said in a guarded voice. But the creature didn't back down, instead a low growl began deep in his chest. Knowing that these creatures understood what they said, Boon went on. "I made an agreement with Sam. I'm friends with you, but in return, you have to leave my kin alone. You can't hurt them."

Boon took a few steps outside, but the creature tensed. "Look, Blackie, I don't have any argument with you. It's Boss, he can't get Clancy."

As he took a few more steps, the creature took a step toward Boon, his hair on his back standing straight up. Boon cursed and put down the gun. "Look, I'll go without the gun. Please let me go. I have to warn Clancy." But the creature didn't back down. Boon took another step, and the creature pounced, knocking him down. Boon put his hands up to protect his face, but the creature stepped back. Boon tried to get to his feet, but was knocked down again.

The creature made a strange noise that didn't sound like a bark or a growl. It sounded like he said a word. Totally freaked out, Boon crawled back to the cabin. The creature circled around him, making the weird clicking sound that sounded to Boon like he was saying something over and over again. As he crawled over the threshold, the creature howled. Boon just lay still, terrified to move. Terrified of what he thought he heard. Terrified that down in the Hollow, the other two creatures were killing his family.

Boon lay motionless for what seemed like hours. The creature lay near him, sniffing at him, then getting up and pacing. It would leave for a few moments, but when Boon tried to move more into the cabin, it was right by his head, sniffing him again.

Finally, Boon heard footsteps coming through the woods. The creature sat down near Boon watching someone coming. Boon called out in a strangled voice, "Stay away!"

The response was a chuckle. "Did you really think they were going to let you go?" Sam asked. He picked up the gun that was lying on the ground and pet the creature. "Go ahead, I'm here now." The creature took off into the woods. "Okay, Boon, you can get up now."

"Why did you let him go?"

"Because my job is to protect them, and they protect me." Sam reached down to Boon, who grabbed his hand and pulled himself up. He held onto Sam's hand, towering above him.

"You have to stop them."

Sam jerked his hand away. "Why would I want to do that?"

"Because I can't be responsible for another death." Sam shook his head and went into the cabin. Boon stood hesitating and then took off toward the Hollow. Sam would have to shoot him to stop him now.

CHAPTER 28

Meg and Reggie had long ago finished their meals and the dishes had been cleared. Meg had told Reggie everything she knew from her first contact with Jake to the flight back from Ireland. Reggie kept asking her questions and going back over some of the details.

"…so I think that we should reconnect with Jesse and get filled in on what's going on here," Meg said finishing up. "Plus, I want to find out what he knows about Dad's accident."

"Okay, let's get moving," Reggie said as he put a large tip on the table. Meg looked at him surprised. "Well, we've been taking up room for a while. Want to make it worth it."

They walked out into the hot day. Reggie squinted against the glare of the sun. "Is it always so hot down here?"

"You're asking the wrong person, Captain. But it's certainly been hot since I got here."

As they got in the car and drove to Creek River, Reggie continued to complain about the heat. Part way around the winding road, Meg pulled over. "What's this?" Reggie asked looking around.

"This is where they found Dad and Sarah. Down that embankment." Reggie got out and looked down the hill. He saw the skid marks and the scars in the hillside from all of the emergency equipment. The tree almost at the bottom of the embankment had a large gouge taken out and a broken branch lying to one side.

Meg walked around the car and stood near Reggie. "I've come by here a couple of times trying to figure it out. What do you think?"

"Do you know if it was raining that day?"

"I don't think it was."

"From the skid marks, looks like Brian swerved and went off the road. I think it was just an accident."

"Then why would my stepmother make it sound so cryptic? And Dad is blaming himself."

"Maybe he got distracted. Let's check things out by the tree." Reggie headed down the ravine and looked back up at Meg. "You coming?"

"I've already done this. Go ahead, see if you find anything."

Reggie got to the tree. He felt the gouges and looked at the embedded paint chips. He walked around going further away from the tree, into deeper woods. Meg watched uncertain as Reggie disappeared from sight for a few long moments. When he reappeared, he came back up the embankment.

"Did you see anything down there?" Reggie asked her when get got back to the car.

"The emergency crew messed evidence up pretty badly when they pulled out the car. The tree is a wreck...," she paused. "What is it Captain? What did you see that I missed?"

"What did you notice about the natural environment?"

"You mean the trees and undergrowth?"

Reggie took a deep breath and slowly released it. "I'm hoping that I'm wrong. But I've seen them before, in Granelle." Meg stood up straighter and looked down the embankment. "First time I saw them was at the old rental you had in Granelle, over on Consul Road. You remember when Grant kidnapped you?"

"What is it?" Meg whispered. "What did you find?"

"The footprints. Those creatures were all over the place down there. You can see it real clear when you get deeper in the woods away from the accident site." Meg took off down the hill. She looked around the ground and then followed the trail like Reggie did. He followed her, knowing that Meg wouldn't just be satisfied with a quick look. He caught up with her where deep, larger footprints were encased in the dried mud. "Riley, this trail is days old now."

"That's what caused Dad to swerve off the road. Those creatures! Did they know it was Dad and Sarah? Could they know that?" Meg asked looking up at Reggie.

"Think we need to find that sheriff. This means that this accident and the disappearances are tied to our cases in Granelle."

"Wait, we need to follow...."

"Riley, don't go off half cocked now. You know as well as I do that they were here the day of the accident. Three days ago now. They are gone or we would have already been attacked. Let's go to Creek River and find that sheriff. Whoever is responsible can't be far away, probably somewhere on this mountain."

Meg nodded and followed Reggie back toward the car. "Dad shouldn't be blaming himself though. If those creatures are involved…."

"They probably distracted him and he ran off the road. Not his fault."

"The big question is, did they know it was Dad? Or was it just a coincidence?"

"The sooner we solve the case, the sooner we'll have the answer."

As they drove the rest of the way to Creek River, they talked about the past, the old cases, and those creatures. Meg told Reggie details about her ordeal in that basement being held by Trevor Grant that he hadn't heard before. She described in great detail the large dark creatures that had a hold over Grant. For the first time, Reggie really listened, not discounting anything she told him. She pulled the car up in front of the small jail.

They both sat there, Meg uncertain about these last details she never told her former boss. "What is it Riley? I got to know all of it, even if you think I won't believe it."

"Last time, I tried to talk to you about this stuff…."

"I was your boss with a different agenda. Now, we are partners, you're the lead investigator. I need to know everything, so just tell me."

"You know that the creature attacked Grant in the end. That's why we weren't killed. Did Jake ever tell you more? About how we were really able to get away?"

"Just what you said, the creature attacked Grant and took off. Grant was hurt so bad and wasn't conscience until he had medical treatment."

"There was a bit more to the story. When I was alone with Sam in the big cage, he had reached out and petted the creature. I saw a bite mark on his hand. When Trevor came back to the house, Jake was there and was trying to rescue us. But Trevor knocked the gun away from him and that creature stopped Jake from being able to get him. There was no doubt in my mind that Grant was going to kill us. He commanded that creature to kill Jake. It was starting to go for him, but then Sam stopped it."

"Stopped it? How?"

"He stood up and said no. He told Trevor that he was the keeper now and commanded that creature to attack Trevor instead. Trevor laughed at Sam, but the creature listened to the kid. I was shocked. But when Jake went for the gun, the creature turned its attention back to him. But Sam was still able to call it off again. He told it to leave Jake alone, told it to leave, and it did."

"But how? How would that kid have been able to do that? And why was he so afraid of that animal three years ago when it turned back up again in Granelle?"

"I think that when Sam got bitten, that creature chose him. Maybe Sam didn't realize that three years ago."

"And now?"

"Now? I don't know. O'Leary was so sure that Sam was the next keeper that he took Trevor's name off the grave in Ireland and gave it to Sam. Jake seems to think that O'Leary disinherited Trevor when he got caught and sent to jail. Then he picked Sam who has some connection to those creatures."

"What do *you* think?"

"I think that those creatures picked Sam over Trevor. I think that O'Leary was just another pawn in their game. I think that the person is really controlled by them, not the other way around."

"Come on, Riley. I'm trying to believe all this, but they are animals," Reggie said in a dismissive tone.

"You've been listening to me up to now, so don't lose me yet. There's another thing that makes that all possible. They have human DNA."

Reggie just stared at Meg, and then shook his head. "Okay, we're back to the old werewolf theory? The one you got from the kook in Albany? What was his doctorate in, mythology?"

"Actually, it was medieval folklore. I tried to show you this then, and you dismissed me. This is too important for you to shut me out now... Reggie."

The use of his first name, surprised him, but then he smirked at her. "Okay, boss. Tell me this other piece of *evidence*."

"These creatures have human DNA. No theory, no mythology, no folklore. All the test reports, from the ones in Ireland, to Granelle, and even here, ALL say the same thing. Somehow, the creatures are part human."

"That's impossible. From a purely biological standpoint, that is impossible!"

"All different labs, all different crime scenes, all the same. Facts, Reggie. Real facts."

"I don't believe it," he said flatly. "There's some mistake."

"Yeah, I thought so too. But you didn't even want to believe that it was the same animal from the DNA reports that were in Ireland and in Granelle. So I never told you about the human piece. But it's back, and it's the same."

"Now, it's here? The same animal?"

"Next generation."

"What does that mean?"

"It's not the same creature that was in Granelle, but an offspring."

"DNA again?"

"Yeah. Now, I think we should find Jesse, so you can see those lab results. And I can confirm with him that those creatures were what made Dad swerve off the road."

"Just one more question. So what if you're right. What difference does it make for us to know that they have human DNA? What does it matter? They are still animals."

"Animals with human intellect. Animals that can control a person, this keeper. Maybe that is significant."

"Or maybe you just gave this person an insanity defense. You go telling this to a defense attorney. That person will spend quality time in a nice hospital instead of behind bars for kidnapping...or worse. Be careful who you tell that to."

Meg hesitated as Reggie opened the door. "Maybe it's too late for that. I think the sheriff has been talking about this in the town."

"Well, let's get to him and make sure he keeps details of this case confidential."

CHAPTER 29

Boon was gone for a long time. Sam made himself something to eat, and then looked through the journals. He wished he could understand the writing for himself and didn't have to rely on Boon to translate the text for him. At least it was better than having Harman do the work. But Sam got the feeling that Boon wasn't really reading the whole journal to him, but carefully omitting certain details.

Sam had always felt a sense of power with being the keeper. But what he was learning from the journals was something deeper, more powerful. It gave him the same courage to stand up to Boon and take authority that he never felt he had before. Part of the power was the fear that others had of the creatures. Sam had never thought to use that to his advantage until Paddy talked about it. Sam went back to the most recent letter from O'Leary that also talked about the power.

Hours later, as darkness was beginning to fall, Sam heard noises from outside of the cabin. He waited, listening at first. The door flung opened and Boon came in. He was disheveled and dirty. Sam looked up from the cot and then began to fold the letters from O'Leary and Donovan.

Boon went to the counter and grabbed his jug. He took long gulping drinks and finally set it down, wiping his mouth with his forearm. He looked over at Sam and narrowed his eyes. "Clancy's missing."

When Sam didn't respond, Boon shook his head and took another long drink. There were noises outside, and Sam knew the creatures had returned. He put his papers and journal back in the backpack. He set it next to the cot and then went to the door. "Maybe it's best if you stay outside with them tonight," Boon said not turning around.

Sam chuckled, "I'll decide what's best. If my presence is bothering you, you can spend the night outside, with them." Not waiting for a reply, Sam stepped out into the night air.

The two male creatures came to him and Sam knelt down. He reached for the alpha who eagerly came to Sam. "What happened? You take care of our problem and now our friend isn't happy?"

The younger male made a low sound and turned toward the woods. Sam looked to where he went and saw the female just inside the woods. Getting up, Sam walked toward her with his hand on the alpha and looked

around. He saw one of the pups near her and looked around for the others.
As he approached, she stood still, waiting. Sam looked between her and the
alpha. Something seemed wrong.

Kneeling down next to her, Sam gently laid his hand on her head and
she sat with a slight moan. He saw a gash on her foreleg and saw how
she held it up. Gently, he reached for her leg and felt around the gash. "I
don't think it's broken," Sam said half to himself. He looked at the alpha
who sat very close watching everything. Looking back at the female, he
asked, "Where are the babies?" She looked at the one sitting near her. "The
others?" She just looked into Sam's eyes and he knew.

Getting up, he ran back to the cabin. Crashing through the door, Sam
ran up to Boon who was still nursing his jug. He slammed him up against
the counter. The big man was surprised, but did nothing to defend himself.
"What did you do?" Sam yelled. "Did you kill the babies? Why is she
hurt?"

"What...?" Boon stammered. His eyes focused on something behind
Sam. Sam, so intent on his own anger, didn't see the dark creature behind
him, waiting for the answer too.

"Did you kill the babies? Did you?" Sam shouted.

"No!" Boon yelled pushing Sam off from him. "I've just been looking
for Clancy."

"What happened? Where are they?"

"I don't know what you're talking about. I went up to the Hollow. Ma
said Clancy left hours before and hadn't come back. They," he pointed at
the creature, "were in the woods. I spent all the hours looking for Clancy. I
went back to the shacks, he still wasn't back."

"Come on then." Sam went and grabbed Boon's shotgun and a lantern.
He heard Boon softly laughing.

"What you planning on doing boy?"

"I'm going to find the pups."

"Find them? In the dark? If they don't know where they are, how are
you going to find them?"

Sam came back over to Boon and yanked the jug out of his hand. He
slammed it on the counter, splashing the whiskey all over. "You and I are
going out there and find them. That's what we are going to do?"

Boon puffed his chest out and stood up straighter. "Who you think you
are boy?"

"I'm the Keeper, that's who I am. And you are going to help me find those pups and kill whoever hurt the female."

"Yeah, right," Boon said sarcastically. He went to pick up the jug and saw the creature still standing, watching. Sam went back to the gun and loaded the cartridges the way Boon had shown him. He stuffed several in his pocket and handed the gun to Boon.

"Let's go," he turned to the door.

"I'm done," Boon said picking up the jug again.

"Then you're dead." Sam laid his hand on the creature's large head. He heard a noise behind him as Boon cocked the shotgun. "You might be able to take out him or me, but not both, and not his son."

"I only need to take out him."

Sam looked back over his shoulder at the shotgun pointed right at the creature. "I told you before to choose your sides carefully. You pull that trigger, you are dead. You might kill 'Boss,' as you like to call him, but then you will die. Is it worth it?"

"And what have I got left anyway?"

Sam turned and went toward Boon, blocking the shot. The creature never moved, never took his eyes off of Boon. "Have you not heard anything that we've talked about, not understood one word of those journals? There is incredible power that belongs to those that protect the creatures. And with that power comes enormous wealth." Sam grabbed the end of the gun and easily pulled it away from Boon who was memorized by the creature's stare. "Besides, do you really think you could kill them? Don't you remember the story in the journal?'

The creature approached Boon, a low growl in his chest. Boon didn't say anything as the creature came closer. Sam stopped him with one move of his hand. He smirked at Boon. "See, the power is mine. I control them and you. Now enough of this, we have to find those pups."

"I can't do this, Sam," Boon said in a quiet voice. "I don't want this power. I just want to go back to my quiet life, with no outsiders."

"Well, it's too late for that. This mountain is now mine. We have an agreement and until I'm settled and able to live on my own, I'm holding you to your word."

"My cousin is probably dead because of them."

"If your cousin is dead, it's his own fault. He should have left us alone. Let's go. If they are hurt, we need to find them now."

Sam picked up the lantern and handed it to Boon, keeping the gun for himself. As they walked to the door, the creature growled at Boon and bared his teeth. Sam looked at him and said, "We still need him. If he crosses a line again…." He looked back at Boon and left the rest unsaid.

The sky was black. There were no stars or moon, and the woods were dark and menacing. Boon knew that his biggest fears were right there with them. Boon stood watching as Sam brought the limping female and the one pup into his cabin. Sam put a blanket on the floor for them, filled a bowl with water, and put some meat scraps near them. Satisfied, he closed the door, so that nothing could get to her or the pup.

Sam shone a flashlight on the lantern as Boon, with hands shaking, lit it. The flame leapt for a moment before settling into a steady flicker. Sam realized that Boon was a bit drunk, but didn't care. He needed Boon to navigate the mountain.

"Okay, let's go," Sam said as he let the creatures lead them into the dark woods. As Sam followed the dark shapes through the woods, he felt completely lost. Branches cut his face and hands, and Boon grunted several times as he too was hit with the unseen branches. Stumbling through the darkness, they had to stop many times because of Boon.

Finally Boon collapsed on the hard ground. Lying on his back on the carpet of pine needles, Boon groaned, "I can't go on any further."

"We have to."

"Look, kid, I haven't eaten since this morning. I'm half in the bag, I keep getting sick. Let me just lay here…maybe I'll do us both a favor and just die."

"Get up!"

Boon flung his arm over his face and moaned. One of the creatures came back and sniffed at Boon. In the darkness, Sam couldn't tell which one it was until he looked up. The alpha turned, walked a few paces, and then looked back at Sam. "We need him." The creature came back to Sam and pulled at his shirt with his teeth. Sam remembered a long time ago, the creature's father doing the same thing. Sam set the flashlight down by Boon's hand. "I'll leave this light with you. If I can, I'll come back later and get you."

"Don't bother." Sam heard him groan out as he went with the creatures into the woods. Without Boon, they sped through the woods, the lantern making weird shadows around them. Sam felt driven by an instinct that was new to him. He felt free running in the dark woods with the creatures on either side of him. Sam began to recognize the terrain and realized they were headed to the den. Sam splashed through the creek and then up the bank. He slid to a stop outside of the small opening. The two males stood waiting for Sam.

Sam put the lantern close to the opening and looked in. In the bit of light, he thought he could see one of the pups. He stuck his head in and touched the little mound. It was cold. Sam shuddered and pulled the little mound out of the den. Setting it to the side, he reached back in to see if the third pup was there. He felt a small movement under his hands. Pulling the little female pup out, he saw she was bleeding and hardly moving.

The two creatures watched as Sam took off his shirt and gently wrapped the wounded pup in it. He knew he had to get her back to the cabin and see if he could save her. But he couldn't leave the dead pup there for someone to find. This is why he needed Boon, he thought! As Sam reached to pick up the dead pup, the alpha came over and picked it up in his mouth. He turned and disappeared into the woods.

Cradling the injured pup, Sam picked up the light with his other hand, "Okay, take us back to the cabin," he said to the other. "We need to see if we can save her life."

The walk back to the cabin seemed to take forever. At first, Sam tried to hurry, but thirst and fatigue weighed him down. The pup barely moved in Sam's arms. Sam figured it was an hour or so later that the alpha returned without the dead pup. When the lantern died, Sam set it down and laid his hand on the creature. He let it guide him blindly through the dark woods until gray streaks broke through the dark night. Relief flooded Sam as he began to recognize the woods near the cabin. He kept up the pace until he reached the cabin and opened the door.

The female was lying with her pup and looked up at Sam. He gently laid the injured pup near its mother. Exhausted, Sam lay on the sleeping bag on the floor near the female and fell asleep. After Sam was asleep, the alpha male laid across the threshold keeping a protective watch over Sam and its mate.

CHAPTER 30

Reggie and Meg met the sheriff at his office before they headed up to the Hollow to talk to Clancy about Sam. Even though Meg had thought Sam was involved, it was hard for her to accept Clancy's positively identifying Sam as the boy that he saw with his cousin, Boon. She needed more information. She had a restless night and it bothered her that the sheriff was late this morning.

"I still think that you should stay here," Jesse said to Meg as he put a water bottle in a canvas bag.

Meg started to defend herself, but Reggie stopped her. "I appreciate your concerns about your mountain people and their ideas of women. But I can assure you that Meg needs to be there."

"It's not just about her being a woman. She's also an outsider. I don't think Clancy's going to take any better to you." He hesitated and then sighed. "He's not too fond of black people either."

"I guess that makes Riley and me good company then. But we know Sam Craig. If that kid that Clancy saw is really him, we will probably be the only ones that will get information out of him. You still have three missing people in Creek River. We're the best you got."

"Let's just get moving," Meg said through clenched teeth. As she followed the men out, she shook her head in disgust.

Jesse was right about the long hike up the mountain. Meg found it tough to keep up with the men. She knew Reggie worked out, but she didn't have time to walk, let alone going to a gym. She took another long drink from her water bottle.

"Better conserve some of that," Reggie said glancing back at her. "It's going to be a long day of hiking."

"I figured there'd be water at the Hollow."

"Oh there is," Jesse said. "But it's from the creek."

"Do people drink from it?" Meg asked with a frown.

"Course, but we're mountain people."

"What difference does that make?"

"Just figured, you being from the city and all...."

"Which means that I can't drink creek water?"

153

"Never mind," Jesse said. "We're almost there now. Clancy has probably seen us coming."

"Jerk," Meg muttered under her breath making Reggie chuckle.

As they came into view of a few rundown shacks, Meg looked around surprised at the condition of the homes. Jesse told them to wait as he walked up to one of the shacks. Meg and Reggie waited quietly, each taking in the small community. Meg saw a few people watching them from a distance. She sat down on a log and took another drink of water.

Jesse came back and looked around before saying anything. "There seems to be a problem. Clancy went out yesterday and never came back. Sometime in the afternoon, Boon came by looking for him and then left, too."

"Who told you this?" Reggie asked.

"Ma Boon. That's Clancy's ma. Everyone calls her that."

"Can I talk to her?" Meg asked standing up.

"Guess it can't hurt none. Let me introduce you though. She might not talk to you even if I tell her its okay. They are very superstitious people."

As they walked over to the shack, Meg asked, "Are they the people that Jake comes to see? The ones that his church tries to help?"

"Yes, these are the folks. He helps them a lot and they all love him here. Okay, let me talk." Jesse stopped her on the small porch. He knocked on the door. "Ma, it's Jesse again. I have someone with me that I'd like you to meet. Is it okay?"

"Boon ain't here," her quiet voice came from inside.

"I know that Ma. But she's a friend of Pastor Jake's. I think Clancy would say she's okay for you to talk to." The door opened and Meg looked down at the tiny woman. "This is Meg. She came down to help Pastor Jake find Erica and the missing kids from town. Since Pastor Jake's wife is hurt, he can't come up here. So, she came up to see if she can help."

"Clancy ain't here." She shook her head and closed the door.

The sheriff shrugged and stepped off the stoop.

"We aren't going to ask her anything?" Meg asked following him back to where Reggie was waiting.

"Won't do any good. She won't talk to us unless her son says its okay."

"But…."

"Ma ain't talkin' to ya, but I will," a soft voice came from behind Reggie. They turned to see a young woman half behind the tree. She glanced around and then continued. "I'm Sissy. Clancy Boon is my pa. He left yesterday and ain't been back. My little sister been gone for over a month."

Meg walked over to her. "My name is Meg. I want to help find them. Do you have any idea where your father went?"

"No ma'am. I heard he went huntin'."

"Do you know what he was hunting?"

"We had bad animals near here. Pa was afraid they'd attack the kids."

"Do you know what kind of animals they were? What did they look like?"

"Ma said they looked like the devil. But pa said they like a huge wolf."

"What happened yesterday that made your father decide to hunt?"

"Well, Boon was here few days back. I don't know what they was talking 'bout. But then this kid come lookin' for Boon. Made Boon really mad and he stormed off. Those wolves was in the woods that day. Pa thought they was here 'cause of the boy. He told my Clint that."

"Who's Clint?"

"My husband."

"Would he talk to me?"

"No, you're a girl. Ya know he be mad if he knew I was talkin' to ya. Pa don't trust no outsiders. Clint's followin' what Pa wants."

"So, who's Boon?"

"He's our cousin. He from the city and be stayin' 'cause of bad stuff that happened to him. He lives all alone in the mountains. Don't like even being with us, and we's kin."

"And that kid was here looking for Boon?"

"Yea, Clint said they had bad words."

"Where does Boon live? I'd like to talk to that kid that was looking for him."

"Only person knows is Pa."

"Why? If he's your relative."

"He doesn't want nobody to know where he is. But from when I see him come or Pa goes to him, its west, deeper into the mountains. Pa goes for almost a day when he sees him. Don't know if its cause it takes that long or cause of the whiskey Boon's got."

"Well, thanks Sissy," the sheriff interrupted. He pointed past her and Meg saw someone coming. He looked mad.

"What's going on?" the man asked grabbing Sissy's arm. "What'd ya doin"?"

"They's friends of Pastor Jake," Sissy replied slipping into the mountain dialect. It surprised Meg. "Pa says he's okay."

"Pastor Jake is, not no girl," Clint jerked her away.

"Hold on now, Clint," the sheriff said as he stepped in front of them. "We only came to try and help find Clancy and Boon."

"Who says they's missing? You Sissy?" Clint glared at his wife. She shook her head.

"No, Ma told me Clancy was missin'. These here people are the law from New York, where Pastor Jake lives. They knows that kid that came lookin' for Boon that day. It may be that boy took Erica and another girl from Creek River."

"How's ya know?" He narrowed his eyes suspiciously.

Meg walked up to them. "That kid is from our town in New York. He was there a few years ago when some people went missing. We've also seen those dark wolves that Ma and Clancy saw. They are evil and are a part of this whole thing."

Clint dropped Sissy's arm and turned to Meg. "Y'all is just a girl. What y'all know?"

"I'm also a police officer," Meg said softly trying to not offend him. "Those creatures are very bad. I want to stop them once and for all."

"Y'all think they had somethin' to do with Erica missin'?"

"Yes, but time is running out. We have to find them all before the next full moon."

"Full moon?"

"According to the legends, that's when that boy will do the sacrifice. To make some kind of pact with those animals."

"How y'all know this?"

"I was taken by the last one who was with those animals and was supposed to be killed. Pastor Jake was the one that found me and saved my life. I only came down here to the Hollow to help Pastor Jake find Erica and save her. But Pastor Jake's wife got hurt because of those animals. I think they tried to stop Pastor Jake from coming back up this mountain, so he can't come save her. That's why I'm here with Captain Bennett," Meg pointed to Reggie.

"Ain't ya fraid they's goin' to get ya?"

"I found out something before I got to Creek River. Someone told me the reason Pastor Jake found me was cause he's a praying man. I think that protected him."

"Pastor Jake always tellin' us'n that God loves us. Don't he, Clint," Sissy said encouraging Meg. "He says prayer can change things."

Clint stood thinking. "What makin' ya think that ya can help without Pastor Jake if he the one with the prayin' power?"

"Well, he says we all got God," Sissy went on.

Clint stood thinking for a moment, then said gruffly, "Nothin' we can do without Clancy here."

"He ain't here," the sheriff said. "Far as I can tell, that makes you the head of the clan right now. You being his son-in-law and all."

Clint frowned and shook his head. "Nope, Clancy wouldn't want all y'all at the Hollow."

"But if Clancy was going after those animals and he isn't back yet, they probably got him. If that happened, he won't be coming back," Jesse said. Sissy gasped and her eyes filled up with tears.

"Clint, y'all got to help um find Pa! Please! I already lost my little sister. Don't make me lose my Pa."

"Sissy, y'all know your Pa don't want outsiders up here."

"But what iffin he's hurt!" Sissy started to cry. "What if Erica's still livin'? We can't turn away the only ones that's here to help us. We all alone here without Pa. We have to find him."

"Sissy, ya know your Pa…."

"Yah, he's a stubborn ole mule! I love him though and don't care iffin he gets mad at me. I'm tellin' you, Clint. Iffin Pa ain't back in the mornin' and you ain't showin' them over the mountain. I'll strap, little Mikey on my back, and I'll do it."

"I won't let ya!" Clint yelled at her. "Y'all is my woman and ya gonna listen to me."

"And that's my Pa that's missin' an my little sister. You ain't stopping me from findin' my kin."

Sissy stomped off into the woods and Clint followed her arguing with her. Reggie and Meg looked at each other and then to Jesse. "Now what?" Reggie asked.

"Well, Sissy's a lot like her Pa. To be honest, she'd be running the clan if Clancy passes, not Clint. Let's see if Ma has some grub. I'm hungry."

"I was asking what we should do."

"Tomorrow morning, the boys will try to help us find Boon's cabin." Jesse started toward the old shack with Meg and Reggie following. "Sissy will have her way. But you better make sure you're all prayed up, cause she'll insist on praying with ya'll before we leave."

"Who are the boys?"

The door was already opened when they got to the cabin. Ma was at a potbelly stove cooking something in a big pot. She told them all to sit and got them food.

"The boys are Clint, his two brothers, and a few cousins of Sissy's. We'll bunk with some of the kin tonight. Meg, I think it's best if you stay here with Ma. Get a good night's sleep. If I'm right, it's probably at least a day's hike to Boon's place."

CHAPTER 31

A round midnight, Jake woke with a start. At first, he wasn't sure what woke him, but he quickly realized that something had changed. A nurse was standing near the bed checking Sarah's vital signs.

"Is everything alright?" Jake whispered.

"I've called the on-call doctor. He should be right here," she whispered back. She wrote something on a paper and stuck it in her pocket. He looked down and realized that Sarah's breathing was more labored.

"Something *is* wrong. Do you know where my pastor went?"

"I think he went to the chapel. I'll see if someone can find him."

"You think she needs him?"

She didn't respond and quickly left the room. Jake took Sarah's hand in his. It was cold and she didn't respond to him. "Honey, I'm right here." Jake continued to talk softly to Sarah, hoping for a response. When the doctor came in, Jake stepped back watching him assess his wife's condition.

As Pastor Walt came in, the doctor turned to Jake. "Mr. Peterson, your wife's condition is deteriorating. Even with the respirator, it's getting harder for her to breath. The internal damage from the accident was so extensive. I'm having a morphine drip administered to help her be more comfortable."

"It doesn't look very good, does it," Jake stated flatly.

"No, I'm sorry. I just want to make her as comfortable as we can."

Jake nodded and turned to Pastor Walt. "Can you call Vivian at the hotel and ask her to come. I don't want her to...."

"I'm here Jake. I'll make the call. Go back to Sarah while you can." Walt watched the young pastor sit and take his wife's hand again. Jake softly began to talk to her about Richie. Walt slipped from the room and prayed before calling the hotel. When Vivian answered, he explained that Sarah had taken a turn for the worse and that she should come to the hospital.

An hour later, with her mother, sister, and husband by her side, Sarah quietly passed away. Jake cried softly while Pastor Walt prayed for the family.

* * *

Sam woke up to the female creature's frantic howling. He jumped from the cot and saw the small creature had died. The female was digging at the door, her sharp nails making gouges in the wood. He went to the door

159

and opened it. The alpha stood there and walked into the room. He picked the small creature up gently in his mouth and went back into the dark night. Sam stood in the doorway and watched the three dark shadows disappear into the woods. The female was still limping. He turned back to the one small creature that stood looking up at him.

Closing the door, Sam scooped the surviving pup into his arms. He lay back on the cot and cried. Just as he was about to drift off to sleep, howling pierced the night. Long echoes of mourning howls bounced off the Blue Mountains. The howling seemed to surround the cabin and Sam shivered at the remorseful cries of his companions. The small creature in his arms whined and barked in response. Sam couldn't help wondering what would happen to them all now.

* * *

Meg woke to howling in the night. Fear swept over her as she wondered where she was. She heard Ma softly praying in the darkness and remembered she was in the Hollow. In the morning, she was going out to face her worst nightmares. She got up and went to the older woman in the cabin.

"Ma," Meg said softly. The older woman reached out and took Meg's hand. Meg sat on the edge of the bed with her. "I'm scared. That's them howling."

"I heared them many nights."

"Are they close?" Meg whispered into the darkness.

Ma listened for a moment. "Miles away. Y'all cold child. Let me make something warm…."

"No, please, just sit here with me."

"Okay." Ma went back to her whispered prayer and Meg sat listening to the faith rising up in Ma. Finally, Ma turned her attention back to Meg. "You's won't find my Clancy. I know, as only a ma could. He be gone."

"But you can't know…."

"Clancy never go for this long. I know." Meg didn't know what to say, so she sat silent. Meg could still hear the distant howling, and some noises of people moving outside in the Hollow. Finally, she found the resolve within herself to try and shake it off. She took a deep breath and went to say something, but Ma stopped her. "I know y'all is a strong woman of the world. Used to standing on ya own with no one to help ya. Ya the law, too. But this fear that got ya's ain't something ya can face alone. It's evil!"

"Nothing in the world scares me, not criminals, guns, nothing. Except them."

"Pastor Jake says that we ain't got to be fraid iffin we have Jesus."

"That's the problem. I don't. I don't even know where to begin."

"Let me tell ya 'bout Pastor Jake's Jesus."

"I don't know…."

"Ain't it time ya stop runnin' child?"

"Running?"

"That's what God says when we's thinkin' we don't need Him." There was a lot of shouting from outside and Meg could hear Jesse telling people to calm down. "Times runnin' out. I heard y'all tell Clint 'bout prayin'. Ya's really want to face this evil without God?"

"I appreciate what you're saying. But I'd be a hypocrite to only be running to God because I'm afraid."

"Best to turn to Him whenever's y'all fears." Something loud banged outside and Meg went to stand. Ma held her hand though. "I don't usually put much in dreams. But I's dreamed that something bad happen to ya's cause ya went alone. Maybe I's wrong to say this. Y'all is the only one who can bring my Erica home. Iffin something bad happen to ya, I not only lose Clancy, but his chile."

"You're putting too much pressure on me. I don't even know if Sam is the one who took her. I…." Someone knocked loudly on the door. Ma let go of Meg's hand.

"Y'all go."

Meg hesitated and the person knocked again. "Meg," she heard Reggie saying. "We're getting ready to leave. Are you up?"

Meg got up and went to the door. Ma lit a lamp by her bedside. Meg opened the door, "It's the middle of the night! We shouldn't leave in the dark."

"Boys think we can follow the howling to Sam."

"I don't have a good feeling about this."

"Well, they are willing to lead us through this mountain. We'd be looking for a needle in a haystack without the help of these people. Even Jesse said he doesn't know these mountains like these people who live in the Hollow."

"But, I'm not sure."

"What's wrong with you, Riley? We actually have some local support and you want to wait?"

161

Meg didn't know how to explain the tumult inside of her. Finally, she just said, "Its dark, Reggie. Those creatures blend into the darkness. Obviously from the sounds of it, something has them riled up. Do you want to encounter them in the darkness?"

"It's only a couple of hours till dawn. Jesse thinks it's going to take us that long just to get on the other side of the ridge. Boon lives probably a half day's walk on the other side of that."

"I don't like this, but give me a few minutes. If you can find some coffee, that would be great."

"Sissy already has a pot going. Just come over there when you're ready. Everyone's meeting there."

Reggie left and Meg stood staring into the darkest part of the night, into the deep woods of the Hollow. She listened to the sounds of Ma rustling behind her, and stepped out onto the porch. She looked up at the star filled night, and felt a warm breeze blow across her face. She closed her eyes and sighed. "Okay God, You've got my attention. Like most, I know I've done wrong and do need Your forgiveness. But I don't know about becoming some crazy religious zealot who gives up my whole life, like Jake did. And I think if I just ask You to be with us tonight that I'm being a hypocrite. But I know enough about this to know that we….I need You to protect me tonight. I'll promise You this, if You help us through this, I will find out more about You. But not from Jake…okay? I promise You that I'll talk to Pastor Ryerson…or maybe even Ma and find out more about Who You are and what you expect. Okay? Is that fair?"

Meg knew she was running out of time. "Maybe not fair, but can You keep me, Reggie, and the others safe from those creatures? Okay, thanks, I think. Ummm…Amen?"

She went back into the cabin and gathered her belongings. Ma handed her a cup of coffee and some wrapped sandwiches. Meg put the food into her backpack and then turned to Ma. "I believe you that I need God with me right now. But I don't know how to do this. So, if you can pray for me, I promise you that I'll look more into this God thing."

Ma smiled and patted Meg's hand. "Same dealin' y'all tryin' to make with God. I pray."

Meg looked embarrassed. "You heard me?"

"Yea, ain't much I don't hear in the Holler."

Meg nodded and went out of the cabin to find Reggie. Ma returned to her bed and her prayers.

CHAPTER 32

Boon sat up with a groan and held his head. Faint, grey light began to break through the darkness of the woods. He looked around and groaned again. As he sat holding his head, he remembered the day before. He remembered that the sheriff was coming on to his mountain to find those creatures because of some accident. He remembered that he tried to warn Clancy that the creatures were after him. But he was too late to warn him.

By now, Boon figured that the sheriff was already scouring his woods looking for those creatures and Sam. Now, Clancy was missing. Like always, Boon got drunk and had become worthless to everyone. Maybe it helped him for a few hours to block out how it was all his fault for letting that fool kid bring those creatures to his cabin because he wanted the promised money. Money that probably didn't really exist!

All these thoughts tumbled through Boon's cloudy, hurting head. He knew that he couldn't accept that money now. No way! Especially cause Clancy was probably dead because of his greed. Boon rolled to his feet and looked around to get his bearings. He stumbled through the woods and saw one the creatures. He mumbled something and kept walking. As he stumbled back to his cabin, he kept an eye on the young creature. Something was wrong. Boon could sense it, and it was making him nervous.

When Boon got to the cabin, he saw the alpha laying in front of the door. It lifted its head and stared at Boon as he came to the door. As Boon reached for the door, it growled, low and menacing.

"It's me," Boon said to him. But the Alpha got to its feet and barred the door. Boon backed up with his hands up. "Sam! I can use a bit of help out here!"

The younger male stood in back of Boon stopping him from retreating into the woods. But Boon held his ground, knowing his safety was in Sam's hands. The door opened, and Boon looked up at Sam. There was a hardness to Sam that Boon hadn't seen before. "What's wrong?" he asked.

Sam put his hand on the large creatures head and said something in the old Gaelic. The creature calmed, but stayed alert. "You ask me what's wrong. Where do I even begin to answer that question?"

"Look, Clancy was in danger."

"From who? Us? Had you just kept quiet, nothing would have happened."

"No!" Boon shouted coming toward Sam. "It was you! You're the one who had to go to the college. You were the one that came to the Hollow. I told you to stay away from my kin. Now, Clancy is gone, probably dead because of them!" He stopped just before them and pointed at the creature at Sam's side.

"If your cousin is dead, it was justified. Two of the pups died, probably due to injuries that Clancy caused. And I hope they did get him," Sam said his eyes narrowing.

"Do you realize that killing Clancy is going to make everything worse for you? They already believe that you got Erica and those other kids. You'll go to jail!"

Sam laughed. "For what? I've got the best alibi. You! I've been with you for weeks now. You know I don't have anyone with me. You know where I was when Clancy disappeared."

"I don't know where they were," Boon hissed.

"I can't go to jail for something an animal did. And they didn't kidnap anyone either."

"Do you think that's going to stop them from trying to convict you? They need someone to blame for this. You are their owner for lack of a better word."

"If anything, they own me. I'm the keeper, and we both know what that means. For now, I need to know where you stand. Are you with us or against us?"

"You ask me that after yesterday?"

"I still need some help. I need to get further into the woods and need to find my way back out again. I need someone to teach me how to survive living in these mountains. That would be you."

"You really think I'm going to help you now? You broke our agreement."

"If anyone broke the agreement, it was you. You turned on us yesterday when you took off for the Hollow. Those pups died because of you…."

"No, they died because you didn't have them with us. You let her keep the litter too close to the Hollow, in that old den where I found you. That was your mistake…or hers. But not mine. I warned you about that."

Sam hesitated and then shook his head. "No, they live by instinct. She would not have come here."

"Then it was her mistake." The creature at Sam's side began to growl again. Boon looked down at him. "Even you must know it's true. You're the alpha, it was your job to protect the pack."

"Be very careful what you say," Sam said in a low voice.

"It's the truth. You and I have been busy trying to keep them safe, yet they run a car off the road, probably kill my cousin, and God knows what else. Now, everything I've worked for is endangered. The law is after you, and they will hunt these creatures down until the last one is dead. So what good is it to be the keeper, have all the money, and yet have to live on the run all the time? Like you said, they are wild and nothing you can do or buy, no matter how far you run, will stop them from reverting to their natural instinct."

"You're out of line."

"Am I? You want us to run further into the mountain. You want to live out your life in isolation. For what?"

"Because for the first time in my life, I'm actually accepted! Don't you see that!"

"Accepted? Is that what you call this?"

"You wouldn't understand. You had a life that you destroyed. I *never* had a life."

"You didn't have a life because of them."

"No, I have a life now because I have them. They are all I need, all I want. I have money too."

"And you live like me. So what good is any of that? Why can't you see what you've become?"

Sam looked down at the creature. "This is all I have left. I'm going to defend them to the end. So, are you going to help me?"

"You're crazy. You've bought the lie from those old journals. This is no life. If you have the money you say you do, leave with me and let's start over somewhere else."

"Boon, all I want you to do is to take us further into the mountains for a while. Once things settle down, we can come back, finish my cabin, and you'll be done with us."

"Things are not going to work out the way you think."

"I'll double the money I was going to give you. I need to protect them. Right now, I can't do it without you."

Boon sighed, "Let's think about this, okay? I need a drink and food. So, let me in the cabin and we can talk this out. If we make hasty decisions, it's going to be bad."

"I'm leaving in a half an hour. You just be ready." Sam stalked off to the woods with the two male creatures following him. Boon sighed and went into the cabin. The female got to her feet and growled at him. Boon saw how her leg was injured and sighed.

"Settle down. I'm not going to hurt you. I just need a drink." Boon pulled out a jug and then set it back down. He poured some water from a bucket into a coffee pot. He turned and saw her sitting near the surviving pup guarding it from Boon.

* * *

Meg looked down the ravine and sighed. It was just another mountain to go down, just to have another peek, just to climb back up again! The sun had barely come up over the mountain and it was already hot and humid. Reggie was ahead of her and she could see him struggling to continue on too. The sheriff looked back at them and then halted the group. Meg sat down on the ground and opened the canteen. The water was still cold as she took a long drink.

"You okay?" Reggie asked as he sunk down next to her.

"I used to think I was in shape."

Reggie laughed. "I can't imagine how I'd be feeling if I didn't work out at the gym. It's more endurance than strength on a hike like this."

"...on only a partial night's sleep," Meg finished.

The boys kept walking to the bottom of the ravine where a creek was running through. They splashed into the water while joking and refilling their canteens. They sat watching in silence. The sheriff walked past them to the top of the ridge pulling out his two-way radio. He walked a distance away and Reggie looked over his shoulder watching. "Something's up. And it's nothing good."

Meg looked over at Jesse. "What makes you think that?"

"The look on his face."

Jesse walked out of their line of vision, and Meg shrugged. "Guess if it's any of our business, he'd tell us."

"He's going to tell us. Not sure he'll tell them," Reggie said nodding toward the boys in the water. After a few minutes, Jesse came back and sat next to Reggie.

"Been a long morning already," Jesse started. "I think Clint and his kin don't really know where Boon lives. They're just hoping we run into him someplace."

"Is that likely?" Reggie asked.

"Nope. Boon can stay hid pretty well. If that kid is with Boon and they are hiding, we won't find either one of them."

"Then, we're wasting time."

"Not necessarily. I was hoping for some sign of those animals again, or maybe Clancy."

They sat in silence for another few minutes. Meg was happy for the break, but knew it was about to end. Reggie shifted and pulled out a granola bar from his backpack. He tore it opened and took a bite. Squinting up at the sun, he finally asked, "So, what's going on in town?"

Jesse hesitated and then cleared his throat. "It's bad news. Sarah Peterson passed away during the night."

Reggie sadly shook his head. Meg took a sharp breath, her eyes filling with tears as she thought about Jake. "Guess we're done then," she said trying to shake off her tears. "Can you get us back to town from here, or do we need Clint to lead us out?"

"Is that what Jake would really want, Riley?" Reggie said looking at her. "Or would he want us to follow this fresh lead."

"Jesse doubts we'll even find Boon. Jake could use our support."

"Jake has Pastor Ryerson, Sarah's mother and sister, and even your dad and stepmother. Right now, they are just trying to make sense of what happened. I've been with grieving families when they've lost someone and so have you. The first thing they will want is for us to do our job and find the responsible party. From what we know, it's those creatures."

Meg looked at Reggie. "This is different. Jake is our friend, and this was his case."

"And if Sarah died because of his involvement, he's going to want justice for her. Crazy people have gone after cops' families before. That means we work harder to find that person. Let me ask you this. What if it was Brian that passed away last night?"

168

"Don't even say that," Meg whispered harshly.

"It's awful to think about. But he was in the same accident. His life was in the same danger. Those that took Sarah's life also hurt your dad."

"So, we hunt them? What about Sam?"

"If he's a part of it, we'll get him too."

Meg got to her feet. "Which way Jesse?"

"Clint!" the sheriff yelled down the ravine. "It's time to get serious. Do you know where Boon lives or don't ya?"

"It's somewhere over that way, sheriff," Clint pointed north.

"Somewhere ain't good enough. Do any of you boys know for sure?" Some shrugged, a few shook their heads. Jesse watched each until his eyes rested on the youngest son of Clancy. He got up and went down the hill to the creek with Reggie and Meg following him. "Okay, Hank where are we headed?"

"He don't know nothin'," Clint said aggravated. "He's just a kid!"

"Hank, which way?" Hank looked at his brother-in-law and then at his feet. "Boy, we ain't got time for this. Your own pa is now missing! Where are we headed?"

"Other side of Shay's pass."

"There's no way Boon's gone that far! Sheriff...."

The sheriff put up his hand stopping Clint. "Truth is, your pa takes you with him. Doesn't he?" Hank hedged and shuffled.

"What does it matter? Can we get moving now?" Meg interrupted.

"Yes, it matters," Sheriff said. "Now, you tell me Hank, did your pa take you there? You know exactly where he lives?"

Hank glanced up at the seething Clint and nodded. "Pa ain't taken me much. But I been there."

"Prove it!" Clint challenged him.

"He'll prove it by taking us there. That's a good half day's walk from here. You up to it?" Jesse asked looking at Meg and Reggie.

Meg walked to the creek with her canteen. "As soon as I get a refill, I'm ready. I want to see those creatures dead by nightfall."

CHAPTER 33

Sam came back into the cabin and frowned at Boon who was just sitting at the table slowly eating some slices of bread.

"Thought you'd be ready to leave by now," Sam said through clenched teeth.

"I think you need to just sit and talk this out with me first."

"There's nothing more to discuss. I've already told you the way it's going to be."

Boon didn't say anything. He took a drink of the strong coffee he made and munched on the buttered bread. Sam pulled out the bread and started making some sandwiches. He kept looking at Boon and finally noticed the old journal on the table.

"What are you doing with that?" Sam asked, snatching it off the table. "You have no right to go into my things!"

"Actually, I got thinking about these books. This Paddy, he had a pretty good life while he was the keeper. Made a bunch of money, got married, had kids. So, I got thinking, why does Sam want to live in the mountains away from everyone when the guy who started the whole thing and his son lived a good life?"

"What are you rambling about?"

"You're so busy thinking about the power part, the being able to make your enemies listen to you by using them to hurt people, you missed something important. The keeper is able to use his power to live."

"Well, that's not the way Trevor lived. He had to live away from people and move around a lot."

"Yeah, but he was crazy. You aren't…at least not yet."

"We need to get moving…."

"Hear me out, will you? Back in the day, the keeper lived in a small town. He had a life, and people knew that the creatures were about, yet they lived too. They made their presence known, but only when needed to keep people from snooping around too much. Sure, they are evil, and you've got to do your part for them, but you don't have to run. That is, if you really believe that they have the power that you think they have."

"You're suggesting we just stay here and fight when the sheriff gets here?"

"No, I'm saying we stay here, and we do nothing when the sheriff gets here. They will hide like they normally do when folks are around. We will just keep building your cabin and say we've been together and know nothing about the accident or the missing people, which is the truth."

"What about all your talk about them wanting to blame someone? About how they will fabricate stuff to make me responsible?"

"Like you said, we've done nothing. You've done nothing. There's no abducted people up here, we didn't cause an accident."

"I don't trust you. You're totally changing everything you've been saying."

"That's because I got thinking about Paddy and realizing what kind of life he had. Besides, if you run, they *will* think you've done all those things. Instead, let them find us building a cabin in the woods, minding our own business."

"No, we're leaving. Get whatever you need for a week or so."

Boon slowly finished his bread and watched Sam. Finally, Boon said, "You still haven't thought this through. What about her?" Sam stopped and looked at the female, remembering her injured leg. "You really think she's going to be able to go far with that leg? And what about the pup?"

"She should be fine, and I'll carry the pup."

"What if she's not fine? You do realize that she's the only female. If infection gets her or if that thing doesn't heal right, then what?" Sam went and knelt down beside her. The gash looked nasty and red. "Did you think of anything to do for her?"

"I don't know what to do."

"Will she let me?"

"Why, what are you planning?"

"It needs to be cleaned and some type of antibiotic needs to be put on it. To be honest with you, you probably should just find a cave near here to hide her and the puppy in for now. I don't think she'll be able to walk very far."

"That's just another trap to get me to stay...."

"I didn't say that, I said leave *her.* If you insist, we'll still go, but find a place for her to be safe. You want me to take a look at that leg?"

Boon got up and went to them, and she began to growl. Sam pet her and talked softly to reassure her. But when Boon reached for her leg, she snapped at him, and he barely pulled away. Boon got a good look at her razor sharp teeth and those glowing red eyes.

"Sorry, I ain't risking losing a hand for her. Let me give you some stuff and see if she'll let you tend to it."

Boon got a basin with some water and a cloth. He instructed Sam to use the wet cloth to try and clean up the wound, but she pulled away from Sam, growling.

"What should I do?" Sam asked.

"Leave her alone. Let me gather some stuff. You go with them and find a place for her."

"I don't like this."

"Well, this is your idea. We could just stay here with her in the cabin. Just wait for old Jesse to show up with whatever help he's got."

Sam sighed and picked up the pup, and led the female outside. The alpha came over and looked intently at Sam. "We need to find a place to hide them and get away. People are coming looking for us."

The alpha took off into the woods, leaving his son to follow his scent with Sam slowly walking with the pup and the limping female. Boon watched from the window until they disappeared. He knew that the creatures, in the end, would kill him for what he did. He had one chance to survive this, and he hoped that Sam was too naïve to figure out his plan.

CHAPTER 34

Jake had gone with Pastor Walt to the Zimmers where his young son was still staying. When he was with Richie, Jake realized how much he had missed him. He broke down when he told Richie about Sarah. They cried together until Richie fell asleep. Jake slept for several hours with Richie cradled in his arms. Exhaustion had finally taken over now that Sarah no longer needed him. When he finally woke up, he found the Zimmers and thanked them for caring for his son for the past few days.

Richie was still asleep when Jake left to go meet Sarah's mother and sister to make funeral arrangements. Although Jake knew they would be headed to New York for a funeral service and internment at his church, there would be a small service for Sarah in Creek River. Jake knew the people of Creek River needed this memorial to show their love and mourn her loss. But having two services was hard on Jake and Sarah's family. The only way Jake knew he could manage was that Pastor Walt would perform the services for Sarah. Millie, Pastor Walt's wife, was also on her way to Creek River with Jake's parents.

The drive to the hotel was long and added more to Jake's doubts and grief. The concierge called the room and let them know Jake was waiting. He sat in the lobby, waiting, wondering what was taking them so long when his cell phone rang. He looked at the New York number and hesitated answering. He didn't want to answer any questions. When it rang the fifth time and the desk clerk scowled at him, he answered.

"Is this Detective Peterson?"

Jake paused at the name and then responded, "Yes, who is this?"

"Mick Finley. I'm doing some freelance for Meg Riley. I've been trying to reach her for days, but she's not answering her cell. I called the Saratoga office number, no one answers there and the voice mail is full. So, I finally tracked you down through the Granelle Police Department. I remembered that Riley told me that you were helping down there."

"What can I do for you?"

"Tell me how to get in touch with Riley."

"I'm sorry, but her father was in a car accident and…."

"Brian? Is he alright?"

"Yeah, he will be…," Jake wanted to add, but his wife would never be, but choked back the words.

"Wow, too bad."

"I guess I can tell her you called…."

"Hold on. Aren't you still working the job?"

"The job?"

"Yeah, the job. Remember, Craig, Donovan, the creatures? You still working the case?"

"I…I have been out of the loop since the accident."

"That bad?"

"Yeah, it was."

"Well, I got some info that might be critical to this. Riley called me about a publishing house in NYC. She said that Donovan was on their payroll. You know about that?"

"Yeah, I was the one who…guess that doesn't matter. What did you find out?"

"Get this, not only is Donovan getting paid by them, but Sam Craig is also on their payroll. On the 990's, Craig was their most highly compensated employee last year. Brought down about a half million, for literally doing nothing according to their payroll office. He sends them these invoices like he's doing work from remote locations. They wire transfer money into an account for him."

"So that's where the money comes from. Is there a way to track how the money is getting spent? Like credit card receipts, hotel bills?"

"Naw, the money goes into Craig's personal account. I've got to get a new subpoena to get into those accounts. But without probable cause, the judge won't sign it. But I got really chummy with the broad in the HR department. Real looker, if you get my drift. Anyway, we go out to dinner, have a few drinks, and she loosens up. Apparently, Craig and Donovan ain't the only ones doing remote work for the publishing company."

Jake looked up and saw his mother-in-law walking toward him. He gestured to her to wait a minute. "You got a name?"

"Guy named Peter Lynch. First bank drafts went to Ireland, then to a US bank, same one Craig uses. But he's new, only been getting paid for like three months. I haven't located him on this side of the ocean, but tracked down some interesting facts in Ireland. Seems his great-great granddaddy is an O'Shea."

"Like in the first keepers, the first clan?"

"One and the same. Thinking how appropriate for him to be making money from the pot his family created."

"How did you track down his lineage? Seems too coincidental."

"You do realize I'm Irish didn't you? Finley? I got a whole clan of my own in Ireland. All I had to do was give my uncle the names O'Shea and Lynch, he filled in the blanks."

Jake looked back up at his in-laws. "I've got to get going. Things down here are a bit of a mess right now. I'll find Meg and give her this information. I'm sure she'll be back in touch with you."

"Do you want me to keep on trying to find Lynch? My bill's getting up there and I need an okay to keep spending Riley's money."

Jake sighed. He had no idea what was going on and didn't want to spend Meg's money. But he knew he couldn't help, not now. "Yeah, go ahead and find him. As far as I know, those girls are still missing."

"Okay. And if you see the old man, tell him to get better. We need him."

"Sure," Jake choked out. He closed his phone and joined his in-laws. He had no idea where Meg and Reggie were, but maybe he could stop by the Sheriff's office on his way back to the Zimmers and pass this information on to Jesse.

* * *

Meg swatted another mosquito on her neck. Her legs and arms were already covered with bites. The day kept getting hotter and muggier. Hank led the way, through thick woods that were, at times, almost impossible to break through. Several times, Clint complained only to be told to shut up by Jesse. Meg wondered how much longer this hike was going to take. She was almost out of water, too.

"How much longer do you think this is going to be," Meg heard Reggie ask.

"Hard to say," Jesse responded. "I'm sure that there are shortcuts that only Boon knows."

"You really think this kid knows where he's going?" Reggie asked in a low voice.

"I think so. Don't let Clint hear you ask that," Jesse broke off from Reggie and Meg. He jogged ahead to talk to Hank. Meg sighed and adjusted the backpack.

"You doing okay, Riley?" Reggie asked squinting at her.

"Sure, Captain. But I could sure go for a swim in some mountain creek. Wish I had taken advantage of it when we had the chance."

"Naw, if you had done that, you'd only feel hotter now." He gestured to the boys in front of them. "Look at them. They all look miserable and hot!"

"Guess so. But that's not going to stop me from taking a dip when we find the next one."

Reggie laughed. "Sure, okay."

They walked in silence for a long time. Meg lost track of the time. Suddenly, it felt darker to her. Meg couldn't explain the feeling, but darker was the only thing that came to mind. The woods felt more sinister and she fell a bit behind. She looked around, and the shadows seemed longer, the air was heavier. It was almost like dusk had fallen quickly, but no one else seemed to notice the change. Meg's pace slowed and fear swept over her.

"Oh God," she whispered. "I think I need some of that help right now."

Meg looked to her left and saw a darker shadow staying with her. She knew that shape and she stopped, paralyzed with fear. "Please, help," her voice barely a whisper now.

"Riley!" She heard Reggie as if from far away yell her name. Her hand slipped to her side, and she pulled out her service revolver. Without taking her eye from the dark shadow, she pointed the revolver. With practiced patience, she waited to see what it was while she slipped off the safety. The shadow stopped, Meg heard again her name being yelled as if from a long way off. Her finger was on the trigger and then she was hit from the side. Her gun fired in the direction of the shadow and the gun bounced out of her hand.

The heavy weight that hit her smelled of darkness, and she knew the smell. The smell of them! She pushed back against the dark shape with her arms and legs while gun fire riddled the air around her. In an instant, the shadow was gone. The gun fire rang in her ears, but she could clearly hear Reggie screaming to stop firing. Meg looked back to where she saw the dark shadow. It was gone. She scanned the woods and saw a person duck behind a tree. A familiar person. Sam!

In a quick movement, Meg was on her feet running toward the tree. Everyone was yelling and Meg could see the dark shadows running away, with Sam behind them. He glanced back once before Meg was knocked down again, this time by one of the mountain boys.

"Get off me!" Meg screamed. "He's getting away!"

Meg pushed him hard and struggled to her feet. But he held on until Reggie fell at her side. "Riley! Meg, are you alright?"

Meg scrambled to her feet and ran in the direction that they disappeared. Then she stopped and spread her arms in exasperation. "Why? Why did you stop me?" she yelled at the kid who lay near Reggie.

"They were after you, Riley. Are you okay?"

"Yes! We've got to get them. That was Sam!"

"Are you sure?" Reggie got to his feet and ran up to her.

"Yes! Let's get moving."

"They're long gone," Jesse said as he came up behind them. "I told Les to stop you. That thing looked like it was going to tear you apart!"

"Yeah, but it didn't. It didn't even hurt me," Meg said slowly.

"Lucky for you," Jesse said. "Well, at least we have a trail to follow."

"Wait, wait," Meg said still thinking it out. "It didn't mean to hurt me. It was like before. Reggie," Meg looked up at him, "You remember before, Sam saved me, and the rest of us in that basement. I think he did it again."

"That thing attacked you," Jesse said as he called for one of the boys to start tracking the footprints in the soft soil.

"No. Sam never intended to hurt me. He was trying to get me to stop pointing the gun...where's my gun." She stopped and went back to where she had fallen. One of the boys handed her the weapon. Reggie was watching her closely, listening to her. "I was standing here. If I saw that creature, I planned on killing it. I was all set, but it stopped me. There has to be more than one. I know I had one of them in my sights."

Meg walked up to Reggie and then pointed to the tree. "When I got up, Sam was right there. He slipped behind the tree. But he must have... we've got this all wrong, Reggie. It's not Sam. It's someone else doing this. Someone who is trying to make us *think* it's Sam."

"What are you rambling about?" Jesse asked annoyed. The boys began to spread out, walking away from them, following the trail. "We saw that kid, you identified him. Now, let's get him and get our people back...."

"Sheriff, hold on," Reggie said in a quiet voice. "You're looking at the expert. She's in charge now."

Jesse grumbled. "I thought Jake was the expert. She's just...."

"Jake would defer to her right now if he was here. I made the same mistake you're making right now, once before. They got away. Let her do what she's good at."

Jesse hesitated. "Those are my people out there, my town."

"Yes, and if you want them back, you have to trust *her*."

Jesse sighed. "Okay, her way."

"Call them back. Let me go ahead, alone."

"Now I know you're crazy!"

"And no one shooting at me either. What was that anyway?" Meg asked walking passed Jesse. "If I got killed, it would have been from them, not Sam. Now, call them back."

Jesse called the boys back. A few didn't listen until Reggie yelled at them. They came sulking back. Meg checked her gun, and then stuck it back in the holster. She went ahead following the footprints, the larger footprints of the creatures and Sam's. When she got to a denser part of the woods, she called out. "Sam, it's me, Meg Riley! I know that you aren't responsible for what happened. Will you come out, so I can talk to you?" There was no reply. "Sam! A long time ago, you told me to trust you and I did. Now, I'm asking you to trust me! Come on out!"

They followed the footprints deeper into the Blue Mountains. Meg was determined to find Sam and help him for saving her life. But those with her had no intention of letting those things live on their mountain. With a hardness that was settling over him after the rebuffs by the outsiders, Clint was determined to make someone pay. If he couldn't get those creatures or the boy, that girl was just as good for him to take his revenge out on. After all, it was because of her that the sheriff was treating him like a child. His eyes narrowed in hatred as he watched Meg talking to Hank who once again took the lead, in the place he should be.

CHAPTER 35

Sam came running back to the cabin with the two males with him. Boon was outside packing another bag when Sam slid to a stop near him. "You're right. They're on the mountain. We just had a run in with them. We've got to move," Sam said in gasping breathes.

"Slow down, boy. You need to catch your breath. Go inside and get a drink...."

"No, let's just go."

"Wait, wait. Where's the female and her puppy?"

"Safe. for now. We've got to get moving."

"Okay, go inside, get a drink, and grab your gear. If you don't get a quick breather, you ain't going to make it far."

Sam nodded and went inside. Boon looked into the woods from the way they had come. The alpha paced in the clearing near the cabin, while the black one waited inside the woods. Sam came out with his backpack and a filled canteen.

"Who were they? Mountain folk or townies?"

"New Yorkers."

"What?"

"That woman cop from Granelle and the Captain. There were others, but those were the two that I saw."

"What's that mean? They really are after you?"

"What that means is that they know that the creatures are involved. That woman cop was nice to me when I was kidnapped, and that Captain helped me out too in the past. She saw me, even called out to me."

"So now what?"

"That doesn't change anything."

"It changes everything. They know for sure that you're involved."

"Let's go before they get here!"

Sam started off away from where he came from. Boon stood rooted, undecided, until the alpha came back to him and growled.

"Okay, okay. I'm coming too. Sam, hold up a minute. You've got to grab one of these other bags. We need supplies if we're going to be gone for a while."

Sam came back and grabbed another bag. Boon handed him a shotgun and held it for a moment after Sam tried to take it. "Be careful with this. I don't want to get shot by you. This is for hunting game, not people."

"They already shot at me. I'll do what I have to if they need protecting."

"They don't need you to protect them. They need you to be alive. Trust me on this kid. These animals can fend for themselves or disappear where no one can see them. Okay?"

Sam didn't respond, just stared Boon down. Boon shook his head and picked up the other two bags. "You might know the New Yorkers, but I know these mountain folk. They know how to take a shot. They will kill you and ask questions later. Please for God's sake, don't play with this gun."

"Let's go. You've wasted enough time today."

Sam turned and walked away. This time Sam didn't stop, but Boon didn't hesitate. Not with the creatures keeping a close eye on him. He'd wait, even if it was overnight, before doubling back on Sam. But if they were that close, it might not take until tomorrow until he was free from his pack with the devils.

* * *

"They's long gone," Clint said as he came out of the cabin. Jesse was still inside looking around.

"Telled you I knows were Boon lived," Hank said taunting Clint. Clint came toward Hank, but Reggie stepped in between them.

"Leave the boy alone," Reggie said in his deep threatening voice.

"Who y'all tellin' me what ta do?" Clint challenged.

"I'm the law. That's who I am."

"Ya ain't nothin' but a no account nig...."

"Clint!" Jesse yelled. "You watch your mouth, or I'll have your hide."

"He ain't got no right! This is Boon land!"

"And last time I checked, you ain't nothing but married to a Boon. Now, stop this nonsense." Jesse turned to Meg and said, "Looks like the creatures have been here. Living here."

"You're kidding," Meg said going over to the cabin door and looking inside. "Living inside?" Meg went in and looked around for a bit. "Reggie, come on in here. You got to see this."

Jesse shrugged and walked over to Hank who was still smirking at Clint. He talked to the boy quietly out of earshot. Reggie went in and found Meg going through a footlocker.

"Look at this," she handed him a leather bound book. "I can't believe it! It has to be one of the journals that Mrs. Flannigan mentioned to me. WOW!"

"You need to back up a bit, you've lost me."

"Mrs. Flannigan is Shamus O'Leary's daughter in Ireland. She told me that O'Leary had these journals that were written by one of the first keepers. That they hold all the secrets…." Meg slumped down and scowled.

Reggie took the journal from her and flipped through it. "Okay, now what?"

"If they're here, that means Sam does have the journals. He has all the secrets and probably knows about the ritual."

"So, he still might be the one who kidnapped the two girls and that little kid."

"I don't want to believe that, Reg. He just saved my life."

"You can't know that. Besides, let's not jump to any conclusions. Unless, he's bi-lingual, he won't know what these journals say anyway."

"Why?" Meg reached back and took the journal from Reggie. She realized it was written in a foreign language. She set it to the side and went back searching through the locker.

"What are you looking for?"

"Mrs. Flannigan said there were several, not just one."

"The rest are probably with Sam."

"Yeah, you're probably right. Did you notice the water bowl and the blanket on the floor? Jesse is right. They've been staying here in Boon's cabin."

"That means Boon's in this mess too."

"I don't understand how Sam could be living with these creatures after what we went through in that basement all those years ago."

"You said yourself that Sam had some connection with them. He was a loner in school, has broken ties with his family, what has he got left?"

"But how'd this Boon character get involved? Sissy said that Boon was a hermit. Why would he let this kid live with him with those creatures?"

"Money does odd things to people, Riley. Certainly, you know that with the work you do with your firm."

"All goes back to that money. Hopefully, Finley will have some answers to that when we get off this mountain."

"If we find Sam, do we need those answers?"

"Yes, if he goes to trial. If he's involved in the kidnappings or if the accident that killed Sarah wasn't really an accident…."

"Okay, let's get moving. I feel like we're up against the clock again in the case."

Jesse came in and closed the door. "I think we need to regroup here before we set off again."

"Okay," Meg said standing and brushing her hands off. "We probably should get moving though."

"Hear me out. We're going to have some big problems with Clint. His ego has been bruised, and he thinks without Clancy around, he should be the boss. There's a bit more to it, but you get the gist."

"A bit more, like I'm black and she's a girl?" Reggie said matter of fact.

Jesse nodded. "Yeah, just didn't want to say it."

"I think we've both had to deal with those types of problems in the past. We can deal with it, but you seem to have another idea?"

"I was thinking of breaking us up. We've really got two separate objectives from what I can surmise. Clancy's still missing, and you've got to find Craig and Boon. I figure if I take one group with Clint, and you take another with Hank, we break up the boys."

"Okay, I take it you want us to follow Sam, and you're going after Clancy."

Jesse started to nod, but Meg interrupted. "But Ma's positive that Clancy isn't alive."

"But what if he is and he's injured?" Jesse asked. "And if he is dead, we need to know how, so we can figure out if someone is responsible for him too. Plus, I still have three missing kids that need to be found. It's too complicated for me to be running all over this mountain chasing those animals with crazy Clint."

Reggie softly laughed. "Crazy Clint. If I remember Sheriff, it was your idea to follow him over this mountain in the middle of the night on his say so."

"A mistake I've regretted since the onset, believe me!"

"Okay, this is your idea. You tell the boys."

"But, the ones that stay with us need to know that we are in charge, not them," Meg quickly added.

"Well, the ones I'm leaving with you won't give you any problem with that. I figure Hank, who knows these mountains as well as his Pa and his three cousins. All Boons. I'm taking Clint, his brother and two friends. I'll spin it so that Clint thinks he's got the better deal, trying to find Sissy's Pa."

"But we got the youngest in the group?" Meg asked.

"Yeah, but these are mountain folk. They are used to hiking and…."

Meg stopped him. "I was actually going in a different line of thinking. It's late afternoon, we've been up since dark, walking for almost twelve hours with very few breaks. What if our group stays here overnight, uses the cabin to rest, and starts out fresh in the morning."

"What are you thinking?" Reggie asked. "The trail will be cooled and it gives them time to get further away."

"I don't think getting far away is what's on Boon's mind."

"What makes you think that?"

"This guy is a hermit. Doesn't want anyone to live near him, wants to live isolated by himself. Yet, look around. What has he taken? Not much. All his cooking stuff, food, probably most of his clothes, and all that ammunition is still here. This guy is coming back to this cabin. And so is Sam." Meg picked up the journal. "He's not going to go too far when he realizes this has been left behind. And Reggie, let's not forget all that money. No one is going to walk away with all that money just waiting for him."

"But he's scared, and he's running."

"He's Sam Craig from Granelle, New York. What does he know about living in the mountains with those creatures?"

"Don't count out Boon," Jesse said. "He's lived a long time up here with very little contact with the world."

"Yeah, but look at this stuff, Sheriff. He isn't living off the mountain. The cabin is put together with supplies from a lumber company. This bed is a real bed. Clothes. Look, he even has some beef jerky, store bought. Sam's bought him off. I feel it."

"Okay, you lead your group your way. I'm taking off with Clint and his boys. Come on out and let's split up. But wait until we're long gone before you mention bunking down for the night. I doubt that Clint's buddies really want to hike all the way back to the Hollow and that's precisely where we're headed."

Meg and Reggie stood with the younger boys as they watched the other group heading back toward the Hollow. Once they were out of sight, Hank turned to Reggie, "They's gone. Wha' we doin'?"

"For now, we're going to see what Boon has that we can make for dinner. Then, we sleep. Sound good to any of you?"

"Really?" one of the kids asked.

"Really," Meg replied. "I want to sleep. So, you've got Capt. Bennett cooking dinner for you."

Reggie looked surprised. "Me?"

"I'm a career woman. I don't cook."

"Okay, Hank, you've got to help me. Let's see what your cousin has for food in here."

CHAPTER 36

Jake didn't know what to do. The plans were made, Richie was in bed, and Jake was restless. He thought about Reggie, Meg, and Jesse being on the mountain still and wondered if they had any success. He wanted to tell them about the funeral plans, but knew he had no way of contacting them. He wanted to tell someone about Mick's phone call… most of all, he wanted to tell Sarah how awful he felt about what happened. His wife, his best friend, was gone, and he was lost.

"Am I bothering you?" Pastor Walt asked sticking his head in the guest room. He glanced at Richie sleeping on the bed. Jake shook his head, but gestured to the hall. Jake stepped out of the room and pulled the door almost all the way closed.

"Do you mind if we go outside?" Jake asked.

"That's fine. I thought you might want to talk to someone." They walked to the back of the house and stepped out onto the deck.

"Guess you heard my prayers. I feel so alone without Sarah. The past few weeks, I've been so busy with the case and didn't get to spend time with her. And now, she's gone."

Pastor Walt sat down in a lawn chair and sighed. "Millie is worried about you. She loves you as if you were one of our kids. How are you really doing?"

"I don't know, honestly. It doesn't feel real to me. I guess it's because we are still down here. I was down here alone for a couple of weeks. It seems so surreal."

"And…?"

Jake sat down in the other chair. "I don't understand why. Why Sarah? Why now? How is Richie going to grow up without his mother?" Pastor Walt just sat quietly, listening. Jake leaned forward and put his hand in his hands. "I remembered how Meg wanted to hunt those creatures. I stopped her. *I stopped her!*"

Jake got up and began to pace. "Why didn't I go after them myself? How many people have to die because of them? And if Sam is responsible… I… don't…."

"Do you really think that Sam is responsible?" Pastor Walt asked in a quiet voice.

"I don't want to believe it. I remember him as that little boy. I remember how lost he was. I was there for that family. I lost my wife because of...."

"You don't believe he is responsible, Jake. I remember the Craigs too. I was their pastor for those years leading up to Sam's mother's death. That boy had a rough time, and it sounds like it didn't get any easier for him as he got older."

"But he's here in these mountains," Jack pointed to the mountain ridge in front of him, "with those creatures! And according to Brian's account, he swerved off the road because of them. He couldn't help Sarah because of them."

"But Brian didn't say that Sam was there. Did he?"

"No, he didn't."

"So, it might have been a coincidence that the creatures were on the road. How could they have known that Brian was going to drive by right then? How would they have even known it was Brian and Sarah?"

"They couldn't have known."

"It was an accident."

"I still need to find Sam. I need to know for sure that he didn't have anything to do with this."

"And what if you never find out? What if they can't find him? Can you live with not knowing?"

Jake didn't say anything for a long moment. "No, I need to know. There's something else too. I got a call today from one of Meg's private investigators. He found the money trail. Sam's been getting money from a dummy company. So has Donovan, and some other guy named Peter Lynch. He's going to check it out further to see if he can find where that money is being spent. But I don't think he has to look any further than a 50 mile radius around Creek River."

"How can you be sure?"

"Simple deduction really. The creatures are here, people are missing, the pattern repeats. The question is, whose money is being spent here? Sam's? Or Lynch's? I'm hoping...no, I'm praying that it's Lynch."

"But why would this other person be involved?"

"Because he's a direct descendent to the original keeper. Probably thinks it's his birthright. I don't know. But Meg and Reggie need this information, so they can find that person. Regardless of my own personal situation, there are still three families with kids that are missing. I can only pray now that God gives them the direction they need to end this, but end it for good."

"Is there any way to get a message to the sheriff?"

"I don't know. I told the deputy about Sarah and hoped that he could radio them on the mountain. But I don't know if they ever got the message."

"We can pray together."

"Yeah, that's all I got left," Jake said glumly.

"Really? Is this really what you think your last option is?" Jake looked at Pastor Walt confused. "Jake, your first reaction has always been to pray. Since when did prayer become the last thing on your list?"

"I guess the past few weeks I haven't turned to God as much as I do as a pastor. I wasn't thinking."

"No matter how hard the situation looks to you right now, God is still in control. You don't have all the answers, so you need to lean on God more than ever, Jake."

"I know what my response should be. But I feel so defeated."

"That's one of the first attacks of the enemy. He makes you feel alone and defeated. But God promises no matter what we see in front of us, He is in control." Jake was silent. Walt saw his face harden. "Jake you know 'that in all things God works for the good of those who love Him.' Trust in Him, no matter what you feel."

Jake leaned against the deck railing and looked up at the mountain. Darkness was slowly descending on Creek River, and somewhere on the mountain were two of Jake's closest friends and the dark creatures. He looked at his pastor and mentor. "I don't know why, but I feel almost afraid for Meg right now. Can we ask Millie and the Zimmers to pray with us?"

"I'm sure they will. But how are you feeling now?"

"This is the hardest thing I've ever faced. I don't know how to get through this. But just having you here tonight reminded me of where my help comes from. I need that, probably a lot in the coming days."

"I'm here. I'll be here until I know that you're on the other side of the chasm. Come on. Let's gather the warriors to get praying, not only for our friends out there," he gestured to the mountain, "but also for you."

CHAPTER 37

The darkness fell fast. Almost too fast for Meg. With nothing else to do and exhaustion set in, the boys turned in for the night. They made makeshift beds on the floor of the cabin with what blankets and pillows they could find. They gave Meg the cot, but she felt odd sleeping in a stranger's bed. With soft snoring filling the room, she tossed again trying to find a comfortable spot. She couldn't quiet her thoughts.

Meg worried about Jake, but knew that Pastor Walt was with him. She worried about Sam being with those creatures and Boon, but Sam had been with them for a while now. She worried about her father, but knew that he was healing. She let her thoughts wander back to the case and the unknowns. After seeing Sam with the creatures, she believed that the accident was just that, an accident. And she also felt that Sam wasn't involved in the recent disappearances, there was something else going on. But she wanted to talk to Sam, make sure he was okay, and pass on the message that Brian had told her from Sam's father.

As Reggie's loud snoring joined the boys', Meg finally got up and stepped outside into the dark night. A damp mist was settling on the woods, and the humidity was thick. Meg didn't want to wander too far from the cabin, but she did walk a few feet away toward the woods. The snoring faded into the background of the night sounds. She looked up at the sky and saw thousands of stars.

Meg heard a soft noise behind her and turned quickly. "Who's there?" she whispered.

"I'm sorry. I didn't mean to scare ya. But y'all shouldn't be out here alone," Hank whispered back.

"I'm okay, Hank. I thought you were all asleep."

"Shucks, hard to sleep with all that noise. My pa, he don't snore…," his voice trailed off.

"What do you think happened to your Pa?"

"I don't know. Pa never goes for long, lest he tells Ma."

"And Ma doesn't know where he is, does she?"

"Nope."

"I'm sorry he didn't come back."

"Ya…like Erica. She ain't come back either."

"Do you think she ran off?"

"Naw. Pa knowed 'bout the boy from town. He was gonna let them court."

"Why? He wasn't from the Hollow."

"Pa thinked that she can do better than Sissy. Have a better life in the town."

Meg was quiet thinking about how that was so different than what she imagined Clancy to be like. Very different.

Hank answered her unasked questions. "Pa, he ain't like what folks think. That's why he let Pastor Jake come. He has to be strong to make sure we have what we need to live, but he's a good Pa. He loves us, in his way. He lets me go to school and learn from Boon. That's why I talk better than most. Since our maw passed, Pa's been quiet, hard like. But he wants me and Erica to have a life away from the Hollow."

"What can you possible learn from Boon? Isn't he a hermit?"

Hank chuckled softly. "Boon's college educated. He ain't from here neither. He's really smart too!"

"But isn't he your cousin?"

"Pa's cousin."

"Oh," Meg replied. She didn't know what to make of Boon and Clancy. So, she went to a more familiar subject. "Did you get to know Pastor Jake at all?"

"Yes'm. He's great! I want to learn to be like him."

"Like him? You mean a minister?"

"Yes'm. These mountain folk know about God, but don't know God. Iffin, I bring them back to God, instead of only one time a year when Pastor Jake comes with his folks, they would know God. You know what I mean?"

"Hmm, not really."

"Well, don't you know God?"

"Of course, I know about God."

"I ain't talkin' about that kind of knowin'. Y'all got the same kind of knowin' that folks have, but don't know Him in a 'personal' way. That's how Pastor Jake says it, personal."

"Do you know God personal, like that?"

"Yes'm. I got baptized too, so all folks know that I know God personal."

"I've seen how Jake is. So, I get the whole personal thing with God. But you're right, I don't know God that way." Meg turned away from Hank. She didn't want to hear any more. It was getting too close to how Jake talked to her about God. She promised God she would hear about Him *if* they got off the mountain safe, but not before.

"Ma'am, I ain't meanin' to push this, but I got a feelin' 'bout y'all. Ya wants to know, but yet, ya is holdin' back. But the Bible says to us that we ain't promised tomorrow."

"Thanks for being concerned about me. But I'm a friend of Pastor Jake's, so I've heard all this before."

"Yes'm. But y'all never faced this darkness in this way afore."

"The darkness?"

"Those dark wolves that knocked y'all down. They is real evil. I learnt 'bout devils in the town school. They is like those in that book. Only they is real. And they's after ya!"

"You can't know that. And Sam stopped them from hurting me."

"Yes'm, for now. But what happens when you face 'em alone? Without that Sam...or God?"

"I don't know, Hank. Maybe we should go back inside now, try to get some sleep." Meg took a step toward the cabin. But Hank stopped her.

"Ma'am, ya can't wait till later. Ya got to make up your mind 'bout God. I is feeling scared and I ain't afeared too much!"

Fear washed over Meg. "I...I'm not scared. I've faced criminals, even was abducted once."

"Yes'm. But this here darkness is not what y'all faced afore. I feel hard pressed to say this to ya. Nothin' but the light of Jesus can break through this darkness that surroundin' ya. I's afeared that ya gonna face it soon. Without that light, they gonna kill ya. That kid thinkin' he can stop um. But he ain't gonna. Ya can't just wait till ya off the mountain. Now's time for you to decide about God."

"That's not the deal I made!" Meg said, her voice rising. "I promised I'd find out more and decide if I get off this mountain, not before."

"Ya have to decide tonight. Or there won't be a tomorra for ya. That darkness is coming back, here to this place. It has a hold on this place cause Boon invited it in. Those animals carry the darkness with em. They's got it from a long time ago from one who made a deal with the devil for his soul." Hank's voice ended in a whisper.

"Are you saying Sam has made a pact with the devil, with these creatures?" Meg could hear the fear in her voice.

"Na, not yet. He's close."

"How can you know this?"

"Sometimes, I have understandin' of things. Ma says I's got the sight. Sam stopped them. I's sees him, in his eyes, sees how he cared that nothin' happen to ya. They got a hold, but not all the way."

"There's no way you can know any of this…."

"Yes'm. I know. They's comin' back!"

Meg didn't know how to respond. After a few moments, she asked, "How sure are you that they are coming back here?"

"Sure as anything I's know. Ya know too. That's why ya ain't sleepin' like the others. It's time to make that choice….ma'am."

"You're just a kid, you can't understand. Religion ruined my life. It was all good until he…changed."

"Knowin' God ain't religion. It's about havin' Someone who loves ya like no person can. It's knowin' that y'all is free from sin, knowin' God got a future for ya, knowin' that no matter what, ya got a place in heaven waitin' for ya. Havin' faith, it's like freeing."

"What do you mean by freeing?"

"Well, I's was kinda a bad kid. I's always had this bad feelin' like guilt, always fearin' someone know the bad stuff I's did. Afraid to be caught. But once I told God I's sorry, didn't matter. My heart was free. I even went to some folks I wronged and told 'em. Made things right with em. First time, Pa ever looked proud of me. But it's in the known' that I's right with God that makes it great. All the bad feelin's are gone, I's free."

"So, it changed you? Made you different?"

"Yes'm. But in a good way."

"Maybe it was good for you. But this religion changed my fiancé. We had a life together. We were partners on the police force. It made him leave me and the force. How is that good?"

"Probably hard for him. But how can he stay if ya was fightin' God? Iffin the life y'all was livin' in sin, how could he stay?"

"What do you mean 'sin'?"

"Was y'all living together like married?"

Meg turned away. "You don't understand. Life is different off this mountain. People live together all the time. You have to know someone before you marry them to see if you can get along."

"Life is all the same under God. Iffin ya'll ain't married, it was sin. Did ya love him?"

"What?"

"Did ya love him?"

"Of course I did. That's why I was so mad when he left."

"Seems to me iffin ya loved him, ya would see how much he loved God. How can ya say ya loved him, but wanted him to stay knowin' for him it was wrong? Iffin ya loved him, ya would have seen how hard it must have been for him."

"He just walked away!"

"Did he? Did he tell y'all about God?"

"Yes, he told me…." Meg stopped and turned back to Hank. "He told me he wanted me to know God too. He wanted us to have this new life. But I couldn't leave the force. I loved being a cop."

"Did he ask ya to stop bein' a cop?"

"No. He never asked me to leave the force. He asked me to consider God. He asked me to marry him now. He wanted to move out, but stay engaged. He wanted me to go to marriage counseling with Pastor Ryerson." Hank didn't say anymore. He stood praying silently for Meg as she struggled with her past. "He…told me he loved me. That he wanted God's best for our lives. I didn't want to hear anything he said. I wanted things to stay the same. But they couldn't. They didn't."

Meg sat down on a tree stump and put her head in her hands. The past caught up with the present. She remembered throwing her engagement ring at Jake and telling him to just leave. She didn't want God. She didn't want him. So, he left and started a new life. Now, he was her friend, her friend who just lost his wife. Hank stood silently watching her struggle.

After several long minutes passed, Hank cleared his throat. "Ma'am, I am sorry 'bout what happened. But we needin' to get back inside. Somethin's feelin' wrong out here."

Meg looked up and then around her. She felt something too, and quickly got to her feet. She grabbed Hank's arm and they headed toward the cabin door. At the door, Meg looked back to the darkness of the woods and saw the red eyes staring back at her.

As the door closed behind her, a howling ripped through the night. The boys awoke and Reggie sat up rubbing his eyes. Meg looked at Hank, "It's them. I know I've been arguing with you. But I think you better explain this to me quick. I can't face this alone, and I'm afraid to die. Please, tell me how to pray?"

CHAPTER 38

Boon stopped short when he saw lights in his cabin. He swore under his breath and grabbed Sam to stop him. "We can't go there now. That's probably the law."

"What are we going to do? We need to get that first aid kit."

"You'd better call them back. If they hear them, whoever it is won't leave if they think those animals are out here."

"They've already been howling, though. It's too late."

"Nah. Whoever it is won't know how close they are. Noises echo off these mountains."

Sam gave a low whistle and called out into the darkness. Boon could barely see the dark creatures as the came close to them. He could sense their tension as they paced around in the woods.

"Okay, now what are we going to do? You need that stuff for your hand," Sam whispered.

"Let's head over toward where we're working on your cabin. We'll hunker down there for the night and see what's going on the morning. Send them to the female and the pup. That will keep them out of sight for now."

"What about your cut? You've been bleeding pretty badly."

"Nothing we can do right now. I'll clean it up as good as I can with water and rewrap it once we get over the ridge."

"But…."

"Look boy, while I appreciate this concern, we don't have any choice right now. Someone is in the cabin. Let's go."

"I want to keep them with us though."

"If people are this close, it's too close. Unless you want to risk that Boss don't want to kill them."

"Let them stay close until we get settled. I don't like that people found your cabin. I thought no one knew where you lived."

Boon started walking and didn't reply. Sam switched on his flashlight and Boon quickly turned. "Shut that off! If we can see that light, they can see this one."

Sam quickly shut it off and reached down until his hand rested on one of the creatures. Boon walked ahead pushing branches and stumbling along. Sam thought quietly and then asked, "Are you going to answer my question?"

"You didn't ask me a question."

"Who knows where you live?"

Boon grunted. "Clancy."

"Do you think that's Clancy? I thought you said he was probably dead?" Sam felt himself getting mad. The creature tensed under his hand. "Who else knew Boon?"

"I have other kin. Do you think that I don't have people who actually care about me?"

"Who else knows? Who is in the cabin?"

Boon stopped and waited for Sam to catch up with him. "I told you that it's probably the law."

"Who would be comfortable enough to be in your cabin?"

"If it was one of my kin, why wouldn't I just go in?"

"I don't know. Maybe you're trying to protect someone else from them. Is that it?"

"We've got enough blood on our hands because of them, don't you think? I don't know who is in my cabin. All I know is that I'm not going to let them hurt anyone else on this mountain. If it's one of my kin, I don't want to see them hurt. You and me had a deal. It got broke when they went after Clancy. I'll do what I need to do to stay alive, but I won't let anyone else get hurt by them."

"This is ridiculous. Your hand…."

Boon turned and walked away stumbling again as he went. Sam watched until Boon was lost in the darkness. Sam looked back toward the cabin and the faint light from the dirty windows. He felt the weight of the shotgun resting in the crook of his arm. He ran his other hand down the back of the creature feeling the thick fur. He looked back toward where Boon had disappeared into the dark, but couldn't even see him.

Sam turned toward the cabin. "I'm NOT going to let people chase me away anymore. I'm tired of running. This mountain is ours!"

As Sam headed toward the cabin, he heard Boon calling to him. But he kept on going until he reached the clearing around the cabin. He looked into the small window and saw several people moving around inside. Boon came crashing through the woods toward him, and Sam said something softly to the creature. It took off with his offspring. Glancing behind him to see where Boon was, Sam walked to the cabin door. Boon grabbed him and started pulling him away.

"No," Sam said, jerking away from Boon. "I'm tired of running. You're the one who just said this morning that I should stop running. Well, I'm done!"

The door opened and light spilled on the two men. Reggie stopped in the doorway, staring at the two men.

"Hi Sam," Reggie said, taking a step outside. "We've been looking for you."

"Why?" Sam asked with a scowl. "Want to blame me for something I didn't do again?"

Ignoring the question, Reggie extended his hand to Boon. "You must be Boon. I've heard a lot about you from your kinfolk."

"Yep, I'm Boon," he responded shaking the outstretched hand.

"I suppose I should apologize for taking over your cabin. But we were tired and thought it'd be okay with you seeing that the boys that are with us are your cousins."

"Well, I need to get my hand tended to." He turned his hand over and showed the deep cut to Reggie.

"Come on in." Reggie stepped aside, so Boon could get into the cabin. After Boon passed him, Reggie faced Sam.

"So, Sam, what do you think we're trying to blame on you?"

Sam hesitated. Then said, "I saw the poster at the community college saying I'm wanted for Bobbi's disappearance. I left her in the parking lot."

"Then why are you hiding out in the mountain? Why didn't you go to the police when you saw the poster?"

"Why would I?"

"Because last time you came to me, I helped you rescue Sarah."

"Not before you accused me of having something to do with her missing. And I got locked in a shed and chased through the woods...."

"You brought that on yourself by running away and breaking into that house. If it wasn't for finding Sarah, you would have faced charges for breaking and entering. You have to admit you haven't always made the best choices. You've got to know that I have to ask you about the missing kids and the accident."

"Why do you have to ask me anything?"

"Because the scenario is the same as the past. There are only a handful of people that know that and you're one of them. And the DNA of those creatures you're with has been found at a crime scene and other evidence was found connecting them to an accident. An accident that left Meg Riley's father in the hospital and took the life of Sarah Peterson."

Sam became very still. The shock showed so clearly on his face that Reggie knew that he didn't know about Brian or Sarah being in the accident. "You didn't know who was in the accident," Reggie stated.

"No," Sam stammered. "Boon told me there was an accident…I didn't know who…."

"Sam, how smart are those creatures? Could they have known that it was them?"

"They're animals," Sam said recovering a bit.

"Yes, they are, but very smart animals. Some of the forensic evidence shows that there are traces of human DNA. While I find it farfetched, that's what the evidence shows. Not only in the offspring, who you are with now, but with the original animals that were in Granelle."

"How do you know all this?"

"It's the evidence, Sam. Do you know where the creatures from Granelle are? Are they in these mountains too?"

Sam heard a noise behind him and figured they were coming back, to protect him. "Look, I don't know anything about what you are saying. I've been hanging out with Boon, nothing has been going on. Go back to New York and leave me alone."

"I can't do that now. Two people that I care about have been hurt by those creatures. You know, Mr. Riley talked to your father. Your Dad asked that when we found you, we let you know that he is sorry. He realized he made some mistakes and wants you to come home."

Sam's hand clenched into fists and Reggie realized it was a mistake to mention Stanley. "Ever since my mother died when I was ten, I've been unwanted. Even though everyone knew it was Trevor that killed her, it seemed that I was always blamed. My *family* never forgave *me* for what happened."

"You know that's not the whole truth. You had problems in school…."

"Not in Granelle, I didn't. What I remember was that I had a crush on a girl who liked the new kid in school. I showed off trying to get her attention and got in trouble. Then, I met Trevor Grant and my life went radically wrong. I didn't ask him to kill Mom, I didn't ask to be kidnapped, and I didn't ask to be the keeper. It happened to me, not because of me."

"I was talking about the problems you had in high school."

"You mean after my abduction when I lived through the most terrifying experience anyone could face. You figured I'd go off to Poughkeepsie and what? I'd live happily ever after?"

"That's a cop out," Reggie replied.

"Is it?" Sam shook his head and saw Meg standing at the door. "Was it a cop out for her?"

"What are you talking about?"

"I know that she killed Trevor, hunted him down with Pastor Jake and her father. But that was okay, right?"

"They didn't hunt him down. They were looking for you. His death was an accident...."

"That's a LIE! I was there! I saw her shoot Trevor, and I saw Pastor Jake shoot the creature. Maybe they are that smart. Maybe they did know who was in the car. A tit for tat, Pastor Jake and Detective Riley killed their father and their keeper. So, they cause an accident to hurt them back. They were left alone until I was finally old enough to know, until I was old enough to care about them."

"Were you there? Were you a part of that accident?"

Sam stood trembling with rage. "I was with Boon," he said through clenched teeth. "How easy it is for you to blame me. Boon said this would happen, that you would come here to this mountain and find someone to blame and that's me."

"We're investigating an accident and searching for several people that are missing. You were the last one to have seen that one girl that is missing."

"No, the last one to see her was the one that took her. Ask Boon. I've been up on this mountain and she's not here."

"Her friends all say she followed you out of that bar. Did you see anyone else in the parking lot? This is why we needed to talk to you, find out if you saw something that might help us track down the kidnapper. You know what it felt like to be taken. Timmy is the same age you were when Trevor took you. We need to find some new leads and you might know something."

Reggie looked past Sam and saw the red eyes inching closer. Meg saw them too and stepped out. "We got eaten up by bugs today and this light is attracting them here in droves. Why don't you come in Sam? I know you saved my life today. I know you aren't responsible for what happened." Sam looked at her and shook his head. "Please Sam, come talk to me. I know that its Donovan doing this, he's trying to get someone else to become the keeper. I went to Ireland with Pastor Jake. We talked to Shamus O'Leary's family. We know all about the legend. We also know that Donovan doesn't think you're doing the right thing and is trying to take the power away from you. So, please come inside…I'll tell you everything I know."

"He can't take it away from me. They chose me," Sam said defiantly.

"But he knows about the ritual. That's how you became the keeper." Meg swatted a bug on her neck. "Well, I'm going inside. If you want to know what Kelly Flannigan told me, you know where I am. Come on Captain, let's get away from these bugs."

Meg walked back inside with a bravado that she didn't feel. Reggie followed her and closed the door. "Now what?" Reggie asked.

"See if he calls my bluff. I had to get you inside. Those creatures are just inside the woods, and they weren't going to wait for Sam to change his mind."

"Let me tell you a few things, so you're not bluffing," Boon said as he sat at the table wrapping his hand in a white cloth. "I read most of those journals, some of them to Sam."

"How could you have read them?" Meg asked coming over. She took the strips of cloth from Boon and began to gently wrap his hand.

"I studied languages and was a history professor. I know Gaelic."

"Why are you willing to help us? Do you know anything about these disappearances?"

"I know the kid didn't do it and two of them that are missing are kin to me. I would have seen something. I just want you to get me off this mountain before those devils kill me. I've betrayed them once already. And for this," he gestured at his hand, "they will kill me."

"What do you mean?"

"I did this intentionally, so we couldn't go on. But when Sam catches on to me, I'm dead."

"What…?"

"Just let him tell us what we need to know," Reggie interrupted. "We can hear *his* story later. Sam may walk in at any minute and we need a cover."

In hushed tone, Boon told them some of the history of the keeper. He hoped he was telling them enough to save them. For the first time since coming to this mountain, Boon felt a need for civilization.

CHAPTER 39

Sam walked into the woods and then waited until the alpha came to him. He knelt down and buried his face into the course fur. He sat down keeping his arm around the dark creature.

"Donovan is turning on me. He's trying to make someone else the keeper. But your father picked me. He made me your protector."

Sam looked toward the cabin. He wondered what Boon was saying to the cops. "Boon's probably betraying us right now. So, we've got two big problems, Donovan and Boon. I wish you could talk to me and help me figure out what to do. Captain Bennett and Meg have been straight with me in the past, but they hate you. Well, they hated your father. I don't know what to do."

The other male came up and lay down on the other side of Sam making him feel safer, protected. He sat for a long time. He saw someone come to the door and look out. Sam sat very still waiting until the door closed again. Lying down between the two males, Sam thought about what Reggie had said. He knew the creatures were smart, that they seemed to understand him. But he wondered if it was true that they were part human. If so.... A few hours later, Sam awoke with a start. The alpha was gone, and the other still lay with Sam.

Sam sat up and looked around. Faint, grey light filtered through the trees. "Take me to your father. We need to stop Donovan. We'll worry about Boon later."

They got to their feet and took off into the woods leaving the cabin behind them.

* * *

Meg got very little sleep. She kept hearing the creature walking around the cabin. It had been over an hour since she last heard it digging at the door. Boon lay awake too, listening. She finally whispered, "Do you think it's gone or just inside the woods?"

"Hard to say," he whispered back. "But even if they are a ways away, they just turn up sometimes."

"Are they going to let us go back down the mountain?"

"Well, we're going to try," Reggie said stretching. "I think by now, Jake needs us. It's time for us to go support our friend and let the locals tend to this."

"But...."

"What? Sam? Do either of you think he took those kids?" Meg and Boon both shook their heads. "Was he really with you when the accident happened?"

"Yep," Boon replied. "He's been pretty intent about building a cabin up here. We've been working on it."

"Then the only reason we'd be staying would be to save him. Do you think he really wants to be saved?"

"No. He believes he belongs with those creatures. He wants to live here to protect them, keep them from being found by folks."

"Then, we need to go be with Jake."

"What about Clancy? He's still missing too and that has nothing to do with the other disappearance," Boon argued.

"Do you want to get off this mountain?"

"Yes."

"Then you need to leave with us. We'll get back to Creek River. You can hook up with the sheriff if you still have a desire to search for your cousin. I know that this is hard, but we did what we were asked to do. We found Sam."

"But the investigation isn't over," Meg interjected. "Those kids are still missing."

"Well, if you still feel a need to continue working on the investigation, talk to the sheriff once we're off this mountain. That creature was walking around this cabin all night. What if they do possess human intellect and the accident was intentional? How long do you think Sam can keep them from going after you...or Jake?"

"If they are that smart, what will prevent them from coming after us in New York?"

"We'll formulate a plan to deal with that once we're home. For now, we need to find out what Jake's plans are and be there for him. Again, once we hook back up with Jesse, either one of you can join him. I'm retired for a reason!"

"Okay," Meg agreed. "Let's pack up."

"What about us?" Hank asked from his spot on the floor between his cousins. "Should we keep on lookin' for Pa?"

The adults looked at each other. Reggie deferred to Boon. "For now, stay with me. Once we're in Creek River, Tom can bring you boys back to the Hollow. The sheriff and Clint were going to keep looking for your Pa."

"Boon, we can bring our ownselves back home. I still worrin' 'bout Pa, that's all."

"Yeah, I know, boy. I'm still worried too. But Mr. Bennett's right. Those devils were around here all night. We need to get back to town."

One of the boys shrugged and soon they all began to fold up the bedding. Boon worked with Meg making some sandwiches. He felt clumsy and his hand kept bumping hers. Finally, Boon went outside with Reggie to see if Sam and the creature were nearby. Meg watched him walk away with a little smile. He glanced back at the door and saw her smiling at him as she quickly turned back to the food.

* * *

Sam had left the two male creatures with his plans. He hoped that they really did understand what he needed them to do. Then, he headed down the mountain toward his car. He practically ran to the car in his desire to get to Langford. He remembered how Boon steered him away from Creek River and Beaumont. So now, he'd go to Langford. Sam hated the long drive, but knew the bias he would face in the two closer towns.

Once in Langford, he found a motel. Looking in the back of his car, he found some clothes and a duffel bag. He took the bag into the office to get a room. The clerk hardly looked at him and hurried through checking him in. Sam knew he was filthy and smelled like the creatures, which is why he decided to get the room before he moved on with his plan. He settled into his room and took a hot shower. After he was dressed, Sam sat on the edge of the bed with his cell phone.

Dialing a number from memory, he waited until he got the voice mail. He narrowed his eyes as he waited to leave a message. "Mr. Donovan, this is Sam. I have the old journals and found a person that was able to translate it for me. So, I know that there is nothing you can do to turn them against me. I am their keeper. Their father chose me. Don't waste those kids' lives trying to stop me. Right now, they are hunting for the person you are trying to get to take my place. Be assured of this Mr. Donovan. You are no longer my attorney. You no longer have anything to do with me or the creatures.

Call off your person and let those kids go or I will come to Ireland and hunt you down. From what I understand, there are still some hounds loose in Ireland that are at my command."

Sam hung up and flipped opened the phone book. He looked at all the attorney listings and found several had offices in the same building. Slipping on a leather jacket, Sam headed out to retain a new attorney.

CHAPTER 40

The hike down the mountain was uneventful. Reggie watched the banter between Meg and Boon with mild interest. A few times, he caught her eye and she blushed. Blushed!!! Reggie could hardly believe the hardened detective he knew was actually blushing. But knowing they were going back to Sarah's funeral kept Reggie from teasing Meg about her attraction to Boon. This funeral was going to be hard.

Back in Creek River, Reggie and Meg walked down the Main Street toward the Baptist Church and the parsonage where they hoped to find Jake. Boon headed with the boys toward the Sheriff's Office, but stopped and called out to Meg. They stopped and waited for Boon to come over.

Hesitantly, Boon said, "I know this sounds crazy, but I don't want you to just walk away and never see you again."

Meg glanced at Reggie who shrugged. She looked back at Boon. "I don't know how to respond to that. You live on the mountain...and I...."

"I know crazy, right? I don't even own a phone. But if you give me your number, I'll go to Beaumont right now and get a cell phone."

"Boon," she said softly. She looked down at the ground.

"Look, I'm not asking you for a lifetime commitment. I'm asking for your phone number. I've wasted my life, but after staring in the face of evil, I want more. I never thought I could feel again after Becky died, but with you...."

"I'm really flattered. What I realized on that mountain was that I've wasted my life too. But what I also realized is that I needed something more than a person, I needed a Savior. I found Him. All those years, I thought I was running from Jake, but I was running from God. Jake tried to tell me, and then a lady in Ireland told me. But when I heard that same message from Ma and from Hank, I knew that it was really God trying to get my attention. Right now, I don't know what that even means. And on top of that, my friend lost his wife. I need to be here for Jake."

"Meg, I believe in God too. You can't live all those years alone in the mountain without knowing God exists. So, why does that need to stop us from getting acquainted?"

"Hank told me there's a difference between knowing about God and knowing Him personally. He explained it, so I really understood it. I'll promise you this, you talk to Hank and find out the difference. I'll probably be here in Creek River until the day after tomorrow or over in Beaumont at the hospital with my Dad. When you have the answer, look me up. Then we can talk about whether we should get to know each other more. Is that a deal?"

Meg stuck her hand out. Boon looked at it, "You serious?"

"Yep."

"Okay. Man, you're tough," he said shaking her hand.

Meg heard Reggie softly laugh as they turned back to the parsonage. "This trip to Virginia has really changed you, Riley."

"I know. In more ways than you can ever imagine, Captain. What about Jake? Do you think he's going to be okay?"

Reggie took a deep breath and took a long moment to answer. "Well, Jake struggled when Sarah was kidnapped. He almost lost his faith. But he has Pastor Walt here with him. Jake has always drawn strength from him. By now, I'm sure other family members are here too."

The driveway at the parsonage was packed with cars and some cars were even parked in the street. The church parking lot had more cars. Meg stopped Reggie as they approached the house. "Maybe we should go to the church first and clean up. We've spent three days on the mountain without showering. We're a mess."

"Do you think Jake is going to care about that?"

"No, but the Zimmers might and so might the family that is gathered here. Reggie, we smell!"

"And it's better to go smelly to the church than a house? Come on, Riley, everyone knows where we were. I'm sure we'll get hustled to the nearest shower."

Meg sighed as she followed Reggie to the Zimmer's house. He rang the doorbell and smirked at her embarrassment. Margaret opened the door, took one look at them and directed them around the house to the kitchen. Meg soon found herself back in the Zimmer's guest room with its own bathroom.

Meg stood looking at herself in the mirror while the shower heated up. Her green eyes looked huge in her face with her long hair pulled back into a messy ponytail. Sunburned, covered in bug bites, she wondered what in the world Boon saw in her. She smiled at her reflection, but then sobered as she remembered why she was here. There were still three missing kids out there someplace, and her friend has just lost his wife.

Meg got in the shower and let the hot water take away the aches and grime. After she dressed, she wandered back toward the kitchen. She found Margaret who ushered her to a table and gave her a bowl full of stew. There was a loaf of Italian bread on the table. Meg sat looking at the bowl, hesitantly.

"Is there something wrong?" Margaret asked in concern.

"I was wondering if Reggie would be joining me and if I should wait," Meg said softly.

"Oh, he just went outside with Pastor Jake. I think they were taking a walk and talking. So, go ahead and eat." Meg still sat there looking at the bowl. "Honey, is there something else?"

"Well…I don't even know how to ask you this."

"Don't you like stew?"

Meg looked up at Margaret's worried face. "I'm so sorry. It's nothing like that. The stew smells wonderful and I'm starving. It's just that…do I need to pray before I eat?"

"Pray before…you mean say grace?"

"Is that what it's called? Are there different names for different prayers? Is there something I should be saying?"

"Oh my! Praying doesn't need to be complicated at all. Aren't you used to praying?"

"No. I wasn't raised in church or with religion. But last night, I prayed with Hank and asked Jesus into my life. I don't want to do anything wrong."

Margaret sat down next to Meg. She took her hand and smiled. "Why don't I pray for the food, so you can eat? Then, I think, we should have a talk about God and what that prayer you prayed last night meant."

Meg looked relieved. "Thank you. I don't know what I'm supposed to do with God now. But I can tell you that I feel such peace and happiness, like I've never felt before. It's like I don't feel guilty about stuff. I want to tell everyone how I feel, but don't know how to explain it."

Margaret said a quiet prayer for the meal and ended by thanking God for the decision Meg made. After she said Amen, she went to the hutch and picked up her Bible. As she shared her own story with Meg, showed her some verses to give her direction, Meg devoured the stew while thoroughly engrossed in every word that Margaret shared with her.

CHAPTER 41

It was a gray, rainy day and the church was packed. Jake sat in the front row with Richie, Sarah's parents and sister, and his own parents. Flanked by those that loved Sarah almost as much as he did, Jake found the courage to be strong for Richie while Pastor Walt spoke of his wife. Even though, Sarah's family hadn't wanted a Creek River memorial for Sarah, Jake knew that these people had loved her too and needed to remember her and celebrate her life.

Among the Creek River residents were the folks from the Hollow. Meg was surprised at the lives that Sarah had touched and knew that in upstate New York, another group of lives had been touched by this woman as well. Some of Meg's sorrow was at herself for missing the chance to have really known Sarah. She also had wished that she could have told Sarah about her recent decision to follow God.

Meg glanced around the church again as Pastor Walt began to read about the resurrection and was shocked to see Sam Craig in the last pew. She almost bolted out of the pew, but restrained herself. Reggie, who was next to her, frowned and nudged her. She looked at Reggie and opened her mouth, but closed it. She was not going to make a scene and ruin this memorial. But she knew there was no way she could let Sam leave without talking to him. If she waited too long, Sam would sneak out the back before she could get to him.

Meg took a piece of paper out of her purse and wrote a note to Reggie. He read it and looked up surprised, then nodded. Quietly, Meg got up and went to a side door of the sanctuary. She knew it lead to the ladies' room and a side exit. She practically ran to get around to the front of the church, but found her heels cumbersome in the ground that was softened by the rain. The rain was coming down in torrents. She hugged the building trying to stay as dry as possible until she was on the front steps, under the awning.

Meg waited trying to catch her breath. She was certain that Sam would be one of the first ones out. As the music started, ending the memorial, Meg heard a car start in the parking lot on the side of the church. She ran down the steps and right in the path of the car, startling the driver. She put her hands on the hood of the car as it abruptly stopped.

Sam stared through the windshield at Meg as the pouring rain drenched her. Afraid he would just take off if she moved, she put her hand up. "Please let me talk to you, Sam."

206

Sam couldn't hear what she was saying, so he rolled the window down. "Can you move? I don't want anyone to see me," he yelled to her.

"I need to talk to you. Please?"

Sam saw a few people leave the church. "Get in the car. Hurry up."

Meg kept her hands on the car as she practically ran to the passenger door afraid he would bolt if she got completely out of his way. She opened the door quickly, got in and slammed it behind her. She hardly was settled as Sam quickly drove out of the drive and noticed a few people looking in their direction.

As Sam drove, Meg buckled her seatbelt, glancing over at him trying to read what he was thinking. Patience wasn't something she was good at, but something about his manner made her wait. This wasn't the scared little boy who she befriended in the basement in upstate New York. This was a grown man who had become hardened by a life that no one should have had to live. Meg thought about their shared experience and realized that she never quite got over it herself, and she was an adult when it happened. She didn't face the rejection of her father, but actually got him back as a result of what had happened to her.

Looking out at the driving rain, Meg realized that they were leaving Creek River and that it was probably a stupid idea that she got in Sam's car. They rode in silence for twenty minutes until they reached another town. Sam drove through the town and then pulled over onto a wide part on the shoulder. He turned and faced Meg.

"Okay, you wanted to talk. So, go ahead. What do you want to accuse me of now?"

Meg looked at Sam and then shook her head. "Nothing," she replied softly. "I really don't know what I was thinking when I saw you. I just felt this need to talk to you."

"Why?"

"That memorial service for Sarah was hard for me to watch. A long time ago, I was going to marry Pastor Jake. But things didn't work out between us. I became really bitter, then he met Sarah. I was jealous of her. After she was abducted and you found her, I felt a bond with her. I was even able to let go of the past and be friends with her."

"What does that have to do with me?"

"I don't know, nothing really. I was struggling with my own grief. She made Jake so much happier than I would have and now…. Then I saw you. I didn't want you to leave without talking to you. I was afraid you would disappear into the mountains."

"So what if I disappear? What difference does that make to you?"

"My dad is still in the hospital and he's blaming himself for the accident. I know that it wasn't his fault…."

"But you think it was mine," Sam said, his voice steely.

"No, I know it's not your fault either. But someone is responsible. I think in many ways you're still a victim of Trevor Grant. You feel some bond to those creatures. But you don't have to live life running anymore. I don't want to see you ruin the rest of your life."

"Ruin? What are you talking about? Haven't you heard? I'm rich. I've got it all."

"If that's true, then why aren't you driving away in your Porsche heading back to one of your houses?"

"I don't have a Porsche or houses."

"That's what I mean. You have all this wealth and what has it done for you? You live on the run, hiding those creatures, and now…."

"What difference does it make to you?"

"You saved my life…twice. I want to help save yours."

"Save me? How can you save me? You brought those people up on the mountain to hunt me down."

"No. I came to Creek River because some kids went missing and the creature's DNA showed up at the crime scene. When we realized you were here in Virginia and that you were identified as the guy with Roberta, I knew we had to find you. Not because I believed you did it, but because I believed that someone was trying to keep the legacy of the keeper alive."

"Why wouldn't you think it was me? After all, I'm with the creatures. I'm in the vicinity."

"Well, there are other factors. Jake and I went to Ireland. We tracked down Shamus O'Leary's family. I talked to his daughter and learned about the journals. You left one up at Boon's cabin. I have it."

"It's mine."

"How did you get it?"

"I found them all at the old house in Granelle when I was there visiting Johnny."

"Why are you here in Creek River?"

"Is this your underhanded way of interrogating me, Detective Riley?"

"No. I want to find a way to end this nightmare. How did you say it to Reggie? Your life went radically wrong when you met Trevor Grant. Well, mine did too. I'm tired of chasing those creatures around, tired of trying to save people. I found something here in Creek River and I want to start over. But I can't until this is over. Right now, you hold the keys to ending this forever."

"Because I'm the keeper?"

"Yes, but someone is trying to stop that from happening. And those creatures…you are the one that can stop those creatures forever."

"Don't you realize yet? They aren't the problem. It's the people that were the problem. The original keeper was evil, not the creatures."

"I've seen those creatures. They reek of destruction and have some kind of evil all their own. I don't understand it all, but you are the one that can stop it."

Sam didn't respond. He sat staring out into the pouring rain. Meg saw the hard line of his jaw and realized that he wouldn't help her stop the creatures. "Sam," Meg said softly, "why are you here in Creek River?"

He looked at her for a long moment before answering. "What difference does it make to you?"

"Well, there are some people that have suggested that you followed Jake here."

"Actually, why *is* Pastor Jake here? Maybe he followed me."

"No, he didn't. He's been coming down to Creek River for the past three summers doing work with the folks up in the Hollow."

"The Hollow? With the Boons?"

"Yeah, he went to the sheriff to see if he could help find a missing little boy from town. He said it reminded him of you."

"It's Donovan. He gave me the name of the guy at the college. He had to have known that Pastor Jake was coming down here. It all goes back to him."

"What do you mean?"

"I came here because Donovan found this guy that is supposed to be an expert on foreign languages, especially Gaelic. He was going to translate the journals for me."

"That's why you came to Creek River?"

"Yeah, only I found out that he is a fraud. He stole all this work that made him famous."

"So, he couldn't translate it for you?"

"He was able to translate some. But then I found out that his translations weren't all that accurate."

"Then who translated them for you?"

"How do you know if they got translated? And why all this interest?"

"I'm interested in them because O'Leary's daughter said that her father read them and it led to him kidnapping Trevor. Those journals and the creatures destroyed his life. He left his wife and child destitute to follow those creatures and do the things that he felt he was instructed to do in those journals."

"So you think I'm turning into O'Leary?"

"I thought it might be possible. But then you saved my life on that mountain. I saw your face and knew that you didn't want to see me hurt."

"But…."

"But, those creatures are still tied to this. The past is repeating itself and we need to figure out why."

"Donovan," Sam said flatly.

"Have you talked to him? Do you know for sure that it's him?"

"I tried to call him, but he is ignoring me. He thinks that he can get someone else to be the keeper, but he is wrong."

"We talked to his son. He claims his father is just this really old man, harmless."

"And you believe him?"

"Not at all. Jake found out that he is getting money from the same publishing house that you are. Why did he set up a dummy corporation to pay you? Why can't you just get your inheritance?"

"Donovan thought it was better that way, to protect me from taxes."

"Or it's about Donovan being able to control the money and you?"

"I don't understand."

"People with money control many things, including other people."

"But it's my money. I control it."

"Do you? What if Mr. Donovan told your company that you were fired. Can they fire you? Would you get your paycheck?"

"He wouldn't do that…couldn't…do…that," Sam ended in a whisper.

"What's the arrangement for the money? Do you even know?"

"Yeah, it's all invested in the company. I draw a salary and have an expense account."

"Who controls the finances for the company?"

"Donovan," Sam said through clenched teeth. He threw the car into gear and hit the gas. Meg felt the car lunge forward and braced herself.

CHAPTER 42

Reggie walked around outside of the church with a cup of punch in his hand, frowning. He checked for the third time to see that Meg's rental car was still in the parking lot. He pulled his cell phone out of his pocket, looked at it, and put it away. He went back into the fellowship hall where people were gathered eating food and talking about the memorial. Looking around, he saw Jake standing with the Zimmers talking to some of the mountain people. Richie was eating a sandwich sitting on his grandmother's lap. As he looked around the room, he still didn't see Meg.

In frustration, Reggie set the cup down on a table and left the hall. He went to the sanctuary and stood looking around, hoping she had come back there. But it was empty. Reggie sighed and went back to the pew where he had sat during the service. As he sat down in the pew, his foot kicked a purse. Grunting, he reached down and pulled it out. Meg's.

Reggie opened the purse and saw her cell phone inside. He pulled it out and opened it revealing all his missed calls and the waiting voicemails from him. He scrolled through the list of missed calls and realized he wasn't the only one looking for Meg. Reggie went outside and stood on the side porch watching the rain for a few long moments.

Finally using her phone, he called back the other number. "Meg, where have you been? I've been trying to reach you for days."

"Finley, this is Bennett. Why are looking for Riley?"

"I don't think that's any of your business, Captain Bennett. From what I've heard you're retired," was the reply.

"Well, I'm back. I'm working on a case in Virginia with her."

"I don't believe it. Not after the history you two have. Besides, Peterson is working with her. I talked to him a few days ago. Where is he? Let me talk to him."

"Do you have any idea what has happened down here? Did Jake tell you anything?"

"He told me that Brian was in an accident and in the hospital. But I can't believe that Riley would let you into her case just because her father was hurt."

"Look, Finley, Meg did ask me to help, but not because of Brian. Brian had a passenger in the car. It was Jake's wife, Sarah."

"Why wouldn't he tell me that himself? Look, I'm coming down there. I need to confirm this...."

"Stop," Reggie sighed into the phone. Mick was about to argue, but there was something in Reggie's voice that stopped him. "Sarah didn't make it. We just had her memorial service down here today. If you don't believe me, her obit is in the Saratoga paper. Her funeral service is up there in a few days."

"Oh man! Why didn't Jake tell me?"

"I don't know. I think he's finding it hard to accept. Seems like Pastor Ryerson is helping him though, but still.... So, that's why Riley called me to come to Virginia. They needed someone else who had worked on those Granelle cases down here to help out."

"I don't even know what to say to this."

"Why don't you just tell me what you were going to tell Riley? I have her phone because she took off following another lead and left her phone behind."

"Did Jake tell you what I found out about the publishing company?"

"No, but with all he's been dealing with the past few days, I'm sure it was the last thing on his mind. Start from the beginning."

Mick told Reggie about the publishing company and Lynch. He even told about his budding relationship with the receptionist. "So, I managed to get a subpoena through the NYC DA's office. I told them that I had evidence that the publishing company was a dummy corporation that was laundering money."

"They believed you?"

"Yeah, I had the records from my girl showing massive amounts of money going in and out of a company that has one employee in an office. So, I told the detective that my client was really Craig."

"Why did you do that? Why not just tell them that you were working for Riley?"

"Well, Riley told me that she was positive that the kid was being used. But with the amount of cash he pulled down last year, sounds like he is in on it. Riley said he was innocent in all this and someone is setting him up. You believe that?"

"Actually, I do believe that too. So what have you found out?"

"That both Lynch and Craig are in Virginia. Not too far from Creek River."

"We know where Sam is, where's Lynch?"

"Tracked some purchases in Beaumont, Langford, and Sweet Briar."

"Where do you think he is staying? That's a lot of ground to cover."

"My guess is to start in Langford. Problem is we don't know what he looks like."

"Give me a list of places he's been shopping at. I doubt too many people down here have an Irish accent."

Reggie went back to the sanctuary to find something to write with in Meg's purse. After he wrote all the information down, he sat in the pew wondering again where Meg was and if she was still with Sam. He got up figuring he would head to the sheriff's office to get some help finding her, when his cell phone rang.

* * *

"Where are we going?" Meg asked still holding on. Sam was driving fast and reckless. While the rain had tapered to a misty drizzle, the roads were slick.

"Langford."

"What's in Langford?"

"My new attorney."

"Can I use your cell phone to call Capt. Bennett? I left my phone at the church, and I'm sure by now he's putting an 'all points bulletin' out for me."

Sam slowed to get his phone from his pocket and handed it to her. "You might not get a signal here. It's spotty in the mountains."

Meg took the phone and was relieved to have a signal. While the signal was weak, she clearly heard the anger in Reggie's voice.

"This service is bad, so don't waste time yelling at me. I'm with Sam on our way to Langford."

"Did you say Langford, Riley?"

Meg grimaced at the use of her last name, "Yeah, Sam's new attorney is there. We think that Donovan is screwing him over financially and he wants to try and stop it."

"Worry more about the case for a minute than Sam's money. Finley called. He's got a lead on a Peter Lynch spending money here in Virginia. He's getting paid from the same company as Sam. And get this…he's a direct descendant to O'Shea, the original keeper."

"You're kidding!" Sam glanced over at her response. "How? That original clan died off."

"Well, apparently not. I suspect that he feels he has a claim to the inheritance and to the powers that everyone seems to think those animals have."

"I can't believe this. Where did he come from after all these years? If there was a legitimate claim…."

"We can ask these questions later," Reggie interrupted. "Don't forget about those missing kids. We need to find Lynch first."

"Okay, where do I start looking?"

"I'm on my way. You just wait for me at Sam's lawyer's office."

"We've wasted enough time. Let me start, you can catch up with me…. Reggie? Captain?" The dead line was her response. She looked at the phone and saw there was still service.

"Lost service?" Sam asked.

"No, I think he actually hung up on me!" Meg pushed the button to redial, but the call didn't go through.

"What was that all about?" Meg ignored him and tried to make the call again, but it went right to voicemail. "What were you talking about? Who is trying to steal the power?"

Meg looked over at Sam who was intently looking at her, not paying any attention to the road. "Sam! Look out!" Sam swerved into the curve causing the car to skid almost hitting the guardrail. "Keep your eyes on the road and slow down! I'll tell you. But, please don't get into an accident."

"Okay, okay," Sam relented as he slowed the car down…a bit. Meg took a breath and told him about Lynch.

CHAPTER 43

After Sam's lawyer called the New York DA's office, the publishing company's assets were frozen pending a full investigation. While Sam argued with his attorney, Meg was relieved that at least Donovan and Lynch would no longer have access to the money, to Sam's money. Meg had tried calling Reggie several times, but he never picked up the call. Frustrated, she called Jesse's office only to be told he went somewhere with Reggie.

Pacing in the lobby of the office building, Meg could do nothing, but wait. Finally, Sam stepped out of the elevator and looked around for her. "Are you going to wait here or go with me?" he asked as he walked up to her.

"Where are you going?"

"To my bank. I need to withdrawal as much money before my personal assets get frozen. I guess I'm lucky I moved my money out of New York. They need a federal warrant to freeze them now."

"But won't taking the money out make you look like you're doing something wrong?"

Sam started walking to the door with Meg following. "The only thing I did wrong was trust Donovan. But I've been living on debit cards and don't have any cash."

"Which made it easy for them to track you," Meg responded without thinking.

Sam stopped short and Meg almost walked into him. "Do you really think that?"

"What? That someone can track you based on electronic payments?"

"Yeah."

"It happens all the time. How do you think we found out about Lynch being down here? It's the same principle."

"So, someone, like Donovan, could be keeping track of where I am and then do stuff to make it look like I did it?"

"Well, that's our theory."

"This is more than just Lynch wanting to become the keeper. It's more like Donovan wants to totally take me out."

"It could be just Lynch…."

"You don't believe that anymore than I do."

"But what sense does that make that Donovan wants to 'take you out?' Why would Donovan do that if this is what O'Leary wanted, and he was his lawyer all those years?"

"The journals."

"What about them?"

"That's when things got weird between us. I told him that I found them and wanted to know everything. He would only tell me bits and pieces. I had these letters that O'Leary left me, but they only come at certain times, again with only pieces of the story. When I told him I had these journals, he tried talking me out of getting them translated. He never wanted me to know what they said."

"Boon told us some of what was in them. If anything, they talked about how great it is to be the keeper. That doesn't make any sense."

"I've done everything that Donovan told me to do, except that one thing. There's something in the journals that we missed. There has to be."

"Well, we can go back and read them again. Can't we?"

"Wait! That one journal we didn't finish. The last one, that one that you found in the cabin. Where is it?"

"I think it's with my stuff at the Zimmer's. Can you read them?"

"No, but Boon can. I have to find him."

Meg didn't know how to respond. The thought of Boon and seeing him again made her feel nervous. Sam didn't seem to notice. "Look, we better get to your bank. Reggie should be here soon, and I have to be ready to leave with him."

"Then, just stay. I don't need you to babysit me."

Sam walked to his car, but Meg followed him anyway. "No, I'm not leaving you right now. I don't know why, but I think I should just stay with you. If Reggie calls, he can find Lynch with the sheriff."

"What is it?" he asked getting behind the wheel.

"It's just this feeling that if I leave you, something will go wrong. I can't explain it. It's weird. So, I'm going with you. I don't want to lose you again."

Sam looked at her and then shrugged. "Okay, it's actually good to have someone who is on my side for a change."

"Well, then we stick together. First, let's get to the bank, then back to Creek River to find Boon."

"Boon's in Creek River?"

"That's the last place I saw him."

"What about Captain Bennett?"

"I'm not worried about him. Lynch is just a person that can be tracked down. I'm more interested in finding out what Donovan doesn't want anyone to know."

"Okay," Sam started the car and drove toward Beaumont. As she looked out the side window, Sam's cell phone rang.

"Finally!" Meg said as she picked up the phone. "Reggie, I've been trying to…. What is it with this signal! I lost the connection again!"

"Well, that's not a very good phone. And we are in the mountains."

"I don't like this. We are totally out of contact with everyone. When we get to Beaumont, I'm going to find a better phone. We have to stay in touch with at least Reggie."

"Do whatever you want. I don't really care either way. There's really no one that I want to talk to."

Meg looked at Sam and saw the hard line of his face. She felt such sadness for the boy she remembered who had become this hardened man. Maybe she could still help him, maybe it wasn't too late for Sam. As Sam sped toward Beaumont, Meg closed her eyes and prayed for him.

CHAPTER 44

"Is communication down here always so frustrating?" Reggie bellowed as he tossed his cell phone on the dashboard.

Jesse glanced over at Reggie and lifted his eyebrows. "Always like this, so I haven't got anything to compare it with."

"Well, now what do I do?"

"What we were planning on doing all along. Check out some of these places and see if we can get a description of this Lynch guy. Do you really need Meg to do that?" Reggie just grunted and looked out the side window. Jesse glanced over again. "She always so impulsive?"

"I don't know what the circumstances are until I talk to her. And no, I don't consider her actions impulsive."

"Taking off from the funeral…."

"She's with Sam moving forward with the case. We've established that the money is key to finding the person who has kidnapped the kids."

"Well, it's not established, yet. We still need all the facts. For all we know, Sam is in the vicinity and has access to money as well."

Jesse found a parking lot in the middle of Langford and pulled in. He parked the cruiser, and the two men got out of the car. Reggie pulled out the list of places that Mick had given to him. After looking at the list, Jesse pointed down the street. As they headed toward the closest store on the list, Reggie wondered what Meg was doing. It certainly did look like she was being impulsive, but he wouldn't betray her to Mueller. He knew she only wanted to protect Sam and in many ways, he did too.

* * *

Meg sat with Sam waiting to see one of the bank officers. The withdrawal of such a large amount of money was causing quite a stir in the small bank. They were waiting for a Mr. Cutler to explain to Sam why he couldn't remove his funds in cash. Finally they were lead down a narrow hallway to an office.

Mr. Cutler's tight smile showed Meg just how concerned the bank was to lose such a large deposit. "Mr. Craig and…," he paused waiting for Meg to explain who she was. She simply smiled back and didn't reply. He cleared his throat and indicated the chairs in front of his desk. "So, I understand you wish to close your account with our bank," he began settling behind the desk.

"That's right, *my* account. I just want my money. So what's the problem?"

"Well, Mr. Craig, we don't keep those kinds of funds in cash at the bank. We cannot simply give you a cashier's check either without having substantial documentation of your identity."

"Look, Mr. Cutler, your bank had no problem taking my substantial deposit or any of my wire transfers from my company. That's my money and you have no legal right to withhold it from me."

Mr. Cutler chuckled. "We aren't withholding it from you, but protecting the interest of the account holder, who *might* be you. So, I'll need...."

Meg interrupted before Sam could erupt and get thrown out of the bank. "Excuse me, Mr. Cutler. But Mr. Craig is right. You have no legal basis to stop him from closing his account with your bank and withdrawing his money."

"Surely, you don't know how banks operate, Miss...."

"Oh, that would be detective." Meg reached into her jacket and pulled out her credentials and laid them on the desk. "I'm Detective Megan Riley from Saratoga Springs, New York. I'm currently working with Sheriff Jesse Mueller over in Creek River on a case. We've traced illegal activities to some people who are trying to defraud Mr. Craig out of an inheritance. My partner in New York and Mr. Craig's attorney over in Langford have been in contact with the district attorney's office in New York City to stop the pilfering of his funds. Now, Mr. Cutler, I don't think that you want me to name your bank as a party to that, do you?"

"Detective," he stammered. "You should have told me who you were before we began this conversation."

"It shouldn't matter. Sam is the only account holder on this account. He has been in so many times, your teller addressed him by name, and he has identity to prove who he is. Certainly, even you know who your largest account holder is, Mr. Cutler."

"I don't know who this young man is. I have never met him before today."

Meg looked at Sam and raised her eyebrows. He just looked back, but didn't respond either way. "So, what I want to know is why are you just being a jerk? Is it because you don't want this sizeable account removed from a bank where your paycheck is contingent on the size of your deposits? Or are you in on the fleecing of his inheritance? Is Peter Lynch one of your new customers?"

"That is preposterous!"

"I will tell you this, if you don't personally close this account for Sam, I will go right over to the courthouse. I will talk to the D.A. here and explain what is happening in New York, I will ask for a subpoena to have your account holders names released to see if anyone matches the names in New York. I will leave your bank so buried in paper work, you'll be retired before you're finished."

Mr. Cutler's cheeks were bright red and he was having a hard time maintaining his composure. "I will have you know that there is nothing out of order in this bank. We just do not have the cash in our bank to cover his account holdings."

"You're complaint was that you didn't know who he was. Now you are back to what the teller said at the window, that you don't have that much in cash. So, what is it? Cash or identity?"

There was a knock on the door and an older woman came in. Mr. Cutler stood and she saw his obvious distress. "Gracie called me and told me there was a problem that I might need to address."

Meg stood and addressed the woman. "I'm Detective Megan Riley from upstate New York. As I was explaining to Mr. Cutler, Sam Craig is trying to close his account here. I'm down in Virginia working on a case with Sheriff Mueller from Creek River. During our investigation, we found that there are some people who are committing crimes using Mr. Craig's money. Before they break into his account here in Beaumont, we are trying to close it. But Mr. Cutler is saying that Sam cannot close his account."

"Derek, what is the problem with closing this account?"

"It's just that the account is so large. As I was trying to explain, we don't have that amount of cash in the bank, nor do we know that he really is the account owner," he said in a tight voice.

"As I tried explaining, one of the men who has been defrauding Sam of his money is in Langford. We came here directly from Sam's attorney's office after being advised to close this account," Meg interjected. "We don't want to cause any problems. My understanding was that once the estate issues were resolved, that Sam would redeposit the funds. But, now that he is getting the run around trying to close the account, so, maybe it won't be advisable for him to deposit his full inheritance here." Meg spread her hands out and then shrugged. She saw the cool look the woman gave to Mr. Cutler.

"Then by all means, Derek, close the account."

"But mother, the account has over $700,000 in it!"

"Mother?" Sam finally said something and looked between them. He smirked a little at Mr. Cutler. "May I say something for myself…Mrs. Cutler?"

"Certainly, but why don't we go into the conference room? I always find Derek's office stuffy."

They went back down the hall into the lobby, where all the tellers were watching. The conference room had several large windows that made Meg feel like they were in a fishbowl. All the tellers and people in the lobby could see them. She knew why Derek had the office down the hall away from everyone.

After, they settled around the table, with Mrs. Cutler at the head and her son sitting on the side near the door. She smiled at Sam. "Alright, what is it you wanted to say to me?"

"I really didn't intend to come here and cause a problem. But I just found out today that the lawyer that I trusted, who did all the estate work for me, has been stealing money from me. I hired a new lawyer over in Langford. It looks like they may have been tracing me by my debit card transactions. So, I need to have cash. While I understand that I have a lot of money here, it is mine and I need it."

"I do understand your concern. The bank will do whatever we can to accommodate your needs. But my son is correct that we don't have that much in the vault. We can give you some cash today. We would have to request cash in order to give it to you all in cash. It will take us several weeks to get that much cash from the reserves. We are also required to report large withdrawals to the IRS."

"But it's still my money."

"Yes, it is. We could do a couple of other things to protect your money if you feel threatened by those you trusted. We could break up the account into smaller accounts and put some in a trust, so that it cannot be touched. You might even want to transfer the funds to another bank."

"Is it alright if I asked a couple of questions?" Meg interrupted the exchange. Sam looked exasperated, but nodded. "The problem is really the size of the withdrawal and having it all available in cash. So, is it possible for you to write several cashier checks that Sam can cash at other banks or here in a few days?"

"Well, that is also a possibility. But does that really make a difference?"

"Yes, the concern is that Sam doesn't want to have an account that can be traced. Even if the cashier's checks aren't cashed, it closes the account."

"The problem would be the sizes of the checks. No bank will cash a check for more than $5,000, so that is a lot of cashier's checks."

"Is it possible for Sam and me to talk in private for a few minutes?"

"Certainly. Derek, I want to talk to you in private as well."

They waited until the door closed. Meg had a plan that she hoped Sam would agree to. They talked for longer than a few minutes. Meg could see the Cutlers talking in the lobby. After a while, she got Sam to agree to her idea. Mrs. Cutler was satisfied with the arrangement and the possibility of the eventual full inheritance being deposited into her bank when they resolved the issues with the trust.

Sam left the bank still frustrated, but with cash in his pocket. Once in his car, Sam drove back to Creek River. As they came into town, Sam finally broke his silence, "I guess I owe you for helping me out with the bank."

"That comes with experience, Sam. I knew you wouldn't get anywhere by just getting angry. And you weren't going to get it all in cash no matter what. The world doesn't operate in large sums of money anymore."

"Yeah, I guess. Still seems wrong that I can't have all my money in cash."

"I know. See that white house by that church? That's where I'm staying."

"Is Pastor Jake going to be here? I'm not sure I want to see him right now. I feel really bad about his wife."

"He might be. You know he wouldn't blame you. That's not the way he is."

"I'm just not ready to see him or to talk to him. Not sure I ever will be. I know you all blame the creatures for what happened, even to your father."

"Look, let's not talk about that right now. I just want to get the journal for you and then see if we can get Boon to tell us what it says. If you drop me off, I'll meet you over by the Post Office."

"Okay, but don't take too long. It's getting late and I want to be back up on the mountain tonight."

Meg nodded and got out of the car. She went in through the kitchen door. Hearing voices in the living room, she snuck through the kitchen and practically ran down the hall to the guest room. She found the backpack she had used that day on the mountain and dumped it out onto the bed. Frowning, she went through everything and didn't see it. She opened the drawer on the nightstand and pulled out a notebook and Bible that Mrs. Zimmer had given her, but it wasn't there either. Turning to the closet, Meg pulled out her suitcase and carryon bag to look through them. She began to get upset and looked through all her clothes. The journal just wasn't there.

Meg went back down the hall to the voices. She found the Zimmers and a few other couples in the living room, and they all looked up at her. "Excuse me. Margaret, can I talk to you in the kitchen for a moment?"

"Sure, dear." She got up and followed Meg.

"I'm sorry to disturb you. But I'm missing something from my room. I had a little leather bound journal that was kind of old. I found it up on the mountain and brought it back with me. Did you by chance see it lying around anywhere?"

"I don't think so. How big is it?"

"It's about the size of the notebook you gave me. It's a handwritten journal. I've got to find it."

"I don't know where it could be. I haven't gone into your room since you came back down the mountain. It's been so busy with the memorial and everything."

"I just hoped that maybe you saw it. I found out who it belongs to and I want to give it back to him."

"Well, I'll keep an eye out for it and let Pastor Zimmer know too. If we find it, I'll be sure to let you know."

"Just so you know. It's written in a foreign language. It's really important that I find it."

Meg went back to the room and looked everywhere again. She knew she was going to have to tell Sam she lost the journal, the journal that they hoped would explained everything.

CHAPTER 45

Reggie was sitting on the side lawn of the Zimmer's waiting for Meg. It was hot outside even in the shade, but he wanted a few minutes to talk to her alone before she went inside. Margaret had been fussing around pulling together a meal for her houseguests from the leftovers at the Memorial Service. Jake had put Richie down for a late nap and had stayed in the room with him.

Finally, Reggie saw her walking down the side of the dirt road toward the house. He got up and met her halfway. As he reached her, Reggie pulled her cell phone out of his pocket and handed it to her. "Next time, make sure you have this thing on you. My first thought was that Sam was the kidnapper, and you were gone again. I don't want to relive that ever again."

Meg took the cell and smirked at Reggie. "I have to say, I never thought you'd be worried about me!"

"Seems a lot of things have changed for us."

"I guess so. This trip to Virginia has definitely changed me."

"Okay, so we need to talk about what happened today."

"Look, I knew as soon as the door closed on the car, I shouldn't have left with Sam. But in the end, it was for the best."

"Problem is it made you look flaky to Mueller. I don't like having to make excuses for you and it discredits you as a detective in his eyes."

"Well, I did call."

"We can go round for round here, but that's not going to get us closer to finding those kids. Fill me in on what's going on with Sam."

"What happened with your leads?"

"Start with Sam, I'll fill you in."

"Can we at least go inside the house? I'm thirsty and it's hot out here."

They walked together back to the house. Margaret looked relieved to see them and came over and hugged Meg. After Meg got a glass of water, they went on the back porch so they could talk. She told Reggie about the money and how Sam had wanted to close his account. She explained the arrangement they made with the bank and how she helped Sam. Then, Reggie told Meg about the dead ends in Langford. The only place that positively said that Lynch was a foreigner was the motel where he was staying. But no one had seen him in days.

Meg was quiet for a few moments and then explained to Reggie about Donovan and the journals. "Problem is that journal that I took from Boon's cabin is lost. I'm positive it's here someplace, but I can't find it."

"Why is it so important?"

"It's just that it belongs to Sam. After seeing how everyone is trying to steal from him, I feel badly that I'm a part of it too."

"It's not like you stole it."

"Didn't I? I took it from the cabin because I knew it was one of the journals that O'Leary's daughter talked about. She said they held the truth about this whole legend. I wasn't thinking about Sam or how it didn't belong to me. I was just thinking that I wanted answers."

"And what's wrong with that?"

"Let's just say, I've developed a conscience down here. Or maybe I feel badly for Sam. He doesn't deserve the life he's been stuck with."

"Yeah, he didn't deserve to be kidnapped and hooked into this. But he is an adult now and is making a choice to be in the life he's in. He has all that money…."

"It's not that simple and you know it, Captain."

"Oh, it's Captain again?"

"Sorry. But you're sounding all bossy. Sam is leading a life that he would never have had to lead if Trevor Grant hadn't killed his mother and kidnapped him when he was ten. Yet, in spite of that, he isn't the suspect. He's innocent in all of this and just wants to be left alone."

"Alone with those creatures. Who are responsible for the accident that took Sarah's life."

"I know all that, and that's what makes this so hard."

"Where does this leave our investigation now?"

"We need to find Lynch and hope he leads us to Clancy and the kids."

"Mueller is ready to go back to Langford tomorrow. Or we can ditch him and follow Mick's leads ourselves."

Meg sighed. "Problem is, I haven't talked to Jake since that day in the hospital when you and Pastor Walt came down. I've got to tell him about what happened on the mountain."

"Talk to him tonight. He doesn't leave for New York until tomorrow with the Ryersons."

"I just wanted to talk to him in private though."

"Why? Oh, is this about your religious experience in the cabin?"

Meg blushed. "It wasn't really like that, Reggie. But yes, I want to talk to him about it. All those years, he tried to get me to see God the way he does and I couldn't. It was as if everyone was telling me and I couldn't understand it. Jake always said he was praying for me, I just want him to hear from me that I finally understand salvation."

"And you don't think someone already told him?"

"No, Pastor Walt and Millie totally understand me wanting to talk to Jake myself. Once I explained things to Margaret, she understands too. They won't tell him because they know how important it is for me." Meg chuckled a bit. "When I first got here, I thought Margaret was this overbearing woman, but she's really so sweet. We've talked so much and she even gave me this really easy-to-read Bible. She's answered so many questions. I'm going to feel really bad leaving her."

Reggie laughed with her. "You getting soft on me, Riley."

"Nope, just saved. Why don't we go in and see if Margaret has supper ready? I never ate lunch."

They went in to see Jake sitting with Richie in the living room. Jake's parents and the Ryersons were with him. Meg made eye contact with Jake's mother who looked away. Reggie saw the exchange and led Meg to the kitchen. "Don't let it bother you."

"I can't do this...."

"What's wrong, dear?" Margaret asked as she came out of a pantry door with a package of napkins.

"It's nothing," Meg said with a tight smile.

"It's something, I can see it all over your face, and I heard what Reggie said. You can tell me."

"Well, I don't think Jake's parents are too happy to see me here. Maybe it would be better if I just took my plate in my room."

Margaret set the napkins down and took Meg's hands. "You are a guest in my house, and you haven't done anything to be ashamed about and hide in your room. The Petersons are leaving to fly back to New Jersey tonight. Right after the meal, Cal will be driving them to Beaumont."

"You don't know the history between me and Jake."

"Yes, I do. Not only did Pastor Jake tell me about your past together before you came, but Sarah also told me. She spoke very highly of you and told me how you two were getting to know each other."

"They did? Now, I'm just embarrassed."

"There's no reason for you to be. You will sit at the table with us, right next to me. Maybe tonight, you'll get the chance to tell Jake about your decision."

"I hope I can. I want to tell him before he leaves and heads back to New York."

"For now, help me finish getting supper to the table."

Meg looked at Reggie who shrugged with a noncommittal look. She picked up the package of napkins and began to place them on the plates on the table. After the meal, Meg disappeared into the guest room. She hunted again for the journal as she listened to the Petersons saying their good-byes to Richie.

Meg waited for a while after they left and then wandered out to the kitchen. Jake was sitting at the dining room table with Richie who was coloring. Jake looked up at her and then quickly looked down. The look made Meg's heart drop. She went to the kitchen and took an apple from a bowl. Feeling nervous, she bit into the apple. She said a silent prayer asking for the right words and went back to the table.

"Hey," Meg said sitting down. "What are you coloring?"

"It's Mickey!" Richie answered with a big smile at Meg. She couldn't help smiling at the adorable little boy who looked so much like Sarah with his big brown eyes.

"That's great and you're doing a wonderful job."

"Thanks!"

She sat for a while watching him color and could feel Jake's unease with her presence. After a few long, painful minutes, Jake got up and went to the kitchen. She heard him getting out a glass and pouring a drink. Richie dropped the crayon and ran to the kitchen to get a drink from his father.

The moment passed as Margaret came in and smiled at her. Meg shook her head and got up from the table. As she was going to leave, Margaret asked, "Did you ever find that notebook you were looking for earlier?"

"No, I've torn the room apart looking for it. I don't remember taking it from the room, so I have no idea where it could have gotten to."

"Why don't we look in the living room? Maybe you did bring it out and just don't remember. The past few days have been very busy around here with extra folks in the house and such."

The two women went in the other room and started looking under furniture. Jake used the opportunity to cut up an apple for Richie and go outside on the deck. Reggie was out there snoring in a lawn chair. Meg heard them leave and plopped down on the couch.

"He doesn't leave until tomorrow. There's still plenty of time," Margaret started looking at all the books in the built in bookcase.

"I thought this would be so easy to tell him. But it's hard to talk to someone who is ignoring you."

"It's been a difficult time for him. Just be patient. The right time will come."

Meg tried a few more times throughout the evening to talk to him, but he seemed to just sidestep her. Finally, he took Richie to his room and didn't come back out. The night had passed and Meg still hadn't spoken to Jake. Sitting out on the deck looking up at the stars, Meg thought about Jake again. She knew he had to deal with his grief. It was so hard to see him suffering and know that she wasn't welcome in his life right now.

CHAPTER 46

Meg wandered into the spare room where Jake was packing the last of Richie's clothes. "So, you're just about ready to leave?"

Jake looked up and then nodded. "This is all our stuff. Pastor Walt and Millie will be traveling home with me."

"That's good. I'm glad that they will be able to stay with you for a while."

"Well, at least until after the funeral. I'm going to have to…. What about you? When do you think things will be wrapped up down here?"

"Reggie and Jesse are tracking down the lead on Lynch. He's been hiding out in a dive in Langford. I think Mick has a lead on where he may have stashed the kids. We should be wrapping it up in a few days."

"Mick," Jake said putting another shirt in the suitcase. "Who would have thought he'd be the one to find those illusive answers?"

"We would have found them if it wasn't for the accident."

"Yeah, maybe. How's your Dad?"

"He should be getting discharged tomorrow to a rehab. Hopefully, he will be able to fly again in a few weeks, so he can go home. But he's done with work. I just hope he can be back to golfing by next spring."

There was an awkward silence between them. Meg cleared her throat. "Jake, there's been something I've wanted to talk to you about."

"I'm not sure that now's a good time…."

"Well, maybe it's not the perfect time. But I couldn't talk to you before the memorial service and you're about to get on a plane to go home, I just need to tell you…."

Jake sighed. "Look, I think I know what you're going to say. I can't do this."

"Part of the problem is you're *assuming* you know what I'm going to say."

"I've noticed you watching me, waiting to be alone with me. This isn't appropriate, not now at least. I can't even think beyond today."

"The door is wide opened and I would have no problem having this discussion with you in front of the Zimmers or the Ryersons. It's not at all what you think. Yes, I was in love with you and was jealous of you and

229

Sarah, but the key word here is 'was.' Something happened to me down here, on that mountain. Out of everyone in my life, you are the one person that I want to share this with, but I haven't been able to."

"What are you talking about Meg? You always talk in riddles." Jake sat wearily on the end of the bed and dropped his head into his hands.

Meg stood staring at his stooped shoulders. His hair was longer than she ever remembered seeing it as it fell forward over his hands. She wanted to comfort him, but didn't move. Her eyes filled with tears at his misunderstanding. "I'm sorry. It really isn't what you think, but I won't trouble you anymore."

Meg walked out of the room and looked down the hall. She didn't want to see anyone, at least not right then. She could hear voices coming from the kitchen. Walking through the Zimmer's bedroom, Meg went out the sliding glass door onto a private deck. After escaping the house, she headed toward the church. She didn't want to go there either, but didn't know what to do.

Finally, she turned to the woods and the mountain. She wandered for a while until she found a huge rock. She climbed on the rock and sat down in the cool of the pine woods. Listening to the sounds of the wind through the pines, Meg wondered if she would ever get another chance to talk to Jake. He was shut down, lost without Sarah. All she wanted to do was tell him how Hank had explained to her about God and about her decision on the mountain. She had also hoped that she could get some advice from him about Boon.

Meg sat there for a long time, until she realized the sun had shifted and that Jake was probably gone with the Ryersons back to New York. As she climbed from the rock, a soft noise caught her attention. Fear shot through her as she realized her mistake. She turned slowly to see the black creature only a few feet from her, watching her. She looked around and didn't see any others, or Sam.

"I feel strange talking to you, but I know Sam does." He cocked his head as if listening. "I'm friends with Sam. I know a long time ago that meant something. I'm not here to hurt you or Sam. I just want to go back to the parsonage."

Meg slowly began to back away. After a few steps, he advanced toward her. The hairs on his neck stood up and his eyes took on a deep red glow. Meg froze. He walked up to her and sniffed her. As he began to growl, she closed her eyes waiting for him to attack. When nothing happened, she opened her eyes and looked around her. He was sitting in front of her, facing away from her looking into the woods. Meg looked up and saw a shadowy figure coming toward them.

"What is it?" she whispered. The creature got up and gently took her jeans in his sharp teeth, pulling at her. "What are you doing?" He yanked again, then turned and growled again at the figure that was coming toward them.

Meg turned and ran with the creature right at her side. As they ran deeper into the woods, he ran ahead of her, and she followed him. Finally, she collapsed in the weeds near a creek. The creature growled again and was near frenzy trying to make her continue to follow.

"No," she gasped. "I can't run anymore."

He pulled at her shirt with teeth, ripping it in his anxiety to get her to move again. She stumbled to her feet and followed, surprised when he disappeared right in front of her. As she stared at the dense foliage, the creature's head appeared. She went to him and saw he was in a small hole. He backed in making room for her. Meg wasted no time, climbing into the small den with him. The space was so small, Meg had to sit with her arms around her legs, bent over to keep from hitting her head on the roof of the cave. Immediately, Meg felt claustrophobic with the large creature right against her. But the fear of who was following them was so much more intense.

Meg tried to calm her ragged breathing, so that she wouldn't be heard. Although alert, the black creature laid down, pressed up against Meg. For a few long minutes, Meg sat listening for sounds indicating they were still being followed. As she was about to say something, she heard a cell phone ring.

"What," the voice was very close. There was a long pause. Meg felt the creature tense near her. She put her hand on his back and gently petting him, trying to keep him calm. "Just deal with it....I'm on the trail of that black creature. Some woman is with it though."

Meg leaned forward to try to see out of the small opened. The creature made a low sound in his throat. Looking into his face, she saw the eyes taking on a deep glow. She turned her attention back to the opening, but couldn't see anything but the thick foliage blocking the opening.

"It's not your concern....No! I dealt with that nosey mountain man. I can certainly deal with a broad....Riley? I don't know who it was....Look, I don't care about some woman. I'll get rid of these hounds, you take care of the financial mess." Meg heard the man start walking away. After a long time, Meg was sure he was gone, but the creature still was tense and hadn't moved.

Finally, she leaned close and whispered. "I think that was Lynch by his accent. It looks like he is hunting you. We need to find Sam."

Meg started to move to leave the small cave, and the creature moved blocking the opening. He growled at her, showing his teeth. Meg put her hands up as if in surrender and settled against the back of the cover. With his body blocking the opening, the creature laid down again watching Meg. A few minutes later, Meg heard the sound of someone walking by the cave again and realized Lynch, or whoever he was, hadn't left.

CHAPTER 47

The plane taxied down the runaway at Albany Airport. Jake watched the trees and building rush by as he looked out of the window. Richie was just waking up next to Millie. As the plane came to a stop at the terminal, they all began to collect their bags. Richie reached for Jake, who picked him up as he handed the carry-on bag to Pastor Walt. They followed the other passengers out of the plane and through an area where others were waiting to board. Reggie's oldest son would be waiting for them on the lower level near baggage claim to give them a ride back to Granelle.

Pastor Walt led them to the escalator to go down to the lower level. Jake shifted Richie to his other arm, so he could grab the handrail. He could see Greg Bennett standing with other people near the conveyor belt looking over their heads to spot the Ryersons and Jake. Their suitcases were already starting to come through the opening from the plane. But Jake was focused on Greg who was the spitting image of his father, and he had the same expression Reggie always had when there was bad news.

When Greg spotted them, he quickly made his way through the crowd and reached the escalator as they were getting off.

"What's wrong?" Jake asked before anyone said anything.

"What makes you think something is wrong?" Greg asked. He reached to take one of the carryon bags from Pastor Walt, looking away from Jake.

Jake put his hand on Greg's shoulder. "I know something is wrong because I know your father. I've seen that look a thousand times."

Greg looked around at the concerned faces. "I guess you didn't get Dad's messages."

Pastor Walt pulled out his phone and turned it on. "We can't get messages in flight," Jake said ignoring the phone. "Just tell us. Is something wrong with Brian? Or your father?"

"No, it's Detective Riley. Dad said they can't find her anywhere. He was wondering if you had seen her before you left."

Millie gasped, "Please, no more." She looked up at Jake and saw Richie looking troubled. "Why don't you men get our bags and let me get Richie something to drink. Come on, honey," she said reaching up to take the small boy from Jake's arms. Jake let her take him and walked a few paces away with Greg and Pastor Walt.

"Okay, what happened?"

"After you left, Mrs. Zimmer went to find her. She said that she was troubled that Detective Riley didn't come out to say good-bye to all of you. Dad thought she was going to try to talk to you before you left. But she wasn't around. The Zimmers got a bunch of people to look all over Creek River and can't find her. Dad and the sheriff are over in Langford tracking down some guy. Everyone has been waiting to hear if you saw her before you left."

"Actually, I did see her about a half hour before we left."

"Oh good," Pastor Walt said smiling. "Then, she told you."

Jake sighed. "Look Walt, like I told Meg, I'm not ready to hear what she has to say. It's too soon. And I'm surprised you would encourage her like this."

"Encourage her? Jake, what are you talking about? We all thought you'd be happy to hear that she finally made a decision for Christ."

Jake looked stunned. "What? That's what she was going to talk to me about?"

"You didn't let her talk to you? Oh, Jake! I know you are mourning Sarah, but I thought you would be happy to hear about Meg."

Jake sat down on a bench and hung his head. The crowd around the baggage claims began to dissipate. "When? When did this happen and how did I miss it?"

Pastor Walt laid his hand on Jake's shoulder. "Well, we all knew, but Meg wanted to tell you herself. But she wanted to wait until after the Memorial Service. Young Hank Boon led her to Christ on the mountain, in the hermit's cabin."

"What made the difference? Why would she never listen before?"

Greg cleared his throat. "Sorry, but Dad's calling again. What am I suppose to tell him?"

Jake reached up and took the phone from Greg. "Reggie, this is Jake."

"Did Greg tell you?" Reggie asked.

"Yes, Meg came into the room when I was finishing packing up. I told her I wasn't ready to talk to her about anything. I didn't listen to her and practically threw her out of the room. She just left. I don't have a clue where she went."

Reggie was quiet for a minute. "Was she upset?"

"I guess she would be now that I know what it was she wanted to talk to me about. Some pastor I end up being when I won't even talk to someone about God."

"Don't start that right now, Jake. It won't help us figure out where she might be. Her car and purse are still at the Zimmer's house. So, it's not like she was planning on going too far. Any ideas?"

"I'd say check with Brian, but if her car is there...."

"We checked there anyway. Her stepmother said she hasn't been there. Jesse and I are heading back to Creek River now. We'll find her."

"Reggie, did you ever find Lynch?" Reggie hesitated a moment too long. "I'll take that as a no. What about Sam and those creatures? Are they still roaming around Creek River?"

"We don't know. But if they are, that might be a good thing. Meg took off with Sam after the service yesterday and they kind of bonded."

"Bonded? What's that mean?"

"It's more than I want to get into on the phone. But from what Meg told me, she and Sam are friends and that means something to those animals. I guess it's like having a mean dog, but if the master says you're okay, you're okay."

"What are you going to do though?"

"Jesse's got an old coon hound that's a good tracker. We're going back to Creek River and hopefully have Meg back to the Zimmer's by supper."

"That old dog didn't find Timmy."

"You're the praying man, Jake. Start praying. Put my son back on the phone." Jake handed the phone back to Greg with a sigh. Pastor Walt patted his shoulder and then went to track down Millie. Jake sat listening to Greg's side of the conversation, knowing that if anything happened to Meg, he was responsible. Closing his eyes, Jake pleaded with God to protect Meg.

* * *

Reggie put the phone back in his pocket as Jesse flew through the winding mountain road back to Creek River. "Anything?" Jesse asked.

"Well, she did have a brief talk with Jake that didn't go very well. Looks like she might have just taken off to cool off."

"Well, she does have a tendency to be a bit impulsive."

"But she's not a rookie. She left everything behind."

"Yep, just like she did at the church yesterday when she took off with the suspect."

"Sam is no longer considered a suspect."

"Maybe not to you, but he will be to me until proven otherwise. He was on that mountain when they all disappeared."

"But as we already explained to you, Sam would have no reason to take those kids and do the ritual. He already is the keeper."

"And Clancy isn't a kid, and he's still missing. He was a clear threat to Craig and those animals. Boon told us that himself. Those are my people that are all still missing."

Reggie wanted to argue, but he knew that Clancy was a different matter. Boon had convinced them that Sam had ordered Clancy stopped and no one has heard from Clancy since. Right now, Meg was missing and he wasn't about to argue with Jesse about Sam. He would deal with that when Meg was found.

As they neared Creek River, Jesse stopped in front of a broken down mobile home. They got out of the vehicle and an old man stepped out onto the dilapidated front porch.

"Where's Tom at?" Jesse asked walking up to the old man.

"Over yonder," he pointed toward a structure that was made from plywood.

As they walked over, Jesse yelled, "Tom Meyer, this is Sheriff Mueller. I need to find Boon."

Tom came out of the shed wiping his hands on a dirty rag. He looked sheepishly at the two law men. "What y'all want Boon for? He done something wrong?"

Jesse stopped a few feet from Tom, halting Reggie too. "Nope. That girl he's sweet on is missing. We need to know if he's shacked up with her."

Reggie started to refute Jesse, but Jesse shushed him. Boon came out of the shack and pushed past Tom. He walked right up to the sheriff. "What do you mean, missing?"

"Just what word don't you understand professor? You know anything about it?"

Boon's eyes narrowed and he looked over at Reggie. "Thought she was with you."

"No, we've been over in Langford," Reggie answered. "Meg stayed here wanting to see off the Ryersons and Jake. Did she come here looking for you after they left?"

"I haven't seen her since we came off the mountain a few days ago. Just been here and there visiting my kin."

"Are you sober enough to help us track her through the mountain?" Jesse asked. Reggie could smell the gin too.

"Guess I am. What makes you think she'd go on the mountain?"

"All of Creek River has been searched. Her car is still at the parsonage. No other place to go unless you walked out of town, but we would have seen her on the way in."

Boon looked between the two and then nodded. "I'll help, but I do it my way. It's my mountain and those creatures are up there."

"Okay, let's go."

"No, I get some kin, and we'll meet you at the parsonage. I take it that's where she was last seen?"

"Yep. And we'll do it your way." Boon nodded and walked back toward Tom.

Reggie followed Jesse back to the sheriff's car and got in. "Think that's a good idea. He reeks of gin."

Jesse drove away and looked back to the trailer to see the old man with a shotgun. "No one knows those mountains like Boon. Since he's also so taken with this girl, he will seriously track her down. It's whiskey not gin… it's hard to tell if he smelled from drinking or from working on the still."

"The still. Are you telling me they are bootleggers?"

"Best ones this side of the mountain."

"And you let them get away with it?

"The Meyers and the Boons are a huge clan and they've been doing this for generations. They don't have much of anything. Those that found God, because of the church, don't run the whiskey, but those that do support the whole clan. You've seen how destitute those Boons are that live in the Hollow. They'd be worse off than they are if I stopped this."

Reggie stared out the window at the mountains. He wanted to argue, but was too old and tired. All he wanted to do was find Meg. Then, he was going to go home to New York. Last thing he wanted was to get involved with bootleggers.

CHAPTER 48

Jesse's old coon hound tracked Meg's scent to a large boulder in the woods. Then, he started trembling and howling. He tried running the other way, pulling on the leash. Finally, Jesse had someone take the old dog out of the woods to bring him home. While everyone was concerned over the dog, Reggie and Boon were trying to look for a trail. Reggie spotted the large footprint before Boon did.

"It was here," he said to Boon as he pointed to the soft dirt near the boulder. Boon knelt down next the print. He saw a few of the smaller footprints left by Meg and followed the tracks with his eyes.

He stood and walked over to Jesse. "There are too many people here. They've been trampling all over the place. You choose two people to stay with us and I will choose two. The rest go home."

One of the townies started to argue and Jesse put up his hand. "Nope, we do this Boon's way. Reggie and Trent, you stay with me. Who you pickin'?"

"Hank and Tom."

"Hank?" the townie complained. "He's nothing, but an ignorant kid!"

Boon just stared at him. Then, he pulled Jesse to the side. "At least one of the creatures is here too. Get those people out of the woods, they are dangerous. This isn't a game."

Jesse nodded and made his deputy take the others back to the parsonage. As Jesse watched them leaving, he heard many complaining they would search on their own, but he noticed more than a few relieved faces in the crowd. Reggie and Boon talked together and looked at the trail that led up the mountain. Once the group was gone, Boon called Hank over to look at the trail.

Hank nodded and Reggie gestured for the others to join them. "This might sound hard to believe, but it looks like Meg is actually with that animal, and they are running from the distance apart and depth of the prints. But it looks like someone is chasing them."

"Where are they headed?" Jesse asked.

Boon pointed up the mountain, "Looks like they are headed to the river pass, near the Hollow."

"And you're sure from the tracks that Meg is with the creature, not running from it?"

"Only way to know for sure is to track them down."

"Let's go," Reggie said as he started up the hill. "She's been gone long enough already, and I want her back tonight."

"Taking this a bit personal? Is it wise for you to go with us?" Trent asked.

Reggie turned and looked him dead in the eye. "You better believe it is. And I'll bet you any amount of money that Boon, Hank, and the sheriff are taking this personally too."

Tom cleared his throat. "I'm on board too. I ain't losing no one else. Let's go."

Tom walked up passed Reggie, who was still looking down at Trent. "What about you?"

"Sheriff picked me himself. I might not know this girly, but I'm kin to the Boons, Tom, and Hank. If they are taking this personal like, then I stand by my kin."

"Then, let's go." Reggie turned and followed Boon who was already way ahead of them following the tracks.

* * *

Meg felt like she was suffocating in the cave between the heat of the day and having the creature lying against her with his thick fur.

"Hey," she whispered. His eyes opened just a slit, glowing red in the cave. "You should be able to lead us around whoever it is out there. Do you know where Sam went? Is he at Boon's cabin?" The creature lifted his head as if listening. "Even if he isn't, I know Boon has guns. I can at least defend myself from that person. Or can you lead me back to the town?"

He turned and poked his head out of the cave opening, then crawled out. Meg crept toward the opening, but waited. A few moments later, he was back. Meg crawled out and went right to the stream. As she reached out her hand toward the water, she stopped.

"Is he around?" she whispered looking at the woods around them. He stood still and alert. Meg's need for a drink overrode her fear. Cupping water, she took a long drink and finally splashed some of the cool mountain water on her face. Once she felt refreshed, she turned to the creature. "I have no idea why you saved me, but I trust you with my life right now. Can you take me someplace safe?"

The creature got up and went to the embankment with Meg following him. He stayed alert, but didn't run like he had to get to the river bed. About an hour later, he stopped near a clearing. Meg looked around, recognizing where she was. "The Hollow?" She looked down at her protector, who was looking up at her. "Okay, this is good. But you need to get out of here fast. They blame you for Clancy...." Meg hesitated for a moment. She knelt down and took his big head in her hands. "I don't know what you or your pack did. People are missing, there was the accident that my Dad was hurt in and Sarah died. This morning I was ready to hunt you down myself. But now.... If you do understand me, find Sam and go as far away from people as possible."

The creature backed away from her with a low growl. Then, turned and took off. Meg stood, trying to watch him until he vanished. She turned and ran to Ma's cabin.

Meg banged on the door and called out for Ma. "Good heavens, what ya doin'?"

"Oh Ma! I was just chased up the mountain by the man I believe kidnapped your granddaughter. I lost him down near where the creek runs off the mountain. Can you please see if Clint and some of the other men can go with me back to the creek?"

"Ya gonna have to go to Clint youself. He won't agree with me since Clancy gone away."

"Which cabin is Sissy's?"

"Closest to the ole well."

"Okay," Meg turned to leave, then turned back. "I just want you to know that I came to know your Jesus, personally. Hank explained it to me and I prayed with him."

Ma's face lit up. "Praise God! I's prayin' ya would!"

Meg startled Ma by giving her a hug. Embarrassed, Ma pushed her to go out the door to find Sissy. Heading toward Sissy's cabin, Meg ran into Clint and a few of his buddies.

"What y'all doin' here? Hank bring ya back?" Clint looked around expecting to see the kid.

"No, I was actually going to your cabin to find you."

"Hmpf. What ya want with me?"

"The man who took Erica just chased me up here. I hid in some cave near the creek until he went away. We need to get him, but alive, so he can tell the sheriff where he has Erica hidden."

"Ya, thinkin' I believe ya?" Clint turned and started walking away with a laugh.

"I don't care if you believe me or not. But I wonder what your wife will think when she finds out how close we are to finding her baby sister and her husband refused to help me…just 'cause I'm a woman."

Clint spun around and got right in Meg's face. "Ya listen good. Ya stay away from Sissy. Clancy ain't here and I'm in charge."

Meg backed away from Clint and shouted, "You're just a coward, Clint! That's why you won't go with me. Hey, are there any Boon kin here that want to bring Erica home?"

Meg saw a few people starting to come out of the woods. She took off to her right into the woods and up the back side of the cabins. Clint yelled and took chase, but Meg was faster. She got to the cabin before he did, shouting along the way. Sissy was standing on the stoop as Meg came to an abrupt stop.

"Sissy," she gasped. "The man who has your sister is down near the creek pass. He chased me up the mountain. My friend, Reggie, and the sheriff went over to Langford…."

Clint ran up beside her and knocked her to the ground. "Shut up! Ya ain't sayin' nothin' to her!"

"No, Clint." Sissy said quietly, reaching down to give Meg her hand. "I done talkin' to you." As Meg got to her feet, Sissy turned to one of her cousins that had come when he heard the shouting and said, "Clint ain't a Boon. He ain't speakin' for me or my Pa. Go get your Pa and come back. We need ta bring Erica home to the Hollow."

"Sissy, ya ain't gonna do this. Ya my woman and Clancy ain't here."

"Ya right. My Pa ain't here. We's deciden what needs to be done. We Boons, not you."

With that, Sissy took Meg by the arm and led her into the cabin and closed the door in Clint's face. Meg looked astonished. "Should you have done that?"

"I ain't got much choice. Erica and Pa are gone. Hank's in Creek River still." There was a slight knock on the door and a man walked in. Meg caught her breath at the resemblance to Boon. "Uncle Si, this here is Meg that's friend of Pastor Jake." He nodded slightly, but didn't say anything. "Okay, tell him."

"Are you sure?" Sissy nodded and went to the kitchen area. Meg told him about being chased by the man up the mountain and how the sheriff was in Langford trying to find him. She left out that one of the creatures led her to the Hollow.

"...so, will you please go with me back down to the creek? I would have followed him myself if I had a gun. He may have had something to do with Clancy disappearing too."

He stood for a long moment considering her. Meg was certain she would be going down alone. Then he simply nodded and walked out. Not sure what to do, she turned to Sissy.

"Was I supposed to follow him?"

"No, he be back soon."

"I don't understand. He's definitely a Boon. How is he your uncle? And why didn't he say anything to me?"

"He's my Pa's uncle. Like cousin Boon, he ain't like outside folks."

"Maybe that's what it was that made me know he was a Boon, his disposition. Boy, he sure reminded me of Boon."

Sissy laughed making Meg blush. "Ya sweet on cousin Boon? Best take care."

"Why?"

"You needin' to wait till Boon talks to you. Iffin he feels the same, he be tellin' ya."

Meg didn't know how to respond, so she went back to the uncle. "Will your uncle actually talk to me, eventually?"

"Iffin, there's a need. The boys will be goin', Lloyd and Silas. He probably went to fetch em." Sissy went over to a side of the cabin that had a curtain drawn. She came out with a shotgun and a box and handed them to Meg. "This is Pa's. I'm askin' ya to find my kin. We ain't got much here, but us."

"I have been doing everything I can to find them." Meg looked into Sissy's bright blue eyes and saw the tears. "I know that Sam, the boy with those creatures, did not take them. No matter what anyone tries to tell you, he doesn't have Erica. I know who is doing it though. I promise I will do whatever I can to bring your Pa and sister home."

Sissy nodded and turned away before the tears spilled down her cheeks. Meg saw her wipe her cheeks as the door opened again. Meg turned to see the uncle and two boys waiting for her. She went to the door and joined the Boons.

CHAPTER 49

"Up this way," Hank called out as he found the trail that had been lost in the dense foliage. Boon caught up to his young cousin and saw the footprint in the softer dirt.

"Looks like they are still heading up to the pass. We've got to keep going." Boon turned to Hank and motioned for him to keep on tracking.

Reggie caught up to Boon and stopped him. "It's going on mid-afternoon. Do you think we really are going to catch up with her before nightfall?"

Boon considered the question and turned to Tom. "You and Hank, head on up to the pass. Even if the path takes you further, wait for us there." Tom just nodded and caught up with Hank.

"Why'd you do that?" Reggie asked. "Why would you split us up?"

"Don't mean to offend you. But they know these mountains, they're young, and tracking is second nature to these mountain folk."

"And?"

"And, this is taking us too long to get up to the pass. Those boys would have been up that mountain by now, all the way to the Hollow, even tracking. You want Meg found by nightfall, then that's how it's going to be done."

"Don't you think you should have discussed this with us or at least told us?"

No. Sheriff said this is my job. Just jawin' with you this long has cost us time. The boys is long gone. Let's go, so they ain't sitting at the Creek for long."

Reggie started to argue more, but the sheriff laid his hand on Reggie's arm and shook his head. Reggie waited until the deputy passed him too before following. Without bothering to look for any more signs of the trail, Reggie followed the three men, vowing again that he was done and back to retirement as soon as he found Riley.

* * *

Meg found these silent men disconcerting. They led her a different way to the Creek Pass than the one the black creature had taken her. But she was fine with it since she didn't want them to see his tracks. Last thing she needed was to explain why she didn't tell them about her companion that had saved her. About a half an hour into their trek through the woods, the uncle stopped and turned around. His eyes narrowed and he said something to one of his sons.

Silas took a few steps back and then ran back to a wooded spot. He yanked Clint out from a thicket of trees. "Get!" he yelled at Clint.

Instead, Clint came down to the uncle. "You's can't do this Uncle Si. She's an outsider. Ya know Clancy be rollin' in his grave iffin he know ya followin' her."

There was silence between them as the uncle stared Clint down. Finally, Clint hung his head and turned away. He kicked a stone and it flew into a tree as he stomped off. Meg watched it all. As Clint started up the incline toward the Hollow, Meg said, "Wait." Clint stopped and looked back. Meg went to the uncle, turning her back to Clint, she whispered, "Did you hear what he said? Did he just say, 'Clancy would be rolling in his grave?' What grave? Sissy just asked me to bring her Pa home. Did anyone ever find him?"

The uncle stood up straighter and shifted his shotgun in his hands. "Get him," his voice was deep. Silas went to get Clint who still stood looking confused.

As Silas reached him, Meg shouted, "Take the gun first." Before Clint could even react, Silas had taken the shotgun from him and began to haul him back toward his father. He stopped him about a foot from the old man.

"Where be Clancy?" the old man spit out.

"How'd I know?"

The old man pointed his shotgun right in Clint's face and put his finger on the trigger. Meg felt her heart begin to race. She truly believed that if Clint didn't say the right thing, he would be shot. Clint realized that too and started stammering.

"Mr. Boon?" Meg quietly said, her voice trembling. "Please wait a minute before you pull that trigger."

The old man glared at her and then spit tobacco. "Where be Clancy?"

"I don't know," Clint whined and fell on his knees.

"Pa, I hearin' someone comin'," Lloyd said. They all looked toward the sound of someone coming through the woods. The person stopped for a moment and then ran up to them.

"Meg!" Hank shouted. "I found ya!" Hank stopped at the sight in front of him. "Uncle Si? What...?" He looked at his cousins and then at Clint trembling on the ground. When no one spoke, he turned to Meg. "What's wrong?"

"Well, ummm, we think that Clint knows what happened to your Pa. Your uncle is trying to get him to tell us."

"Pa? You know were Pa been? Why...?" Realization hit Hank and he took a step away from them. Meg watched Hank uncertain of what was going to happen. Finally, in a rage, Hank turned back to Clint grabbing the shotgun from Meg's hands. With tears coursing down his face, Hank put the gun against Clint's head. "I always knowed y'all hates my Pa. Ya had no right...."

Meg grabbed the gun and jerked it from Hank's hands as he pulled the trigger. The shot flew off into the air and hit a branch. "Hank, no! Don't ruin your life over this piece of garbage. You don't even know if he did anything."

"Ya, we's does," Silas said as Tom came running at the sound of the shot. He took in the scene and didn't say a word. Hank turned and disappeared into the woods.

"Even if you know for sure that he killed Clancy, you can't let Hank murder him. He will spend the rest of his life in jail. Besides, don't you think you owe it to Sissy and Ma to know where his body is? Don't you think your women would want to give him a proper burial?"

Meg looked around and didn't see Hank. Tom pulled her away from the Boons. "The sheriff and your friend are just behind us. We've been looking everywhere for you. What happened and how did you end up with Uncle Si and the boys? Did Clint really kill Clancy?"

"I don't have time to explain all this to you. Go back and get the sheriff, so he can stop them from killing Clint. I'll explain the rest when Reggie gets up here. But hurry, I don't think I can stop your Uncle if he decides to shoot him."

Tom took off running, and Meg turned back to the Boons. The boys had pulled Clint to his feet and dragged him to a tree. Meg ran up to stop them, but Uncle Si grabbed her. His grip on her arm was strong and unyielding. "Y'all right. We's known first."

Meg could do nothing while the boys beat Clint within an inch of his life. Finally, in a heap on the ground, Clint was begging for mercy with broken bones and blood pouring down his face. Lloyd came over and took hold of Meg so his father could speak to Clint. Pressing the shotgun to Clint's forehead, Meg heard him ask again where Clancy was and again, Clint said he didn't know.

As Meg struggled to get free from Lloyd, to her relief, she heard Jesse shout. "Si Boon, that's enough!" The old man looked up as Jesse, Reggie, and the deputy came up to them with Tom. He scowled at Tom. "If Clint broke the law, I'll deal with him."

"Not till he says where Clancy be."

"The law's the law even in the Hollow."

Reggie walked over to where Lloyd was holding Meg. Silas lifted his gun and pointed it at Reggie. The sheriff pulled out his revolver and pointed at Silas.

"Stop, everyone! Just stop! Please!" Meg shouted yanking free from Lloyd and stepped between Reggie and Silas. "We don't have time for this. Mr. Boon, did you forget the reason you were going with me? Erica. We have to find that man who has her. If Clint did kill him, Clancy's gone, we can't save him. But we still have a chance to save Erica."

"This be our kin, we does it our way."

"While I'd love to see you put a bullet in his head Uncle Si, he ain't worth losing you or your boys," Boon said as he walked into the group. His sudden appearance surprised Meg. Tom didn't say that Boon was with them. As he walked up to Meg, he looked down at her and she blushed. He smirked at her and then went up to his uncle and took the shotgun from him. "The law will take you away from your mountain and kin because of him. The sheriff's a good man, let him deal with Clint."

Si said something to Boon that Meg couldn't understand. As Boon replied, he yanked Clint to his feet. Clint moaned as Boon dragged him over to Jesse and the deputy. The deputy took out his cuffs, but Jesse stopped him. "Before I can arrest him, what evidence do you have?" He directed his question to Meg.

Meg looked at Boon, then at Si and his boys, who stood apart from them. Like Silas had already said, they knew that Clint had killed Clancy and so did she. "He told us that Clancy was in a grave. He wouldn't tell us where."

"Who fired the shot we heard?"

"That was me…and Hank. It was an accident."

"Where'd the boy go?"

"I'm not sure. He took off when he was told his Pa was dead. From the direction he went, he probably went to the Hollow."

"Okay, let's get him out of here before the entire Boon clan comes and lynches him."

"But wait! That guy, Lynch, he's up here on the mountain. He chased me up here. If we can catch him, we have a chance to find Erica, Bobbi, and Timmy."

"I'll leave that to you and Reggie…and the Boons. You've got enough help here."

Meg walked up to Jesse, so that the Boons couldn't hear her response. "Sheriff, if you leave, it's just me and Reggie, who they consider outsiders. They almost killed Clint, how are we going to stop them if we run into Sam or Lynch?"

"You're both officers of the law…."

"Do you think they will care?"

"Look, if we don't get Clint back to Creek River, he will be killed. Boon stopped this one, but probably won't be able to stop Si once the rest of the clan is here. I'd really rather arrest Clint than that old man."

Meg sighed as Jesse grabbed Clint's arm and started directing him back down the mountain path. "I can't walk far," Clint mumbled.

"It's either that or your in-laws will kill you. I can't stop the mob once Hank tells them what you've done."

Mumbling again, Clint started walking supported by the deputy. Reggie came over to Meg and watched them for a bit. "You sure that you saw Lynch?"

"Well, I doubt there are any other people on this mountain with an Irish accent. It has to be him. I heard him on his cell talking about taking out the creatures."

"How in the world did you find your way back up the Hollow? Jake always had to have Tom bring him up."

"That's a story for another time," she whispered.

Boon had come over and was listening to her. She didn't realize he was right behind her until he spoke. "It was them, wasn't it?"

Meg jumped, and turned around and saw Tom, Boon, and his kin standing right behind her. She wanted to lie, but knew she couldn't, not now. "Yes, but he saved my life. You can't hunt him, and we now know he didn't do anything to Clancy."

"But they are dangerous, and they are up here on this mountain."

"I told him to find Sam and hide. He protected me and brought me to the Hollow where I was safe."

Boon stood looking down at her, "You don't know them…."

"And you do? All I know is that I didn't even know that Lynch was in the woods about to grab me. But that creature warned me, brought me up here and protected me. Then he led me to the Hollow."

"Which one was it, Blackie?" When she crossed her arms and wouldn't answer, he nodded. "Had to be. I doubt Boss would have cared what happens to you."

"Why do you think the black one would?"

Boon shrugged and then turned to his kin. "Okay, everyone keep a look out for those animals, but for Meg's sake, don't shoot unless they come at us. Do you think you can show us where you saw that guy?"

"I already told your uncle. We were headed that way when we realized Clint was following us."

"He wasn't with you?"

"No, he was behind us. Mr. Boon called him out and he started yelling at them for going with me."

"Huh." Boon started leading them back down the hill. Meg stood frowning as the Boon men passed by her veering away from where the sheriff had disappeared with Clint. Reggie watched her and then looked at Boon's back as he started walking away. He looked back at Meg who was thinking. He was just about to say something when Meg took off after Boon.

Running past the other men, Meg ran right in front of him and stopped him. "Did Clint know about the creatures?" He tried to walk around her, but she grabbed his arm. "Stop! Did he know?"

"Everyone knew about them. They were up at the Hollow with Sam when he came looking for me."

"No, no. Your timeframe is wrong. Ma saw the creatures up at the Hollow before Jake ever came here. When we were in Ireland, he told me that the first day that he went to the Hollow, Ma told him that she had seen the devil. But nothing happened." Meg turned to Tom. "How long before Pastor Jake came did Erica disappear?"

"A couple of weeks, maybe," Tom answered with a shrug.

"You were the one that brought Pastor Jake up the mountain?"

"Yep."

"And Erica was already missing?"

"Yep."

"Where are you going with this, Meg?" Boon asked. "Aren't you just wasting time? Let's get to the pass and find that guy you saw."

Meg went to say something else, but stopped and reconsidered. She watched the men go on ahead of her, except Reggie. Something was still missing, something she still needed to work out in her head. Meg had gotten so used to bouncing ideas off her partners, first Jake, then her Dad, and most recently Reggie. She glanced over at Reggie and saw he understood.

Once the others were out of earshot, Reggie looked down the hill and quietly asked, "Okay, Riley spill it."

Tom glanced back at them, and Meg took a tentative step forward as if they were following. "Think about this for a minute. Hank said he always knew that Clint hated Clancy. While I know that Donovan was the one that set this whole thing up, got Sam to come here to meet Roscoe Harman, sent Lynch here to stage the whole thing, but how does Lynch know how to get around this mountain? As many times as Jake has been here, Tom has always had to bring him up to the Hollow."

"But does Jake know how to get around this mountain?"

"No, he didn't. Tom always had to show him. And someone who does know this mountain had to show Lynch and whoever that person is knew Erica Boon, and that she was in the Hollow."

"Do you think Clint did more than kill his father-in-law?"

"No. I think he took advantage of the situation. But someone in the Boon clan is helping Lynch."

Reggie stared at the spot where the Boons had disappeared in front of them. "Guess they're doing more than running whiskey. Which one?"

"I don't know. But I'm praying it's not one of them or we are walking into a trap."

"It wouldn't be all of them."

"But do you think they would defend us or their kin if it came down to it?"

Reggie didn't respond, but checked to be sure his gun was loaded before he followed the Boons toward the pass.

CHAPTER 50

Jake put Richie down for a nap and then went down to Pastor Walt's office. "Any word?"

"Nothing yet," Pastor Walt was sitting in his recliner, a worn Bible on his lap. "Stop beating yourself up, Jake. You didn't do anything wrong."

"I should have realized Meg wasn't trying to…. I wish I could just talk to her. Make sure she's alright. I want to talk to her about her decision and see if she understands it."

"You will have plenty of time for that. Besides, Mrs. Zimmer had a long talk with her and gave her some guidance."

Jake sat down in the easy chair near the window that matched Pastor Walt's recliner. He stared out the window and realized that the tops of some of the trees were beginning to show color. Pastor Walt watched him for a few long moments, before turning back to his Bible. He read for a while and then looked up at Jake. "Have you thought about when you want to go get Buddy?"

Jake sighed, "I forgot all about him and Felix. I guess I should get them soon. It's just…."

"There's no rush. Steve has been taking great care of Buddy and going over every day to feed the cat."

"Yeah, but that old dog probably just wants to go home. And Felix, he's going to miss Sarah so much." Jake's voice broke at the mention of his wife's name.

"Why don't you wait a few days? I'll call Steve and let him know you're staying at our place until after the services."

"I don't know how I'll be able to do this Walt."

"You will, one day at a time. You'll do it for Richie. For today, just be here. You know how Millie likes to spoil Richie…and you."

Jake sat silent for another long moment. "I don't know how I could have gotten through arranging everything if you and Millie hadn't come to Virginia."

"That was all Meg's doing."

"As much as she has fought me over my faith, I still can't believe she called you to come."

"She figured you would need your own pastor down there. She knows how close our families have been since you became my associate pastor all those years ago."

"And then, she's still working on the case with Reggie, of all people. From what I've heard, they've been getting along great, too. No one down in Creek River even knows that when she was a cop, Reggie fired her and then totally disregarded her as a private investigator." Jake shook his head and laughed softly. "Seems like that old captain we knew has mellowed in retirement."

"Well, he doesn't have the responsibility anymore. He made a choice to help Meg and it wasn't something that was required of him to do. From what I heard, he let her be in charge and has been impressed with how she has been handling the case. Maybe they have both mellowed."

"Is that the way it is for you now? No responsibility, so you can choose how you want to serve?"

"I guess so. The church had a lot of responsibility, personalities, people in different places with God, and they all expect me to have all the answers."

"Yeah, I know that one. I remember that when Sarah was abducted, it took a long time for some people to realize I was human and made some mistakes when I got involved in looking for her. I even lost some parishioners, but gained new ones. I wonder how losing her will affect my ministry in this town."

"I've been thinking about that myself."

"It's going to be tough, isn't it? I took that mission trip, I got involved in helping down there, I went back to police work. I can almost hear the eldership now." Pastor Walt sat silently, waiting. "When Jesse Mueller gave me that badge and swore me in, it felt great. I got caught up in the investigation. Then, I got that call...."

"Did this make you reconsider the call on your life?"

Jake hesitated. "Losing Sarah has made me reconsider everything. It's been more about how I took back that badge, not about being a minister. Ever since I saw Sarah in the hospital bed fighting for her life, I've been begging God to forgive me. If I had just left it alone, come back to New York, Sarah would be alive, and so would our baby." Again, Walt waited. "Now, Meg is missing because of me. Walt, what am I going to do?"

"You need time to grieve. Take Richie and go visit your family in New Jersey. The church will understand...."

"Take a sabbatical? Like I did three years ago? If I do that, I will no longer be the pastor of Granelle Gospel. There is no way that they will continue to look at me as a person that can lead the congregation."

"It's not the same thing as what happened before. You lost your wife. The congregation will understand. They love you and Richie. There has been such an outpouring of love for you, like I haven't ever seen in Granelle."

"So, there's not one person in Granelle that will blame me for Sarah's death?"

"I know one...you."

Jake sighed and leaned back in the chair. "What am I suppose to do, Walt?"

"Get through today. His grace is sufficient for today."

CHAPTER 51

Boon was standing on the edge of the creek when Meg and Reggie finally caught up with the Boons at the pass. Uncle Si and the boys were looking for tracks to figure out in what direction they should head as Tom took a long drink from the cold spring water.

"What happened when you were here?" Boon asked. "Need to figure out where this person may have gone."

Meg pointed on the other side. "I was over there, running up the hill and then the creature disappeared into a hole. There's a small cave over there." Meg stepped on a large rock in the stream to get to the other side. She went up to the tall grasses and pushed them aside to show Boon the opening to the cave.

Boon followed her and knelt down to see inside the dark interior. "The den. This is where she had her pups."

"Pups? How many of these creatures are there?" Meg asked, her voice shaking a bit. Boon got back up and brushed the dirt from his hands.

"They're forming a nice pack."

"But I was told a long time ago that they couldn't breed. Because they are a hybrid animal they can't have offspring."

"Who told you that?"

"A professor at a college in Albany."

"Well, apparently, he was wrong. What else did he tell you that you believe?"

"I…. Does it really matter?"

"I thought that as a detective you would have sorted out the fact from fiction a long time ago when it came to these creatures."

"It's not that simple. Certain facts don't make sense. And you know that the legend we knew that was passed down is different than those old journals told you about. Anyway, how big is the pack now?"

"I saw three adults, and there were three pups."

"Were? What happened?"

"I thought Clancy had found them. Two pups were killed, the female was injured. I don't know what happened to them after that."

"I don't understand. Did Clancy kill them? Is the female alive?"

Boon looked mad and started walking away. Meg grabbed his arm. "Look, I need to know what's going on, so we can figure this out."

"I don't know! I assumed that Clancy killed the pups, but I never found out what happened. I went to the Hollow to warn him and he was gone. I assumed the creature got him, blamed myself, and then got drunk. When I finally sobered up, she was gone and so was the pup. I don't know where Sam took them. Now with Clint going to jail for killing Clancy, my whole theory about them is wrong."

Meg dropped her hand and looked back at the den. She looked around for Reggie and saw Tom sitting on the bank of the creek staring at them. The intensity of his look set her back a bit, it was almost a warning. She started saying more to Boon, but he had stomped off following his uncle. Reggie was standing near Tom and took in the whole scene. He caught Meg's attention and shook his head, just slightly. She just figured it out… and so had Reggie.

Turning, Meg called out to Boon and ran to catch up with him. "Wait." Boon stopped, but didn't turn around. Meg heard Tom coming up behind her too. "Boon, you can't blame yourself for what happened with Clancy. It wasn't the creatures or Sam who killed him. It isn't your fault. It was an outsider who came into your family. Let's just focus on finding Lynch."

"You're an exasperating woman!"

"Why? Because I'm allowing you to be human?"

"You don't get it. My whole life imploded because I got drunk all those years ago. I lost everything. Seems my response to anything is just, just get drunk."

Meg put her hand on Boon's arm, "But it doesn't need to be that way…."

Boon shook off her hand and walked up to his cousins who had found footprints leading back toward Creek River. Tom was right next to her, but she ignored him and told Boon to stop being stupid. Boon didn't acknowledge her. Instead, he caught up to his uncle, who was starting to follow the trail.

"Hold on a minute!" Meg yelled, making Uncle Si stop and squint up at her. She turned and headed back to the small cave.

"What's you doing?" Tom asked, stopping her with the barrel of his shotgun. The reaction didn't surprise Meg and she pushed the gun out of her way. She looked Reggie right in his eyes, and he pulled his revolver out.

When Tom grabbed her to physically stop her, Reggie pointed it at Tom. "Let her go," he said his deep voice like steel. Meg grabbed the barrel and yanked it out of Tom's hand. She heard the Boons shouting behind her as she wrestled with Tom. Reggie pulled him off from Meg and restrained him, bringing him to the ground. He yelled and struggled, but couldn't move under Reggie's bulk.

The boys pointed their shotguns at Meg, but one word from their father, they just froze. Uncle Si waited a few paces away. "What are you doing?" Boon yelled at them. But Meg ignored him and went over to the old man. She asked him to talk to her where Tom couldn't hear them. They walked a few paces away, but both were able to watch Reggie sitting on Tom.

"Did you know?"

The old man looked at her, "Not sure. Figurin' though."

"Mr. Boon, I figure the way he reacted, that Clancy's got to be buried right here in the Pass. But I can't let you and your sons kill Tom, anymore than I could let you kill Clint. We need to get the sheriff. He probably isn't all the way down the mountain yet."

"We's take care of our own."

"You can't. There will be evidence that can be destroyed if you and your kin find the body. We need the evidence in order to get a judge to send them to jail. This goes further than Clancy too, I believe that Tom has been taking money from Lynch to take your Erica and those kids from town."

Meg waited for him to say something, anything. But he didn't. But Boon came over. "I don't know what you think you're doing, but…."

"Hush!" the old man spit out at Boon. "Boy's done killed Clancy and brung shame on us."

"What is he talking about?" Boon asked Meg.

"I think that Tom was bringing Lynch up the mountain to try to set up Sam for these kidnappings. Somehow, Clint figured it out and used it as an excuse to kill Clancy to pin the blame on someone else. But I need to keep Tom alive, until we get to town, in order to find out where Lynch is holding Erica, Bobbi, and Timmy."

Boon looked at his uncle and then to Reggie who still had Tom pinned to the ground. He walked over to Reggie and said, "Let him up."

"We are trained…."

Boon pointed his gun to the back of Tom's head. "He ain't going anywhere. Let him up."

Reggie got up and yanked Tom to his feet. Tom looked indignant and tried to brush leaves from his shirt. "You got about ten seconds to tell us where Erica is."

"I ain't knowin' what y'all talkin' 'bout. Y'all want ta believe outsiders over ya own kin?"

"Kin? Last time I checked you were a Meyer, not a Boon."

"I's kin to you. Blood kin, just 'cause I ain't a Boon in name, don't mean nothin'."

Boon dropped his gun and grabbed the front of Tom's shirt, yanking him close. "I've spent that past two days with you. You knew how I was blaming myself for Clancy. All along you and Clint were responsible and you let me...." Boon pushed him, and he fell hard on the ground.

"If anyone's an outsider, it's you, Boon! Or should I say Larry. That's what you was called till you killed your wife and kids."

"Enough," Uncle Si said getting between them. He looked up at Reggie, "We done doin' it ya way."

"I ain't lettin' ya kill him, Mr. Boon. But we need to find those kids sooner than later. I'm tired and just want to get back to my own mountain."

Uncle Si nodded his understanding and motioned his boys over. Lloyd came over and yanked Tom to his feet. Silas laid his shotgun to the side.

"Let me go first," Boon said his face full of rage. Meg ran up and got in the middle of the men.

"Stop. We don't need to do this! Just sit him over by that tree and watch him. I found something."

"Nothing short of finding Clancy will stop...."

"That's just it. I'm pretty sure I just did. Reggie, can you come with me and look? And the rest of you, just guard him for now. Mr. Boon, can I count on you to keep your nephew and sons from doing anything?"

"Sure y'all find Clancy?"

"I found someone. Can you just wait?"

"Yep," Uncle Si directed Silas to get his gun and the two boys hauled Tom to a tree and kept him there.

"What are you thinking?" Meg asked Reggie as they walked back toward where she found the body.

"I was thinking that I'm sick of Virginia and want to get home to Vanessa. I don't care if some moonshiner is beaten up by his kin for killing one of their own and helping kidnap some kids if it means I get home that much sooner."

"Reggie, you're a decorated officer...."

"Retired. I'm here for you, in place of Jake, and once we are off this mountain, I quit."

"Well, not so fast, Captain Bennett. I think I found something in the den." Reggie turned his attention to the small opening in the mountain. Meg knelt down and pushed the tall weeds away. "Off to one side, there's a lot of loose moss. I dug down a bit and hit a body."

Reggie pulled out his cell phone. He stuck his head in the hole and used the light from the phone to shine it around the cave. He saw where Meg had found the body and crawled back out.

"We can't dig anymore without destroying the scene. What made you think to look here?"

"It was a couple of things. When I was here earlier with the creature, it really stunk in there. I thought it was just him, but when I saw the reaction from Tom, I figured that Clancy was in there somewhere. But I knew for sure when Boon told me about the puppies being killed and the female being injured. Great place to put the body if you're trying to pin the blame on Sam and the creatures too."

"What are we going to do now? They won't leave until we know that this is Clancy for sure. We can't do any more damage to the scene. I'm not sure that the Boons will let us take Tom down to Creek River without getting retribution for Clancy's death."

"Maybe Boon can help us."

"I'm not so sure about that. He wants revenge too. Guess he was closer to Clancy than most thought."

"Cause Pa's only one who gave Boon understandin' when he had the accident," a voice said from behind Meg. She turned quickly pulling out her revolver to see Hank standing near them. "Y'all found Pa?"

Meg put down her gun. "I think we did. But we can't be sure until we get the sheriff back up here. If we do anymore digging, we will ruin the crime scene and Clint and Tom will get away with murdering your Pa."

"Uncle Si gonna see them ain't touchin' nothin'. I knowed that ain't right."

"You were all set to put a bullet in Clint's head. What made you change your mind, son?" Reggie asked.

"God. I went and ask Him, and 'member, Pastor Jake sayin' that God makes things right. He says somethin' bout God repayin' bad that's been done to us. Nothin' badder than killin' one's Pa."

"You're right, there's nothing worse." Reggie stood and put a hand on Hank's shoulder. "But how do we convince your Uncle?"

"I will."

"How?"

"Clancy's my Pa."

Meg watched as young Hank walked over to his uncle and pulled him aside. As they talked quietly, Reggie nudged her and dropped his voice. "Okay, if Hank can convince the Boons to get the sheriff and bring him back, how are we going to do this?"

"I guess one of us will stay here and the other will go down with Tom and bring back the sheriff."

"And the Boons?"

"I guess we divide and conquer. Leave some, take some."

"Somewhere is the illusive Mr. Lynch too. Let me stay here with Boon and one of the boys."

"Why?" Meg asked turning her attention back to Reggie.

"Way I figure it, Boon's too mad at Tom to go with him, the old man and one son can easily keep him in line, and I don't want Hank here when we bring his father out of the cave."

"Why would you stay and not me?"

"I've seen you and Boon together. Right now, I need both of you to stay focused on the case and not each other."

"Are you kidding? The way he's been acting since we ran into him on the mountain, I'm having second and even third thoughts about…."

"Figure that out at another time. Right now, we need to wrap this part of the investigation up. If you stay in Creek River, maybe you can get out of Tom where those kids are."

"Stay in Creek River?"

"Meg, you realize by the time we get done here, it's going to be the middle of the night. I don't want to have to worry about you again. Plus, you have to call Jake. He's worried sick about you and feels horrible that he didn't give you a chance to talk to him before he left."

"Jake? He's worried?"

"Yeah, he's still your friend. Remember?"

Reggie went over to Si and Hank. He told them of the plan and it was agreed. Boon argued as Meg stood quietly by watching the mountain men. She thought about Jake and Boon. Boon glanced over and saw her watching him. The look on her face bothered him, so he stopped arguing and walked over to Silas who would be staying at the pass waiting for the sheriff.

CHAPTER 52

The trip down the mountain was uneventful. Tom knew he couldn't escape the Boons and even worse, the law. All the years of running bootleg whiskey and committing other minor crimes had gone unpunished by Jesse Mueller. But kidnapping and murder were crimes that the sheriff was dead serious about seeing prosecuted.

Clint, whose wounds had been treated by the town doctor, sat in a holding cell. He hadn't spoken a word since coming off the mountain. He sat listening while Meg gave her statement to Jesse about finding the body. When Uncle Si and Lloyd walked past him to the sheriff's office, he turned white. Meg sat at a deputy's desk watching him and didn't miss the reaction.

After talking to the Boons, Jesse called the State Police to assist in recovering the remains in the cave. Meg went into Jesse's office after he made the call and closed the door.

"We still haven't found those kids. Are you willing to let me interrogate Tom to see if he will crack?" Meg asked.

"He probably won't talk to you."

"Maybe he will if we can cut him a deal."

"What kind of a deal?"

Meg sat down in the chair in front of his desk. "We both know that it was Clint that wanted to see Clancy dead. We don't know if Tom is even involved in the murder. So, we can't just offer him a deal that doesn't allow the prosecutor's office to try him for some degree of murder or manslaughter. But if he agrees to tell us everything he knows about Lynch and the kidnappings, maybe we can offer him a lighter sentence."

"We don't make those kinds of decisions here."

"Can you call the D.A. and ask him if you can deal? I'm afraid that if Lynch knows that we have Tom and Clint in custody, he may kill those kids. Or he may just take off leaving them locked up someplace."

Jesse sat thinking about it. Finally, he sighed. "You know the biggest thing I had to deal with here is running whiskey. I figured they weren't hurting anyone. If you had told me when Erica went missing that my own people were responsible for any of this, I would have kicked you out Creek River."

"I never cared much for Clint," Meg replied as she stood. "But it surprised me that he would kill Clancy. And I never would have thought Tom would have been involved."

Jesse stood up, "Let's go find out why."

"What about the D.A.?"

"I got about a half hour before those state boys get here from Beaumont. I figure if Reggie don't want you back at the mountain pass, you could be doing something useful, like finding Erica and bringing her back to Ma and Sissy. Gonna be really hard on Sissy, finding out her man's the one that killed her Pa."

Meg didn't respond to that as she followed Jesse to his makeshift interrogation room that was formerly the supply closet. One of the deputies brought Tom into the room still in handcuffs. He glared at Meg, but sat in one of the chairs in the room.

Jesse turned another chair around and straddled it. Meg stood with her back against the closed door. "So, seems you've been pretty busy lately."

"You ain't got nothing on me. She's lying," Tom whined.

"She is? That's not what your Uncle Si and cousin are telling me."

"They never liked me."

"Aw, Tom, I grew up here in Creek River. My own Pa was sheriff before me. Now who's lying?"

"It's that Larry Boon. He's the outsider, and he's turning my own kin 'gainst me."

"What I see is that Boon is always helping you, Tom. I always find him at your place when he's in Creek River."

"Cause he's a drunk! He just comes to get his booze."

"He wasn't drinking this morning when I came lookin' for him. He was fixin' that still of yours. Helping you. Just like Cousin Clancy was always watching out for you and helping you. Then, you did him wrong. Took his little girl and then helped Clint kill him. Why? Why'd you do it?"

"I ain't done nothing wrong. Just doin' what I always done. Helpin' folks, showin' them the mountains."

"Leading strangers to the Hollow ain't helping folks. It's turning on your own kin."

"He told me that he wanted to see real mountain folk."

"Who? Lynch?"

"I ain't sayin'. I don't have to talk to the law about nothing." Tom stuck his chin up in the air and wouldn't look at Jesse.

"Sure, you don't have to talk to me. But this will be the only chance you get. Soon as those state men get here, you'll be in Beaumont. Then off to the state penitentiary. Even if you didn't kill Clancy, and we find out it was Clint, and you knew what he did, it's as if you did it yourself," Jesse stood as if to leave.

"I didn't kill Clancy." Tom looked up at Meg. "I didn't want to go up the mountain today. You did this to me. You had to go up there alone!"

"You're wrong," Meg countered. "I didn't do this to you. You did this to yourself. How much did Peter Lynch pay you to turn your back on the Boons?"

"I didn't…."

"You know what you did and so do I…and so does Uncle Si. If Erica, Bobbi, and Timmy die because you became a traitor, it's as if you killed them too." Not taking her eyes off from Tom, she asked Jesse, "Sheriff, does Virginia have the death penalty?"

"Yeah, it does," he replied.

Meg continued, "You'd be responsible for the deaths of four people. Two of them would be your own cousins. Right now, the Boons have already convicted you. The best thing that could happen to you is if you confess, help us bring those kids home. Maybe the state of Virginia would show you some mercy and lock you up for the rest of your life."

Tom wasn't following her, but Jesse was, so he made it simpler. "You tell me what Clint did and how you are involved, so I don't have to charge you with Clancy's murder. Then, if you tell us where Lynch has those kids and we find them alive, I don't have to charge you for those murders either."

"I don't know anything," Tom said growing more indignant.

Meg sat down in the chair that was close to Tom. "I'm going to have a nice little talk with Clint. And if he tells me it was you who killed Clancy, I'm going write that down and have him sign it. Then, the state police will arrest you for killing Clancy and Clint will go free."

Tom didn't respond, he looked down at the floor. Jesse looked at his watch and motioned to Meg. They were running out of time. Jesse pushed his chair to one side. "Guess that's it. Detective Riley, go get a statement from Clint. I'll have the state men take Tom over to Beaumont to see the judge. Once we have Clancy's body, Tom will…."

"I didn't know he was gonna do it," Tom said in a quiet voice. "I don't think Clint knowed he was gonna do it either. They had a fight. Clancy kept askin' questions about Erica. I was getting' scared 'cause I kept havin' to go up to the Hollow with them church folks. Clint known that I feared Clancy and guessed I knowed what happened to Erica."

There was a knock on the door and Jesse looked at Meg. "What happened?" Meg asked in a soft voice. Jesse went to the door and asked the deputy to wait for a minute.

"Clancy thought them devils did somethin' to Erica and was gonna hunt 'em. Clint was gonna go with him, but Clancy said no. Clint don't listen so good. He followed him to the Pass, like he did today. Clancy found one of those pups near the creek and kilt it. He heard the others and went to the cave, but then he sees Clint followin'. He calls him out and then calls Clint bad names. Says he can't live in the Hollow no more."

"They had a fight?"

"Yep, whiles theys fightin' that momma devil shows up and goes after Clancy, but he hits her with this shotgun. As he turnin' the gun to shoot, Clint hits Clancy with a big rock from the creek. Smashes him bad. He throws the rock at the momma, but hits another pup that cried and falls over. The momma grabs the hurt pup and disappeared quick, but Clint says she's hurt. Then, he runs away and comes to me at my Pa's." The knock came again and Jesse slipped out of the room.

"You went back up the pass to help him cover his crime."

"He was scared 'cause he ain't sure if he kilt Clancy. It was gettin' dark, but he needed to know if he was alive. When we got there, he was dead, so we hid him, then put him in the cave the next day."

"What happened to Erica?"

Tom sighed and looked up at the ceiling. "That Lynch guy seen her in the woods. She was sneaking down to town to see that boy. I told him to leave her alone, but when I heard she was gone, I know'd he took her."

"What about Timmy and Bobbi?"

"Don't know 'bout 'em."

"Did you know he was going to kidnap them?"

"No, I swear I don't. He jus' want me ta take 'im up the mountain. I figure' he did somethin' with Erica when I heared she was missing after he paid her so much attention."

"When was the last time you saw Lynch?"

"A few days ago. I asked him what he did with Erica and he ignored me."

"So, it wasn't you he was on the phone with when I was hiding in the pass?"

"No, I ain't talked ta him since a few days ago."

"Do you know where he is staying? Did he tell you that?"

"The Inn in Langford. He said he doin' somethin' at the college, helpin' out with somethin' Irish, and he liked our mountain. Wish I never took him up there."

"What was he doing at the college?"

"I don't know. Think it had somethin' ta do with Boon. Ya know he used to work there?"

"Yeah, I heard that. Do you know if the person he was working at through the college was named Harman?"

"Naw, some name like rascal. Least, that's how I remember it, Rascal. What's goin' to happen ta me now?"

"You helped cover up a murder. I'm not sure how it works in Virginia. But if you are honest with the D.A., tell him everything, maybe he can cut you a deal. You'll have to have a lawyer too."

"Do y'all think ya can find Erica now?"

"I don't know. But at least you gave me a few other places to look for her. And if it helps me find her, I'll tell the D.A. that part too."

Meg got up and went to the door. The deputy, who was in the other room, came in and took Tom back to a holding cell. The sheriff's office was empty except for two deputies left to guard the prisoners and Boon. He was sitting on a bench near the door when Meg came out of the room and went over to the deputy. Boon watched her as she talked to him for a moment. Then, she took out her cell and made a call.

"Hey, Jake," she said. "Guess I've got lots of explaining to do." She laughed softly at what Jake said as she walked over near Boon to leave the office. She looked surprised to see him. "Hold on a second." She cupped the phone. "What are you doing here? I thought you would have gone back up the mountain with your cousins."

"No. I thought it would be best to stay in town with Hank."

Meg looked around. "Is he still here too?"

"He said he needed to talk to the preacher, so he went to the church. I thought I'd just wait here for you."

"Oh," Meg hesitated. "I've really got to talk to Jake about a few things. But…can you hang out for a few minutes? I want to talk to you about something."

Boon shrugged. "I guess I can. I've waited this long."

Meg went back to the call and walked outside. Boon scowled as she left wondering why she needed to talk to Jake in private. As he looked around, he realized Clint was watching with a satisfied look on his face.

CHAPTER 53

After making sure that Hank was safe at a relative's house in Creek River, Meg went with Boon to the college. Boon couldn't believe he was going back to that school. But there was no one else who could go with Meg. The two deputies had to stay with Clint and Tom until the sheriff got back from the mountain. Right now, Boon didn't trust anyone else in his family until he saw where they stood with Tom.

Boon was glad they were already in her car heading to the college when Meg told him that Tom had told her that Clint had killed Clancy. All he wanted was to avenge Clancy's death. But he knew that killing Clint wouldn't bring back Clancy, and it would only ruin what chance at life he might be able to have now. He glanced at Meg as she drove and still felt like a foolish schoolboy.

Boon almost hoped that they wouldn't find anything at the college because that meant she was another step closer to leaving Creek River, Virginia, and him.

"I'm sorry about Clancy," Meg said looking over at him.

Her comment startled him because he realized he had been staring at her. "It's not your fault."

"But that doesn't mean I can't feel bad for you. I heard that Clancy was more than just a cousin to you, that he was a good friend to you when a lot of folks turned their backs on you."

Boon's jaw's clenched and he looked out his side window. "Yeah, he never blamed me for anything. He told me to come to his mountain, helped me build my cabin even. He was a rock, not only for me, but everyone at the Hollow. I don't know how they will survive without him."

Meg waited for a moment, each lost in thought. "He reminds me of Reggie."

"Reggie? That big guy with you?"

"Yeah. He seems all tough and blustery. To most, he's a big pain in the neck. He even fired me from the police force. But he's really come through for us down here. He's been a real friend to me these past few days. Yet, he practically had my head for taking off with Sam after the memorial service. I see him so differently now."

"Hmmm, I feel the same way about Clancy. I think a few of our Meyer relatives will be glad to hear about his demise. But to me, Ma, Sissy, and a few other folk on that mountain…." He stopped getting choked up.

"I'm sorry I mentioned it. I didn't mean to hurt you."

"Naw, you didn't hurt me. The hurts been there since he disappeared. I knew then that he was dead. He would never get lost on that mountain, and he would never allow himself to be taken anywhere. I've already been grievin' him."

Meg didn't say anymore. The silence between them was comfortable, each lost in thought without feeling the need for conversation. As Meg came over the hill, the old buildings of Creek River Community College came into view. The light from the sunset shone on a few windows, tinting the side of the main building in reds and oranges.

"Where should I park?"

"Just pull into the main lot. The History Department is in that old stone building."

Meg pulled into the lot and parked. "Look, we haven't talked about this, but you can't just go in all Wyatt Earp on me."

"Wyatt Earp?" Boon burst out laughing. "What made you come up with that one?"

"I don't know," Meg chuckled getting out of the car. "Maybe it's the beard. But seriously, don't pull your weapon. We can't have a shoot out here. I understand that there is bad blood between you and Harman, but I need to find out if he is involved in these kidnappings."

Leading the way to the building, Boon replied, "Right now, I'd be happy to take my rage out on Harman. But I'll try to control myself. I used to be a gentleman."

The building was locked, but Boon smiled and led her around to a side entrance. He found that was also locked, but took her to the back of the building.

"He's not even here. No one is," Meg sighed, still following Boon.

"You can get a lot more information from people who aren't present."

"What do you mean by that?"

The heavy wooden door was also locked. Boon looked around and shook his head. "You would think that they wouldn't do this, but they still do." In between two stones in the wall of the building, Boon pulled out a twisted wire. He wiggled it around in the skeleton keyhole and unlocked the old door. "Presto, my dear! Let's see what that rat has hiding in his office."

Meg hesitated. "You do realize this is breaking and entering, don't you?"

"And the sheriff is on the mountain dealing with a murder. I doubt us breaking into my old employer's building to see if we can find out anything about the kids that are still missing will cause him to issue a warrant for your arrest."

Meg sighed and followed him into the building. The old stone building was cast in shadows and darkness as the sun began to set. Even though it was dark, Boon found his way through the building like he was there yesterday, instead of ten years ago.

"Do you even know which office is his?" Meg whispered, her voice echoing through the empty hallways.

"Of course I do. It was mine," his voice was hard, and he didn't whisper.

"Oh."

The door to the office was locked. Boon pulled out a beat up wallet and fished around in it for a minute. He pulled out a key. "Let's see if they ever thought I'd come back." The key turned easily.

"They never had you turn in your keys?"

"I did, but I had two copies of this key. At that time, I planned to come back and destroy all of Harman's work. But after spending time in rehab and spending time with Clancy, I figured that one day the rat would be found out. God, I hope that time has finally come."

Meg didn't know how to respond, so she followed him into the office. The room was growing dark as the sun was almost gone. Boon walked to the windows and pulled the blinds, and then turned on a small desk lamp.

"So, what exactly am I looking for?"

"Anything that has the name Peter Lynch, Robert Donovan, or Sam Craig on it. Well, actually anyone else's name that he shouldn't have in here."

Meg went to a filing cabinet and found it was locked. She took a paper clip and jimmied it opened. "Bravo, learning bad tricks from me?" Boon asked laughing.

"Nope, I learned that one from Jake when I was a rookie."

Meg didn't see Boon's smile disappear at the mention of that name. He turned his attention to the desk drawers. After ten minutes of searching, Meg pulled out a file that was in the bottom of the cabinet.

"Roberta Jackson."

Boon looked up from a folder he was reading. "What?"

"Roberta Jackson. Bobbi as she's known in town. She was one of Harman's students in the spring semester. Her file was all by itself in the bottom of the cabinet."

"Misfiled?"

"I don't think so." Meg brought the folder to the desk and put it under the light. "There are faint pencil marks that have been erased on the side of an essay she wrote. I can't quite make it out."

"Let me see." Boon took the page out of the file and lifted it before the light. "I think it says Beaumont. Wasn't that where she disappeared?"

"Yeah, at a club where she had just met Sam."

"This was under the drawer in the bottom of his desk." He turned the folder around so Meg could see it.

"Sam! He does have a file with Sam's name."

"He was working on translating the journals from Gaelic. He has the notes in here. But he also has all the information about Donovan in Ireland and that guy, Lynch."

"Is there a number for Lynch?"

"Plan on calling him?"

"No, but the state authorities can trace calls made on that number to cell towers. If we can see where the calls are coming from, we can narrow down where he has been."

"That's such a long shot. Just like you tracing those credit card sales all over Langford."

"Well, do you have any better ideas?"

"You're the detective, not me."

"It's so frustrating! We've been down here for weeks and are no closer to finding them then before we went to Ireland. We know who, we know how, and we even figured out the motive. But where is he and where did he hide them?"

"Wouldn't the most logical place be on the mountain?"

"Not really. If they managed to get away, they would easily find their way to safety, but Lynch wouldn't be able to find them. It would have to be a place where he could contain them. But everywhere we checked in Langford was a dead-end."

"What makes you think he's in Langford? You saw him this morning on the mountain."

"No credit card charges were made here."

"And like I said to Sam, go to Beaumont or Langford to spend your money."

"What do you mean?"

"When Sam came to me and told me that he was wanted for questioning in Bobbi's disappearance, I told him to go to the bigger towns to buy supplies. I didn't want anyone looking for him in Creek River or the mountain. I actually told him to go to Langford because it was that much further away and Bobbi went missing from Beaumont. Simple deduction, if you're not a kid, like Sam."

"So, you're theory is that Lynch was spending money in Langford to draw suspicion away from here? Creek River?"

"That's what I did for the creatures."

"But Creek River has been searched, multiple times. They aren't in town…or are they?"

Boon sat stumped. "Okay, again. You're the detective. Do you really think…?"

" Lynch couldn't be seen in town. So, that leaves out the center of town. The shacks that lead out of town are all locals. But like the mountain, if Timmy, Erica, and Bobbi are being kept in town, they can easily escape and get help. That leaves one place, that even if it's searched, they might still be hidden. How well do you know this campus?"

Boon stood up and the chair flew back. "Here? But, how…."

"Harman," Meg let that sink in for a minute. "This greedy professor whose big research breakthrough that he stole from you still has him working in a backwoods community college. Donovan sent Sam to this town, to talk to this professor, where it is known that Pastor Jake comes every summer to help the folks in the Hollow."

"The connection is Harman."

"And Jake. Because without Jake to put the pieces together with our old cases, Sam wouldn't have been a suspect. Lynch wants his claim to the keeper's legacy back. Donovan for some reason, has turned on Sam, so he sets it all up. Only they need someone here to help set the stage."

"That would have been Tom."

"No, that still would have been Harman. The expert in Gaelic, who wrote a book on the Creek River wars. Tom didn't want to be involved. He just wanted the money that Lynch paid him as a guide to help the clan. But how much more money is Harman getting for his role?" Meg asked more to herself.

"But how does this help him in the long run?"

"Maybe you don't know how rich Sam really is and how much money Donovan has been able to steal from him through that fake publishing company. With Lynch on the payroll, a lot of cash has been funneled to this 'rat' in exchange for Erica, Timmy, and Bobbi."

"But...." Boon got out from behind the desk and came around to Meg. "Money? He had my research and book. That should have...."

"Harman isn't you. He couldn't follow the book with any other works. So, he had to turn to something else to become rich. Maybe he did think he could use the old keeper's journals to gain more notoriety as an expert in history. But Sam didn't come back, so.... Professor Boon, how well do you know this campus? Where could Harman have hidden three kids?"

"Don't you think that someone would have heard them if they were on campus?"

"When Sam was a little boy, one of the keepers kidnapped him...and me. We were held in a basement and drugged. Donovan was the lawyer for that man. He knew what was going on and how to perform the rituals. With him behind this whole thing, those kids could be in the next room, and we wouldn't know it."

Boon stood staring at her. "You were kidnapped? But how?"

"I'll tell you about it later, if you still want to know. For right now, we need to find those kids before Lynch or Harman comes back."

"Wait, if you're right about all this, wouldn't Lynch be here? On campus?"

"No, he's staying in Langford.... Oh, God, he's been staying right here in Creek River all along."

"Lurking in the woods, watching the town."

"The creatures must have known that and that's how that black one was able to save me today."

"And maybe they were trying to save your dad that day too."

"What? How do you figure?"

"Your father and Sarah were hurt really bad. The sheriff said they found footprints and signs that those creatures were right there at the accident scene, waiting."

"Dad said that too. He said he wasn't able to get help for Sarah because they were guarding the car."

"Guarding or protecting?"

"I need to find Sam."

"First, let's find those kids. But I want to have my gun. I'm not walking into an ambush unprotected."

"Okay, but don't shoot unless you have to. I want them both alive. I have to know for sure if those animals were really trying to save my dad."

CHAPTER 54

Sam sat on the knoll with the black creature watching the police as they took the body out of the cave. Sam wrapped his arms around the neck of the creature. A few times, he saw Reggie looking around, but Sam knew he couldn't see them. As it got darker in the woods, it was more difficult for Sam to see what the men were doing. His car was still hidden between that cave and the town. He hoped that the car was hidden well. If they found it....

It was time to get moving. He figured it wouldn't be long until they came looking for him, blaming him and the creatures for the death of whoever they found in the den. Getting to his feet, Sam brushed the leaves from his clothes. He let the creature lead him through the darkening woods to the new place where they were hiding. At least tonight, he would stay with them in the cave. Tomorrow, he would head back toward Boon's to see what he could salvage to start over.

* * *

Reggie saw the red eyes up the mountain watching them. He figured that Sam was close by, but couldn't see him. Just those eyes. He didn't say anything to Jesse or the others involved in the recovery. There was enough work to do without them focusing on Sam. They didn't need him now that Tom confessed to helping Clint bury the body in the cave. They had their suspects in custody already.

But Reggie felt bad for Sam. For all the blame that always fell on him and how he was wasting his life with those creatures. Reggie wondered if Sam had stayed in Granelle four years ago, like his friend had wanted him to, if that would have made any difference. He remembered how hard Sam had become. At this point, Reggie felt that Sam was a lost cause. He would end up like that hermit that Meg had a crush on.

"What you looking at?" Jesse asked as he walked over and looked up the mountain.

"Nothing really. Just thinking about that kid, Sam."

"We may still have some questions for him when this is all said and done. I know he wasn't responsible for Clancy, but there are still those others that are missing." Reggie grunted his disapproval. "I know that you and Meg think he's not involved there either. But her own daddy told us that his animals were there when he had the accident. Don't be so quick to dismiss his involvement in the accident that took Mrs. Peterson's life."

"As you just said, it was an accident. Even if Sam was a witness to it, which Boon already told us he wasn't, he can't be held responsible. There was no crime committed."

"I'm not saying there was. But you can be sure that once things settle down around here, we are going on a hunt for those animals and rid them from our mountain."

Jesse turned and walked back to the state troopers. Reggie sighed, knowing that his return to retirement in upstate New York would have to wait. He was going to have to hike back up this mountain tomorrow and find that kid. Maybe if he was lucky, Meg and Boon would take the trip for him. Either way, Reggie felt he owed it to Sam, for all that kid had been through, to warn him that they were being hunted…again.

* * *

"Shhh!" Meg whispered loud as Boon knocked into a table. The thud didn't make a lot of noise, but it echoed in the hall.

"It's not like I did it on purpose," Boon whispered back.

Meg wanted to just shut him up, but he couldn't really see her in the dark and talking would just make more noise. They had already searched through the unused offices and classrooms. She skirted around the table that Boon had walked into. He led her to stone stairs that went to the administrative office. Meg leaned over the banister and saw the offices and sighed.

"Boon," Meg said stopping on the stair. He shushed her. "Boon, there's no one in this building. It's a waste of time."

"I thought we had to be quiet." Boon stopped on a stair just below Meg. The moon was coming out and it reflected on the marble floor just below them.

"There wasn't anyone upstairs. Down there it's all offices. Since summer classes just ended, they wouldn't be hidden in the offices. I think this building would have just been too busy a few days ago to be the place. Where else on campus could Harman have hidden them? Someplace that is secluded?"

"Wouldn't it make more sense to have them in the building his office is in? He'd be able to keep tabs on them."

"Maybe too obvious and if Lynch is staying here too, that would be too close for comfort."

"Well, there are three other buildings on campus. We can look in them. They aren't as easy for me to get into though."

"Would there be an extra set of keys in the office to all the buildings and maybe a floor plan?"

"I don't know."

"What about a maintenance office? Is that in this building?"

"Roger didn't really have an office. It's just a spot near the boiler that he kept tools, and there is a table of sorts."

"Where's the boiler room?"

"In the basement."

"Are there any other rooms down in the basement?"

"I only went down there once and that was years ago."

"Okay, let's check it out." Boon led her to the door where they came in.

"I thought we were going to the basement."

"The basement of Ellison Hall. That building over there." Boon pointed to the building the furthest from them.

"Maybe we should look in the administration offices first to see if there is a set of keys before we leave the building. I don't want to expose ourselves in the open and then have to come back to find keys anyway."

Boon stood staring out at the moonlit parking lot and grounds. Meg had turned away, heading toward the offices. "Wouldn't your car being all alone in the parking lot give us away? If anyone is on this campus, they already know we are here too. Or at least someone is here."

Meg stopped for a moment, then kept walking. "Let's just find those keys."

"Okay, I guess. Seems like we are just wasting time. It's almost totally dark out there, so it's got to be close to ten. The sheriff should be back in town by now."

Meg found herself getting irritated. "What's your point?" She turned the handle to an office and found it locked. She went to the next one and it was locked too.

"Was thinking that maybe a real law enforcement officer would have more luck figuring out where they are." Boon led her down a narrow hall to a counter.

"A 'real law enforcement officer' wouldn't be here right now because what we are doing isn't legal. They would have to wait until they had probable cause and get a warrant from a judge to search the premises."

Boon jumped up onto the counter and spun around. He dropped on the other side. "If what you are saying is true, then…."

Meg followed him over the counter. She glared up at him. "Why don't you just stop talking? Nothing you are saying is helping."

Meg shook her head and walked over to a desk. As she started looking through it, Boon went to a wall and turned on some overhead lights.

"What are you doing?" Meg jumped up from the chair.

"Like you said, your car is a dead give away. We might as well use a light, so we can see."

"That's a huge difference. Anyone driving by would think that the car was broken down or someone is working late. Shut the light off!"

"Relax, Meg. There are no windows. The light can't be seen from the outside and if someone is in this building, we've already made enough noise to tip them off."

Boon went back to the counter and started looking around underneath it. Meg sat back down and pulled open a drawer. Ten minutes later, Meg found a set of keys hanging from a nail on the back of a closet door.

"Think these might work?" Meg asked showing Boon the keys.

"Possibly." Boon took the keys from Meg and looked through the large ring of keys. "Looks like it is every master key on campus. Offices, closets, buildings, cabinets. How are we going to be able to figure out which one opens the buildings?"

"The larger keys are probably the building keys. The little ones would be just desks, so we eliminate those right away."

Boon shook his head. "Seems like it would be easier to break a window and climb in."

"Let's just figure out which key might open Ellison Hall."

There was a loud bang somewhere in the building. Meg motioned to shut the lights off and ducked behind one of the desks. Boon hit the lights and crouched behind the counter. They heard voices echoing in the open hall. Lights came on in the hall and spilled into the reception area. Meg looked around the corner of the desk and saw Boon slipping behind the other desk, out of sight.

The voices drifted away, and Meg got out from behind the desk. She crept to where Boon was and whispered near his ear, "Where's the front door?"

Not saying anything, he went back to the counter and quickly climbed to the other side. Meg followed, knowing that if they stayed they would easily be found by whoever came back into the college. Quietly, they got to the front door and stepped into the night air.

Meg motioned for him to follow her to the side of the building. She peeked around the corner to the parking lot and saw another vehicle parked near hers. She gestured to Boon, who shrugged and shook his head. She mouthed 'woods,' and he nodded.

Surprising her, Boon grabbed her hand and took off. At the side of the building, he glanced around the corner. Seeing no one, he practically yanked Meg to the woods. Once inside the woods, he let go of her hand and crept around to see the back of the main building.

"Look, Harman's office." Meg looked to where Boon was pointing and saw a light on in the office.

"You sure it's Harman's?"

"It used to be my office. Of course, I'm sure." Meg watched the light for a moment and then she headed toward the other building. "Where are you going?"

"We still need to check out Ellison Hall."

"If that's Harman or that other guy, don't you think they will be heading over there if those kids are here? Why not wait and see what's going to happen first?"

Meg thought about it for a moment and then nodded. "Guess we've waited this long already. But let's get deeper in the woods, not too deep."

As they walked back a few yards in the woods, Meg pulled out her revolver. Boon looked at her with a question, which she either ignored or didn't see.

CHAPTER 55

Reggie was relieved to see Creek River. He started heading toward the Zimmer's and the guestroom, but Jesse stopped him. "Come to the office first. The state men might need a statement from you before they take off for Beaumont."

"Can't they get it in the morning when they come back for Clint and Tom?"

"Actually, I've convinced them to take them tonight. We just aren't equipped for these kinds of crimes. Besides, I don't think I'd be able to keep the Boon kin from lynching them."

Reggie sighed and followed the group back to the Sheriff's Office. Town folks were hanging out near the office. Word had quickly spread through town that a body had been found on the mountain. Several people were circled around a young woman who was smoking. Hank was standing with some men that bore a strong resemblance to Boon and Clancy. The hearse had been parked near where they came out of the woods. As the vehicle passed the growing crowd, the men removed their hats and they reverently watched the taillights as the hearse left town.

The closer they got to the Sheriff's Office, the larger the crowd grew. Reggie even saw the Zimmer's in the crowd. "Who'd ya find, Sheriff?" a voice called out from the crowd. There was silence as they waited for an answer.

Jesse walked up to the door and stopped only a moment. "I'll be out in just a minute. I've got to get these state boys out of here first."

"Was it Clancy? Boy should knowed what happened to his Pa."

Jesse didn't answer and went into the office. Reggie stopped for a moment and looked at the crowd of people before following him in and closing the door. He looked around the room and frowned. The troopers were doing paperwork and getting ready to take Clint and Tom. Reggie heard someone mention Meg's name and walked over to Jesse and a deputy.

"...she left with Boon," the deputy said. Jesse saw Reggie and shook his head.

"What's up?" Reggie asked.

"Meg's following a lead with Boon. I have to make sure that our suspects get safely out of town, and then we will go track them down."

"You think there's a problem?"

"Don't think so, but she's with Boon."

Reggie didn't like the sound of that. He started to ask something, but one of the troopers called Jesse away. The deputy went back to his paperwork he was filling out. He knew he couldn't leave because of the crowd outside. So, Reggie found himself sitting on the same bench that Boon was using several hours before. He called his wife and told her that he planned on seeing when he could get a flight out to Albany, New York, in the morning. Then, he called Jake and gave him an update on the case.

Finally, the troopers were ready to transport the prisoners to Beaumont. They took Clint and Tom out the back door to the waiting cars. Jesse watched until their cars were well on their way out of town, and then turned to his deputies. "Guess it's time to let folks know about Clancy. Let me do the talking."

Reggie waited until Jesse and his deputies were outside, then he followed. The crowd had doubled since they had arrived. There was silence as Jesse went to address them. He started, then stopped when Hank moved forward a bit. Jesse stepped off the wooden planking and walked up to Hank.

He put his hand on the boy's shoulder. "Hank, I'm sorry to have to tell you, but it was your Pa that we found at the Pass. If you want me to, I'll go up to the Hollow in the morning and talk to Ma and Sissy with you."

Hank hung his head, and an older man came behind him. "Thanks for the offerin', but us Boons, we gonna take care of our own."

"I understand, Eli. Do you know where Uncle Si and Lloyd got to?"

"Nope. Ain't seen Boon neither."

"Sheriff," Hank looked up. "I's got to know. Was it Clint?"

The crowd grew still, almost too still waiting for that answer. Reggie actually put his hand on his gun. Jesse took a deep breath, "He's being charged with murdering your Pa. But it will be up to the law in Beaumont to find him guilty."

"Tom?"

"He's being charged with knowing and helping Clint hide your Pa after he was dead."

Hank nodded and then turned away. Eli still had his hand on the boy's shoulder and followed him. A few other men standing near them went off with them.

A voice from the other side called out. "What about my boy, Timmy? Did they do something to him too?"

Reggie noticed the young woman from before, still holding a cigarette. "No. This had nothing to do with Timmy, Erica, or Bobbi." The crowd began to murmur again. Jesse quickly added, "But we do have some new information and have some people following up on it."

The woman began to cry. Reggie saw Mrs. Zimmer going toward her as another woman took her in her arms. With that, Jesse turned and went back into the office with his deputies and Reggie followed them.

"Okay, Jesse, where's Meg?"

"She told Earl that she had a lead at the college. It sounds like Boon's old enemy has gotten involved with that Irish guy we were looking for in Langford. They left hours ago, and haven't come back."

"Old enemy? What's that about?"

"Back ten years ago or so, Boon was a professor at the college. He was drinking a lot in those days. He was involved in a fatal car accident that killed his wife and kids. He went off to a rehab for a while. His assistant, Roscoe Harman, finished the work they had been doing. I agreed with Boon that Roscoe stole the work, but the university didn't see it that way. They published it under Roscoe's name and gave no credit to Boon. When he got out of rehab, his entire life was gone, family, work, friends. That's how he ended up on the mountain with his kin."

"Boon? That hermit? We talking about the same guy?"

"Yes, sir. Drink can destroy a whole life. I've seen it over and over again here."

"And how is that Roscoe guy involved with our suspect?"

"Earl's a bit sketchy on the details, but said that Meg told him that she was going to the college. Asked if there was any way that one of my guys could go with her because she had a lead on the missing kids from Tom."

"But they had to stay here with the prisoners."

"So, she took Boon 'cause he knows the college very well."

"That doesn't sound like a good idea," Reggie said frowning.

"Seems to me like Meg is always making rush decisions that aren't always the best."

"Sometimes, but she is trained and knows what she is doing."

"Would have been better for her to wait until tomorrow when someone from my office could have gone with her."

"You are the one who left her down here to follow any leads on getting those kids back. Let's see if we can track her down." Reggie called Meg's number, but it went directly to voicemail. "All I want to do is go to bed, but I think we should at least go to the college and see what's up."

"You do realize it's almost midnight. What are the chances they are still there?"

"If they aren't there, then we can just go to bed and figure it out in the morning. If they still are, then maybe they are on to something and can use some help."

Jesse moaned. "Figured you'd say that. Hiking up that mountain twice in one day…. Okay, let's go before I change my mind."

* * *

"This is ridiculous," Meg said getting up. "I doubt that Harman is still even in his office. For all we know, he's over in Ellison Hall and we are sitting here getting eaten up by mosquitoes for nothing."

"What are you going to do?"

"I'm going to Ellison Hall to that cellar and see if those kids are there."

"But…."

"You can stay here if you're afraid."

Boon was on his feet. "Afraid? I'm here, aren't I?"

Meg shrugged and walked off following the perimeter of the parking lot inside the woods. Boon grumbled behind her. Meg stopped short and Boon almost ran right into her.

"What…?"

"Shhh, look," she whispered. From a distance, staring at them were two sets of red eyes. Meg quietly walked up to them, and they never moved. She looked back, but Boon hadn't followed her. She knelt down next to the black creature and put her hand on him. "Is Sam here too?"

"Yeah, I'm here," Sam said from somewhere deeper in the woods. "What's going on here?"

"I'm not 100% sure, but I have a gut feeling that this may be where those kids are being held."

"Based on…?"

"Harman's mixed up with the guy from Ireland that is trying to take your place as the keeper."

Sam was quiet for a minute. "Who was in the den?"

"Clancy. It looks like his son-in-law killed him."

"Not the creatures," he said flatly.

"No, they weren't involved, but I heard the one puppy was killed and another one hurt during the altercation that took Clancy's life."

"She died too, later that night."

"And the other one and their mother?"

"They are fine and in hiding."

"I'm sorry to hear they died."

"Why? What difference does it make to you?"

"Because, this morning, he saved my life," Meg said, petting the creature again. Sam came up to her and looked down.

"He saved you?"

"Yes, from Peter Lynch. It's made me wonder if Lynch was in the woods that day of the accident, like he was this morning. Could the creatures have been protecting my Dad and Sarah?" Sam didn't say anything, just kept staring down at the creature. The alpha male moved away from them, heading toward Ellison Hall. "Sam, is that possible? Can we have been wrong about all of this?"

"No, we aren't wrong. The journals prove that."

The black creature, standing near them, began to growl. They both looked to see where the alpha went. They saw a car pull into the lot. Meg saw the lights on the roof.

"Let me and Boon check it out. You stay here in the woods with them. Sam, I really want to talk to you about all of this. So, please don't just take off."

"Boon? Is he here too?"

"Yeah, he's back there. Just go, I don't want the sheriff to see you. He's not convinced that you are innocent."

"Are you?"

"Yes."

"And them? Are you convinced that they aren't involved?"

"The only thing I wondered was whether they had gotten Clancy. Now go!"

Sam disappeared and the black creature went with him. She heard a shrill whistle and saw a blur heading toward the direction of the sound. She figured the alpha male was heading back to Sam. She looked back to see Boon behind her again. "Thought you weren't afraid."

"I betrayed them, so I'm not thinking they will be too happy to see me."

As they made their way through the woods, Meg saw Reggie in the parking lot peeking into her car windows. She moved faster and was about to yell out to him, when she heard shots ring out. Reggie and the sheriff both went down. Meg wasn't sure if it was in reaction to the sound or if they were hit. She pulled out her revolver and ran toward the building.

CHAPTER 56

Jake woke up with a start. His heart was pounding and for a few long moments, he wasn't sure where he was. The light from the alarm clock showed it was almost mid-night. He had gone to bed only an hour ago and his sleep was filled with vivid dreams. The last one ended with a nightmare. The fragments of dream began to drift away, but somehow it was filled with red eyes looking at him through the woods. He listened to the sound of his young son sleeping in the double bed next to him. Trying to let that sound soothe his wildly beating heart, but it only brought up the pain he had been trying so hard to forget.

Jake realized his life would never be the same again. Now that he was back in Granelle, he thought about all his options. He knew the one that made the most sense was the one that Pastor Walt had suggested. Go to New Jersey and visit his family for a month. Then, come back to Granelle and start life over as a widower pastor of the small church. But was that really what he wanted, or was that the convenient response?

Jake had prayed and there was no clear answer. Part of his problem was Meg. He had been totally wrong about her. She was still in Virginia trying to close *his* case. It had been exhilarating to have a case of his own again. But the calling on his life....

He threw back the covers and got up. The bright moon spilled light into the room, the Ryerson's guest room. Another thing that bothered him was his house. How could he live in Sarah's house when she would never come home again? The only thing that was his from before his life with her was his old dog, Buddy.

With so much of his future undecided, Jake knew only one place where he ever felt peace in troubled times. He could hear Pastor Walt snoring from the other room. Jake put on a light jacket over his tee shirt and sweats. Slipping on his sneakers, he left the old parsonage and went next door. Granelle Gospel Church's steeple was lit up and Jake used his key to open the front door. He walked into the sanctuary and took his old seat, fifth row back on the right side. The place he would sit when Pastor Walt was the senior pastor. He looked up at the old pulpit and the wood cross hanging on the wall behind it. Jake sat there for a long time. Finally, he put his head in his hands and prayed.

* * *

"Where they hit?" Boon asked as he collided with Meg.

Meg stood still, staring at the two figures on the ground next to her car. More shots rang out. She turned to Boon. "Stay here."

"No, if you're going, I am too."

"I'm trained to handle this. I don't want to have to worry about you getting shot. Stay here!"

Meg took off toward Ellison Hall, still staying in the woods. As she got closer, she saw that both Reggie and Jesse were fine. They both had their guns drawn and were looking for the location of the shooter. Meg pulled out her cell and saw several missed calls, but ignored them. She called the Sheriff's Office.

"Earl, this is Meg Riley. Shots have been fired at Creek River Community College. The sheriff and Reggie Bennett are behind a car, and someone is shooting at them. Assistance is needed immediately." He said he would be right down and hung up. She looked at the main building to see if she could see where the shots came from. Even though there was a light in Harman's office, it didn't help her to see where the shooter was.

Meg made her way cautiously to Ellison Hall. Behind the building, she was blocked from the parking lot and the main building. Using that to her advantage, she tried a few windows, but nothing was opened. Tucking her gun in her waistband, Meg tried to open a door, but it was locked too. She thought about Boon's suggestion to break a window, but the shooting made even the wildlife go silent. She stood still listening and could hear the sheriff whisper something. It was just too quiet to break a window. She tried the door again, feeling in her pockets for anything that she could use to jimmy the lock.

Hands reached around her and she reacted by bring her elbow back and slamming the person in the stomach. Boon fell hard on the grass behind him. He went to say something, and she was on top of him with her hand over his mouth. He looked up at her with giant eyes. She put her finger to her lips and shook her head. He reached up and removed her hand. With his other hand, he showed her the keys.

Meg helped him to his feet, but cautioned with gestures for him to be quiet. He nodded and tried a few of the bigger keys in the lock. Meg kept looking around them. She saw the red eyes looking from the woods. She wished she had warned Sam about their eyes. Maybe that's what the shooter had been aiming for.

Finally, one of the keys worked, and they slipped into the building. Boon locked the door behind them. "Where's the basement?" Meg leaned in to whisper in his ear. Boon nodded and led the way.

The only way down was through a service door that was locked. Boon started trying all the keys, while Meg quickly looked into rooms on that floor. She looked at a front window to see Reggie still hiding behind her car. She hesitated for a moment...her *rental* car! Thank God, she got the insurance! Her next thought was, what was taking Earl so long to get to the college. She went back to Boon who was still trying keys and looking very frustrated.

"What's upstairs?"

"Classrooms," he whispered back.

"Any other way down?"

Boon just shrugged and kept trying keys. Meg watched for a few minutes, then went back to the window. She saw Jesse was looking for a way to get to the main building, but there was no cover from whoever was shooting. He would have to be totally exposed to risk getting there.

Meg saw an exit at the end of the hall. She went to it and looked around. There was a small utility shed a few yards from the door. If the shooter was focused on the men, she might be able to get there and then to the main building without being seen. Maybe, but unless Earl showed up pretty quickly and was on the ball, that shooter could be getting in a better position to shoot the men. She couldn't wait for someone else to rescue them.

The crash bar across the door warned of alarms, but that might be good if they were tied to an alarm company. Meg pulled out her revolver and leaned against the door. She looked down the hall at Boon who was still trying to get the right key. He looked down and saw her and started to get up when he figured out what she was doing.

"Boon if you follow me, I'll shoot you myself. Find those kids, let me do my job," Meg shouted to him as she crashed the bar and ran out of the building.

She got behind the utility shed and watched the door close to Ellison Hall. Boon didn't follow her...yet. She looked around the side of the building and saw Reggie looking right at her. The alarm went off sounding shrill against the quiet night. Meg only hesitated for a moment before taking off for the main building. With her back against the building, she had a clear view of the sheriff. She pulled out her cell and called Reggie.

Before he even said anything, she whispered, "I've got a clear shot of Jesse, tell him to move." He just barely moved when another round of shots were fired, blacktop chipping off and hitting him in the face and arms. The shots were coming from an upstairs office that was dark.

Meg slid down to the back door and looked in the window. There was no one there.

She slipped into the building and held the door, so she could close it quietly. Looking up the stairs, she knew that she couldn't go that way and she also knew there was more than one person here. She went further into the building back toward the reception area. The marble and stone staircase was opened underneath and there was a small door under it. Meg got under the stairs. She heard movement from upstairs and saw a shadow right above her.

Meg put her hand on the handle of the door and it turned. She heard the person coming to the staircase. She slipped into the dark opening and quietly closed it behind her, then turned the little lock. In total darkness, Meg listened at the door. Someone walked past the door going toward the reception area. After she heard the footsteps go back to the back of the building, she felt around her. As she stepped back, there was nothing behind her. For a moment, she felt a grip of fear, but shook it off.

Feeling around with her feet, she realized it was steps behind her. She turned around and took a step down and felt around her. The wall to her left dropped off and was opened. She made her way down the staircase carefully. When she finally was on solid ground, she still had no idea where she was. There were no windows and the faint light from the door at the top of the stairs was gone.

Walking forward, Meg reached a stone wall. Turning to her right, she only found more wall, so she went left. She followed the wall until something was in front of her. She reached in her pocket and flipped opened her cell phone. The faint light guided her down the wall to a corner. Surprised, the phone shone on the face of a boy with big blue eyes. He was gagged and bound sitting on the concrete floor in the corner of the room.

"Timmy?" Meg whispered. The big eyes filled with tears and he nodded. "I'm a detective, but there's a bad person upstairs. I need to make sure it's safe before I get you out of here. Okay?"

When he nodded, the tear rolled down his cheeks and into the gag. Meg quickly looked around, and then she heard the doorknob being turned. She got under the opened stairs and pulled out her gun. She pressed herself up against the wall as an overhead light came one. She looked up through the wooden slats. A person stepped out onto the top step and looked down.

Meg wanted to look around the room to see if the girls were here too, but kept her eyes on the perpetrator. The light snapped off again and the door closed. The total darkness of this room was a bit unnerving. Using her cell phone light, Meg made her way around the room. Timmy was alone in the room. She went to him and untied the ropes that held him.

Before taking off the gag, she whispered, "You have to be very quiet. The man upstairs has a gun. Nod if you understand." Timmy nodded and Meg took off the gag. He took a couple of ragged deep breaths. "Two girls are missing too. Have you seen them?" He shook his head.

The cell phone light went out. Meg sat quiet, listening to the sounds of the building. She could still hear someone walking around. But she heard some noises from outside too. Part of her felt like just staying right where she was until Reggie or Boon found her, but another part knew that she had to get Timmy out and safely back to his mother.

"We're going upstairs. Be very quiet, no matter what you see or hear."

The boy nodded again. She stood and took his hand. She got to the stairs and let go of his hand to get her gun. She crept up the stairs with Timmy holding onto the back of her shirt. At the top of the stairs, she turned to listen at the door. It was silent. She waited, not wanting to alert anyone on the other side of the door. Before she could do anything, she heard loud bangs from the other side. There was yelling and something crashed. She felt Timmy cringing against her back, but she didn't move or let on that they were there.

When she heard Reggie calling her name, Meg opened the door a crack. She didn't see anything. Leading with her gun, she opened the door and looked into the hallway. She heard yelling above her on the second floor. Movement by the door caught her attention and she saw Boon coming in with his shotgun. He just stared at her and then ran up to her and enveloped her in a big hug.

Embarrassed, Meg pulled away. "I thought something happened to you when I heard all the yelling and crashing."

"Umm, no. Did you find the girls?"

"The girls? Oh, I couldn't get into the basement."

Meg reached behind her. "They must be here someplace. I found Timmy down there."

"Down there? That's a downstairs." Boon looked behind her at the dark opening, and then saw Timmy hiding behind her. "Hey, Timmy, do you remember me?" Timmy looked shyly up at Boon and then nodded.

"Do you know what is going on? Who is the shooter?" Meg asked to get Boon's attention back on her.

"I don't know. I just got in the building and am so relieved to see you."

They heard people coming to the stairs. Timmy pulled back behind Meg, trying to hide. She just let him, knowing how scared he was and knowing the feeling. Meg could only see someone in handcuffs being led out by the two deputies. When she saw the sheriff and Reggie, she turned to Timmy. "It's okay now. The sheriff is here with my friend. Do you want to go home?" Looking up at her, he just nodded again.

"What's wrong? Why won't he talk to us?" Boon asked concerned.

"He's been missing for a couple of weeks, probably traumatized by being held captive in that room. It's pitch dark down there, no windows, and he was tied up and gagged." Meg knelt down in front of him. "It's okay now. No one is going to hurt you."

Jesse and Reggie heard her talking and came down the hallway. She stood up and Jesse saw Timmy. "You found him! We've been looking everywhere for you, Tim. Boy, is your momma going to be happy to see you!"

"Can I go home now?" he asked in a quiet voice.

"Sure, let me see if Earl is here still…."

"Sheriff, can I talk to you a minute first?" Meg asked. Jesse nodded a bit confused. She took him to the side, leaving Timmy standing with Boon. Reggie joined her. "Those girls have to be here too. We found some notes in Harman's office that showed he had knowledge of each of these kids and ties to Lynch too. Who did you arrest?"

"It was Harman. But let's get that kid home, and then we can get your statements."

"Wait, who was the other person?"

"Other person? The only one here is Harman."

THE HOLLOW

"We heard two people come in. They were talking. Someone else is here in this building and aren't you forgetting Erica and Bobbi? If we found Timmy here, it's highly likely that the girls are here too."

"Where was Timmy?"

"There's steps going down to this small room. He was bound and gagged, sitting on the floor."

"Alright, we'll look around. Boon, do you know your way around here still?" Jesse went over to Boon. He looked down the stairs as Boon answered.

"Not as well as I thought I did. I didn't know this room existed. But call Dr. Gregory, I'm sure he will come right over. He's not going to want any negative publicity for the college and will do whatever you want to help. Come on into the office, I know where we can find his number."

Meg went back to Timmy and smiled at him. "How would you like to call your Mom and tell her you've been found? I've got a cell phone."

Timmy nodded and Meg handed him her phone. She showed him how to use the phone. But he was shaking so badly, he couldn't dial it. Meg looked up at Reggie as she asked Timmy his number. He started crying when he couldn't remember. Meg put her arm around the small boy and led him to the door.

"Reggie, I'm just going to take him home. Is my car drivable?"

"If what you said is true, are you sure you want to leave?"

"I know those girls are here, but I can't just leave Timmy to wait until someone else is free to bring him home. Just tell Jesse to start in the basement of Ellison Hall. I've got a gut feeling about it."

"Sure thing."

Meg walked with her arm around Timmy. When she got to the door, Reggie called out, "Hey." She turned back to look at him. "Nice work, Detective Riley."

She smiled. "Thank you, Captain."

CHAPTER 57

Meg never made it back to the campus. By the time she got to the Novak's house to bring Timmy home, she knew he needed medical care. Instead, she picked up his mother and drove them both to the hospital in Beaumont. Severe dehydration and starvation combined with post traumatic stress disorder was the diagnosis. Meg made sure that there was a cot for his mother to stay close to him before heading down to the E.R. to check on the two girls who had been found behind the boiler in Ellison Hall.

As she headed back to Creek River, exhaustion was setting in. It seemed like a long time ago that she tried to talk to Jake, but it was less than 24 hours. The sun was just coming up as she took that last bend and saw Creek River spread out before her. She drove the rental into the church parking lot and turned off the engine. She sat listening to the sound of the engine cooling and wondering if the sheriff ever found Peter Lynch.

Meg figured she would worry about that later. Right now, she wanted food and sleep in any order she could get it. As she walked toward the parsonage, someone was sitting on the back deck and got up to meet her. She almost moaned that she was going to have to talk to someone. She didn't think she recognized the person though.

"Hey. You look exhausted."

Meg stopped and stared. "I must be more tired than I think."

He laughed. "Naw, it really is me. Mrs. Zimmer offered me a shower and clean clothes. I borrowed a razor. What do you think? Do I look like a college professor?"

"Boon? I can't believe it. You look like a totally different person!" Meg walked up to him and put her hand on his cheek. She laughed out loud. "You don't look like a Boon anymore!"

"Well, maybe you should call me Larry."

"Larry?" Meg started laughing hysterically. "I'm sorry," she gasped. "I'm just so tired. It's hard to think of you as Larry."

His laugh was deep. "That's my name and the one I went by for years."

A window popped open next to them and a rumpled Reggie scowled at them. "Do you seriously need to do that this early in the morning outside of my bedroom window?" Meg laughed harder. "Can you just bring her inside, so I can go back to sleep for a few more hours?"

Boon led her to the deck. "You better get yourself under control. The Zimmers are still sleeping."

"What were you doing? Sleeping on the deck?" Meg asked.

"I wasn't planning on it. I was going to just wait for you to come back."

"And then what?" Meg began to get her laughing under control.

"I haven't quite figured that out. Why don't you get some sleep? Maybe we can talk in a few hours."

Meg yawned. "Probably a good idea. But you might have to introduce yourself to me again. I don't think I'll remember who this stranger is." She started cracking up again, and he shook his head as he led her into the house. She went down the hallway to her assigned room, still laughing softly. He watched her until the door closed.

* * *

Meg's cell phone was ringing and it sounded like it was from a long distance away. She fought to wake up from a dream. Finally, she looked at the phone to see it was from Jake. "Hey."

"I heard you broke the case last night."

"Yeah, that's what the rumor is."

"To think they were right in Creek River the whole time. We went all the way to Ireland for nothing."

"Actually, you did make the right choice to go to Ireland. That's how we found out about the publishing company that led us to Lynch."

"We could have found out about him through other means…."

"Jake, don't second guess yourself. Going to Ireland was an important part of solving the case. To be honest, it was the start of my realization that I needed God too. You're still a good detective you know."

"But…."

"But nothing. All the decisions that you made from the beginning were just as important as mine in the end. Face it Jake, we've always been good partners."

"Telling me that makes the decision that I need to make even harder, you know."

"Oh yeah, and what's that decision?"

"I'm thinking about going back to police work." Meg hesitated, not sure how to respond. "Do you think it's a bad idea?"

"I don't know what to think. I thought that being a minister was something you were called to, like that's what God wanted for you. The people in Granelle love you and that life seems to fit you so well."

"I know. Things have changed with Sarah gone."

"All the more reason to stay in a safe, non-life threatening job for Richie."

"I'm not making any rush decisions. In fact, after the memorial service and burial tomorrow, I'm taking a month sabbatical to visit my family in New Jersey. While I have the church here, I don't have any family."

"I didn't think about that. I guess having extended family would be good for Richie."

"My Mom already said she would help out with him if I moved back to my hometown. Dad told me that there is an opening on the police force, or I could easily get a job in a church down there. I just need to make sure that's what God wants me to do and not what is convenient for me."

"I hadn't thought about that. The convenient thing, instead of what God wants."

"So, Reggie's coming home later today. When are you coming home? Will I see you before I leave?"

"Reggie's leaving today? I didn't know that. Guess I'd better get out of bed if I want to say good-bye."

"What? It's after noon!"

"Yeah, but I didn't get back from the hospital until this morning."

"I was hoping to see you before I left for New Jersey. I know we have talked on the phone, but I still feel I owe you an apology."

"You don't owe me anything. But I doubt you'll see me before you leave. Dad is still in rehab and I want to be close by in case my stepmother needs something. Plus, there are a few details that I want to close in the case. As far as I know, Lynch hasn't been found."

"That's what Reggie told me earlier. But there's something else you aren't saying. Why else are you staying in Virginia?"

"Well, I need to find Sam. I haven't even said too much to Reggie about this. But yesterday morning, I had an experience with one of those creatures. He saved my life." There was silence on the other end. Meg could hear Jake breathing, but he didn't respond.

"When you find them, finish the job like you said you were going to before we went to Ireland," his voice broke. She knew the wounds were too raw and fresh to mention her theory about the creatures.

"I'll let you know how it turns out. I better go talk to Reggie before he leaves without saying good-bye to me. You know how he can be."

"Okay. Promise you'll call me after you kill them. Do it for Sarah's sake…and Brian's."

Meg closed her eyes. Yesterday morning, she would have promised him that, but not today. But she couldn't hurt him anymore either. "Jake, you take care of yourself and Richie. Let me know what you decide about your plans."

"You didn't promise."

"Because I don't want to lie to you. Let me find Sam and talk to him. I want to find out the truth." Jake didn't respond and for a moment, she thought he had hung up on her. "I'm sorry that I can't promise you this, but there are so many questions that I need answered before I can make a decision to just…kill them."

"You had no problem with making that decision before. You were even going to hunt them down in Granelle. Why not now, when you know they are responsible for my wife's death?"

"I'm not sure they are. In fact, I think they were trying to protect them. Let me find out for sure. If they were, I will hunt them down for you, but I need to be sure." Again, Jake was silent. She could feel his pain and knew that two days ago, she would have felt just like he did. "Do you trust me, Jake?"

Jake sighed. "You know that I trust you."

"Then, pray for me. Pray that God shows me the truth, so I will know what to do. Trust me. If they are responsible for Sarah's death and are evil like we always believed, I'll go up on that mountain with every Boon kin I can find and take out the pack."

"I wish you would just do it without the hesitation. But I'll leave it with you for now. Please let me know what you find out when you see Sam."

She heard Reggie laugh down the hall. "Okay, I'll definitely call you when we get back. It sounds like Reggie is getting ready to leave. So, I'll call you later."

Meg waited a long moment after hanging up, wishing she could just promise him that she would end it once and for all. But she had her doubts now and couldn't just kill them, not until she was sure.

CHAPTER 58

Meg took a quick shower and put on fresh clothes. Feeling more herself, she went into the kitchen to find the Zimmers and Reggie having lunch.

"Thought I wouldn't get to see you before I left for the airport," Reggie said as he took another handful of potato chips.

Sitting across from him at the table, she put a couple of slices of bread on a plate Mrs. Zimmer put before her. "Had to get my beauty sleep. What time do you have to leave?"

"In about an hour. Rev. Zimmer is going to take me to the airport in Langford. Can't wait to see New York." Meg laughed as she made her sandwich. "What are your plans?"

"I'm actually thinking about staying down here in Virginia for a while."

Everyone looked at her surprised and started asking questions all at once. Meg laughed, "Okay everyone, I'll explain. But first, is it alright if I stay here for a few more days? I'm not sure if it's better for me to stay here or over in Beaumont."

"Well, of course you can," Mrs. Zimmer said. "But why Beaumont?"

"My first reason is that Dad's in Beaumont in rehab. Looks like he might be there for another few weeks. But there are a few loose ends I need to get tied up here in Creek River, so that's why I'd like to just stay with you for a couple of days."

"What loose ends?" Reggie asked as he picked at the chips.

"First is Sam and the creatures. I've got to talk to Sam and make sure he's okay."

"I agree with that one. You need to know that once this is all settled. Jesse and some of the men are going up in the mountain to hunt them."

"Oh no! They can't!"

"Why?" Pastor Zimmer asked perplexed. "I thought they were bad."

Meg looked panicked, but then took a deep breath. "Because I think we've been wrong about them all along. But until I talk to Sam, I won't know for sure. I need to find Boon and see if he can take me up the mountain to find Sam. Do you know where he went?"

"I think he's over with some of his kin on the other side of town," Margaret said getting up and taking some of the dishes with her to the kitchen.

"When can we find out? I need to talk to him...."

"Slow down, Riley," Reggie said with a chuckle. "I know you're anxious to see him, but it's not like he's going to take you up there today." She opened her mouth to say something and saw the look he was giving her. "That was first, what other reasons are you staying in Creek River for?"

"Have you talked to Jesse about Lynch? Did they ever find him?"

"Nope, don't know where to even start looking."

"I think the case against Harman will be better if we have Lynch for leverage. And he has a great deal of Sam's money."

"That's up to the feds to find him and arrest him. Money laundering is a different case."

"I know, but he was the one that took those kids to begin with. I just want justice for them and their families."

"Feels like there's a number three coming up. Spill it, Riley, why are you really looking to stay down here in Virginia?"

Meg blushed and then shook her head. "Nothing that is your concern."

"Seems to me like you turned into my concern the minute my feet hit the ground in Virginia. It's that mountain man, isn't it?"

"Look," she said dropping her voice to a whisper. "I have no idea if I even want anything to do with him. But if I do, I don't want all of Creek River to know. Okay?"

Reggie looked toward the kitchen where the Zimmer's were putting away the lunch foods. "Okay, I won't say anything about Boon to anyone. As long as you call me first and let me know what you decide. You owe me."

Meg stared at him and then laughed, "My proxy father?"

Reggie smiled. "No, just your old friend who wants to be sure that you are okay. Fair enough?"

"Fair enough. Who would have thought when you fired me all those years ago that you would care about my love life?"

CHAPTER 59

It took Meg all afternoon to track down Boon. She was still surprised to see him clean shaven and dressed in regular clothes instead of workpants and plaid. But it was a pleasant surprise. Meg talked to Hank for a while who was struggling with the death of his pa. Boon and Meg finally agreed to meet in the church parking lot at sunup to head up the mountain in search of Sam.

Leaving him at Eli's house, Meg went to the Sheriff's Office to give her statement on the events that took place the day before. She spent a couple of hours filling out paperwork and finalizing any last questions. Meg was disappointed to hear that Peter Lynch had taken a flight out of Langford yesterday afternoon heading to Dublin. Now, he was out of their jurisdiction. The State Police were trying to see if there was enough evidence to tie him to the abductions, but so far, Roscoe Harman wasn't giving up his accomplice. There was no evidence that tied Robert Donovan, Esq. to any of the disappearances. She hoped and prayed that somehow he would be held responsible for the way he handled Sam's inheritance.

Meg was exhausted when she got back to the parsonage in time for dinner. She excused herself to go to bed, knowing she needed a good night's sleep for the hike the next morning. Meg woke up before her alarm and got ready without waking the Zimmers. Mrs. Zimmer had made a bag lunch for her and Boon. She grabbed a knapsack and put the food in it with a water bottle. She made sure her revolver was tucked in the bag too, but if she was right, she wouldn't need it.

When she reached the parking lot, she was surprised to see Hank with Boon. "What's up?" Meg asked.

"Since we're headed up the mountain, Hank wanted to go with us, so he can go home. A few of the uncles went up to the Hollow yesterday and told Ma and Sissy about what happened, but wouldn't let Hank go. So, against Cousin Eli's wishes, I'm taking the boy home. They need him now that Clancy's gone. And I agree that he is needed there now."

"How's Erica doing? Anyone hear from the hospital?"

"Sissy is there with her. She should be ready to leave today or tomorrow. Then, she'll be going home to the Hollow too."

296

Hank didn't say anything, but nodded from time to time at what Boon told her. "Okay, let's get moving. Where do you think Sam might be?"

"My guess is, near my cabin or the one he was building for himself."

"That's a half day's walk, isn't it?"

"Nope, more like a day, depending on how fast you walk. I would usually stay in the Hollow overnight when I needed to come to town for any reason."

"Let's get moving then."

They walked in silence for a long time. Meg really wanted to talk to Boon, but didn't want to say much in front of Hank. The boy was quiet the entire walk. Instead of taking the faster way past the creek pass and the cave, Boon took a longer walk to the Hollow. Meg didn't notice since she didn't know her way through the mountains, but Hank did. When he realized it, he simply said thanks, and Boon nodded.

It was late morning and starting to get hot when they saw the first shack. Although Meg was relieved for the break, she had wished they were further up on the mountain and finding Sam. Ma came out and welcomed her grandson home. Seeing her brought the first tears that Hank had shed, and Boon pulled Meg aside.

"Emotion isn't something we're very good at showing. I think we ought to just keep on going. They live up here alone for a reason. Do you mind if we give them their privacy?"

"They are your family, and I'll do what you think is best for them."

Boon nodded with a tight smile. "Wait here. I just want to let Ma know, so she doesn't feel obliged to us."

Meg waited near the well and saw a few kin beginning to come around. As Boon walked back over to her, she saw they headed to Ma's cabin. Once they were out of earshot Meg asked, "What were they doing?"

"Showing their respects to Hank. Even though Uncle Si is the elder Boon, it's going to fall on young Hank to take the place of his father."

"But he's just a teenager."

"Yeah. But one that is the best hunter and tracker in the family, loves his kin, and will take good care of them. Plus, he has a strong faith in God. Seems like that last one ought to be enough for you."

"Wouldn't have been a few weeks ago, but I guess you're right. Let's find Sam. I need to know."

"Okay, before we get up there, I think we need to talk about this whole thing."

"What's to talk about? Blackie, as you call him, saved me. It made me think that I owe at least him, even if it's just a warning that the sheriff wants to hunt them down. I need to make sure Sam is okay after all the time we spent together the other day."

Boon didn't respond and for a long time, they walked in silence. Meg kept looking at him because he looked so different. After a while, they stopped to eat their sandwiches that Mrs. Zimmer had made.

"Alright, already!" Boon finally exclaimed. "What is wrong? Why do you keep looking at me like that?"

Meg looked surprised and then tried not to smile. "Well, maybe I was just really overtired yesterday, but do you really want me to start calling you Larry?"

He stared back at her and she actually giggled making him scowl. "If you don't like that, you can call me Professor Boon."

"Professor? Oh yeah."

He looked mad. "Yes, Professor Boon, that's what my students will be calling me in a few weeks."

Meg stopped giggling. "You got your job back?"

"They need a new professor with good ole Roscoe on his way to jail. Yesterday, I was able to show the chancellor proof that the book that Harman wrote was actually mine. I was really sloppy with my work, but my wife wasn't. She actually sent copies of my original ideas and research to herself that predated the work that Harman did by years."

"That's great," Meg said smiling. "But I still want to call you Boon."

He shook his head as he got up and walked away. She started giggling again. "Hey, Larry! Wait for me."

The afternoon quickly passed as they hiked to the old cabin. As they got closer to the cabin, Meg saw one of the creatures. It was the alpha that she had seen with Sam near the college. She nudged Boon and pointed him out.

"Wish we had found Sam first. I'm not sure I'll be welcome."

"Sam!" Meg yelled making Boon jump. "It's me, Meg Riley! I told you the other night that I wanted to talk to you."

"Can you please wait until I am actually in my cabin before you alert the entire pack that I'm on the mountain?"

"Do you really think they didn't know you were here before I yelled?" Meg saw the alpha take off into the woods. They got to Boon's cabin without them seeing Sam or any of the other creatures.

Boon opened the door and looked around. Nothing had been moved since he had left days before. Meg found the nearest place to sit, while Boon looked around. He got her some water and then cleaned up a few things.

Finally, Meg asked, "Okay, how long until we go find him? He's obviously close by or the creature wouldn't be here."

"We wait. He knows we're here."

Boon had made them something to eat from his stores of food in his cold storage under the cabin. Meg really took in the whole setup and was impressed by how he was able to survive all the years on the mountain. She fell asleep on the bed that she had been sitting on. Boon sat in the chair at his table watching her sleep for a while. Then, he took the old jug that still was about half full with bootleg whiskey and took it outside. As he dumped it, Sam showed up. He showed only a little surprise at Boon's change in appearance.

"You come looking for me? Or you just back?" Sam asked stepping out of the darkening woods.

"Actually, I did come looking for you and so did Meg. She's inside."

"Dumping the whiskey? You finally found a reason not to drink?"

Boon noticed a hardness to Sam, but didn't want to indulge it. "Might say that I found a reason in what I've seen in the past few days. Why don't you come inside? We've got a few things that we wanted to talk to you about."

Sam shrugged and followed Boon inside the cabin. Boon saw the red eyes of the creature watching him. Meg woke up as they walked in and was happy to see Sam. She actually got up and hugged him. It set Sam back for a minute.

"I'm sorry. I had wanted to come find you yesterday, but it got too late in the day. We found the missing kids at the college."

"Really?" Sam stood by the door, glaring at Boon.

Meg went to Sam and pulled him into the small room. "Just relax. I wanted to talk to you. I wanted to tell you that we solved the case and that you weren't even a suspect. You'll never believe what happened."

Sam sat down on his old bedding and listened as Meg told him all about Clint. He was surprised when she told him that Harman was involved with Lynch. When she finished, Sam sat quiet for a few minutes.

"So, where does all this leave me?"

"Right here," Boon said from his place at the table.

"I don't get it. What do you mean?"

"Harman's arrest left a vacancy at the college. I was able to show them that the work was originally mine. So, I'm moving back down the mountain. I figure there's no one else that would want this cabin, but maybe you."

"I guess that explains the way you look."

"Yeah, can't look like an old hermit if I'm helping shape the minds of today's youth."

Sam didn't smile. "But what's the catch, Boon?"

"There is no catch. The only reason I survived up here was my cousin Clancy. He's gone now."

"How much is this going to cost me?"

"I have a source of income again. I still own the house in town. I was only renting it to some people."

"Sam," Meg interrupted. "You do need to know that the sheriff told Captain Bennett that he was going to hunt the creatures.

"It wouldn't be the first time they've been hunted. Probably won't be the last. We'll be fine."

"I've got to know though. Did you think about what I said? Is it possible that the creatures were trying to protect my Dad and Sarah?"

"I don't know. I know that they possess power, they are really smart, and according to you and the journals, they're even part human."

"That's hogwash," Boon answered. "It's all the legend that the original keeper told to get folks scared. It wasn't true."

"You read those journals to me yourself. You know they are true!"

"Well, I believe they are true too," Meg said. "I have DNA evidence that shows they have human strains. I've heard that they are part wolf and part werewolf. A hybrid beast that helped the first keeper amassed a great fortune. I know from what O'Leary's daughter told me that it destroyed her whole family."

"It was her father that destroyed the family, not those animals," Boon said. "They are a hybrid animal, but not what you think. There was a final journal that I had just started to read before everyone showed up on the mountain. Paddy found that his father was a liar. The fortune didn't come from being this great man who made a deal with the devil for wealth, but he stole it from his English landlord."

"No, that's not true," Sam said getting to his feet. "Meg has that last journal. Did you bring it?"

"Had it. I'm sorry, Sam. I've torn my room apart at the Zimmer's and still don't know where it is. Maybe someone took it from the room."

Boon got up and went to a footlocker. "No, it's right here." He started taking everything out of the big chest, but it wasn't there.

"You're not going to find it there. That night I spent here with Reggie and the boys, I took it. I told Sam that I had it the day of the memorial service when we went to Langford together."

"But I know what it said. Do you remember how the early journals talked about the black potatoes and how everyone was starving? I explained that it was during the Irish Potato Famine."

"I remember, but…," Sam started.

"Let me finish. The men in Ireland didn't own the land, but their English landlords did. They didn't care that the potatoes were rotting in the field, they didn't care that the Irish folks were dying from starvation. They wanted their rents paid. The Irish lost the land that they farmed and had to go to workhouses. Remember, Paddy talked about that. But they never had to go. Because he found out that when Mr. Bledsoe came to collect, his Pa locked him up."

"It was the werewolf that he locked up."

"No, he was a man. He held him captive, just like the future keepers would take people captive, he made up all that ritual stuff to scare people. He didn't want them to know the truth. He kept him locked up until he was begging for freedom. O'Shea made him give him money, lots of it, in exchange for what he thought was freedom. That was how he got his money and the screaming and howling the townsfolk heard was Mr. Bledsoe."

"That makes no sense, Boon. If what you are saying is true, who are the creatures? Where did they come from?"

"I don't know. I never finished reading the journal, and now it's gone." Boon looked over at Meg with a scowl.

"It's got to be someplace at the Zimmer's house. I promise I'll find it once we get back to town," Meg said.

"Don't bother, it doesn't matter to me," Sam shrugged. "I know that they are here, that they have saved me, and that I have a place with them. That's all that matters."

"Oh, Sam, I wish I could do more for you. There is a whole life waiting for you."

"My life is waiting for me, in those woods. No person ever made me feel like I belonged the way I belong with them. And even if my money gets tied up for a long time, I have this mountain now. That's if you haven't changed your mind about me staying in the cabin."

"No," Boon shook his head. "It's all yours and aside from a few personal things, everything in it. We just need to stay here overnight, and I'll pack my belongings in the morning. I'll probably have to come back up for some stuff. But I'll put what we can't carry in the shed, so it's out of your way."

Sam just nodded and went to the door.

"Wait," Meg said going up to him. She remembered the ten-year old boy that he was as she looked up into the man's face. "I'm going to stay down here in Creek River for a while. Would it be alright if I came up to visit from time to time?"

"Why?"

"Because, a long time ago, you saved my life."

"And?"

"We made a connection in that basement in Granelle. I just have this feeling that I want to know where you are and that you're okay."

Sam kept looking down at her. "You'll never find you're way back up here alone."

"No, but I know a mountain man that can bring me up here from time to time. And if I'm here in Creek River, you can always find me too."

"You're leaving in the morning?"

"Just the mountain, not the town."

"I'll let you know tomorrow." With that Sam, slipped out into the night.

CHAPTER 60

The next morning Meg kept looking for Sam. She went a ways into the woods calling his name, while Boon packed up some personal things. When he was ready, he found Meg walking in the woods, visibly upset. "He told me he would be here in the morning."

"Well, we can wait a little while longer. If we wait too long, we'll have to spend the night in the Hollow and I would prefer to just go back to town."

"Can you look around too? Please?"

"Okay, but if he was around, you would know it."

Boon walked around to the other side of the cabin and poked around the woods. He went back to the cabin and on the back side of the shed was a piece of paper hanging on a nail. He read the first few lines and found Meg.

"I think this is Sam's answer to you."

Meg took the paper and read it.

Meg,

> *I don't know why you feel that we are connected. If anything I'd think you'd want to forget that dump in Granelle that ties us together to the past. Seems that Trevor messed up both of our lives. I really am happy living with the pack. They accept me and I feel safe. I won't tell you to stay away, but I won't come looking for you either. If you are on the mountain, you are a friend. I guess that means Boon is a friend too. Thanks for the warning about the sheriff. But he won't be able to find us.*
> *Sam*

Meg was crying as she finished reading the note. Boon put his arm around her and she let him hold her for a long time. Finally, he asked if she was ready and she nodded.

Boon picked up a large backpack and put it on his back. Meg took her little knapsack with belongings that he had also filled. He had made some dried meat sandwiches that he knew wouldn't taste that good, but at least it would get them back to civilization.

It was close to dusk when they finally reached the last slope that lead to town. Meg turned around and the black creature and another were standing together across a knoll from them.

Boon looked up to see why she stopped and saw them. "Well, look at that, it's Blackie."

"Who's that with him? The other one? The female?"

"Nope, never seen her. Looks like he might have found himself a mate."

"But she doesn't look like one of the creatures."

"She's pure wolf. Seems like they are going to grow the pack. I don't know how long it will be safe to come up here into the mountain. Maybe the sheriff is right."

"No, we promised Sam."

"If they are breeding with wild wolves, what will that make their offspring? Some other creature, with no connection to Sam? Will he even be safe?" They took off and disappeared quickly into the thick woods.

"Is what you told Sam about the lost journal the truth? Did you really read it?"

"Yes, it was the truth. But like I said, I never finished it. So, I don't know what they really are."

"For Sam's sake, I have to find that journal. I have to know the truth so he can be set free."

"Set free? You make it sound like he's in bondage."

"He is, but the truth in that book has the power to break this stronghold from his past. I have to find it. I have to know what it says. I have to prove to Sam that he doesn't have to live in this darkness."

"I thought you were okay with them now that Blackie saved you."

"Yeah, I thought so too. But I can see him for what he really is now. It's like I was blind to it before. He's like an angel of darkness, an evil dark creature that has taken Sam, pretending to be my friend."

"Huh, that sounds like this quote, but a little mixed up. I actually think it might be from the Bible."

"Yeah, what's the quote?"

"Hold on," Boon dug around in his backpack and pulled out a little book. Meg looked at it and saw it was a small New Testament. He started flipping through the pages.

"You have a Bible?"

"Yeah, most of the town is Baptist. I got this one when I was baptized. Here it is, 'For such people are false apostles, deceitful workers, masquerading as apostles of Christ. And no wonder, for Satan himself masquerades as an angel of light.' It's like you said, they came to Sam as light, but they really are darkness."

"Can I see that?" Boon shrugged and handed her the little book. She looked down at the pages as she said, "I wish I could have seen them for what they are before we saw Sam. They are always just out of reach, always on the edge of destruction. They have this stranglehold on Sam, and he can't get free. When that creature bit him in the basement when he was ten, it was like Sam got infected."

"Aren't you being a bit melodramatic?" Boon turned away to get out of the woods. Meg looked around and saw the alpha male staring at her.

As Meg stood there, a strength rose up in her. The creature lifted its head and howled, and the woods turned a bit darker. But she stood facing the darkness, the last ray of sun hit the golden edge on the little New Testament, and just for a moment, a light shone around Meg.

Looking up to the top of the knoll, she saw more creatures join the alpha. "I'm going to find the truth about you." His eyes turned a deep red, and even from the distance, it was as if she could hear the warning growl. "I have the power that Jake had before. I have the power of prayer that broke your stronghold in Granelle. I'm not going to let you have Sam. I'm going to get stronger. I'm going to get all the answers, and I'm going to come back."

More books
by
Ladean

The Hollow: The Keeper's Legacy is the third book in Ladean Warner's series. *The Keeper of Darkness* and *Beyond the Keeper's Gate* can be found on her website: ladeanwarner.com.

Her next book, *When She Cries*, will be available soon.

To stay in touch with Ladean, follow her on Facebook or sign up for her updates on her website.

http://ladeanwarner.com

http://opendoorpublishers.com